HEART QUEST™

HeartQuest brings you romantic fiction
with a foundation of biblical truth.
Adventure, mystery, intrigue, and suspense
mingle in these heartwarming stories of
men and women of faith striving to build
a love that will last a lifetime.

May HeartQuest books sweep you
into the arms of God, who longs for you
and pursues you always.

A Victorian Christmas Cottage

CATHERINE PALMER
DEBRA WHITE SMITH
JERI ODELL
PEGGY STOKS

HEART
QUEST™

Romance fiction from
Tyndale House Publishers, Inc.
WHEATON, ILLINOIS

Visit Tyndale's exciting Web site at www.tyndale.com

Discover the latest about HeartQuest Books at www.heartquest-romances.com

"Under His Wings," "Christmas Past," and "A Christmas Hope" edited by Kathryn S. Olson; "Beauty of the Season" edited by Chimena Kabasenche

Designed by Melinda Schumacher

Library of Congress Cataloging-in-Publication Data

A victorian Christmas cottage / Catherine Palmer . . . [et al.].
    p. cm.
    Contents: Under his wings / Catherine Palmer — Christmas past / Debra White Smith — A Christmas hope / Jeri Odell — The beauty of the season / Peggy Stoks.
    ISBN 0-8423-1905-0
    1. Christmas stories, American. 2. Historical fiction, American. 3. Love stories, American. I. Palmer, Catherine, date.
PS648.C45V515   1999
813´.0108334—dc21   99-34158

Printed in the United States of America

05   04   03   02   01   00   99
9   8   7   6   5   4   3   2   1

CONTENTS

Under His Wings

CATHERINE PALMER

For Richard McClure
A true gentleman

CHAPTER ONE

*May the Lord, the God of Israel, under whose wings you
have come to take refuge, reward you fully.*
RUTH 2:12

1870—BRACKENDALE MANOR IN CUMBRIA,
NORTHWEST ENGLAND

A light glimmered in the kitchen window. Lord William Langford, the earl of Beaumontfort, breathed a sigh of relief, shouldered his hunting rifle, and trudged through the deep snow around the perimeter of Brackendale House. Annoyed to find his country home shut up tight the very evening before he was due to arrive from London, the earl made a mental note to have a chat with Yardley about the matter. The butler should know better than to lock all the doors and abandon the place. What if someone should need lodging?

Stamping his boots on the stone step, Beaumontfort gave the kitchen door a good pounding. There, that should register his displeasure over the entire situation. No doubt whoever had remained in the house this evening would spread the word among the permanent staff that, upon his untimely arrival in Cumbria, the earl had been miffed indeed.

"I say!" he called, giving the wrought-iron handle a jiggle. "Do be sensible and open this wretched door."

Bad enough he'd missed his shot at a large deer poised on the shore of a half-frozen tarn at the outskirts of his property. There would be no fresh venison for the table tomorrow. An unexpected snowfall had shrouded trees and blanketed the roadway, making travel chancy at such a late hour. The whole situation had been compounded by his horse's stumble, which nearly sent the earl head over heels and caused the poor animal to pull up lame. Leaving the creature at the deserted stables, he had trudged through the snow, with hopes of a hearty welcome from the small staff he kept in permanent residence at the House. Instead, he found his own home shut up for the night. Abominable.

Restless with the plans, ambitions, and goals that filled his London life, the earl had been felled recently by a minor illness that unexpectedly had drained him of vigor. The doctor had prescribed nothing more than a strong dose of peace and quiet. A few hours of amusement, perhaps a chat with a friend or two, and a great deal of rest would be just the ticket. Beaumontfort decided upon a visit to his country home—a place where he surely would be welcomed and tended to by his devoted staff. So where were they?

"Are you quite deaf?" Beaumontfort cried, giving the door another hammering. When no one answered, he strode to a diamond-paned kitchen window. His feet were nearly frozen, and he could hardly feel his fingers inside his gloves. The fire sending a wisp of smoke from the manor's chimney would warm him—if he could ever get inside.

Lamplight shone through the soot that coated the thick glass panes. He could not discern anyone inside, but he felt confident Yardley would not have left a lamp burning unattended.

The earl tapped on the window. Nothing. His ire rising, he lifted his riding crop and gave one of the small glass panes a good whack. It broke loose from the leading and fell to the stone floor with a crash.

"Oh, what have you done now?" The female voice was angry. "You've broken the window! Wicked man! Be gone at once. Shoo!"

Beaumontfort peered through the empty pane into the

kitchen. At that moment, a single, large brown eye filled the leaded diamond. Startled, the earl took a step backward.

"Good heavens," he exclaimed. "What on earth?"

"Who, don't you mean?" The brown eye blinked. "It is I, Gwyneth Rutherford of Brackendale House. You have broken the earl's window, sir, and Cook will be jolly angry tomorrow, I assure you. I trust you're prepared to pay for a new pane, because I shall not take responsibility for your vandalism."

"Vandalism? Upon my word—"

"I know 'twas you who broke the window. Don't even attempt to deny it. I was standing directly before the fire stirring the stew when I heard the pane fall to the floor. And I can promise you that the earl's glass windows—"

"Enough about the earl and his blasted glass windows, girl. Open the door and let me come in."

"Certainly not!"

Beaumontfort gritted his teeth. He was not the sort of fellow to lose his temper easily. In fact, he admired the young woman's loyalty to the household and her determination to keep out vagabonds. All the same, his toes were likely to begin to chip off inside his boots at any moment.

"My dear woman," he began, calming his voice. "I have journeyed all the way from Kendal this day, losing my path twice, encountering a raging blizzard, having my horse go lame, and failing to shoot the deer that would have been my dinner on the morrow. I have not eaten for a good six hours, and I am ravenous. Should you fail to open this door at once, I am likely to bash it in."

The brown eye grew larger for a moment. "Were you shooting on the earl of Beaumontfort's manor? That's poaching, you know. Highly illegal. 'Tis a blessed thing you missed the deer. No one but the earl and his own personal—"

"I *am* the earl of Beaumontfort!" He jerked off his glove

and pushed his signet ring into the open diamond. "And I am the lord of this manor. I have the right to shoot my own deer, break my own window panes, and—if perchance God still looks favorably upon me—enter my own home. Would you be so good as to open the door, please, Miss Rutherford?"

"M-Mrs. Rutherford," she stammered. The brown eye vanished from the window, and in a moment the door creaked open.

Beaumontfort pushed it back and stepped into the warmth of the cavernous kitchen at the back of Brackendale House. The woman, a slender creature garbed in a plain brown plaid dress and white apron, gave him an awkward curtsy. He would have preferred to ignore her and proceed directly to his private rooms, but the earl knew she was his only hope for a decent meal.

"Mrs. Rutherford," he said, striding across the stone floor toward the hearth. "I don't recognize you. You must be new on staff. Do be so good as to prepare a platter of cold meats for my evening repast. I should like a loaf of fresh bread, as well, and perhaps some gingerbread. And could you please enlighten me as to the reason Yardley locked all the doors and vanished? I'm due to arrive in Cumbria tomorrow morning."

"Tomorrow is not today, sir," she said. "Mr. Yardley ordered the house prepared for your arrival, and then he gave the staff the evening off. After all, you'll be in residence until after the new year, will you not, sir? With all the guests and parties and dinners you'll be having here, no one on staff will have a moment to himself until you've gone away to London again. You keep only a small permanent staff here, sir, so all of us shall be required to labor long hours. This is a night for the village families and, no, you may not have fresh bread because all of Sukey's children *and* her husband have come down with influenza. She was unable to bake anything at all today, but I can pour out crumpets."

Beaumontfort turned from the fire and stared. What an impudent young woman. What utter candor. . . . What astonishing beauty.

Mrs. Rutherford's clear, rose-cheeked skin was set off by a wealth of coal black hair swept up into a knot from which stray wisps drifted around her fine little chin. Her lips, though softly pink, expressed confidence and determination. Framed by a set of long black lashes, her intelligent brown eyes met his in an unwavering assessment. The earl felt suddenly not so much lord of the manor as an insect specimen on a skewer. He actually had the urge to wriggle in discomfort as she continued to look him over.

"They were quite wrong about you," she said suddenly. "They told me you were old and crotchety. You aren't old at all."

"Quite crotchety, though."

Her lips parted in a radiant smile that crinkled her eyes at the corners. "Perhaps you are, sir. But 'tis nothing that cannot be cured with a strong dose of cheer and good humor."

"Actually, I was thinking more along the lines of a strong dose of hot tea."

"Exactly," she said. "Nothing warms the heart like tea. Do seat yourself beside the fire, sir, and I'll give my stew a stir. After that, I shall put on a kettle and carve a bit of beef from the shoulder we had this evening. Would you like crumpets?"

"Indeed. Have we jam? I do enjoy jam with my crumpets." Beaumontfort settled into a large square-backed wooden chair and bent to tug off his boots.

"Allow me, sir," Mrs. Rutherford said, kneeling at his feet. "Strawberry jam. And 'tis truly delicious. You really must come out to Brackendale Manor in the springtime, sir. This year the whole village went into the hills and valleys to pick strawberries, and I can tell you I never had such a lovely time in my life." She pulled off one boot, and landed on her backside in a heap—though she never stopped talking for even a breath. "I used to live in Wales, and we don't often find wild strawberries there—at least not in the mining areas. 'Tis dreadfully rocky, and one wouldn't want to picnic as your staff did by the lake. We had singing and poetry and games. You would have loved it."

"Would I?"

She glanced up, as though she'd forgotten to whom she was speaking. "Anyone would. Even crotchety old earls."

"I'm forty-one, Mrs. Rutherford."

"I'm just past thirty," she said, setting his boots near the fire. "But I'm not crotchety in the least."

"Then why are you alone here in my house whilst the rest of the staff have taken the night off to be with their families?"

"My family is only Mrs. Rutherford, my late husband's mother, though she is more than dear to me," she said, standing and giving him a gentle smile. "She can hardly keep her eyes open past seven, and so the cottage grows a bit quiet in the evenings. I thought I should like to keep myself busy and help out in the village if I could. Mr. Yardley gave me permission to gather up the leavings in the kitchen each night and take them down to the village to feed the hungry."

"Leavings?"

"Scraps of potato, bits of meat, bones, bacon ends, carrots, turnips, that sort of thing."

"I received no word that the villagers were hungry."

"Then you are ill informed." Turning, she began to stir the stew in the large black cauldron. "Honestly, some families are barely getting by," she said softly. "Poor Sukey won't be able to work again until her family is recovered from the influenza. Her husband is an ironmonger, and he's terribly ill at the moment. She's frightened, poor thing. Without their wages, how can they hope to feed all the children? They have five, you know, and one is just a baby. So I gather the leavings into a pot each evening and boil a big stew. Then I put on a kettle of tea, collect the lumps of leftover bread, and carry it all down the hill in the vegetable man's wagon."

She hung the dripping ladle on a hook beside the fire and vanished into the shadows of the pantry. Beaumontfort wriggled his toes, decided they were thawing nicely, and stifled a yawn. Rather comfortable here in the kitchen, he thought. Though he longed for time to relax, he didn't often take time away from his business. Most evenings in London, he entertained guests at home or ventured by carriage through the grimy streets to his gentlemen's club or to some acquaintance's house. Life had not always been so.

"You look a hundred miles away, sir," Mrs. Rutherford said, returning with a plate piled with thinly shaved cold meat. "Might I ask where your thoughts have taken you?"

"Here, actually. To Cumbria. When I was a boy, I roamed the Lake District entirely alone. I wasn't earl at that time, of course, and I had few responsibilities. I was merely William. Nothing more ponderous than that. Often I vanished for days at a time, and no one bothered to look for me."

"Goodness," she said, sifting flour into a bowl. "I should have looked for you at once."

He glanced up, surprise tilting the corners of his mouth. "Really, Mrs. Rutherford?"

"I wouldn't want you to feel lonely. A child should have the freedom to explore the world a bit, but he ought to know he's loved at home, as well."

The earl considered her words. Unorthodox, but charming. "Have you children, madam?"

"No, sir." She bit her lower lip as she stirred in some milk.

"Nor have I. Never married, actually. Haven't given it much thought, though I've been advised I should. Heirs, you know."

"Yes, sir."

9

"Should I ever have children, I would permit them to explore the dales and fells," he mused, recalling his own wanderings across valleys and hills covered in feathery green bracken. "I would give them a boat and let them row out on the tarns."

"Did you have a boat?"

He nodded. "Two dogs, as well. One of them could go right over a stone fence in a single leap. But the other . . . I had to slide my arms under his belly and heave him over—a great mound of slobbery fur, gigantic ears, long pink tongue, cold wet nose—"

Pausing, he realized the woman was laughing. "Oh dear, I can hardly stir the crumpets." Chuckling, she covered the bowl with a dish towel and set the batter on the hearth to rise. "We always had corgis. Such dogs! They're more like cats, you know, always nosing into things they shouldn't. And terribly affectionate. We had to leave our corgi in Wales, Mrs. Rutherford and I, when we came to England. Griffith was his name, and such a wonderful dog I have never known. Although they do shed, quite dreadfully."

Beaumontfort took a sip of the tea the woman had just poured for him and felt life seep back into his bones. He couldn't remember the last time he'd sat before a fire in his stocking feet. The aroma of fresh yeast rising from the crumpet batter filled the air, and the sweet milky tea warmed his stomach. The sight of the slender creature stirring a hearty stew, pouring his tea, and tending the fire transported the earl to a time and place he could hardly remember. Maybe it was one he'd never known at all.

"How have you come here, madam?" he asked her. "And why?"

"God sent me." She pushed a tendril of hair back into her bun and settled on a stool near his chair. "You see, many years ago Mr. and Mrs. Rutherford and their two sons left Cumbria and journeyed to Wales to find profitable work. After a time, the men became partners in a coal mine, and the sons married."

"One of them was fortunate enough to find you?"

"My husband was a good man, and all I have ever desired in life is the warmth of home and the love of family. The Rutherford men labored in the mine until an explosion took their lives." For a moment, she twisted the end of her apron string. "After that, the coal mine began to fail. Miners were afraid to work it, you see. Mrs. Rutherford decided she must return to England, where she owns a small cottage and a bit of land. She urged her sons' wives to return to our own villages where we might find new husbands. My sister-in-law agreed to go, but I would not. And so I came to Cumbria."

"But you told me God sent you."

"Indeed he did. Mrs. Rutherford had taught me about Christianity. My family had followed the old ways, a religion with little hope and even less joy. But Mrs. Rutherford explained things I had never heard—how God's Son came into this world to suffer the death I rightly deserved, how Christ rose to life again, how his Spirit lives inside every believer. I became a Christian, but I hungered to learn more. After my husband's death, I couldn't bear to part with Mrs. Rutherford. She'd become more than a mother to me—the only family I really knew. Though she was quite firm in ordering me back to my own village, I begged her not to send me away. Her God had become my God, you see, and that bonded us. I told her I would follow her to England and make her people my own. And so we journeyed here together, Mrs. Rutherford and I."

The earl sat in silence as the woman rose from her stool and began pouring batter into crumpet rings on a hot griddle. As a boy, he'd become acquainted with a village woman very much like the elder Mrs. Rutherford. Her husband had been a distant cousin of little means, but they had welcomed their landlord's child into their cottage during his long country rambles. Reading from her Bible, the dear woman had taught William the message of salvation—and he had become a Christian. Could the woman in his half-forgotten past be the same Mrs. Rutherford who had been like a mother to this intriguing lady?

"Where is the cottage in which you live?" he asked, straightening in his chair. "Is it just beyond the village, down a dirt lane lined with lavender? Has it a thatched roof and climbing roses near the front door? Pink roses, I think. Yes, and stone walls with small windows?"

"Have you been there, sir?" She slid the steaming crumpets onto a plate and turned to him, wonder lighting her brown eyes. "I understood you never went down to the village. People say you're always so—"

"Old and crotchety?"

"Busy," she said with a laugh. She scooped a spoonful of strawberry jam onto his plate and set it beside the platter of cold meats on a small table near his chair. In a moment, she had ladled out a bowl of savory-smelling stew. The table's boards fairly groaned under the feast laid upon them, and Beaumontfort anticipated the meal as though it had been prepared for a king. More than that, he looked forward to further conversation with Mrs. Rutherford of the sparkling eyes and coal black hair.

"I hope I'm not too crotchety to be joined at high tea by a woman of your fine culinary skills," he said. "Will you sit with me, madam?"

She swallowed and gave him another of those awkward curtsies. "Thank you, sir, but I must take the leavings down to the village," she said softly. "It has been a difficult year, and many depend upon me."

"And then there's Sukey with her influenza-inflicted family."

"Yes, sir."

He studied her, wondering at a woman who could so easily warm his feet, his stomach, and his heart—all at a go. This brown-garbed creature was nothing like the bejeweled court ladies who often accompanied the earl to the opera or the theatre. They would label her plain. Common. Simple.

Beaumontfort found her anything but. She had enchanted him, and he meant to know how she had managed it. Was it the faith in Christ that radiated from her deep, chocolate-hued eyes? Was it her devotion to her mother-in-law? Or was it simply the crumpets?

"Before you leave," he said to the woman bending over the stewpot. "You tell me you work in the kitchens?"

"Yes, sir. Almost a year." Drinking down a deep breath, she lifted the stewpot's arched handle from its hook. "I'm usually in the larder. Butter, you know. I'm very good at churning."

As she started across the room, the earl could do nothing but leap to his stockinged feet and take the heavy pot from her hands. *Fancy this,* he thought, realizing how fortunate it was that the house had been empty on this night. He carried the stew out the door into the dark night and across the wet snow, soaking his stockings and chilling his toes all over again.

"Mrs. Rutherford, you will work henceforth in the upper house," he instructed the woman as she lifted her skirts and climbed aboard the vegetable wagon. "Mrs. Riddle will see to the transfer of position in the morning. Perhaps you could polish the silver in the parlors. Better than churning butter anyway. I shall tell my housekeeper to put you there, if you like."

"Oh, no, sir! Please, I cannot leave the kitchen. Cook needs me in the larder, and Mrs. Riddle will be most displeased to have her staff turned topsy-turvy." She gathered her gray wool shawl tightly about her shoulders. "What about the leavings? The villagers depend on my help. Mrs. Rutherford and I . . . well, we also eat the leavings, sir. We have hardly enough money to buy food."

"You'll earn higher wages on Mrs. Riddle's staff, and I'll instruct Cook to allow you the leavings as she has." He picked up the horse's reins and set them in her gloved hands. "But you, Mrs. Rutherford, and the other Mrs. Rutherford . . . I'm afraid I must address you by your Christian name, or we shall be always in a muddle."

"Always, sir?"

"When we speak together. You and I." He felt flustered suddenly, as though he'd said too much. But why shouldn't he have what he wanted? He was the earl of Beaumontfort, after all, and she was merely . . . what had she called herself? Ah, yes. Gwyneth.

"You and Mrs. Rutherford will be sent a portion from my own table each day," he said quickly. "Good evening then, Gwyneth."

He swung around and headed for the kitchen door again, hoping no one had noticed the earl of Beaumontfort traipsing about the vegetable wagon in wet stockings.

"Good evening," her voice sounded through the chill night air. "And thank you . . . William."

❄

"Again, Gwynnie?" Mrs. Rutherford trundled across the wooden floor of the single large room in her thatched-roof cottage. In her arms she carried a heavy basket covered by a white linen embroidered with a large monogrammed *B*. She set the gift on the pine table beside the fire and turned to the chair where her daughter-in-law sat paring potatoes.

"But 'tis t' fourth evenin' in a row t' earl has sent us dinner," she said in her native Lakeland lilt. "Whatever can it mean? And look at you, my dear, you've peeled t' potato until there's almost nothin' left of t' poor thing."

Gwyneth studied the small white nubbin in her palm and realized that most of the potato now lay in the bowl of parings. She tossed the remainder into a pot of bubbling water on the fire and sank back into her rocking chair. "Oh, Mum, I haven't wanted to trouble you, but everything has become difficult at the House. Terribly difficult."

"Don't tell me Mrs. Riddle is treatin' you ill again." The older woman sat down on a stool beside the chair and took Gwyneth's hand in both of her own. "That housekeeper has no heart. I can't imagine how she rose to such a position. Has she been spiteful to you?"

"No, 'tis not that. Mrs. Riddle is as unkind as ever, but 'tis not her at all. 'Tis—"

"Nah, for why would we have such feasts brought to us each night? Is it Mr. Yardley, then? Is he tryin' to woo you, my dear? Heaven help us, that butler is old enough to be your grandfather and thrice a widower already."

"No, no." Gwyneth lifted the old woman's hands and held them against her cheek. "'Tis nothing of the sort. 'Tis just that everything is suddenly so . . . so confusing. For one thing, I've been promoted into the upper house."

"But that's marvelous!" Her olive green eyes brightened. "Why didn't you tell me?"

"And I've been assigned to polish the silver in the parlors." Agitated, Gwyneth rose and began to set out the meal they had received from Brackendale Manor. Lamb! When was the last time she'd eaten mutton? Oh, why was the earl doing this?

"Silver polishin's t' easiest work in t' house," Mrs. Rutherford said. "How lovely for you!"

"And my wages are increased."

"Wonderful!"

"No, Mum. You don't understand."

"I can see that, my dear." After she'd offered the blessing for the meal, Mrs. Rutherford fell silent.

Gwyneth picked up her fork, wondering how she could explain the whirlwind that had blown through her life since

15

that evening in the kitchen with the earl of Beaumontfort. Her tidy, intimate world had been tossed into disarray like a haystack in a storm.

It hadn't always been so. From the moment Gwyneth had stepped into the snug stone cottage with its tiny windows and blazing fire, she had felt at home. Just as every piece of sturdy white china nestled comfortably in the old Welsh dresser, so Gwyneth's life had been ordered and tidy. On Mondays she baked, and on Fridays she washed. And every Sunday she and Mum walked to the village church to worship their Lord. Each day had its familiar, if sometimes lonely, routine. Gwyneth swept the floor each morning with the straw broom that hung beside the fire, and she nestled under the thick woolen blankets of her narrow bed each night. Nearby in her own bed, Mum would snore softly, a gentle reminder that all the world was at peace.

Now Gwyneth cut a bite of mutton and then another and another, unable to eat anything. Her stomach churned and her palms were damp. She wished desperately that she could similarly divide her thoughts into neat little squares that could be easily managed.

"Gwynnie." The old woman's hand stopped the knife. "T' good Lord is never t' cause of confusion and despair. What troubles you? You must tell me t' truth. All of it."

Gwyneth lowered her hands. "I explained to you about the night I served crumpets to the earl. Now, do you know he must have them every day for tea? And Mrs. Riddle does *not* appreciate my presence in the upper house, because I didn't work my way up as the other girls did. I've been assigned the silver polishing, the rug beating—all the easiest work. Every night this wonderful food is brought to our door. And every day when I'm polishing in the parlor, the earl . . . well, he says good morning to me, and he asks after you, and he inquires as to the health of Sukey's family, and he wonders whether I still think him crotchety—"

"Crotchety?"

"Yes." Gwyneth stuck a bite of lamb in her mouth. "Crotchety."

Mrs. Rutherford looked across at the sweet woman whose confusion was written clearly in her brown eyes. Mum gave a slight shake of the head and resumed her dinner. The forks and knives clinked in the silence of the room, while Gwyneth pondered her turmoil. How silly to be upset when all was going well. Had she no confidence in her Savior's ability to guide her life?

"I understand what troubles you, Gwynnie," the old woman announced finally. "T' earl of Beaumontfort has taken a fancy to you."

"To me?" Gwyneth gave a laugh of disbelief. "Absolutely not! He likes my crumpets, 'tis all. I gave the man a warm supper on a cold night, and he wished to reward me for my loyalty. But my promotion has not brought me joy as he had hoped. On the contrary, I'm resented and envied by the rest of the staff."

"Do you wish to go back to t' kitchen, then?"

"How could I? The earl would be most offended. Did you know that each evening I find twice the leavings I did before he came? Certainly he has companions who visit him for shooting and riding and playing at chess. He brought his personal staff from London, as well. But I'm quite sure they are not eating such great quantities of food. Mum, I believe the earl has ordered Cook to leave out more than usual."

"Aha, 'tis just as I hoped and prayed then. Wee Willie has grown up into a fine man and an honor to t' titles bestowed upon him when his dear father passed on, rest his soul."

"Wee Willie?"

"T' earl, of course. I knew him when he was but a lad. You must accept t' blessin' God has chosen to lay upon you, my dear. Soon enough t' staff will come to accept you in t' upper house, you'll see."

With a yawn, Mum set her plate in the dish pail and started for the narrow bed across the room. It was just past seven o'clock, and Gwyneth knew there would be long hours of silence ahead. Too much time to think lonely thoughts.

She lifted another bite to her lips, but her focus remained on the flickering fire. For an instant she imagined she'd caught sight of the exact spark that twinkled in the earl's blue eyes when he strode into the parlor each morning. He always spoke to her so briefly, and her replies to him were properly humble and sparse. Yet their few words had become the high point of each day to her. How could she have allowed it?

Dear Lord, she poured out, *'tis not the resentment of the staff that troubles me, is it? 'Tis not the easy labor and extra food. 'Tis him. For the first time since my husband died, I feel alive in the presence of a man. Oh, God, why does it have to be the earl?*

"I'll just put out t' lamp, my dear," Mrs. Rutherford called. "We don't want to use up what's left of our oil."

"No, Mum."

"Would you fetch a bit more coal for t' fire? 'Tis so chilly—" She paused, listening. "Now who could be outside at this hour?"

At the sound of a knock on the door—though she had no idea of the nature of their visitor—Gwyneth's heart clenched tightly, and her hand flew to the stray tendrils that had slid from her hair.

"Glory be," Mrs. Rutherford said as she peered through the small window beside the door. "'Tis wee Willie himself!"

CHAPTER TWO

Gwyneth set her knife on the plate and wiped her hands on her apron as Mum opened the front door. Oh, she was a mess—her fingers wrinkled from the starchy potato water, her sleeves damp to the elbows, her skirt hem muddy from trekking through the village with the night's leavings. She had no gloves, no time to do up her hair, and she felt quite certain she smelled of onions. Why now? Why him!

"Mrs. Rutherford?" the earl's deep voice sounded across the room.

"She's just finishin' her dinner," the older woman answered. "I shall be happy to—"

"But it's you I've come to see, of course," he cut in. "I had spoken with Gwy—with your daughter-in-law of your earlier life here in Cumbria, Mrs. Rutherford. I wondered if you might be the dear woman I recalled from my boyhood rambles. And indeed you are. You used to feed me strawberry tarts in the summertime and strong tea in the winter. Do you remember?"

"Aye, of course," Mrs. Rutherford said. "How could I forget wee Willie and his two great hairy dogs muckin' up my fresh-mopped floors? Do come inside out of t' chill, boy."

19

Gwyneth rose from the table as Beaumontfort spoke for a few moments with his equerry, who waited outside. Why had the earl come to their cottage? Couldn't she at least have worn her blue dress on this day? Heavens, she was in her stocking feet!

Oh, Father, he didn't come to see me. Please keep my thoughts in order. Please help me to be humble and to think of Mrs.—

"And I wished to see your daughter-in-law, of course," the earl said, stepping into the house and shutting the door behind him. "Gwyneth has been a most welcome addition to my household staff, Mrs. Rutherford. I have never seen the silver gleam as it does these days."

Gwyneth flushed and attempted one of her hopeless curtsies. No one taught children such manners in a Welsh mining village. Her legs felt as tangled and limp as a bowl of hot noodles. She drew the best chair before the fire for the earl.

"My lord," she managed. "Welcome to our cottage."

"Thank you, Gwyneth." His blue eyes met hers, and she recognized the spark she had seen in the fire. "I was just down from the House having a look round the village, as you recommended."

"Oh, sir, I didn't—"

"A most useful suggestion." He gave her a smile that carved gentle lines in his handsome face. "I have called on the family of Sukey Ironmonger. It appears her children are well and her husband is on the mend. He plans to return to his labors at the smithy tomorrow, and Sukey will return to my kitchen. I believe we shall have fresh bread again at Brackendale."

Gwyneth tried another little bow. "Many thanks for your generosity, my lord. The extra leavings have been greatly appreciated."

"And t' lovely meals here at t' cottage, too," Mrs. Rutherford put in. "You're too kind."

"Not at all, madam. Do be so good as to join me here by

the fire, both of you. I should like to discuss a certain matter of some urgency."

Gwyneth shot her mother-in-law a look of desperation, hoping she might be allowed to go out for more coals or something. But Mrs. Rutherford, her face wreathed in smiles, settled in the rocking chair and picked up her knitting as though this were merely a neighbor come round for a spot of tea. Willing her heart to slow down, Gwyneth took the only other chair in the house.

How fine the earl looked in his black frock coat and starched white collar. His dark hair, perfectly trimmed, framed the deep-set blue eyes that had so entranced Gwyneth. But it was his hands, his strong fingers ornamented with a gold signet ring, that reminded her of his stature and wealth. She must not forget the vast gulf between them.

"First, I wish to offer my condolences to you on the loss of your husband and sons, Mrs. Rutherford," the earl began. "Your return to the village has been the cause of much speculation. I am told your situation in Wales grew bitter indeed."

"'Twas I who was bitter." The old woman studied the fire as her needles clicked softly. "When I first returned to England from Wales, sir, I felt quite sure t' good Lord had forsaken me. I had nothin' left. My few savin's were lost to me, along with t' only family I'd ever known."

"My deepest sympathy."

"'Twas a low time, but only because I'd taken my eyes off t' cross of Christ. God himself suffered greater loss than I ever did, and willin'ly, too. Slowly, I began to understand that he'd given me a new home and a new family. Here I am in t' dear cottage I have loved all my life. And Gwynnie has become my daughter, my friend, and at times, even my mother—tuckin' me into bed at night and makin' sure I eat my vegetables."

The earl looked at Gwyneth. "Well done, madam."

"'Tis I who have reaped the blessings of my life with Mrs. Rutherford. She has always been so kind to me, and I'm happy to do what I can for her."

"Which is why I have come with a proposal." He shrugged out of his frock coat and cleared his throat. "I, ah . . . but I'm afraid I missed my tea earlier today. Might you prepare some crumpets, Gwyneth?"

"Of course, sir, at once." She leapt to her feet, thankful to have something to do with her hands. "And tea, my lord?"

"Only if you'll agree to return to your previous form of address."

"Oh, sir, I—"

"William is my name. I should thank you to use it."

"Yes, sir." She raced to the shelf where they kept their dry goods, her mouth parched and her heart slamming against her chest. It had been so different between them in the kitchen at Brackendale House. Gwyneth hadn't thought of William as the earl, and she hadn't noticed his blue eyes or the way his skin looked just after his morning shave. She'd given little heed to the breadth of his shoulders or the warm timbre of his voice. He'd been merely a man with wet stockings and an empty stomach. Now she knew he had the power to turn her life . . . and her heart . . . upside down.

"I don't suppose I could place a request for one of your strawberry tarts next spring, Mrs. Rutherford?" he was asking. "Seeing you again, I can almost taste them."

She laughed. "Ah, wee Willie, you were a bold thing even then. Yes, I'll make you a plateful of tarts—as long as you promise not to eat them all at a go."

"No, madam, I shall be a good lad, as always."

She chuckled, a welcome sound in the usually quiet cottage. "Whatever became of those two cheeky dogs that always roved about with you? Long gone, I suppose. You know, Mr. Rutherford and I had a fine dog in Wales."

"A corgi, I understand."

"Aye, Griffith was a dear dog. And do you still like to splash about in t' tarns? Boatin' and fishin' and such?"

"I rarely have opportunity these days. I'm very busy. Even crotchety, some say."

Gwyneth glanced across the room to find him eyeing her, a grin lifting the corner of his mouth. She covered the crumpet batter with a cloth and set it on the hearth. The man might be here another hour or more. She must relax. She simply must.

"And how is your new position suiting you, Gwyneth?" he asked as she sat down again. "Yardley speaks well of your services."

"I'm grateful, sir. Mum and I have creditors in Wales, and the increased wages will be most helpful."

"Good. Then you will not object to yet another increase in your income." He leaned back and propped his feet on the hearth. "I shall explain. My brief illness this autumn necessitated a period of rest, and I was compelled to leave London before the culmination of the holiday season. Such a breach of custom has left my acquaintances in want of my company and my business colleagues feeling the absence of my usual generosity. All this has led me to the decision to host a ball this Christmas Eve. Guests will begin to arrive from London the weekend before. This will mean a good bit of work—organizing the staff, planning meals, scheduling entertainments, and the like. I am assigning the responsibility to you, Gwyneth."

Her heart faltered again. "Me, sir? But Mr. Yardley is your butler."

"Yardley is a good man, yet he's getting on in age. He's just buried his third wife, and he's distracted. In fact, I believe his mental faculties are not in top form."

"Oh, dear." Gwyneth thought for a moment. "I'm quite sure Mrs. Riddle—"

"My housekeeper has enough work on her hands. I want fresh ideas. I want efficiency. I want loyalty, intelligence, and a keen wit. In short, I want you."

"I've only just come out of the larder into the upper house. In the eyes of the staff, I'm a kitchenmaid, my lord."

"My name is William." His blue eyes flickered. "Are you rejecting my proposal, Gwyneth?"

"No, but—"

"Good, then I shall inform Mrs. Riddle in the morning." He slipped the gold links from his cuffs, tucked them into his pocket, and rolled up his sleeves. "Do you know what I discovered today? My ice skates. I was searching for my old boat—the one I used to take out on the tarns—and I found the skates hanging from a nail in the stables. Not the least bit rusted! Do you skate, Gwyneth?"

"Never."

"You must learn. It's good fun."

She knelt before the fire and began to pour crumpets into the rings on the griddle. Skating? Planning the earl of Beaumontfort's Christmas ball? Whatever was this man thinking? Although she needed the wages, Gwyneth felt strangely hemmed in by his generosity. Did she want to plan a grand party? Did she even know how? Life had been much simpler when she labored in the larder and took leavings to the villagers by night.

Gwyneth glanced up at the earl, who had slouched down in his chair and closed his eyes. Good heavens. Was he going to sleep? She looked over at Mrs. Rutherford. She snored softly, her knitting forgotten in her lap.

How often had it been just so in their small house in Wales? The family dozing by the fire as Gwyneth boiled up tea or fried sausages. The dog watching with hopeful eyes. Her husband with his coal-blackened hands folded on his chest, always so exhausted. She had loved him well, though never with a passion that made her pulse flutter.

Dear God, why does the sight of the grand earl make me feel as though I've just run a mile—breathless, dry of mouth, and completely light-headed? I know he's a good man, she prayed as she turned the crumpets, *but he's beyond me. Lord, why have you put him into my heart in such a powerful manner? You must want me to touch his life in some fashion. Perhaps I'm to lead him to you, Father. Is that it? Please show me!*

"You look a hundred miles away," the earl said in a low voice. "May I know where your thoughts have taken you, Gwyneth? I once shared mine with you."

She lifted her eyes to find him leaning forward, elbows on his knees, hair softly tousled. He looked nothing like an earl and everything like a dear, comfortable, wonderful man.

"You're in need of a good jersey," she said without preamble. "A jersey knitted of sturdy brown wool, with long sleeves and a rolled collar to keep you warm in winter."

"You were thinking of me, then?"

"Actually, I was praying." She slid the crumpets onto a clean plate. "I was asking God why he has sent the earl of Beaumontfort into a small cottage with two plain widows who have nothing more to offer him than tea and crumpets."

"You offer yourselves to me, both of you. I shall never forget the kindness of Mrs. Rutherford. And you . . . I came because I wanted to talk to you."

"Sir . . ." She gathered her courage. "I am not as well educated as you are. I have read few books, and I know little of the wide world. I have no coy speech to entertain you nor quaint stories to charm you. Moreover, I am not an organizer of Christmas balls, my lord."

"You've been feeding half a village on the leavings from my household. And my name is William."

"I feed them stew made of scraps, and you are the earl of Beaumontfort. How can I call you William?"

"Precisely because I am the earl, and I have commanded you to."

"Commanded?"

"Asked. It is also my role to employ competent assistants. Do you doubt my ability as an overseer of my properties and entertainments?"

"No, sir. William."

He gave a soft chuckle. "Good, then you'll take the position."

Gwyneth handed him the plate of crumpets. "Do you make it a practice always to get exactly what you desire, William? Or am I the sole recipient of your incessant demands?"

"Incessant? I hardly think—"

" 'I should like some crumpets, Gwyneth.' 'I'm assigning the position to you, Gwyneth.' 'You must learn to skate, Gwyneth.' 'I command you to call me William, Gwyneth.' " She dropped into her chair, folded her arms, and stared at him. "And I have *not* offered myself to you. I offered crumpets to you. That's all. Crumpets."

"You amuse me, and that's a gift whether you intend it or not."

"A gift is something given from one friend to another. And friends do not issue commands."

"No? Then perhaps I've never had a friend. I've commanded people all my life, and they've always obeyed. Until now."

He was still smiling at her, and she noticed a tiny globe of strawberry jam at the corner of his mouth. Leaning across the space between them, she brushed it away with a napkin.

"Love is kind," she said, softening her voice. "Love does not seek its own way. 'Tis gentle and forbearing. A true friend would lay down his life, never expecting anything in return."

"As you did for Mrs. Rutherford."

"As she taught me to do by living out the words of the Holy Bible. By her example, Mum showed me how to be a servant. I'm willing to be your servant, my lord, but unless

26

you learn to stop issuing commands, you shall never have me for a friend."

"A friend." He mused for a moment, a knuckle pressed against his lower lip. "My father instructed me never to trust anyone too much. I was taught to depend upon myself, upon my own keen wit, in order to minimize the risks in life. Like a strong fortress, I was to keep my walls high and well guarded. Casual acquaintances are acceptable. But true friends do not fit comfortably into such a picture."

"Nor does God." She tore off a piece of crumpet. "How can you allow the perfect and almighty Creator of the universe into your heart, if you cannot admit even one silly goose of a human?"

"You are no silly goose." He studied her, his blue eyes absorbing her face, her hair, her lips. "Gwyneth, do you know why I came to Brackendale this winter?"

"You said 'twas to recuperate from your illness."

"My physician recommended rest, and I warmed to the notion. I recalled a time when Christmas did not mean balls and grand parties and gold-wrapped gifts. When days were simple and carefree. When my world was . . . different." He let out a breath. "Life has become complicated. Demanding. On my journey to Cumbria, I dreamed of a small fire, a warm drink, a pleasant chat. Rest. And somehow . . . I have found those things only with you."

Gwyneth swallowed the bite of crumpet and felt it lodge like an acorn in a drainpipe. *With her?* What was the man saying? What did he want? Surely he knew she was nothing to him. She could never be his peer, and she would refuse any relationship that smacked of scandal. She took a sip of tea, praying the crumpet would dissolve.

"My businesses are prospering," he continued, oblivious to the fine sheen that had broken out on his companion's brow. "To enrich the family's coffers, I have employed capable managers, esteemed barristers, and astute accountants.

My oversight of their activities is helpful, but hardly essential. In fact, I often find myself at loose ends, wanting something . . . and not quite certain what it is."

Gwyneth swallowed the bite of crumpet. This was a matter she understood perfectly. Perhaps he was the earl, but William was also a man who needed a sympathetic ear. That she could give him.

"You feel as though something is missing in your life," she said softly. "When I was a girl in Wales, I knew that sentiment well. I ached inside with a loneliness I could not fill with chores, entertainments, acquaintances, or any sort of busyness. My mother had died when I was wee, and I began to believe 'twas the love of a family I lacked. So I sought after a family in the same way you seek to fill your own emptiness. I married a good-hearted coal miner and believed I soon would have children."

"But you did not?"

"At the time I had no idea that a fever my husband had in his childhood meant he could never father children. When I learned the truth, I was angry, and I felt betrayed. How could he fail to give me what I wanted most? But then Mum put her arms around me, and as I wept bitter tears, she told me that a baby would never complete me. Six babies would never complete me. 'Twas not an emptiness of heart that plagued me, Mum said, but an emptiness of soul. When I welcomed Christ in, I found the most blessed fullness. My anger toward my husband faded, and I discovered joy in the family I'd been given."

"But then you lost your husband."

She nodded. "'Twas the end of what little dream I had left, I thought at first. My family was gone." She gave a little smile. "And what earthly future could I have? Who would ever marry a penniless widow past the age of thirty? No man in his right mind, I would think. So, when Mum told me she was returning to England, I knew I wanted to go with her. She is my family now—more than family enough to keep me content. And the love of Christ fills my soul. I need nothing more, William."

Glancing at him, she hoped he believed her. What she had told him was true—all of it. Christ did fill her, and she had been content. *Had been* until this long-legged man with a deep voice and blue eyes had walked into the kitchen in need of food, drink, and . . . and things she ached to give. A listening ear. Warm arms to hold him. A soft cheek against his neck. Gentle words to comfort and strengthen him.

What was wrong with her that she wanted more? God had blessed her with salvation. He had given her home and family. Gifts more precious than diamonds and gold.

"Your faith is all you need?" William asked. "Perhaps that's my failure. I am a Christian, Gwyneth, but I have little time for matters of religion."

"Then your faith must be shallow."

"Shallow?" He looked offended. "I don't think so. I have quite a deep belief in God."

"My lord, have you ever truly loved someone?" She searched his face and clearly read the answer. "I didn't think so. True love demands time. If I love someone—as I love Mrs. Rutherford, for example—I want to spend time with her. I want to know her better day by day. We enjoy our hours together and, as a result, our devotion to each other grows. Were I to tell you that I have little time for matters of friendship with Mrs. Rutherford, you would surmise that I do not truly know her well, nor do I love her as I claim."

He mused, his focus on the fire. "You speak frankly with me, Gwyneth."

"Aye. 'Tis the only way I know to speak."

"Then I shall be honest with you." Leaning forward, he met her eyes. "I do not believe you are perfectly content. I believe your faith sustains you and fulfills you, but I also discern a longing you cannot disguise. I saw it that night in the kitchen when I asked you to stay and take tea with me. You're lonely."

Gwyneth clasped her hands together, praying for divine assistance. How could she admit what he said was true? She wanted to be completely satisfied in Christ. Honestly she did.

"Do you deny it?" he asked.

She glanced at Mrs. Rutherford, who was snoring softly, her knitting needles askew on her lap. What good would it do Gwyneth to acknowledge her true feelings to the man? Why did he even want to know? What on earth had led her into this dreadful circumstance?

"No," she said, "I cannot deny I am lonely at times. But I've come to understand that I can choose to wallow in unhappiness or seek after the joy in life. I choose joy."

He smiled. "Which is the very reason your faith is real and not a contrivance. Will you do something for me, Gwyneth? When you are lonely, will you feel free to seek me out and speak with me? I should like to . . . to listen to you."

She moistened her lips, trying to think how to respond. Of course she couldn't go traipsing up to the earl of Beaumontfort every time she felt a little low. He was not her close acquaintance. He could not be her confidant.

"Gwyneth?" He reached out and laid his hand on hers.

"'Tis impossible. You and I—"

"Not impossible. You tell me my faith is shallow, and you urge me to grow deeper in Christ. You insist this will fill the emptiness inside me. Yet you resist taking the hand of a man God has sent to relieve your own loneliness."

"God has not sent you to me, sir," she argued. "You are my master, and I am your servant—nothing more."

"Perhaps he didn't send me to you. Perhaps there's nothing I can do to enrich your life. But God sent you to me, that much I know. Gwyneth, you have filled my stomach, warmed my heart, uncovered my flaws, and challenged my faith. And I like that. Very much."

Standing, he took his frock coat from the back of his chair and slung it over his shoulder. "Consult with Mrs. Riddle in the morning," he said as he headed for the door. "She'll instruct you on planning the Christmas event. Use the grand ballroom, and see that Yardley selects a tree large enough to hold all the candles. We've nearly a thousand of them. I want venison, veal, pheasant, and boar—" He came to a stop, swung around, and tilted his head. "Am I issuing commands?"

"Yes, sir," she said.

"Hmm." He pulled on his coat and cleared his throat. "Gwyneth, you may do whatever you like to ensure that joy reigns at Brackendale this season."

"Thank you," she said, rising. "I shall see to it that this is the best Christmas ever. For you, William."

❉

"Sir, as head housekeeper under the earl of Beaumontfort for fifty years," Mrs. Riddle began, "I must—"

"You refer to my late father," Beaumontfort cut in, turning toward the woman from the desk in his study. "I am earl now, of course, and I have been earl for three years."

Mrs. Riddle's pinched lips turned a pale shade of ivory. They hardly parted when she spoke. As a boy, Beaumontfort had found it fascinating to watch her form words through the tiny slit between them. Now her affected mannerism merely irritated him.

"Yes, my lord," the woman continued with a deferential nod. "As head housekeeper under your father *and* you, and as an employee of Brackendale House for fifty-three years, I must take it upon myself to speak boldly."

"Certainly, Mrs. Riddle. For I am quite confident your words will be both gracious and charitable."

The lips tightened. "I must inform you, sir, that the kitchen-maid whom you directed to plan your Christmas ball is incapable of carrying out the assignment."

"Kitchenmaid, Mrs. Riddle? I don't believe I gave that assignment to a kitchenmaid. Gwyneth Rutherford is under your employ in the household staff, is she not? I understand from Yardley that she is performing her duties quite admirably."

"Gwyneth Rutherford has only the experience of a kitchenmaid, sir. She hardly left the larder during her tenure at the House, and before that she was merely a housewife. She has no training in matters of such consequence as the entertainment of your friends and colleagues. Furthermore, she is Welsh."

"Welsh, is she?" He tapped the nib of his pen on the blotter. "Interesting. Perhaps we shall have Welsh caroling."

"As you know, my lord, the Welsh are . . . they are an unrefined people. And Gwyneth Rutherford hails from a mining village far less prosperous than our own."

"Ah, yes, I'm given to understand that her late husband was part owner in a coal-mining venture. Which reminds me . . . you did send round for that coal delivery, didn't you, Mrs. Riddle?"

"Of course, sir."

"The house seems a bit nippy of late. Do be good enough to lay a fire in the gold parlor. I shall take my tea there this afternoon."

"Yes, sir." Nostrils rimmed in white, the housekeeper stared as if daring him to give another order. He might be earl, but she clearly considered herself queen.

"And send Gwyneth Rutherford to my study, please. I shall welcome firsthand news of her progress on the Christmas ball. Now that you have mentioned it, my dear Mrs. Riddle, I believe that Welsh caroling would add the perfect touch to our festivities. Thank you for your ever-wise contributions, madam, and good afternoon."

Before she could respond, he turned back to his writing

desk and dipped his pen in the crystal inkwell. For the three years he had visited the country house as earl, Mrs. Riddle had been a pebble in his boot. In fact, he clearly recalled disliking her when he was a boy. Hadn't he once put a toad in her pocket?

As the woman left the study, he considered what action he might take to replace her. The house had rarely been calm under her reign. The small staff labored in peril of losing their positions, fearful lest Mrs. Riddle dismiss them for one reason or another. Yet, how could Beaumontfort release such a long-term employee? An unmarried woman of Mrs. Riddle's age would have little hope for a comfortable life . . .

The earl's thoughts focused on old Mrs. Rutherford, whose own widowhood and poverty placed her at great risk. How many women, he wondered, lived on the edge of starvation in the village below the great house? He pondered Gwyneth's efforts to help by carting leavings through the mud from home to home. The Beaumontfort family had never paid their villagers much heed, employing them as land tenants and household staff but rarely deigning to offer a helping hand. Perhaps, like Gwyneth, he should do something to assist.

Could *she* manage Brackendale House? Already Beaumontfort sensed the respect the staff paid her. She was well liked for her charity work, and Yardley insisted she was working diligently on preparations for the Christmas ball. Why not provide Mrs. Riddle a rent-free cottage and a small yearly purse? Why not place Gwyneth Rutherford as head housekeeper at Brackendale? Why not, indeed?

"My lord." Her voice drew him out of his thoughts. "You sent for me?"

"Gwyneth." He turned to face her. "Gwyneth, I have come to an important decision."

"Yes, sir, so have I." She took a step into the room. "I wish to resign my position at Brackendale House."

Chapter Three

R esign your position?" The earl stood to his full height. "Why would you do such a thing, Gwyneth?"

"'Tis best, my lord." She smoothed the white apron of her uniform and prayed for the words that would make him understand. "Mrs. Riddle is displeased with my work."

"That woman does not—"

"*And* I feel that my presence may become the cause of unrest among the household staff. Mrs. Riddle tells me I am resented." At the dark look on the earl's face, she took a step toward him and laid her hand on his arm.

"William, from the moment I chose to follow Mrs. Rutherford to England, I knew God intended me to be a servant. I will not go against his plan. As a servant, I can reach out to others and help them. In some small way, I can minister to their needs. But as organizer of your Christmas festivities—"

"You are serving me." He squared his shoulders. "Which is exactly why I placed you in that position."

"Is it, William?" She lowered her hand. "You knew I had

no experience in such matters. I am not the best choice. I still don't know why—"

"Have you posted the invitations?"

"Yes, sir."

"Have you ordered the meats?"

"Yes, but—"

"Are the candles brought down from the storage rooms?"

"Of course, my lord."

"Then you are performing your duties as expected. I refuse to accept your resignation. You are my servant, Gwyneth. Mine." He jabbed the air with a forefinger. "You will do as I command. And leave Mrs. Riddle to me. Is that clear?"

Gwyneth lowered her voice. "I am *God's* servant above all. If I can serve my heavenly Father best as a kitchenmaid, then that is where I shall work."

"But that's preposterous."

"You would do well to revisit the moment of your salvation, sir, and determine to whom you committed your life. If 'twas to Jesus Christ, then you must stop placing yourself and your own desires first. You must remember that hungry villagers are more important than Christmas balls. And you must understand that my purpose in life is not to promote myself or raise my wages or win the companionship of the earl of Beaumontfort. 'Tis to honor Christ and serve my fellowman."

"You told me your deepest desire was to create for yourself a family."

She swallowed at the truth in his words. "My own desires fall second, sir, when my purpose is to follow my Lord."

Before he could argue further, Gwyneth gave him a curtsy and headed for the door. She knew he had ordered his afternoon tea in the gold parlor, and she could see the maids laying out the cup, saucer, and silver implements as she slipped from the house. Let the earl of Beaumontfort take his tea and issue his commands and be as crotchety as he liked. She could not afford to alienate the other staff in the House and lose all hope of providing for Mrs. Rutherford in her declining years.

Not only did the two women face the struggle for survival that every commoner endured, they also bore the burden of the failed coal mine in Wales. The property sat unused—the land amassing back taxes and much of the now-rusted equipment in arrears. Each month they sent a little money to their creditors, but it was never enough. Somehow, Gwyneth must continue to earn a decent living.

Most important, she would not go against God's purposes. William might be earl, but his interest in her was clearly far too personal. And she would not set aside her commission to honor and care for her mother-in-law in favor of a brief romantic whim that could lead to nothing of profit. She must step away from the House—and its master—and try to think.

Stopping at the center of a narrow bridge on the outskirts of the village, Gwyneth drew in a deep breath. In her haste, she had left behind her woolen wrapper and gloves. An icy chill crept through her fingers as she set them on the iron railing and studied the glassy tarn beneath the bridge.

In deciding to resign her position at the House, she had confided her concerns to Mrs. Rutherford. Now those fears rose before her again. Mum had insisted that Gwyneth must follow her conscience, and God would provide. But what work could a poor widow find in the middle of winter? How could she earn enough wages to sustain two women who still owed such a debt in Wales? And how could she bear to surrender the joy that flooded her heart when William called out to her in greeting each morning or stopped by to chat with her each afternoon?

A gentle cascade of snowflakes sifted down from the leaden skies, dusting the bridge's black ironwork and sugarcoating the sleeves of Gwyneth's dark blue uniform. She closed her eyes and tried to gather her thoughts. With a shiver, she folded her hands against her mouth and exhaled to warm her fingers.

"Praying again, Mrs. Rutherford?" Gwyneth opened her eyes in surprise. The earl of Beaumontfort skated out from under the bridge, circled around on the frozen tarn, and came to a skidding halt that sent a spray of shiny crystals across the ice. A crimson scarf fluttered against his black frock coat as he held up a pair of skates. "These belonged to my little sister. Might I interest you in a brief turn around the lake?"

What an impossible man! He must have forgone his tea to follow her. She leaned forward, elbows on the rail. "Is that a command, my lord?"

"An invitation, friend to friend."

"No thank you, then. I'm quite chilled to the bone, and I'm on my way home for tea."

A frown darkened his face. She lifted her chin, fully expecting a barked command to follow. He set his hands on his hips, eyed her for a moment, and then let out a breath.

"Please?" he asked.

With a laugh of delight, Gwyneth clapped her hands. "Well done, William! Perhaps there's a human being inside that frock coat after all."

"Of course there is. Now will you come down and join him on the ice, or will he be forced to climb onto the bridge and sweep you off your feet?"

She pretended to consider for a moment. "Hmm. You know, I've never been swept off my feet."

"I have," he said. "Once."

The light in his eyes sent a flush of heat to her cheeks. Alarm bells clanged inside her. This was the earl, the lord of the house, the master of Brackendale Manor. She couldn't forget the differences between them, the hopeless and overwhelming chasm. He could not be allowed to woo her with entrancing words. She could not be seen alone in his company. Tongues would wag, gossip would fly, and her example of servitude would become a mockery.

"I left my wrap and gloves at the House," she said quickly. "'Tis too cold for skating, and I really must be going home."

"Don't go, Gwyneth." He skated toward the end of the bridge, paralleling her as she headed for the road. "I'm asking you to stay. I must speak with you."

"'Tis not proper."

"Balderdash." He caught her arm and swung her around to face him. "I want to be near you, Gwyneth. Is that so much to ask?"

She lowered her head as he held up the skates once again. Unable to respond and quite certain this was the worst mistake of her life, Gwyneth took them from him. Before she could bend to tie them on, he was kneeling at her feet.

"You took off my boots once," he said. "Let me learn to serve."

As he wrapped the leather straps over her shoes, she laid one hand on his broad shoulder to steady herself. She could see the top of his head, dark hair thick and rumpled, falling a little over his ears. It was all she could do to keep from threading her fingers through it and giving his hair a tender tousle.

William had been a boy once, roving about the tarns alone. Perhaps he was still a boy at heart—a lad in need of a good friend, a companion as loving and comfortable as his two dear dogs. She could be that to him, couldn't she? Merely a comrade, a chum?

"Gwyneth." Still kneeling, he took her hand and pressed his lips to her fingers. "Gwyneth, I won't command you to stay on at the House. I'll beg you instead. When you're there, the rooms seem brighter somehow. Warmer. Filled with life. I hear you laughing now and again, or singing some little

Christmas carol, and my heart lifts. I have lived my whole life with purpose and fortitude, plans stretching endlessly before me. But I have always been so restless. *Servanthood* and *godliness* and *family* . . . these are new words to me, Gwyneth. I drink them in like a man dying of thirst. I crave them, even though I cannot fully comprehend them. If you leave the House, if I cannot see you each morning, I shall be forced to relinquish that which lies just at the edge of my grasp."

"And what is that, William?"

"Hope. Faith." He lifted his head. "Perhaps . . . love."

"No," she said. "Not that."

"Why not?" Standing, he slipped his arm around her waist and urged her out onto the ice. "You asked me if I had ever loved anyone. I have not—not in the way you describe it. And I've begun to wonder if it is only the Sukey Ironmongers and the Mrs. Rutherfords who have the right to love. Perhaps that emotion is unavailable to men such as I."

Gwyneth closed her eyes and gripped his coat sleeves as he guided her across the tarn. How on earth could she concentrate on what he was saying when she was likely to land on her backside at any moment? She tried her best to keep her legs straight, but her ankles were determined to turn in, and her knees wobbled like jelly.

"Will you relax?" he asked, his breath warm against her ear. "Can you trust me to support you?"

"I'm trying, William, but 'tis treacherous here on the ice. I'm afraid I shall tumble."

"I'm quite strong enough to protect you, Gwyneth. Here on the tarn . . . and at the House. Won't you open your eyes?"

Her heart hammering, she looked up at him. Snowflakes drifted silently around them, a shrouding mist that enveloped the trees and hillsides in downy white. Warmth seeped through Gwyneth's limbs and heated her cheeks. How could it be that the chill had vanished so quickly? Her hands clasped in his, they glided beneath another bridge and past a tiny island thickly grown with gorse.

The village lay in a dale just beyond the lake, its thatch-roofed houses wearing snowy white caps as stone chimneys breathed wisps of pale smoke into the evening air. To Gwyneth the little town seemed distant, almost as far away as the grand manor house reclining in luxury on the hill. Lamps had been lit in the parlors there, and no doubt the staff was in a flurry over the disappearance of the earl just at teatime.

"And what is so amusing?" William asked.

"Did I laugh?"

"Indeed you did."

"I was picturing Mrs. Riddle in a grand kerfuffle. She'll be wringing her hands and shouting at Cook to boil another kettle of water for your tea. Poor Mr. Yardley will send the dogs to track you soon." She shook her head. "Oh, dear. If Mrs. Riddle learns you were out on the tarn with me, the fault will lie on my shoulders. And rightly so. I should be pouring Mrs. Rutherford's tea, not skating."

"You're not exactly skating, Gwyn. You're clinging onto my arm for dear life."

As she gave a laugh of protest, he swung her away and put her into a twirl that nearly sent her spinning out of control. With a chuckle, he caught her close again and kissed her cheek. Then he tucked her under his arm and set off down the length of the tarn at a speed that sucked the breath right out of her lungs. It was all she could do to stay upright as his long legs ate up the ice, whisking her past another small island, around an inlet lined with snow-laden fir trees, and out again beyond the shadows of a hut built at the water's edge.

"William!" she gasped. "I can't... I'm going to... don't let go!"

"Never." He skated her around a bend and onto a stream

that led away from the lake. "I used to fish this beck in the summer."

"That hill . . . that's where we picked strawberries last spring."

"Which puts me in mind of your crumpets and jam. I can almost hear my stomach grumbling at the thought."

As his stride slowed, she laid her head on his shoulder. How lovely to have a small tradition shared between them. The thought of baking crumpets for this man filled her with tenderness and longing. And those powerful emotions led her to the realization that all too soon he would be gone again.

"Why didn't you come to Brackendale last spring?" she asked.

"Duty, of course. But I shall never miss another spring in Cumbria," he vowed. "As long as I may pick strawberries with you."

"Oh, William. Really, I cannot." But even as she said the words, she ached for his promise to come true.

"And catch fish with you in summer," he went on. "And roast chestnuts with you in the autumn."

"And skate on the tarns in winter?"

"As long as it's with you." He was hardly moving forward now, as the stream narrowed and the sky darkened toward nightfall. "Gwyn, say you'll return to the House. I need you."

He stopped beneath the arching bare branches of an old oak tree. How could she turn him away? Yet, where could this growing intimacy between them lead? Not long after the new year began, he would go away to London. She would have no Christmas ball to plan and no position in the kitchen. Mrs. Riddle's wrath would burn unhindered. And loneliness would wrap around Gwyneth's heart once more.

But had she not told this man it was her purpose to serve? He stood here in the twilight pleading with her to help him.

He needed her for reasons she could not fully understand. And she must serve.

"I shall return," she said.

He let out a breath. "And I shall be your guardian. You have nothing to fear."

Nothing but the loss of your smile, she thought. *The absence of your laughter. The disappearance of the joy and warmth and fun you have brought into my life.*

"I hope Mrs. Rutherford hasn't drifted off to sleep without her tea," William said as he took Gwyneth by the shoulders and turned her away from him. To her surprise she realized she was facing her own little cottage, its thatched roof wearing a cap of snow. "This was the path I used to take as a boy. Mrs. Rutherford would spy me splashing through this very beck, and she'd invite me to her cottage for tarts."

Gwyneth wanted to tell him a hundred things—that she was afraid to lose him, that this past hour had been the most enchanting of her life, that she would pick strawberries at his side until not one remained on the hillside, that tears of joy and blessing filled her to overflowing. But she swallowed her words and climbed onto the snowy bank.

"Good night, Gwyn," he said, lifting a hand in farewell.

She tried to speak, but nothing would come. As she turned toward the house, she saw him skate into the darkness.

❄

"I plan to put sugarplum trees down the center of every table," Gwyneth said, reading from her long checklist. The head cook peered over her shoulder as they stood beside the kitchen fireplace. "That means we shall need to make hundreds of sugarplums. Have we currants and figs?"

"Currants, yes. Figs, no."

"But how can we have sugarplums without figs?" Gwyneth lowered the list and studied the elderly woman whose olive green eyes peered at her from a wreath of wrinkles. "Oh, Cook, we've sixty people coming for the Christmas ball."

"I'm afraid you'll have to take a carriage to t' shops in Bowness on Windermere." Cook gave a shrug. "You've got to have figs."

"Figs and almonds for the sugarplums, ribbon for the table, gold paper for the name cards, and a hundred other things. But how can I leave Mrs. Rutherford? She was not feeling at all well when I arrived home last night."

"Had you not been out frolicking until the wee hours," Mrs. Riddle intoned as she approached them from the stairwell, "you would have been available to help the dear woman." She held up the skates Gwyneth had worn the evening before. "These straps are wet. Sukey Ironmonger told me you returned the skates to the House this morning. Perhaps they were in use at the same time as these?"

When the housekeeper lifted the earl's skates, Gwyneth knew her flaming cheeks gave away the truth at once. Carefully folding her list, she lifted up a prayer for wisdom and charity. Though she would like nothing better than to lash out at the thin-lipped woman, she was reminded of her precarious position in the House.

"I fear my mother-in-law may have contracted the same influenza that felled Sukey's family," Gwyneth said. "I shall be attentive to her, of course."

"As well you should. She graciously took you in when you had no family and no home of your own. But then, perhaps you wormed your way into her good graces, just as you have done with others here at Brackendale Manor."

"Madam, I have never been deceitful in my dealings with anyone."

"You are aware, Gwyneth Rutherford, that it is against the rules of the House for fraternization to occur between employee and employer." The housekeeper's pursed lips hardly moved as she spoke. "An infraction is grounds for immediate dismissal."

"Yes, madam. Of course."

"Oh, do let her be, Riddle," Cook spoke up. "If t' earl chooses to take Gwynnie out for a bit of a skate, why should it trouble you? She's a good girl, that she is—takin' t' leavin's into t' village of an evenin', goin' to church every time t' doors open up, workin' her fingers down to t' nubs on this Christmas ball. You know she came all t' way from Wales to look after old Mrs. Rutherford, and not t' other way round. She left her family and country behind her, and she's always been a fine, hard worker. T' whole village will assure you that Gwynnie's a good girl. You leave her be, Riddle, or you'll have me to answer to."

Mrs. Riddle stared down her nose at the little cook. "Watch your tongue, Cook, lest you speak out of turn and jeopardize *your* position."

"I've been workin' at t' House nearly sixty years, Riddle, and I'm not afraid of t' likes of you."

"No? Though I came here after you, it was I who rose through the ranks to the superior position. As housekeeper, I am well within my rights to discipline you for insubordination."

"I should think plannin' all my menus and pokin' your pointed nose into my vegetable storage bins and castin' fear into my poor wee kitchenmaids would keep you busy enough, Riddle. I'm not afraid of you, and I never will be. With Gwynnie, here, I've a chance to show what I know about good cookin' for t' Christmas ball. She's let me plan my own menu for once. We're havin' ham, boiled fowls, tongue, chicken pie, roast pheasant, galantine of veal, and boar's head. We're havin' fruited jellies, prawns, raspberry cream, and meringues. We're havin' lobster salad, charlotte russe, and mayonnaise of fowl. And we're decoratin' t' tables with sugarplum trees. Now how do you like *that*, Mrs. Fiddle-Faddle?"

The housekeeper lifted her chin and pressed her lips into a tight white line. "Don't forget who's in charge here, Cook," she said. "As for you, Gwyneth Rutherford, a fortnight beyond the new year, you will see your last of the inside of Brackendale Manor. Once the earl leaves for London, you and your wicked attempts to woo his good favor will be quickly forgotten. Your low, immoral behaviors will be revealed to all within this House and the village. And you will find yourself cast out into the winter winds to straggle back to Wales where you belong. Do I make myself quite clear?"

"Yes, madam, that you do."

Without another word, the housekeeper turned on her heel and marched back up the staircase. Cook thumbed her nose at the retreating shadow as the kitchenmaids emerged from hiding places to which they'd fled at the sight of the formidable woman.

"Good riddance, Fiddle-Faddle," the cook said with a snort. "Don't let her trouble you, Gwynnie. She's just talkin'."

"She means what she says." Gwyneth shut her eyes and leaned against the long oak worktable. "Oh, Cook, 'tis a hopeless situation, no matter how I choose. I tried to step away from the Christmas ball, but the earl refused my resignation. And yet, every day that I remain, Mrs. Riddle grows more angry."

"Jealous, don't you mean?" Cook took the list from Gwyneth's pocket and spread it on the table. "She knows she's almost done for. She and Yardley and I—we were all hired on by t' present earl's father when he was but a very young man. 'Twill not be long before Sir William finds himself a bride and she sets about cleanin' t' House of its cobwebs, if you know what I mean. I'd put my wager on you for t' housekeeper's position. T' earl likes you, and you've done good work for him. Don't look so surprised. Sukey will fill my place, and one of t' younger men will take on the butler's duties. That's the way 'tis."

Gwyneth took the old woman's hand. "The earl is a good man. He will not set any of you out of the House without seeing to your needs."

"I hope you're right. But we don't know him well, for he doesn't come regularly to t' House."

Gwyneth gave the woman's hand a squeeze. He would come to Brackendale in springtime, in summer, in autumn, and in winter, he had promised her. But that was last night on the frozen tarn when they were nothing more than a man and a woman alone together on a chilly evening. Would Gwyneth be head housekeeper one day? Was that what William planned for her?

Oh, Lord, I'm so confused! I cannot take Mrs. Riddle's place. But if I don't hold some position here at the House, Mum and I will live in fear of our lives. The debt on the coal mine grows in spite of my payments, and you know how I labor for every tuppence I earn here at the House. Yet how can I recommend myself to the earl without being accused of improper behavior? Already the skating has been brought to light. Nothing will escape the prying eyes—

"You look as if you're ready to wilt right onto t' floor, Gwynnie," Cook said. "Come now, what's this about crackers here on t' list?"

"Crackers?" Gwyneth focused again on her Christmas plans. "Oh, yes, Mr. Yardley told me about them. They're a sort of toy. You pull them on each end, and when they pop, small toys fall out. I understand that Queen Victoria adores them."

"Hmph. You'd better hurry out to t' stables and arrange for a carriage. You won't find crackers for sale in our little village. 'Twill be a journey to Bowness for you, my dear."

❄

"James!" The earl of Beaumontfort spotted one of his grooms at the end of the stables. "Have you been out? What is the condition of the roads?"

"Good afternoon, my lord." The man removed his hat and gave a bow. "T' main thoroughfares are traveled enough to be passable, sir. But t' lanes and byways are treacherous."

William studied the steel gray skies. "I'd say we're in for another snow."

"Yes, my lord."

"We've had more snow this year than normal, haven't we, James?"

"Yes, my lord."

As usual, no one on the earl's staff gave more than a deferential answer to his inquiries. There would be no conversation about the coming storm, no musings as to its impact on the activities surrounding the manor, no queries as to the master's plans for the evening. Nothing. It wasn't proper.

William studied the young groom, whose nervous twisting of his gloves revealed his eagerness to be off. Rarely before had the earl wished for conversation with his staff—or with anyone, for that matter. Too busy, of course. Important matters to attend to. Business to be transacted. Perhaps if he returned to London, his hours would fill quickly and there would be no time for loneliness and longing. No desire for camaraderie, friendship . . . or love.

"James," he said suddenly, "have you a family? A wife, perhaps? Children?"

The man's eyes narrowed in wariness. "Yes, my lord."

"A wife then?"

"Yes, my lord."

"How many children?"

"Three, sir."

"And . . . ah . . . do they play in the snow? Your children?"

"Yes, my lord."

"I see. Very good, James. Do take care of them."

"Yes, my lord. I will, sir." He gave another little bow.

William let out a breath. "I was considering a ride, but perhaps that would not be prudent. What do you think, James?

Should I ride, and if so, which of my horses do you find the most surefooted? And can you tell me your opinion of the stables, James? Do you think them warm enough, or should I consider a stronger door?"

The groom glanced over the earl's shoulder as if he wished he could run for cover from this unexpected battery of questions. "Ridin', sir, would be . . ." His eyes brightened. "I say, there's Gwyneth Rutherford. What's she doin' out here in t' stables?" Catching himself, he addressed the earl again. "Ridin', sir, would be ill advised under t' circumstances."

William turned to find Gwyneth marching purposefully down the long row of stalls. Spotting him, she gave a silent gasp, pulled up short, and clutched her shawl against her throat. With an unconscious attempt to smooth her hair, she continued on more slowly.

"My lord." She gave the earl a curtsy. Her technique had improved, he noted wryly. "James."

"Mrs. Rutherford," the men replied as one.

"My lord, I must request permission to take a carriage to Bowness on Windermere," she said, her focus on the earl. "We need figs and ribbon and crackers and all manner of items for the Christmas ball. Really, I must go straightaway. You cannot imagine the kerfuffle I'll be in if we don't have figs for the sugarplum trees."

As James headed into one of the stalls, a tickle of amusement lifted the corner of the earl's mouth. "Sugarplum trees?"

"I must put something down the middle of the tables, of course—for decoration. Cook tells me 'tis always done. We won't have fresh fruit at this time of year, and I had hoped for something festive." Her brown eyes lit up. "Sugarplums! I loved them as a child, didn't you? We used to have them at dinner on Christmas Day, so delicious I could hardly wait."

"Visions of sugarplums danced in your head?"

"Exactly!" She laughed and reached out to touch his hand. "Please, you must let me take a carriage. If possible, I shall be away only this one night. Mum isn't well, you see, and I dare not leave her alone for long."

"Not well?"

"I fear she may have the influenza."

"I shall take you to Bowness myself," he announced. "James, ready a carriage."

"No!" Her cry rang through the stables. Grabbing his sleeve, she pulled him closer and stood on tiptoe to whisper into his ear. "I cannot go away with you, William! Think of it, please, and reconsider your order at once."

"You would rather go with James?" he murmured back, rather enjoying the moment of intimate tête-à-tête.

"James is a groom. I can go with him, of course. But not with you!" Her voice trembled a little. "Please, do not insist upon this, William. I beg you."

He considered for a moment. It would be most enchanting to spend an entire afternoon in the presence of the witty and straightforward Gwyneth Rutherford. He could take her to dinner at some little inn near the lake. They might stroll the shops together the following morning. Bowness was a lovely town, and he would buy Gwyneth anything she desired.

But the look in her eyes reminded him once again that her commitment to her faith took precedence over all else. She would not raise eyebrows with imprudent behavior. Her duty came before any sort of frivolity. She was a servant, demonstrating her commitment to Christ in word and deed. And it was this very quality that drew him to her.

Dear God, he prayed, awkward at the unfamiliar step into the world of the invisible. *Please grant me wisdom. Teach me to walk with you as Gwyneth does.*

"How may I serve you best?" he said, taking her hand and looking into her brown eyes. And then he knew. "James, will the carriage be safe enough along the main road to Bowness?"

"Yes, my lord," the groom replied, emerging from the stall.

"Take Mrs. Rutherford's list, then, and purchase the goods she requires." He handed over the sheet of paper she had brought. "But first, see that she is escorted safely home this afternoon. Her mother-in-law is ill."

Giving Gwyneth the most formal of bows, William forced himself to turn and walk away. He heard a breath of relief escape her lips, and he knew his prayer had been answered. Though it was not the answer he liked nor the path he would have chosen, he understood that to serve God and to truly honor and respect this woman, he must give her up.

Chapter Four

"However do you know so much about all these people?" Gwyneth sat beside her mother-in-law in their little cottage and sorted through the responses to the earl's Christmas invitations. The room was warm and cozy this night with the women's chairs pushed close to the fire and the crackle of the flames to cheer them. Their wooden floor had been swept clean, their dinner dishes washed and put away, and their shutters latched against the winter wind.

Gwyneth held up a missive inscribed with grand flourishes of black ink. "Now, tell me about this gentleman, Donald Maxwell. Who is he?"

The old woman's knitting needles clicked as the length of brown wool on her lap wove into a complex pattern of cables and fisherman's knots. "Donald Maxwell is a baron of very little means and very great ambitions," she replied. "He's a distant cousin to t' earl, but you'd think he was king by t' airs he puts on."

The effort of conversation sent her into a fit of coughing that made Gwyneth's heart ache. "Here's a clean hanky,

Mum. Shall I pour you another cup of tea?"

"Thank you kindly, Gwynnie. Oh, me, I do hope I'm past this before Christmas." Setting her knitting aside, she accepted the cup with both hands. "Does it seem cold in t' house to you, my dear? I can't seem to stay warm."

"I'll fetch more coal." On her feet at once, Gwyneth threw her shawl over her shoulders and hurried outside. As she scooped a hod full of coal from the bin outside their cottage, she scanned the narrow road to the village. Empty, of course. The earl had not come to visit the two women again, nor had he spoken more than a word of greeting to Gwyneth at the House each morning. She remembered well the evening she had made him crumpets before the fire. And she recalled their breathtaking skate across the lake and down the beck.

With her refusal to accompany him to the town of Bowness, the earl of Beaumontfort's attentions to her had ended. She should be grateful.

Clutching the hod close, she pushed back into the room. She must not think about the man. How could she be so ungrateful as to desire more than God had given her? This cozy cottage and Mrs. Rutherford were enough. *Dear Lord, please let them be enough!*

"Donald Maxwell did his best to woo t' earl's wee sister when she came of age," Mum was saying as Gwyneth stoked the fire. "But Lady Elizabeth would have none of it. She married a fine young fellow from Yorkshire, and a good thing, too."

"I've never seen Lady Elizabeth."

"A true beauty, and very sweet. Once Maxwell knew he'd lost her, he set about to match his own sister to t' earl."

Gwyneth sat down again and studied the letter's elegant penmanship. "I didn't realize any woman held the earl's affections."

"Oh, he doesn't take them serious, Gwynnie. At least, that's t' word in t' village. Some say our master will be a bachelor for t' rest of his days. But you can be sure any number of women would marry him at t' drop of a hat. He's a good Christian, he's rich, he's landed, he's becomin' to look upon, and he's kind. What more could a lady want, I ask you?"

"Nothing more," Gwyneth answered softly. "Nothing at all."

Hoping her mother-in-law could not read the message in her tone of voice, she sorted through the remainder of the letters. She couldn't afford to dwell on the impossible. There was work to be done, after all.

In one pile she placed the letters from those who had accepted the invitation to the Christmas ball. In another, she placed the regrets. To her way of thinking, it seemed half the English peerage would be coming to Brackendale Manor in less than a week. She could only pray she'd be ready for them.

"Do *you* find t' earl becomin' to look upon, Gwynnie?" Mrs. Rutherford asked. "Or is he too old for your taste?"

"Old? He's only just past forty," she answered absently. "He's certainly not old, and I, for one, cannot imagine how anyone finds him crotchety. I've never known a man who enjoyed a laugh more or one who took such pleasure in—" She glanced up. "The earl is agreeable."

Mrs. Rutherford chuckled as she turned her knitting to start another row. "Agreeable, is he? More so since he met you, I'm told."

"Who would tell you such a pointless piece of nonsense as that?"

"Sukey Ironmonger. T' dear girl dropped in on me t' other day, and she told me t' House is fairly aglow with your preparations for t' ball. Everyone's in high spirits. Do you know t' earl himself has been speakin' quite plainly with his staff, askin' questions and seekin' advice as though he were no grander than a common gent? Sukey says last week he went down to t' village and had a look round at t' ironworks, t' mill, and all t' shops. He's ordered his footman to write up a list of all t' widows and elderly who can't provide for themselves. Word has it, he's going to establish a fund. Can you credit that? A fund for t' elderly."

Gwyneth tucked a strand of hair behind her ear and placed the letters in her workbasket. "The earl of Beaumontfort is a good man. I have no doubt that he'd care for the villagers."

"He didn't before." Mrs. Rutherford gave a cough. "T' villagers say 'tis you, Gwynnie, who've done it. You've changed t' earl."

"I've done nothing but my duty," Gwyneth insisted, "and you've dropped your hanky again, Mum. I do wish you'd look after it. Here, take mine. Look, this is a letter that came in the post today. Perhaps 'tis from your cousin in Ambleside."

Before Mum could go on with that ridiculous blather about Gwyneth's effect on the earl, the younger woman crossed the room to lay out their nightgowns and slip the coal-filled brass warmers into their beds. Enough was enough. The gossip had to stop before her reputation suffered.

If so many women in London were eager to marry William, why didn't he just choose one of them? Let him marry Donald Maxwell's sister. Better yet, he could just stay a bachelor, and then she might see him now and again, or speak with him . . .

No, there must be no further dalliances with a lowly housemaid. The earl had made his request to see Gwyneth alone, she had spurned him, and that was that.

"Oh, dear God, this cannot be!" Mrs. Rutherford gasped and began to cough. "Oh, Gwynnie! Gwyn!"

Doubled over in pain, the old woman clutched at her chest as Gwyneth raced across the room to her side. "What is it, Mum? Take a sip of tea. Please, you must calm yourself. Whatever is the matter?"

Mrs. Rutherford took a drink as Gwyneth patted her on the back. A hand on the fevered forehead told the dire news. "Mum, you've taken a turn for the worse. You must come and lie down. I'll fetch the apothecary at once."

"No, no." Mrs. Rutherford squeezed Gwyneth's hand as her coughing subsided. "No, I cannot. Cannot rest. This letter . . . 'tis t' news I feared. May God have mercy upon us, Gwynnie. We're ruined."

❄

Beaumontfort paused at the edge of the wooded copse and studied the little cottage by the stream. In spring, he recalled, the climbing rosebush by the door would be lush and green, its long, arching canes loaded with pink blossoms. In summer, the lavender that lined the narrow lane would display a mist of heavenly purple flowers. By autumn, the trees surrounding the cottage would cast their red and gold leaves into the beck, and a wisp of pale smoke would waft from the brick chimney.

Gwyneth would be there, too, tending Mrs. Rutherford, carrying the leavings to the villagers, peeling potatoes for dinner. All the things that made her common . . . and somehow so dear to him.

Would he see her again? Could he ever bridge the gap between them? Or must he ride back to London, immerse himself in business, and fall into his bed exhausted and unfulfilled each night?

"Sir?" His footman gave a polite cough. "Shall we return to t' House now? 'Tis past ten o'clock."

Drawn from his reverie, the earl surveyed the small hunting party that had followed him through the woods that afternoon. As members of his loyal staff, they were always polite, always distant, always obedient. Was this type of demeanor what Gwyn had meant by servanthood? Was this the way one served the Lord?

Would she do everything Christ asked of her without response, without even a word of personal emotion—as these who served the earl of Beaumontfort did? He searched the faces of the men. Tired and cold, they obviously longed to hurry to their homes in the village and prop their feet before the fire. But as servants of the earl, they would suppress their own wills and do only his bidding.

They were good men, yet he did not truly *know* any of them. Was this what God expected of those who served him? Distant, mute, impersonal obedience?

"Take the deer back to the House," he told the hunters with a wave of dismissal. "And then go home to your wives and children. Inform Yardley I shall return within the hour."

"Yes, my lord." The men bowed, and without further word, they turned their horses in the direction of Brackendale Manor.

Beaumontfort let out a breath that misted white in the chill evening air. What sort of deity would wish his servants to function silently before him? What kind of master enjoyed absolute power?

He didn't.

Do you, Lord? he prayed, lifting his eyes to the dark branches woven overhead. *Is that what you want of me? Or do you long for something more of your servant? A friendship born of intimacy? A passion for conversation and communion? An end to loneliness through the fulfillment of genuine love?*

Beaumontfort couldn't deny he felt very alone these days. In fact, he would trade all his slavish staff for one hour with someone like Gwyneth Rutherford. Someone who would talk to him, challenge him, even dispute him. She was bright and witty. She possessed depths he had only begun to explore. Her loyalty pleased him, and her faith intrigued him. In his mind, she had become very real, very human, and more than a little desirable.

All that, and yet she was a servant. God's servant. And his.

He glanced over his shoulder at the silent forest. Though he could see none of the retreating hunters, he knew that if he set one foot into the little cottage, rumors of his presence there would fly through the village before dawn. Gwyn had made it clear she wanted no private moments with him. She wanted nothing, in fact, but the security of her job.

Blast! He gave the slender tree trunk nearby a shove, which sent a flurry of snowflakes drifting onto his hat and coat. He was master, wasn't he? Why should he care what the villagers said about him? He wanted to speak with Gwyn. He wanted to see her, ask the questions that haunted him, touch her hand, look into her brown eyes.

And, by heaven, he would.

Stalking through the iron gate at the edge of the property, he marched up the lavender-lined walkway and gave the heavy wooden door a sharp rap. "Mrs. Rutherford," he announced, "it is I, the earl of Beaumontfort. Open, please."

He waited a moment, listening. Nothing. Surely they were inside. He knocked again. When no one answered, he stepped to one side and peered between the shutter's slats through the tiny, glass-paned window. The two women were huddled before the fire, Gwyn's arms around Mrs. Rutherford, whose knitting lay amid letters scattered across the floor.

Beaumontfort frowned. Gwyn had told the footman in the stables that the old woman was ill. He shuddered, recalling the devastation that disease had caused in his own life.

Trying the doorknob, he found that it turned easily. The moment he leaned inside, he could hear sobs and cries of anguish. "Mrs. Rutherford?" he called out. "Are you all right?"

Gwyn lifted her head, her cheeks wet with tears. The moment she spotted him, her expression darkened. "What are you doing here?" she demanded.

"I was passing by. I thought to look in on Mrs. Rutherford."

"At this hour? Nonsense!" Gwyn leapt to her feet and waved her arms at him. "Get out, William! Leave us at once. We've enough trouble on our hands without becoming the scandal of the whole village. You march straight out that door, sir, and do not set foot inside our home again!"

Lest she become even more agitated, Beaumontfort exited the cottage. But as Gwyneth made to shut the door, he grabbed her arm and pulled her outside. On the doorstep, she jerked out of his grip and pushed the heel of her hand across her damp cheek.

"Don't ever come here again!" she cried. "I cannot bear to see you, and I won't have Mum subjected to gossip. You have no idea—"

"Then why don't you tell me," he cut in. "What's happened that has left you in tears? Is it her health? I can fetch a doctor from Bowness on Windermere. I have every—"

"Our troubles are none of your affair, William. I can accept no further favors from you. The villagers will accuse me of acting improperly with you, don't you see? There is nothing you can do for us. Nothing!"

"I can do anything for you. Anything you need." He touched her cheek. "Please let me help you, Gwyn."

She shook her head. "Truly you cannot. When I learned I would never have children, I thought my dreams were dead. And then our men were killed in the mine explosion, and I believed we were ruined for good. But God sheltered us under his wings. He brought us here to Cumbria, he gave me a position at the House, he provided us this . . . this beautiful . . . dear cottage . . ."

Covering her face with her hands, she gave a sob that wrenched his heart. He slipped his arms around her and drew her close. "Gwyn, you must speak openly with me. Is it Mrs. Rutherford? Let me carry her up to the House. I'll send for a doctor at once. I'll ride to Bowness myself."

Her fingers clutched the fabric of his hunting coat as she pressed her cheek against his shoulder. For a moment she said nothing, swallowing her tears and trying to stem the flood of emotion. He clutched her tightly, aware of the fragility of her thin frame and the threadbare fabric of her dress. She was poor and cold and in need.

God, I can do so much to help this woman! Show me how to reach her. Let me touch her life as she has touched mine.

"No," she said, pushing him back. "We must trust God to provide. Go home, William. Leave us in peace."

"God has provided already. Can you not see that God has sent me to you, Gwyn? I want to help. I care about Mrs. Rutherford. I care about *you* . . . very much."

Her eyes focused on his as he cupped the side of her face in his hand. She reached up, covering his fingers with hers and pressing her cheek against his palm. Her flesh was so soft. Her heart so pure. What more could he desire in life than this woman's presence? He ran his thumb across the delicate skin beneath her eye, absorbing the dampness of her tears and the gentle brush of her lashes.

"You have become precious to me, Gwyn," he murmured. "I treasure you, and I long to keep you near."

"No, you cannot—"

"I should not have asked you to go with me alone to Bowness. I beg your forgiveness."

"You have no reason to abase yourself. I'm naught but a poor widow, William. I'm your servant—"

"And I am yours."

"No."

"Yes. I *will* serve you, Gwyneth, as long as I may honor you as you honor me."

"To honor me, you must leave me in peace. Great trouble has fallen upon us, and we have little hope of redemption."

"Tell me your trouble."

"A letter came from Wales. 'Tis the coal mine. We owe a large debt—property taxes and machinery that remains in arrears—and we cannot meet it. Now we have learned that our creditors are demanding immediate satisfaction."

"Can you answer their demand?"

"No." She twisted her hands together. "Mum is beside herself with despair. I fear for her health. I must go inside."

"Stay a moment longer. Let me help you, Gwyn. I shall put one of my barristers onto the matter. Perhaps there is something I can do to relieve the situation."

"Do you wish to purchase a failed coal mine in Wales?" she asked, her dark eyes imploring. "I think not. You're a businessman, that much about you I know for certain. Your properties flourish, your investments grow, your wealth increases. To risk your finances by helping two poor widows pay their debts in a useless Welsh mining venture would be heedless and foolish. Ridding ourselves of the property is our only hope for salvation, but who would purchase a mine in which no one dares to labor? Of course you will not do it. You're a good man, William, and an honorable landlord. But I do not believe you will act recklessly out of a misguided ambition to assist a penniless widow who has briefly captured your fancy. I cannot blame you. Mrs. Rutherford will not hold you responsible."

"Gwyn, you must give me time. Allow me the opportunity to think this through and make a plan. I can help you; I'm certain of it."

She shook her head. "You must go now, William. Please go."

"Why do you push me away? Do you care so little for me?"

"And how shall I care for you? As one friend for another? No, for you are a man, and a lord, and by far my superior in situation."

"Care for me as a woman cares for a man."

"And become your mistress? Your illicit lover? Is that what you suggest?"

"No, of course not," he protested.

"But what other hope is there for association between a man of your rank and a woman of mine? My God does not permit any intimacy between unmarried men and women, William. And I cannot disobey his command. I am his servant."

"And mine!" He caught her roughly in his arms. "I want you with me, Gwyn. I have the wealth and power to overcome any obstacle between us. Allow me to make this happen. I shall take you into my home and provide a place for you there as my guest. I'll care for Mrs. Rutherford. Every need will be met. Everything you dream of—"

"Honor. Faith. Servitude." She gripped his coat sleeves. "Those are my desires, William! When I gave my life to Christ, I laid aside any earthly dreams of passion or wealth. I cannot obey my heavenly Father and obey you at the same time. How can you say I would be your guest? No one would believe such an arrangement between us—not even I."

"You misunderstand," he said.

"Do I? I understand that you ask of me more than I can give you. I must choose Christ, William! Let me go. Let me go!"

Pushing out of his arms, she rushed into the cottage and slammed the door shut. Breathing hard, he listened as the iron bolt dropped into place. To serve Christ or the earl of Beaumontfort—was that the choice he had given Gwyn?

Dear God, what have I done?

CHAPTER FIVE

I understand the Rutherford cottage is to be sold." Mrs. Riddle stood in the foyer, hands tightly clasped, as Gwyneth twined swags of pine branches along the banister. "How very sad for you both."

Gwyneth bit her lip to keep from responding. The housekeeper's delight was evident in her tone. She soon would be rid of the upstart Welshwoman who threatened her position at Brackendale House. Rumors had been flying that Gwyneth was to succeed Mrs. Riddle as head housekeeper by the start of the new year. Nothing the young woman said would stop the gossip, and Mrs. Riddle's agitation grew by the day. Gwyneth knew she would like nothing better than to dismiss her rival. Perhaps now that the Rutherfords' meager hopes had died, Mrs. Riddle hoped to purchase the cottage for herself. Gwyneth wouldn't put it past the woman.

"I'd always believed that cottage and t' lands around it belonged to Brackendale Manor," Sukey Ironmonger said as she pinned a red silk ribbon to the swag. "It's built so near t' village. Everyone assumed it was a part of t' earl's holdin's. I wonder if he even knows he doesn't own that land."

"Of course he knows," Mrs. Riddle snapped. "The elder Mrs. Rutherford, you see, was married to the earl's cousin. On the matriarchal side, of course. Hardly any money at all, I'm afraid, but there was that cottage and bit of land. *Was*, I say, as it soon will pass from the hands of the Rutherford family forever."

Gwyneth's scissors dropped suddenly from the first landing to the marble floor below. At the clang of metal and spray of marble dust, she clapped her hand over her mouth. Mrs. Riddle gave a snort of disgust.

"You really must be more careful, my dear," she said. "Any further mishaps like that, and I shall be most reluctant to write you a favorable reference."

"I should be pleased to write Gwyneth Rutherford a reference myself—if she needed one," Beaumontfort said, striding into the foyer as three footmen bore his coat, top hat, and gloves behind him. "You needn't trouble yourself so greatly in these matters, Mrs. Riddle. Yardley, where's my coachman? I gave instructions that he await me at ten sharp."

Gwyneth crouched behind the banister and tried her best not to look down at the earl. They had not spoken since the night she had rejected him a second time, and she doubted that he would ever speak to her again.

Though their future hung in the balance and the young woman's heart was breaking, nothing good could come of a relationship between them. What sort of man was the earl to suggest such an arrangement? She could not move into his home without arousing all manner of suspicion, and no one would believe she was merely a guest. No, the two women must seek shelter beneath the wings of their heavenly Father, and no one else.

"Ten o'clock, yes, my lord," Yardley was saying. "Ten sharp. I'll just have a look out front for him."

Gwyneth tucked sprigs of pine branches into the swag and kept her eyes shut tight. *Let William go away. Take him away, Father. Don't let me have to hear his voice or think about him. I can't think about him.*

"Gwyneth," the earl called up the staircase. "I should like to have a word with you, please."

She raised her head, certain her cheeks were flaming red. "My lord, I—"

"About the Christmas ball," the earl amended.

"Yes, sir. Of course." Smoothing her wrinkled apron, she hurried down the stairs, aware that the eyes of all the staff were upon her. Did they know the earl had been at her cottage? Had they learned of his proposal? Or were they merely curious at the unexpected affinity between their master and his maid?

"In the front parlor, please," he said, pointing. It was a command, not a request.

She knitted her fingers together and held her breath as he stepped into the room after her. The door stayed open behind him, though he placed his back to the hall so that no one could hear their words.

"The guests will begin arriving soon," William said. "I am assuming that all is in order."

"Yes, my lord. I have arranged for a small musical concert of Christmas hymns and various amusements in the parlor this evening as your visitors arrive. Tomorrow night, Christmas Eve, the ball will begin at eight o'clock with a meal, proceed through the dancing, and end with a nativity play performed by the village children. The footmen have laid out logs for a bonfire on the lawn. The following morning—"

"Gwyneth, I owe you a profound apology," William moved forward, stopping only a pace from her and dropping his voice. "I came to your cottage the other night seeking nothing more than to speak with you. I hoped to better understand your faith in God. And I confess that I desired to be in your presence because I . . . because I have grown to care for you. Instead, I stepped beyond the bounds of gentlemanly behavior. My offer of assistance was well intended but poorly thought out. I am certain you misunderstood my meaning, for I would never suggest any imprudent action. I have—" he lowered his head—"I have been brought to the edge of despair at the memory of your reaction to my hasty and ill-considered words."

She longed to reach out to him, to brush back the lock of hair that had fallen across his forehead, to touch the hands that gripped his gloves so tightly. Instead, she stared down at her own shoes.

"I have been praying earnestly to God in these last few days," he went on, still unable to meet her eyes. "And it has become evident to me that in the years since my conversion to Christianity at the feet of your mother-in-law, I have strayed from that conviction. Unlike yours, my faith in Christ has not borne fruit. My purposes have been selfish and my actions worldly."

"The coachman is here, sir!" Yardley called through the open parlor door. "Three minutes past the hour, my lord."

"One moment," the earl returned. He raked a hand through his hair. "Gwyneth, I want you to know that I have asked forgiveness of God for my heedless notion that you must serve me as you serve him. I ask forgiveness now of you."

"You have it," she said softly.

"So readily?" He lifted his head. "How is your faith so easily followed?"

"'Tis never easy to follow Christ, William. Do you think it has been easy to give up my dreams of husband, children, and home? Do you believe 'twas easy to leave Wales and accompany Mrs. Rutherford to a foreign land? When you made your offer of refuge that night outside the cottage, 'twas all I could have hoped for, wasn't it?"

"Do you care for me then? Even a little?"

"More than a little." She looked away. "Though you may deny it, I have seen the fruit of the Holy Spirit in your life. You are well known for your intelligence and honesty. But you have shown yourself to be good, kind, and generous, as well. More than that, you have made me laugh. I shall never forget you."

"Five minutes past the hour, my lord," the butler called. "The coachman awaits."

"In a moment, Yardley!" William barked. He took her hand. "Gwyneth, how fares your mother-in-law?"

"Better, I think. Her spirits have rallied."

"And you?"

She shrugged. "I wait upon the Lord."

"Never again shall I seek to make you serve me, Gwyneth. But may I ask you to trust me?"

"In what?"

"In all things."

She nodded, understanding the meaning of his request. He would never dishonor her. "Good day, my lord. May you go with God."

He squeezed her hand. "Yes, with God—to whose path I have recommitted my life. Forgive me, Gwyneth. Trust me. And if you can, love me."

Without waiting for a response, he made for the parlor door. "Yardley, where is my hat?"

"Just here, my lord. And your coat, as well. We are expecting snow, sir, a good bit of it, I should think."

Gwyneth leaned against a settee upholstered in gold brocade and drank down a deep breath. Forgive him? Yes, that was easy. William was a man, as confused and uncertain as she in the matter of this strong emotion that had sprung up between them. He had spoken in haste, and he had apologized. Of course she could forgive him.

Trust him? That, too, was easy. He had proven himself honorable and good. She had no doubt he would labor for the welfare of all those around him.

Love him?

Dear God, yes, I love him! How easily I have loved this man from the moment we met. Why have you allowed such an impossible emotion to creep into my heart when I had believed myself beyond the tender feelings between a man and a woman? Is this some test of my faith in you, Father? Oh God, you know I love you more than I love any human. My spirit serves you, and only you. My devotion to you will never cease. I beg you to end my torment!

Before emotion could overwhelm her, Gwyneth squared her shoulders and returned to the foyer. As she crossed to the staircase, she spotted the earl speaking in earnest to a pair of visitors who had just entered the House. The newcomers made a sight that fairly took her aback.

The young female of the pair wore a bright green silk gown trimmed with countless rows of lace upon the skirt, which was dotted with satin bows. The hat perched on her head bore such a great number of ostrich plumes that it threatened to fly away of its own accord. The gentleman had bedecked himself in a fur-collared, pinch-waisted coat, a pair of checked wool trousers, and a large, bow-tied cravat. A mound of oiled black curls perched atop his scalp, looking as though they might slide off *en masse* with just the tilt of his head.

"Mr. Maxwell," the earl was saying, "and Miss Maxwell, this is an unexpected pleasure. Welcome, of course. How good of you to come all this way."

"But my sister and I received an invitation to your Christmas ball, Beaumontfort," the gentleman replied. "Did you not receive our response?"

"No, I cannot imagine—"

"I am certain Mr. and Miss Maxwell are expected," Mrs. Riddle interrupted the earl. "They are your cousins, are they not, my lord? Their names would have been included on the list of those invited to the festivities."

"Quite right," Beaumontfort said uncertainly. "It has been several years since our last meeting, has it not, Maxwell? You and your sister are looking well. I believe you have grown taller, Miss Maxwell."

"Yes," the young woman said with a blush and a giggle. "Yes, indeed."

Miss Maxwell, Gwyneth thought. So this girl was expected by some to wed the earl. A striking beauty in her elaborate gown and hat, she clearly had the power to attract attention to herself.

"I beg your pardon, my lord," Gwyneth said, stepping forward to address the earl. "Indeed, Mr. Maxwell's acceptance to the ball has been registered. Rooms are prepared in the east wing."

"I see," Beaumontfort said, a question in his blue eyes.

"Yes, my lord," Gwyneth went on. "I wrote the invitations myself, sir." She dropped him a curtsy before addressing the visitors. "Have you and Miss Maxwell baggage, Mr. Maxwell? I shall send a footman."

The man's eyes lit with pleasure. "Thank you, madam. How good of you." He glanced at the earl. "Would this, perhaps, be Mrs. Gwyneth Rutherford? Mrs. Riddle has told me all about you."

"Indeed!" Beaumontfort exclaimed. "Maxwell, again I am astonished. How is it that you know Mrs. Riddle?"

His cousin smiled, revealing a set of very large white teeth. "Do you forget that I was brought up on a small estate near Ambleside? Whilst you and your family gave little heed to anyone outside your social circle, those of us less richly blessed in lineage played our part in the local community. Mrs. Riddle's sister served my mother as housemaid. The elder Mrs. Rutherford's husband owned property adjoining ours, and their two sons were my close companions."

"In fact," he continued, addressing Gwyneth, "your husband was, at one time, my beloved boyhood friend. I miss him greatly, and I was deeply saddened at the news of his tragic death in Wales. I consider you a dear reminder of him."

At that, he took her hand and kissed her fingers with a flourish. Half amused and half repelled by the unctuous man, Gwyneth tipped her head and pointed the way to the staircase. "Mrs. Wells will guide you and your sister to your quarters, sir."

"Until later then, Mrs. Rutherford, Mrs. Riddle. Good morning to you, Beaumontfort." Donald Maxwell lifted his chin and ascended the stairs as his sister gathered her many skirts to follow him to the east wing.

The earl tugged on his gloves and adjusted the leather fingers. When the visitors were well out of earshot, he turned to his housekeeper. "Mrs. Riddle, I am quite convinced I did *not* invite Donald Maxwell."

"You did, sir," the housekeeper countered. "Wasn't his name on the list, Gwyneth?"

"Yes, madam. I posted his invitation with the others. Shall I fetch the original orders?"

"No, no, of course not," Mrs. Riddle said. "My lord, Mr. Maxwell is your closest living relation. I am perfectly certain you invited him."

He glowered up the stairs in Maxwell's direction. "Just see to it that the man is keenly observed. On our last encounter, he attempted to rob me of something very dear."

With that, he stepped out of the foyer, leaving his staff standing openmouthed behind him. Gwyneth lifted her skirts and brushed past Mrs. Riddle. The name of Donald Maxwell had indeed been on the invitation list—but it had *not* been written in the hand of the earl of Beaumontfort.

As she climbed the stairs to resume hanging pine swags, she felt her spirits girding up for war. Though she could not be certain what Mrs. Riddle had up her sleeve, it was apparently something that involved Donald Maxwell and his sumptuous little sister. What did the housekeeper hope to gain from an alliance between the earl and Miss Maxwell? Did Mrs. Riddle suppose that her relationship with the Maxwells would ensure her position in the House, were there to be a marriage? Did she believe that Donald Maxwell could somehow speak on her behalf—or that he had the power to harm the earl? Or was there another scheme of which Gwyneth could hardly guess?

Gwyneth was well aware she dwelled on the brink of poverty and could afford to risk nothing, but she also knew she would do battle with the devil himself to protect the man she loved from further hurt. If Donald Maxwell had once tried to steal the hand of the earl's sister, what wouldn't he do?

❄

"You must go to t' Christmas ball tonight, my dear," Mrs. Rutherford said from her chair beside the fire. "He'll be lookin' for you."

Gwyneth listened as her own knitting needles clicked in time with Mum's. "You are being very silly," she said softly. "It must be the influenza that has addled your senses."

"I'm not ill, and I'm not addled." The dear woman's voice was more tense than usual, and Gwyneth wondered what had upset her. "You planned t' ball, so you'll be expected to see it off without a hiccup. Besides, t' earl invited you personally. Did you not say he wanted you to be there for a special reason?"

"He invited *us*. He wanted us both to be there, Mum."

"Then we'll go together."

"Nonsense. You're hardly able to walk five paces without a fit of coughing. You gave me such a fright the other day, I won't even think of letting you out of the house. You'll sit right there, and knit your jersey, and have a cup of good, hot tea."

"I only frightened you because I lost my way for a moment. When I read that letter from Wales, somehow I forgot altogether that my life rests in t' hands of almighty God, and I'm not to worry about t' food I shall eat nor t' roof over my head."

Gwyneth turned her knitting and threaded the length of soft blue wool through her fingers. "We'll be all right, Mum," she said gently. "I feel certain of it. If we can find a wagon on its way to Wales, we can transport most of our things. Once the cottage is sold—"

"I'll not go back to Wales," Mrs. Rutherford said, a quaver in her voice. "I'll stay here in Cumbria where I was born and bred, and here I'll die. You shall go on to your family alone. My God will provide."

"I won't leave you, Mum. I promised you that long ago." Gwyneth's knitting blurred as tears filled her eyes. "You are my family. Your God is my God. I shall die where you die, and I'll be buried beside you. If you will not go with me to Wales, then we shall stay here. Together."

For almost a minute, the two worked at their knitting in the silence of the little cottage. Nothing but the crackle of the fire on the hearth and the tapping of a bare branch against a windowpane disturbed the quiet. Gwyneth focused on the simple arrangement of pine boughs that covered the mantel, their fresh-cut branches scenting the warm air.

"Christmas morning soon will be upon us," Gwyneth said softly, "and I have nothing to give you, whom I love so dearly."

"Nothing but your honor and respect and constancy," Mrs. Rutherford answered with a smile. "You are t' light of my old age, Gwynnie. How I thank my God for you!"

"And I, for you. I shall speak to Sukey's husband tomorrow. Jacob Ironmonger is a kind man. Perhaps he knows of someone who will take us both in."

"We'll be just like t' holy family in Bethlehem, knockin' on doors and askin' to be let inside."

"If a stable was good enough for the King of kings to lay his head, I'm sure you and I can make do." Gwyneth lifted her chin. "I have considered applying for a position at the stocking factory in Ambleside."

"Will you leave your place at t' House?"

"I shall have no choice after the earl returns to London. Mrs. Riddle will not allow me to work in the larder again, of that I am certain."

"My dear, I must tell you of somethin' that has come to pass. T' housekeeper stopped by here this very evenin' while you were deliverin' t' leavin's in t' village."

Gwyneth's heart clenched. "Mrs. Riddle came here? Whatever for?"

"T' cottage." She swallowed. "I have sold it."

"To Mrs. Riddle?" She leaped forward in the chair. "I *knew* she was planning to do something like this. How could you let her take your home, the place where you gave birth to your children, this beautiful, dear cottage? Oh, that woman is the most wicked—"

"Not *her*," Mrs. Rutherford said. "Mrs. Riddle brought along a visitor. He was t' one who bought t' cottage and land."

Gwyneth knew at once of whom the old woman spoke. "Donald Maxwell."

"T' very chap. I've never been fond of him, not since he tried to woo t' earl's sister. He was deceitful and canny about it. But he offered me a fair price."

"Did you take his money?"

"Nay. I told him I would speak with you first, but I know I shall accept his offer. He comes tomorrow mornin' with t' papers I must sign."

"On Christmas Day?"

"Try to calm yourself, my dear. T' price will make a start on t' debt we owe in Wales. How could I say no?"

"Because . . . because he is not a nice man and . . . and the earl doesn't like him and . . ." She stood and tossed down her knitting. "I do not trust him, Mum! And I do not want that man to take land that rightfully belongs to you. Mrs. Riddle invited him here—not the earl. He's come at her bidding, and I know she's behind this offer on the cottage. She knows that if we sell the cottage we must move away. And that secures her position as head housekeeper. But I fear she has greater schemes than this. If the Maxwells live so near the earl, Mrs. Riddle can arrange regular meetings between them, and perhaps a marriage. I feel certain she and Donald Maxwell are plotting together on these plans that will benefit them both! You mustn't sell the cottage to him. You must—"

"Calm yourself, child." Mrs. Rutherford stood and slipped an arm around Gwyneth's shoulder. "I am forced to take what I can get for t' property. There have been no other offers. I have no choice."

"You must have a choice! There must be *something* you can do."

"Only one thing." Her eyes misted. "I can fall upon t' mercy of t' earl. I can ask you to go to him and plead with him to give us aid. My husband was his cousin. He's my relative, though distant, and I feel sure he would help two lonely widows. If you implore him, I know he'll ask nothin' in return."

Stricken, Gwyneth searched the worn face before her. "You want me to beg?"

"Go to t' Christmas ball tonight, Gwynnie. When you find t' earl, sit yourself near him, no matter how it looks to t' others. Lay yourself at his feet, if you must. He's been kind to you. Ask him to pay our debt and allow us to live t' remainder of our days in t' cottage." A tear made its way down her weathered cheek. "I know of naught more we can do, Gwynnie. We have no other hope. I know he cares for you—I have seen·it in his eyes. And he himself has fond memories of this cottage. For the sake of his own family's holdings, perhaps he would help us."

"But you said God would provide."

"He has. He provided Donald Maxwell. And he provided t' earl. Now we must do our part."

Gwyneth clutched the woman's frail shoulders. Mum had no idea of the words of passion, anger, forgiveness, and rejection that had passed between her and William. If Gwyneth went to him, what would he think of her? That she was using his kindness to save herself? That she cared for his financial assistance but not his person?

Oh, God, surely you cannot expect me to go before William and beg for mercy! Surely you cannot mean to make me do this! Show us some other way. Provide another answer . . .

"You could wear your blue dress," Mrs. Rutherford said. "And I shall let you borrow my brooch. How will t' earl resist you?"

CHAPTER SIX

Mortification shrouding her like a black shawl, Gwyneth stepped into the foyer of Brackendale Manor and removed her bonnet. The attendees gathered would recognize at once that she did not belong among the landed gentry and peerage who graced the halls. Her gown was of simple blue muslin, its neckline graced with nothing more than a single row of handmade lace. Though she had put up her hair in a braided knot, she had only a thin blue ribbon to adorn it. Her gloves were threadbare, her slippers worn at the toes.

She eased past the elegant company and edged her way along the side walls, wishing she could disappear altogether. She must find William, plead with him to spare the cottage, and then escape into the blessed darkness of night. If only she could accomplish her task without drawing attention to herself. If only her plight were not so extreme. If only she were not reduced to crawling on her knees . . . begging . . .

Mum's favorite passage of Scripture slipped into her thoughts. *If any man desire to be first, the same shall be last of all, and servant of all.* Servant of all. This was Gwyneth's aim and her commitment—to serve Mum, and in serving her, to serve the Lord God.

"I am quite fond of the theatre," a woman said nearby. "Although I confess I do not like to go *every* night, as Fanny does."

"I protest!" another responded in a peal of laughter. "I certainly leave my calendar free for opera."

"And for Christmas balls," a gentleman said. "Does not the manor house appear grand this evening, my dear Fanny? I believe Beaumontfort has employed a better staff than last year. I understand that later we are to have a small nativity play performed by the village children. True meaning of Christmas, and all that. Splendid notion, don't you think?"

Feeling that every eye in the room must be upon her, Gwyneth slid past the group. She spotted the earl's footmen tending the gathering, and she wondered what they must think of her to appear in this company without her dark uniform and white apron. Did they know she had been invited as a guest? Doubtful. And she would never admit that their master had committed such a breach of etiquette.

Lifting up her hundredth prayer for divine assistance, she at last located the earl of Beaumontfort. He was surrounded by a bevy of beautiful young women, among them Miss Maxwell. Her arm looped through his, she leaned against his shoulder and chatted as though she were the fox that had captured the prize rooster. Donald Maxwell stood not far away, his oily curls agleam in the lamplight as he regaled a group of men with some story they found highly amusing.

"And a pathetic fire that fairly belched with smoke!" he was saying as Gwyneth moved past him. "The old woman insisted she must have at least a hundred pounds for the place. She would not take less! And I told her I could give no more than seventy-five."

"Seventy-five! How much land did you say there was?" another fellow demanded, much diverted. "I believe you could be tried and hanged for robbery, Maxwell."

"At least one hundred acres of prime forest, and the property can boast a fair number of streams. Once I have torn down the cottage, I shall build myself a manor house to rival Brackendale itself."

Choking with disbelief, Gwyneth lowered her head and slipped around the man. Seventy-five pounds? How could Mrs. Rutherford have agreed to such a paltry sum? She had indeed been robbed—and by a man who meant to pull down the cottage at the first opportunity. Her resolve strengthened, she made for the earl.

"Mrs. Rutherford!" he exclaimed on seeing her. "I am delighted you have come. Ladies, may I present Mrs. Gwyneth Rutherford."

The women curtsied. "Have we not met before?" Miss Maxwell asked. "You have a familiar look about you."

"Indeed, madam, I am—"

"Mrs. Rutherford is my dear friend," Beaumontfort said. "She assists in the management of my household."

Seven pairs of incredulous eyes fastened on Gwyneth. "You *assist* the earl?" Miss Maxwell asked.

Gwyneth tried to smile as she glanced at William in a silent plea for assistance.

"In fact, I could not manage my affairs without her," he said. "The decor is splendid, Mrs. Rutherford. Magnificent. You have outdone yourself."

"Thank you, sir." Gwyneth let out a breath, trying to make herself relax. It was useless. The women clustered closer, like wolves around a wounded lamb, moving in for a kill.

"Is your husband a friend of the earl's, then, Mrs. Rutherford?" Miss Maxwell asked. "I find this association most fascinating."

"I am a widow. I come from Wales." Her speech sounded

plain and inelegant. "And if I may—"

"Wales?" The women looked at each other as though this in itself were a grand joke. "But how marvelous! Yet, you must find our company vastly boring, for we have nothing so amusing as your Welsh log-tossing games."

As the women giggled behind their gloves, Gwyneth turned to the earl. "My lord, if I may speak with you a moment, I would be much obliged."

"Indeed, I had been hoping to speak with you, Mrs. Rutherford. Excuse me, ladies." Without hesitation, he detached himself from the astonished Miss Maxwell and escorted Gwyneth to a corner of the room. As the orchestra struck up the notes of another dance and revelers filled the floor, the earl took Gwyneth's elbow and turned her to face him.

"My lord," she began, "I have come tonight to beg a kindness of you."

"And I, of you." He smiled, his blue eyes warm. "But first I must tell you that you are truly lovely, Gwyn. I confess I feared you would not come."

"I would not have, sir, but Mrs. Rutherford has asked me to speak with you."

"Your mother-in-law? How fares the dear lady? I trust she is much improved." At Gwyneth's acknowledgement, he made as if to steer her through the long French doors into a less crowded parlor.

But she held up her hand. "My lord—"

"Call me William."

"You asked me to trust you, and in this matter I can hope for no other champion."

"But first, I must champion my own cause." He took her hand. "Gwyneth, I have been thinking and praying about my future. About your future." He touched her cheek. "About our future."

"Announce it then!" someone shouted. "Announce it,

Maxwell! Share your good news."

At the raised voice, laughter, and cheers, the orchestra faltered and the dancing stopped. In a moment, Donald Maxwell was lifted bodily onto the dais and saluted with a round of applause. The earl slipped a protective arm around Gwyneth as he focused on the interruption of the evening's festivities.

"All right, all right!" Maxwell said to the crowd. "Beaumontfort, I am asked to give out my news for all to hear. You should have been the last to know—and therefore the most surprised—but at the behest of my friends, I shall tell you."

The earl's jaw flickered with tension. "What news, cousin?"

"We are to be neighbors once again, sir." The man gave a dramatic bow. "Although my family's property near Ambleside was swallowed up some years ago by Brackendale, recently I have arranged to purchase land adjoining yours. I mean to bring my sister to Cumbria and build for us a house that will rival any in the Lakelands."

At the applause, the earl set Gwyneth aside and walked toward the dais, his presence parting the crowd as though it were the river Jordan. Broad-shouldered, eyes flashing, he stepped onto the dais beside his cousin. The smaller man touched his oiled curls as the earl regarded him.

"Welcome to Cumbria, Maxwell," Beaumontfort said. "I am certain you will make your presence felt."

"Thank you, my lord. Yes, indeed."

"And may I ask the location of your new property? For I cannot recall any land for sale in these parts."

"Indeed, sir, in that you are mistaken." Maxwell lifted his chin. "I am buying the cottage and nearly one hundred acres belonging to Mrs. Rutherford. The property lies near the village, and it possesses a fine prospect of Brackendale Manor. I believe we shall see one another's lights of an evening. My sister and I will, of course, welcome you to visit us as often as you like. Indeed, my lovely sister—"

"Mrs. Rutherford's cottage, did you say?" the earl demanded.

"Yes, sir."

Gwyneth saw the earl's focus dart toward her. She covered her mouth with her hand and shook her head. How could it be undone now? No matter that she throw herself on the earl's mercy, his cousin had announced ownership. Begging would accomplish nothing. Even prayer seemed hopeless, though she shut her eyes and poured out her soul.

"And when did this transaction occur?" the earl was asking.

"This evening before the ball. Mrs. Riddle was good enough to—"

"Riddle is behind this?" His voice rose. "To what end?"

"She said she hoped merely to assist me in establishing a permanent connection to this district."

"And to assure her own permanent station, as well," the earl said. "You wish to purchase Mrs. Rutherford's land, cousin, and I assume you have seen to the welfare of the woman herself?"

"She'll have the purchase price. Why should her welfare be any of my concern?"

"Indeed. Of course not," the earl said. "She is merely an old woman of little wealth and even less import, is she not?"

As the men continued their discussion, Gwyneth gathered her shawl about her. It was no use now. She must return to the cottage and help Mum pack their trunks. In the morning, she would go down to the village to inquire after lodgings from Sukey Ironmonger's family. At least this one night, the two women would be safe in the cottage. But on the morrow . . .

"I heartily congratulate you," the earl announced, clapping his cousin on the back. "You have chosen a remarkable piece of property, Maxwell, and one that will give your family much pleasure for years to come."

Lowering her head, Gwyneth made her way through the crowd. Mum would be asleep by now, nodded off with her knitting on her lap. The fire would be low. She would stir it. And perhaps make a cup of tea.

"I see that I was quite mistaken in my estimation of your character, Maxwell," the earl said. "In offering to buy the cottage and land for a sum generous enough to retire Mrs. Rutherford's debts, you prove yourself a worthy gentleman indeed."

"Generous?" someone cried. "He is paying a mere seventy-five pounds for the entire property."

"Seventy-five?" The earl's eyebrows lifted. "Surely you must be mistaken, for I am certain my good cousin would offer no less than seventy-five *hundred* for such a finely situated estate."

Gwyneth paused and tried to make sense of the earl's words. She had heard Maxwell give the sum at seventy-five pounds. Was William so naive as to believe well of his cousin? Or did he hope to humiliate Maxwell into paying a greater price? Either way, all was now lost. The cottage would be razed, and she and Mum would have no choice but to leave the Lake District.

"Seventy-five hundred?" Maxwell said in a strangled voice.

"Surely no less, for you have seen what excellent forests, lakes, and streams the property boasts. Indeed, Maxwell, you are a fine fellow, and I shall welcome you as my neighbor. Shall we not all congratulate such an esteemed man?"

As the crowd began to applaud, William gave Maxwell a firm handshake. Then the earl stepped off the dais and searched the room. Though she could see the earl making his way through the crowd toward her, Gwyneth knew they must not be seen together. Indeed, she must race back to the cottage to inform Mum of this turn of events, for no doubt Maxwell would come this very night to clarify the matter.

"Seventy-five hundred pounds?" someone said as she passed. "It must be a very fine estate indeed."

Confusion welling up inside her, Gwyneth grabbed her bonnet and hurried out the front door. She had hardly passed halfway down the gravel drive when she heard William calling out to her. *Dear God, send him away! His society must not see us alone together. He will be humiliated—*

"Gwyn," he called, "stay a moment. I shall speak with you."

She halted and stuffed her bonnet onto her head, the ribbons dangling loose down her dress. As she tried to tie them, he caught her hand and pulled her close.

"Gwyn, why do you leave me?" he demanded. "Why must you always run from me?"

"Oh, William, those people—"

"Those people matter nothing to me. They require my acquaintance in business, they imagine themselves graced by my presence and I by theirs, they consider themselves my peers. Yet not one of them can I call a true friend. Not one has warmed my heart or tended to my spirit as you do, Gwyn. You are beautiful and good, and I cannot bear—"

"Beaumontfort!" Maxwell barked as he and his company of friends approached. "Do you mean to have the Rutherford property for yourself, as your father took my family's lands so many years ago? I assure you, my determination to regain my foothold in Cumbria remains unchanged. You were born to title and property, but I shall have them both in the end."

"By deceit and treachery, Maxwell?" The earl nodded. "Indeed, such actions do befit your character."

"You refer to my legitimate pursuit of your sister."

"My sister was but thirteen years old when you set your sights upon her. Can the pursuit of a mere child be called legitimate? I think not."

"Had you not interfered—"

"I shall interfere in your machinations as often as I find them odious, cousin!" The earl turned to Gwyneth. "Please return to the House, madam. I fear these matters do not become the sensibilities of a lady."

"Thank you, my lord, but I shall go home to my mother-in-law instead," she said.

When Maxwell cut in with a curse, Gwyneth tugged her bonnet down over her ears and raced down the driveway.

❄

"I cannot understand the earl's purpose," Gwyneth said, kneeling at Mum's feet, "for you are certain the offer was seventy-five pounds."

"Aye, Mr. Maxwell said it must be seventy-five and not a farthing more." Mrs. Rutherford's gnarled fingers clutched Gwyneth's. "Oh, my dear, I am not pleased at t' idea of that man comin' here again."

"Nevertheless, he will come to clear the matter. And we must think how to speak to him. Did William mean to humiliate his cousin into raising the offered price?"

"Nay, for then Mr. Maxwell would reject t' purchase of t' property—and who will buy my land if not Mr. Maxwell? Everyone will have heard of our debts now. No one will want t' cottage for so great a sum, and we shall be turned out with nowhere to lay our heads. Oh, did you not speak in private with our dear Willie? I was so certain he could help us. Did you not go to him and kneel at his feet and beg?"

"I did go to him, Mum. But we had no chance to speak before Mr. Maxwell—"

At the hard knock on the door, Gwyneth grasped both her mother-in-law's hands. "'Tis him. I can think only that we must accept the original offer and trust in God's sufficiency to meet our need."

Steeling her nerves, she rose to her feet and threw open the door. But no one was there. Gwyneth searched the dark, crisp night. Icy tree branches creaked in the breeze. The half-frozen stream trickled over smooth stones with a soft gurgle. A tiny tug at her hem drew her attention.

"Good heavens!" She knelt and scooped up a small brown-and-white puppy that stood wagging its tail and gazing up at her with huge brown eyes. "What has brought you out on this cold night?"

"He has come about t' cottage and land," Mrs. Rutherford said firmly from her chair before the fire. "You must take it, Mr. Maxwell. We agreed to t' seventy-five pounds, and that's all I have to say."

"But this isn't Mr. Maxwell at all! 'Tis a small puppy. And he's wearing a red bow!" Cuddling the tiny ball of fur, she hurried to Mrs. Rutherford's chair. "Look at him!"

"A corgi!" The old woman laughed in delight. "A corgi has come to us!"

"All the way from Wales, I might add." The earl of Beaumontfort walked into the cottage and removed his top hat. With a smile on his handsome face, he gave the women a bow. "A blessed Christmas to you both. I hope my gift gives you great pleasure."

"*You* brought him?" Mrs. Rutherford gathered the puppy in her arms and began to weep. "Oh, Gwynnie, didn't I tell you our Willie was a good man?"

"'Twas I who told you."

"Indeed, we both love you, sir!" Mum held out her hand to the earl, who knelt at her feet. "But what of your ball and all your friends? Have you left them?"

"Those people are not true friends. I put on the Christmas ball to make amends for abandoning them in the midst of the London social season. Tonight, after Gwyneth had gone away, I realized the gathering's purpose was completely mercenary—on the part of the host *and* his guests."

"Really?" Mrs. Rutherford asked.

"Indeed, the ball was intended to solidify business relationships rather than to honor faithful and beloved companions. But here, in this small, quaint cottage, I have discovered more of friendship and warmth and family—greater rest—than I have ever known."

"My dear boy, how good you are."

"It is you who truly are good."

"Ah, what a fine lad, is he not, Gwynnie? And to bring us this wee dog! We have missed our beloved corgi so, and now you have given us this sweet puppy."

"But what of Donald Maxwell?" Gwyneth asked. "Surely you know he offered only seventy-five pounds for the property. Mum and I have no choice but to accept Mr. Maxwell's—"

"You will be hard-pressed to find him. The man has ridden for London this very night. To avoid publicly exposing himself for the cad that he is, Maxwell had no choice but to gracefully remove himself from the agreement—an action that will allow me to step in as benefactor." The earl smiled. "Mrs. Rutherford, why did you not come to me with your plight at once?"

"But why should you take pity on a poor widow who can offer you naught in return?"

"Dear lady, you have given me two gifts more wonderful than I could have imagined. When I was but a lad, you taught me about God and led my feet onto the path of Christianity. Though I strayed, I have found my way again. My eyes now look only to Christ for guidance."

"Bless you, my boy."

"And as for the second gift." He stood and held out one hand to Gwyneth. "I have no certainty that I may claim it. Yet I am here to plead for the single joy that will give my life abundance beyond measure."

As Mrs. Rutherford's eyes crinkled with pleasure, the earl

dropped to one knee at Gwyneth's feet. She could hardly remain standing as she gazed down into blue eyes filled with such passion she feared she might drown in them. He drew her hand to his lips and kissed her fingers.

"Gwyneth Rutherford," he said, "from you I have learned the true fulfillment that can come only through servitude. You have served me well. Now I beg that you will join me in a life of mutual submission. Will you consent to marry me?"

Unable to stand any longer, Gwyneth fell to her knees and threw her arms around him. "William, I could wish for nothing more than to live as your wife! But how can it be right?"

"How can it be wrong?"

"Your society will—"

"My society will soon understand the welcome news that the earl of Beaumontfort has taken a wife. They will convince themselves that such an unexpected union arose when the earl purchased a valuable property adjoining his estate. In addition, he has assumed responsibility for a Welsh coal mine, which he intends to make profitable once again. Not only did the earl enrich his holdings, but he took upon himself the welfare of his relatives by wedding the younger of the two. How very noble of him, they will say. What a fine fellow—and how clever to enrich himself in such a fashion."

Gwyneth swallowed. It was possible the peerage would accept this explanation. And after all, perhaps it was the truth. Could this be the reason for William's pledge?

"I doubt that my society will realize," he continued, "that the riches I have gained have nothing to do with lands and cottages. I have found the rest and quietude I sought in coming back to Cumbria. More important, I have discovered their source. And that is you, Gwyn. I love you as I have loved no other. Please say you will abandon all hesitation and become my wife."

"I shall," she said, holding tightly to his hands.

Was it possible that God had heard and answered the secret plea of her heart? Had her heavenly Father truly blessed her with the home and family she had so desired? She was young enough yet that there would be children. And laughter. And skating parties, picnics, and strawberry picking.

Oh, yes! But more than that . . . God had brought her love. True love. She looked into William's eyes as his lips met hers. How blessed. How wonderful. How—

"Glory be, Gwynnie, t' puppy has hold of your knittin'!" Mrs. Rutherford cried. "T' earl's sweater will be in shreds! Help, help!"

"My sweater?" William asked.

"'Twas to be your Christmas gift!" Gwyneth exclaimed, leaping to her feet in pursuit of the rapidly unraveling sweater. The puppy took off around the table, trailing blue yarn that wrapped around the wooden legs. Flapping her skirts, Gwyneth raced after the scamp who scuttled underneath the bed. William got down on all fours and felt around in the shadows just as the pup bolted out the other side, her knitting in a tangle around his feet.

The puppy barked with excitement and bounded between William's legs. As the yarn tied the earl's legs together in a hopeless knot, Gwyneth fell back against a chair, consumed with giggles. Mrs. Rutherford chuckled as she made a swipe after the furry brown bolt of lightning. The sound of laughter filled the air and drifted like a warm blanket of hope as snow began to fall on the Christmas cottage in the woods.

RECIPE

❄

*I love the visual image of hot crumpets drizzled with melting butter. Give
these a try, and then curl up with your sweetheart for a truly English
teatime!*

GWYNETH RUTHERFORD'S CRUMPETS

1 tsp. active dry yeast
1 tsp. sugar
¼ cup warm water
⅓ cup milk
1 egg, lightly beaten
4 tbsp. butter, melted
1 cup unsifted all-purpose flour
½ tsp. salt

Mix yeast with sugar; add water and let stand 5 minutes until foamy. Stir in milk, egg, and 1 tbsp. melted butter. Add
flour and salt. Using a wooden spoon, mix until well
blended to make a smooth batter. Cover the bowl with a
cloth towel, and leave in a warm place to rise until almost
doubled (45 minutes to 1 hour).

With the remaining melted butter, thoroughly coat the insides of several crumpet rings, 3-inch flan rings, or clean
tuna cans with both ends removed. Also use the melted butter to grease the bottom of a heavy frying pan or griddle. Arrange as many rings as possible in the pan.

Over low heat, heat the rings in the pan. Pour enough batter
into each ring to fill it halfway. Cook for 5–7 minutes, until
bubbles appear and burst on the surface. Remove rings and

turn the crumpets. Cook 2–3 minutes more, until lightly browned.

Repeat with remaining batter. Serve crumpets hot and generously buttered.

A Note from the Author

Dear Friend,

I've always been fascinated by the biblical romance of Ruth and Boaz. Their love story provided the inspiration for "Under His Wings." This bold, enterprising, and very determined woman was willing to submit herself to God's leading in every way! She left her homeland and family to follow her mother-in-law into a brand-new world. She was obedient to Naomi's guidance—even in the matter of love.

And what a man Ruth got! Wealthy, respected, and intelligent, Boaz fell head over heels for the lovely woman who labored in his fields. By mutually submitting to God's plan, these two formed a marriage that resulted in the birth of Jesus Christ many generations later. Now that's a Christmas love story!

My prayer today is that you and I can learn to release the tight control of our own lives and let God lead us where he can use us for his glory.

Blessings,
Catherine Palmer

ABOUT THE AUTHOR

Catherine Palmer lives in Missouri with her husband, Tim, and sons, Geoffrey and Andrei. She is a graduate of Southwest Baptist University and has a master's degree in English from Baylor University. Her first book was published in 1988. Since then she has written thirty books and published more than twenty. Catherine has also won numerous awards for her writing, including Most Exotic Historical Romance Novel from *Romantic Times* magazine. Total sales of her novels number close to one million copies.

In addition to *A Victorian Christmas Cottage*, her Tyndale House books include *Finders Keepers, Prairie Rose, Prairie Fire, Prairie Storm, The Treasure of Timbuktu, The Treasure of Zanzibar*, and novellas in the anthologies *A Victorian Christmas Tea, With This Ring*, and *A Victorian Christmas Quilt*.

Catherine welcomes letters written to her in care of Tyndale House Author Relations, P.O. Box 80, Wheaton, IL 60189-0080.

Christmas Past

DEBRA WHITE SMITH

Dedicated to my father,
Gaylon L. White

CHAPTER ONE

ATLANTA, GEORGIA
NOVEMBER 1890

Davis McCumby's heart palpitated with dread and anticipation. At last, Madeline Devry had arrived. At last . . . at last. From the cottage window, Davis watched her disembark the carriage. As the evening sun enveloped her in golden light, he thought of sonnets, of rhymes and rhythm. She gracefully straightened her mink-trimmed cape, bestowed a distant smile on the coachman, and turned toward the cottage.

"Dear Lord," Davis breathed, "please tell me you're bringing my sweet, godly Madeline back to me. Oh, Father, tell me she hasn't forgotten you. And please, please tell me she won't try to sell this cottage. You know I promised Mrs. Pritchard I wouldn't let her sell it. She was as loving to me as my own parents. I simply cannot go against her wishes. Oh, Lord, I don't want to have to battle Maddy over the cottage."

With these prayers tormenting his soul, Davis noted that Madeline's appearance hadn't changed much in the last ten years. Her dark, wavy hair was the same. Her flushed cheeks were the same. Her thin, rosy lips were the same. She had always possessed an arresting quality in her candid demeanor and charming personality that enchanted many men, including Davis.

As she walked toward the front door, Davis's gut twisted. Her hesitant knock seemed to scurry straight into his heart. In an attempt to get control of himself, Davis didn't answer immediately. Another hesitant knock. Davis took one step toward the door just as the knob rattled. Knowing she was about to enter left his knees weak. Madeline's shoes tapped against the wooden entryway. Davis gripped a dining-room chair, determined to get his equilibrium before she discovered his presence.

She turned toward the parlor as if she were basking in the essence of her childhood. Davis's spirits soared. Perhaps Madeline had come home to stay—unlike the other hurried visits during the last ten years when she had merely made a guest appearance, kept her distance from him, and hastened back to New York.

As he continued to soak in the image of her standing in the entryway, Davis began pleading with his Maker once more. "Oh, Lord, please don't let her want to sell this cottage . . ." But despite his prayers, something in the pit of Davis's stomach tensed in uncomfortable dread, and he felt as if he were a warrior preparing for combat.

❈

Riveted in haunting memory, Madeline watched the smoldering fire cast flickering shadows across the dimly lit parlor. With a reminiscent ache, she recalled a Christmas ten years before when she and Davis McCumby, both teenagers, had attended her mother's annual party. That party had marked the end of their childhood friendship—the years in which they had been inseparable. For that night Davis had tried to kiss her.

Swallowing against a throat tight with emotion, Madeline both anticipated and dreaded seeing Davis. During her visits in the past, she had avoided him as much as possible.

Their relationship was simply too awkward, too confusing, and Madeline never quite knew what to say when they met.

"I've been waiting for you," a familiar voice said from behind.

Startled, Madeline stilled herself before she could turn around to face the boy of her childhood, the teen of her adolescence, the man she had yet to know. Davis McCumby. She felt him watching her, felt his presence like a nuance of the past, and knew she could not avoid him.

Slowly she faced him. Davis stood near the cottage's baroque dining-room table and warmly appraised her. Silently, she returned his appraisal and grappled for something to say.

Her childhood friend hadn't changed much since the last time Madeline had glimpsed him riding across the plantation during one of her visits with her grandmother. Even Davis's choice of clothing was the same—a floppy, white shirt with wide cuffs and snug-fitting riding pants. The only thing different was the black patch over his eye. Somehow the patch obliterated any traces of the boyish appeal he once held, even as a man. Instead Davis appeared a bit dangerous—much like a lean pirate who has come on land with the sole purpose of stealing a maiden's heart. And the warmth in his gaze left Madeline wondering if she were the maiden of choice.

Her stomach churning, she posed the first question that popped into her head. "What happened to your eye?" The prying query, so inappropriate among New York society, startled even her own ears. Had Madeline shed every vestige of propriety when she stepped into the cottage in which she grew up?

"I was involved in a carriage accident about six months ago. It cost me my eye. But I'm the fortunate one—" He halted abruptly, squinted, and looked around the cottage's interior of pine walls and rich tapestry. With a short wave of his hand, he said, "Your grandmother never changed a thing after you left for New York." He spoke the unnecessary words as if to parry any more comments about the carriage accident.

"Yes, I noticed," she replied, her mind wondering about the details of the accident. Someone else must have been involved. But who? Was that someone severely injured or even killed? But instead of further pursuing the subject, she said, "The cottage is as quaint as it's ever been, don't you think?"

"Quaint?" One brow quirked upward, and some of the warmth seeped from his expression.

Madeline recalled that night ten years before in this very cottage when Davis had teasingly raised one brow during her mother's Christmas party—right before he tried to kiss her. Her pulse jumped in memory of Davis's playful youth. But now he seemed tainted by cynicism.

"Yes . . . quaint . . . compared to—" Madeline pressed her lips together, instinctively staying her comments of the homes she frequented in New York. "Compared to the plantation mansion . . . uh . . . *your* mansion."

As if he were determined to make her plight as awkward as possible, Davis crossed his arms and silently appraised her. Once again he narrowed his eye as a certain chill crept into its depths. Madeline felt as if she were simultaneously engaging in two conversations with Davis—one spoken, the other unspoken. And as their terse undercurrent of communication continued, Madeline sensed in an uncanny way that he had read her mind concerning the New York homes.

Flustered all the more, she wondered why their conversation was acquiring an unfriendly nuance. These were difficult circumstances, to say the least; being unfriendly only added to the difficulty. As Grandmother Regina Pritchard's sole heir, Madeline had arrived in Atlanta for one specific purpose: to sell her grandmother's possessions, including the heirloom cottage, and immediately turn over all profits and all inherited sums to the person to whom they rightfully belonged—Madeline's mother, Lily Pritchard Wilson. Ten years ago, Regina Pritchard had coldly disinherited her widowed daughter and shut her out of her life when Lily chose to remarry and move to New York. Even though the marriage and move did occur only a month after Grandfather Pritchard's death, the whole ordeal left Madeline riled just thinking about it. Although she did care for her grandmother, Madeline could never deny where her allegiance lay. In short, her grandmother had behaved despicably—and for no good reason.

Squaring her shoulders, Madeline decided to plunge into a discussion of the necessary facts with Davis. The sooner she could get down to business and sell the cottage, the sooner she could return to New York and the society functions she adored.

"From what I understand, your family arranged to purchase the final acreage of Grandmother's cotton plantation within the last few months?" Madeline questioned, relying on the sophisticated composure she had honed to perfection.

"Everything but the cottage and ten acres. Your grandmother wanted it that way," he said evenly, a defensive edge hardening his voice. "I watched her cry many days and nights because she missed you and your mother so much. And I think she would have preferred that you keep the plantation, but she knew you would probably want to sell it, and she wanted a say in who it went to."

"That's understandable. I'm glad your family bought her out," Madeline said quickly. She really wanted to argue passionately that her grandmother in no way loved her mother. But she swallowed her objection and chose instead to continue in the original vein of their conversation. "That's one less chore for me. Now I only have to worry about soliciting a buyer for the cottage," Madeline rushed, not certain of the words tumbling from her.

"By all means," he drawled, his expression darkening all the more. "Let's save you a chore." Gripping the back of the dining-room chair until his knuckles were white, he clenched his jaw as if he were trying to maintain composure.

"I didn't mean it in that fashion," she snapped, peeved with him for taunting her. "It's just that our families' association goes back so far that your buying her out is ... is ... simply the appropriate thing for the whole situation." Unnerved by Davis's steady scrutiny, Madeline turned her back to him and studied the cozy parlor, decorated with her grandmother's elegant touches. Even with her back to him, she felt Davis's presence like a force from her past. A distracting, disturbing force. They had once been the best of friends, until that fated year when Davis was seventeen and Madeline fourteen, and Davis had coldheartedly broken their friendship. Nothing between them had been the same since. What had once been a carefree acquaintance turned stilted and stale. Even now, Madeline felt like a disappointed fourteen-year-old, confused and uncertain of Davis, the very person she had once been the most sure of.

None of these musings from the past relieved the tension crawling up Madeline's spine. She had obviously offended Davis without ever intending to. Turning back to face him, she desperately grappled for any excuse to make a civilized exit from this encounter, but she could conceive of no means of escape that wouldn't seem abrupt and rude.

Then as if heaven were extending a branch of mercy, Anna McCumby entered the dining room and deposited a silver tray laden with a coffee urn and cookies on the oversized table.

"Anna!" Madeline exclaimed. Rushing to the wiry cook's side, she embraced the woman who had sneaked her more childhood cookies than she could ever count. "I didn't realize you were here."

"Oh, yes, I'm always here. Good to see you," Anna said thickly.

Madeline pulled away to notice a tear trickling down the wrinkled face. Davis's aunt looked to be ninety, although Madeline knew for a fact that she couldn't be more than sixty.

"I'm so sorry," Madeline said. "I know you're going to miss Grandmother terribly. The two of you were like sisters." They fell into another warm hug.

The McCumbys and the Pritchards dated back over a century to produce a bond almost as strong as blood. From one generation to the next, the McCumbys had worked in various capacities for the Pritchards. At the end of the Civil War, the McCumbys even pooled their own inheritance with Pritchard money to pay the imposed taxes. Miraculously, the Pritchards were among the few Atlanta families who were able to hang on to their plantation, and during the Reconstruction, they successfully rebuilt their cotton business.

Her own eyes stinging, Madeline released Anna.

"I will miss your grandmother," Anna said, reaching deep into her apron's pocket for a handkerchief. "But I should be comforting you."

Davis produced a dry cough.

Madeline, gritting her teeth, wondered how a cough could sound so challenging. Davis obviously thought very little of Madeline's affection for her grandmother. She bit her tongue to stop herself from asking why he was even here. Madeline could easily deal with his father on any business, specifically the selling of the cottage. She hoped the McCumbys would buy the cottage. Then Madeline could wrap up her business and return to New York.

Ignoring Davis, Madeline laid her mink muff and black lace reticule on the end of the dining table and draped her mink-trimmed cape across a chair. "May I serve, Anna?" she asked, reaching for the silver coffeepot.

"Of course, dear, of course." Anna claimed one of the dining chairs.

Deftly, Madeline poured three cups of the fragrant coffee and laid one of Anna's famous pecan crisps on each saucer. Her mind insisted on stubbornly reminding her of the past, and she recalled that Christmas ten years past when she had spilled similar cookies in the fire. The Christmas Davis had almost kissed her . . .

Escorted by holiday laughter and merriment, the two had stolen away to the kitchen in search of Anna's pecan crisps. They found both Anna and the cookies, then settled into the chairs in front of the kitchen fireplace, while Anna delivered a new tray of holiday treats to the guests. At least, Davis settled in his chair. Madeline, a victim of her very first corset, had collapsed into the chair and spilled her cookies across the hearth. When she and Davis both reached for the cookies, their hands touched, their gazes caught and held, and if not for Anna's return, their lips would have likewise met. . . .

The memory left Madeline feeling as if a cloud of butterflies were flitting through her midsection, despite her outward composure. Disgusted with her own reaction, she firmly reminded herself that she had been one step removed from childhood on that occasion. Now Madeline was a woman who could never be attracted to the likes of Davis McCumby. They were from completely different worlds. Compared to the refined men who courted her in New York, Davis McCumby, with his day's worth of dark stubble, appeared a ruffian. They had been nothing more than childhood friends. Period.

"I'll have two cookies," he said, settling into a nearby chair like a wary panther preparing for battle.

Sipping her coffee, Anna mischievously eyed him over the brim of the cup. "That means four, Madeline," she said.

Without looking at him, Madeline stiffly passed the whole

cookie plate to Davis.

A tentative knock sounded on the front door. "That's probably the coachman, wanting to know where to put my trunk." She stood, glad for any reason to distance herself from Davis. "I forgot all about him."

"Here. Let me take care of it." Anna jumped to her feet and gently nudged Madeline back into her seat. "You've had a long journey. You need the rest."

As if she were still a child, Madeline mutely obeyed. And once again, she was alone with Davis. Stirring a spoonful of sugar into her coffee, she focused solely on the dark liquid. But her thoughts rested with the "pirate" sitting next to her. Silently, he sipped his coffee and menacingly munched the square cookies. Madeline wanted to scream as the tension mounted.

Out of desperation for something to say, she decided to discuss selling the cottage. She assumed anything would be better than the torment of this smothering silence. But she was wrong.

Chapter Two

Madeline nervously cleared her throat and glanced toward Davis. "I was wondering if perhaps you and your father had thought of buying the cottage. Since you own the rest of the land—"

"You haven't even visited her grave and already you want to talk business?" he muttered furiously.

Davis's words arrested Madeline's proposal, and her anger flared at the contemptuous twist of his lips. What he said was true, but Madeline didn't regard the situation in the same light Davis obviously viewed it. For very practical reasons, they had been forced to bury Regina Pritchard before Madeline arrived. Madeline intended to visit the grave alone and in her own time.

"No, I haven't visited the grave, but I plan to," she challenged. "I just want to be alone when I do. Saying good-bye is an intensely personal thing. I don't want anyone else there when I do it."

"Then I'll leave and give you the opportunity." He started to stand.

"You still haven't answered my question." She refused to allow him to dismiss the issue at hand. "Whether or not I have visited the grave has no bearing on my question. I still would like to know if the McCumbys are interested in buy-ing the cottage."

He scrutinized her incredulously, as if he were completely disillusioned with her. Madeline wanted to shrink away from the shame he imposed upon her and, at the same time, heatedly jump to her own defense.

"No, we don't want to buy the cottage," he said firmly. "You know your grandmother wanted you to have the cottage. It was her last wish. This place has been in the Pritchard family for over one hundred years. Your great-grandfather built it with his own hands. You were raised here. Your grandmother lived here the last few years of her life. She wanted you to keep it," he insisted, as if the repetition would somehow change Madeline's mind. "She even hoped you'd spend your summers here."

"But it doesn't rightfully belong to me," Madeline snapped. "It should have been left to my mother."

"It would have been if your mother hadn't walked out—"

"Walked out?" Madeline exclaimed. "She didn't walk out. She finally gained the courage to pursue her own life, some-thing Grandmother never allowed her to do." In agitation, Madeline clenched and unclenched her fists against her skirt's woolen nap.

"She chose a horrible time to decide to pursue her own life," he said caustically. "Your grandfather hadn't been dead a month—"

"But my father had been dead eleven years. And for eleven years, my grandparents dictated—"

"They dictated nothing!" Davis jumped to his feet, and his chair toppled over. "They gave her a home and supported her. And your mother selfishly repaid that by doing what she wanted with no thought for how it affected the rest of us."

"'Us'?" Madeline forced herself to rise slowly. She refused to give Davis the satisfaction of seeing her lose her composure. Even though she was calm outwardly, inwardly she reeled with anger. "You sound as if you were injured as well. That's preposterous. You were only a boy."

"I was seventeen! I was a young man." He stalked toward the doorway as if another second of her presence would choke him.

Madeline followed.

At the door he abruptly turned to glare at her. "And I was in love with you," he said deliberately.

Madeline's cheeks cooled as the blood drained to her feet. No matter how hard she tried, she was powerless to drag her gaze from his. Once again she remembered that moment when he almost kissed her while standing in front of the kitchen fireplace. Madeline had felt exactly as she felt now, as if Davis's blue eyes were the waters of a heaving, azure sea—a sea in which she was drowning. But now, one of those eyes was covered with a black patch that created an air of mystery, of past pain, of a man . . . a real man.

"I had promised myself I would do everything in my power to cherish you and allow you to grow up before I proposed. I also vowed to protect you . . . even if it meant protecting you from myself. And your mother took you to New York and turned you into a society snob. I must have been crazy to ever think of marrying you." He grimaced as if the very words left a bad taste in his mouth.

"A society snob!" she shouted, forgetting her vow to maintain composure. "You were the one who turned into a snob before we moved. I thought you were my closest friend, but you barely said two words to me at my grandfather's funeral!"

"I owed it to you to keep my distance because of the way I felt about you," he said as if she were daft.

"Well, your keeping your distance crushed me!" she said in the aching voice of a fourteen-year-old. "And you have no right to behave so . . . so despicably. This is beyond unreasonable—"

Before Madeline realized his intent, Davis rushed toward her, gripped her upper arms, and peered deeply into her eyes. Unable to look away, Madeline felt as if she were the prisoner of his scrutiny. And what she saw spilling from his soul was a mixture of torment and anger and questions . . . questions . . . questions.

At last, one of those questions posed itself on his lips. "Tell me, Maddy," he said, part challenge, part plea, "have you also forgotten God?"

Madeline's chest tensed. She recalled her passionate devotion to God when she moved to New York. Before her grandfather's death, he had dubbed her his fellow prayer warrior. Yet somehow, that passion for God had faded. Presently she couldn't remember the last time she had prayed, seriously prayed, about anything.

Stumbling backward, she said, "Of course . . . I . . . I haven't forgotten God!"

"I find that hard to believe," he said, as if the very admission wrenched his spirit.

Her mind whirled with new fury. "How dare you judge me! You . . . you . . . "

"I'm not judging you," he blurted out, his nostrils flaring with renewed anger. "But it seems to me you're more interested in money than in fulfilling the dying request of a saint of God."

Madeline remembered that night before she and her mother left for New York. Madeline had hovered near the top of the cottage's stairway and listened as her "saintly" grandmother slapped her only daughter and further demeaned her with a horrid tongue-lashing. In her tender youth, Madeline had silently cried with her weeping mother, who desperately begged Grandmother to understand that she needed a life of her own. Once they had settled for bed, Madeline listened into the wee hours as her mother gently sobbed herself to sleep. That night Madeline vowed blind loyalty to her mother, even if that loyalty brought her grandmother's disdain.

Blinking her eyes against new tears, she gritted her teeth. "My grandmother was far from a saint!"

"Who says?"

"My mother says. I say. The very fact that she disinherited my mother says."

"Well, *I say* that I felt Mrs. Pritchard sobbing in my arms the day you left for New York! *I say* I saw her weep many tears on the church altar for you and your mother! *I say* I listened to her retell the same agonizing stories from both of your childhoods! And *I say* the woman I loved as much as my own mother *was* a saint of God!"

Astounded, Madeline watched Davis as he passionately defended her grandmother. How could he be so blind to her true nature?

Finally he paused as if he were digesting the whole situation and formulating a plan. Madeline squirmed inside, dreading what he might say next. If he were so ardent about her not selling the cottage, would he somehow hinder her attempts to do so?

At last he spoke, slowly, deliberately. "I want you to know that I'll do everything in my power to stop you from selling this cottage."

Those words confirmed Madeline's worst fears. "You wouldn't dare!"

"Oh, yes, I'd dare. I'll do more than dare. I'll follow through. The day she died, your grandmother made me promise that I wouldn't let you sell this cottage." He waved his arm to punctuate his words. "I told her that I couldn't imagine you'd try to do such a thing. But she insisted until I promised."

"You can't stop me!" Madeline stomped her foot. "There's nothing you can do—"

"I'm personal friends with the owner of the only daily papers in the area—the *Atlanta Constitution* and the *Atlanta Evening Journal*. The same man owns both papers," he said with a satisfied smile. He reminded Madeline of a smug tomcat who's just outwitted a defenseless mouse. "All I have to do is drop a word to him and ask him to influence the weekly papers in the area. No newspaper in town will run an ad."

"What about the real-estate agents? There must be over thirty of them!" she countered, matching his smug expression.

"If I have to, I'll pay a visit to each of them as well. I know several of them personally. The ones I don't know, the owner of the *Constitution* does know. By the way . . . ," he added as if the thought had just struck him, ". . . I'll make sure they understand that the McCumbys will refuse to give any buyer the right-of-way to access the cottage by crossing our land. By the time we get through, you won't have a chance to list with any real-estate agent."

Madeline pictured the public tree-lined lane that ran in front of the mansion now owned by Davis's family. In order to access the cottage, which sat a few acres behind and to the west of the mansion, it was necessary to turn onto the small carriage path that crossed the McCumbys' land. Without right-of-way across the plantation, no one could access the cottage.

"But that's . . . that's . . . that's despicable," she accused.

"No! It's honorable." He pointed his finger directly at her nose. "I promised your grandmother. I will keep my promise. Whether you know it or not, she was loved and respected in this town. She received from the town and my family what her daughter and granddaughter refused to give her."

"Well, I promised my mother I would sell the cottage and give her the money that rightfully belongs to her! And whether you know it or not, my mother is loved and re-spected in New York City, and she has received from New York what my grandmother and your family refused to give her!"

"If you're so sure your mother was right, why did you bother to visit your grandmother at all?"

Madeline remained silent, not certain she understood all the implications of her visits. She had been distantly fond of her grandmother despite the family disagreement, and she did enjoy visiting Atlanta. Aside from that, her mother had insisted that she visit. Madeline, who had never gone against her mother's wishes, assumed that her mother sim-ply kept her best interest in mind. But had there been other motives?

"Your silence has answered my question more than any words ever could," Davis said in a tormented yet livid tone. "Apparently you and your mother wanted to do whatever you could to ensure that your grandmother would not disin-herit you as she had your mother. I dare you to tell me I'm wrong," he challenged, as if he wished she would attempt to deny his infuriating accusations.

Gaping, Madeline resisted the urge to rip a flickering can-delabra off the wall and hurl it at this person who had once been her best friend. She refused to give him the satisfaction of further arguing. "Get out!" she demanded, stomping her foot once more. "Just—just leave!"

Abruptly, Davis jerked open the door, stepped through it, and slammed it behind him.

CHAPTER THREE

Davis paused outside the door and contemplated stalking back into the cottage to shake some sense into Madeline Devry. How could he have ever thought that ten years in New York would leave her unchanged? Davis scanned the rolling countryside—the barren trees, the setting sun, the horses in a distant pasture. And the land, forever unchanged, seemed to mock him.

He thought of his adolescent reaction to Madeline upon her arrival and wanted to groan in disgust. How could he have been so naive? But the whole afternoon as he waited for her to arrive, all Davis could picture was the evening he had found her gently weeping in their church just before her move to New York.

At the time, Davis's whole existence seemed bathed in sobs. Only hours before, he had listened as Mrs. Pritchard tearfully poured out her heart regarding her daughter's impending move. Davis could trace the beginning of his resentment toward Madeline's mother to those very hours.

The day he found Madeline crying in the church he had been assisting their pastor in some repairs. She was draped

117

over the altar, silently pouring out her heart to God. Davis almost rushed to her side but refrained. Any attempt to comfort her would have been futile. Already a young man, he was in love with her. And in his estimation, a fourteen-year-old girl was still too young to return that love. Davis had known then that he could never again be her mere chum. Any contact with her would have been colored by his feelings. Therefore, Davis had closed the church door and allowed her to weep. He knew her heart was breaking over the recent death of her grandfather coupled with her mother's decision to marry and move. But there was nothing Davis could do about it. He remembered dashing aside his own tears that day. Even now, his eyes stung with the memory.

Gritting his teeth, Davis stomped away from the cottage. The Madeline of his past, that guileless, godly young girl, had turned into what seemed to be a scheming, ruthless socialite who would never drape herself over an altar in prayer.

Davis would never allow her to sell the cottage. Never.

❄

As soon as Davis closed the door, Madeline whirled around to run up the stairs, only to face Anna and the coachman directly behind her. Both wide-eyed. Both apologetic.

"I'm so sorry," Anna began. "I didn't know when we came down the stairs that—"

"It's all right." Madeline wearily rubbed her brow and blinked against the threatening tears. Anna McCumby didn't have one deceitful bone in her body. She would never intentionally eavesdrop on anyone. Madeline looked to the meek coachman, hoping he wasn't the gossiping sort. A few words here or there might set the whole town buzzing with "the latest" about Pritchard Cotton Plantation. "I'll get your tip," she said thickly, rushing into the dining room where she had laid her reticule.

In a matter of minutes Madeline had paid the coachman, and Anna had cleared away the coffee cups. Madeline stepped into the kitchen, which was full of the smells of rising bread and chicken broth, to observe Anna efficiently washing the coffee cups and stacking them in the cabinet.

"I'm going upstairs to rest awhile, Anna," Madeline said. "And then if I have time before dinner, I may visit Grandmother's grave."

With a sad smile, Anna nodded. She hesitantly glanced into the glass-front cabinet, then peered at Madeline as if she were lost in confusion. "I don't know what all that was about between you and Davis, but I think you need to know that the man paced around here all afternoon waiting for you. I think he was really looking forward to seeing you."

Madeline suppressed the urge to roll her eyes. "I appreciate what you're trying to do, Anna. You always were the peacemaker. But—"

"No, I'm serious. I'm not trying to make peace. I'm simply stating the truth." Anna's honest expression almost convinced Madeline, but the memory of Davis's scornful words obliterated any possibility of Madeline's being convinced.

Not desiring an argument with Anna too, Madeline simply said thanks and exited the kitchen. Head bent, she walked toward the stairway, trudged up the stairs, and entered the room she had occupied during childhood. As in the parlor, dining room, and kitchen, everything in this room remained the same. The lace curtains, the ornate dresser and bed, the fireplace full of glowing embers.

Numbly Madeline took off her plumed hat and tossed it onto the bed. Seconds after easing into the ancient rocker sitting beside the window, Madeline's hands started trembling. Her throat constricted, and she began gently rocking as she hugged herself. The confrontation with Davis had taken far more out of her than she wanted to admit. She had pulled together every scrap of her composure to prohibit herself from sobbing the minute Davis slammed the door and stalked away. But the time for composure had ended. Madeline was alone now. And the tears could no longer be denied. As they silently trickled down her cheeks, Madeline bit her lips until she tasted blood. The tears prompted more emotions, and the trembling drastically increased.

The years peeled away. Madeline was a lonely four-teen-year-old who had just bid farewell to the man who had been the only father she ever knew—her grandfather. Desperately, she had wanted to cling to Davis, sob against his shoulder, and hear him say everything was going to be all right. But Davis had barely looked at her during the funeral. After it was over, a hurried "I'm sorry" was all he produced. Today's pain, Davis's rejection, his unfair accusations were heightened by his dismissal in the past.

But today Davis had also told her he loved her all those years ago. Once more, Madeline remembered that Christmas Eve by the kitchen fireplace when he almost kissed her. After that night, their whole relationship had changed, or worse, disappeared. Davis had unceremoniously distanced himself from her. Could what he said today have been true? Could he have vowed to protect her . . . even from himself?

Standing, Madeline stared out the floor-to-ceiling window, which overlooked the pecan and peach orchards. In the distant northeast, Stone Mountain hovered like an ever-present sentinel, guarding Atlanta. To the west of the peach orchard, the cotton fields of red soil rested after their recent harvest. Instinctively she peered toward the old woodshed that had provided hours of childhood fun for Madeline and Davis. Many times they had dragged sticks of wood from that shed to outline a "house" or create a make-believe railroad track.

A movement near the shed's doorway caught Madeline's attention. Through dusk's shadows, she strained to see a man, dressed in a white shirt and dark riding pants, open the shed's door as if to enter it. It was Davis. There was no mistaking his silhouette. As if he sensed her watching him, Davis turned and looked straight toward her window. Madeline caught her breath and her stomach twisted. She only heard two sounds—the lazy fire's gentle crackling and her own heart pounding in her ears.

Something in the deepest cavern of her soul tugged her toward this man from her past. Instinctively she stepped toward the window. At that instant, Davis abruptly walked into the shed and snapped the door shut behind him.

❄

Davis paused a moment to allow his eyes to adjust to the shadows in the woodshed. Moments ago as he approached the woodshed, he had felt as if someone were watching him, only to look up and find it so. Seeing Madeline standing at her window had stunned him. The uncanny experience left him feeling somewhat disoriented. And he was plagued with a sudden onslaught of doubts regarding his former assumptions about her. Could a person really change as much as he thought Madeline had changed? Beneath all the societal finery, could the old Madeline still exist?

Out of habit, he sat on a large log standing on end. During the last year, this woodshed had become his prayer closet. The log upon which he sat served sometimes as his stool, sometimes as his altar. Unlike recent days, this time Davis didn't exactly know what to pray. After Mrs. Pritchard's death, he had prayed that Madeline would come. God answered that prayer. Davis had also prayed that their reunion would be both comforting and joyous. He wondered if God had even heard that one.

With a stab of guilt, Davis wondered how much of his argument with Madeline he could truthfully blame on God. Davis had lost his temper. He was also highly disillusioned by what his dear, sweet, childhood friend had grown into.

Even though Madeline had shunned him during her past visits, Davis had hoped that today would be different. That the rift of their teen years could be mended. That they could move forward like two mature adults. That perhaps Davis could finally realize his decade-long dream of marrying Madeline.

He chuckled dryly, amazed at his own naïveté.

At once, he wondered if today's conflict with Madeline was God's way of showing him he should indeed marry Faye Allen. Faye lost much more in that carriage accident than he did. She lost the ability to walk. The ethereal, fragile blonde would probably never have an opportunity to pursue marriage unless Davis proposed. He was the guilty one in that carriage overturning. He had been driving. Even though Faye and her family held the strong conviction that the whole thing was a freak accident and that Davis was in no way to blame, he still felt that it was his responsibility to provide Faye with a home and a husband. But he had yet to formally propose to her. Davis had spent several weeks seeking God's guidance. Was today God's way of showing Davis he would never have a future with Madeline, the woman he had once vowed to marry?

As dusk turned to night and the woodshed darkened, Davis felt as if he were choking on the damp odor of freshly cut wood. In distress, he dug his fingers into his hair, rested his elbows on his knees, and remembered the night of that Christmas Eve party ten years earlier. . . .

When he had arrived at the party and seen Madeline all dressed up, looking so grown up, he should have run. But Davis, already in love with his childhood friend, had instead embraced the opportunity to tuck her soft hand in the crook of his arm and mercilessly tease her, while his heart raced with admiration for the young beauty she had become. . . .

Wanting to thrust such agony from his thoughts, Davis straightened and bolted from the woodshed into the cold night air. He blindly pursued the night until his lungs felt they would explode from the frosty air, until his cheeks burned from the cold breeze tormenting them, until his soul numbed with the pain of his horrid predicament.

And despite himself he once again remembered. He remembered an icy night ten years before when he had likewise tried to run from his emotions. Running hadn't worked then. It wouldn't work now.

Chapter Four

Madeline was fourteen once more. The night before their departure for New York had arrived. Sadly, she trudged toward the stairs, wiping away a sorrowful tear. She cherished every sight, every smell of that dear old cottage. The hallway rug tickling her bare feet. The smell of the lemon oil the maid used to clean the pine walls. The sight of the balcony banister gleaming in the moonlit corridor. If only her mother would change her mind.

She was about to descend the stairs in search of a glass of milk when she accidentally overheard her mother and grandmother arguing. Not wanting to eavesdrop, Madeline turned back toward her room but couldn't move. The ugliness spewing from her grandmother paralyzed her in dread disbelief. Stunned, Madeline gripped the balcony banister and listened in disgust. Her mother was barely able to defend herself in the face of the livid accusations. . . .

"You care nothing for me or this plantation!"

"But, Mother—"

"You never have. You never loved me!"

"Yes, I—"

"No! Don't lie to me!" The sound of her grandmother slapping her own daughter made Madeline's insides twist with nausea.

Yet Mother's soft weeping did nothing to stay the older woman's fury.

"Stop your crying!" Another slap. "Just stop it! I'm the one who should be crying. I'm the victim. Not you! You're leaving me—your poor widowed mother—to marry that—that—*Yankee* . . . and taking Madeline with you." Grandmother's voice cracked on a sob. "After your father's death, she's the only light left in my world—"

"Well, what about me, Mother? Am I no light to you?" The broken words, barely audible, made Madeline want to fling herself down the stairs, throw herself into her mother's arms, and declare her undying love to the woman who bore her.

"No!" Grandmother barked out. "Not now. Not after this betrayal. You are nothing to me!"

"Would you please just leave me alone?" Mother choked over a new sob, and Madeline cheered the first signs of her bravado.

"This cottage belongs to me. I have a right to enter any room I choose! . . ."

And the argument continued, leaving Madeline feeling as if she would explode with grief. Her palms grew clammy. She gasped for every breath. Her legs trembled uncontrollably.

From the corner of her eye, she saw a shadowed figure walking up the hallway. She knew the man was Davis. Without a thought, Madeline hurled headlong toward him. Somewhere between the banister and the time she fell into Davis's arms, Madeline had aged from fourteen to twenty-four. Now she stood within the circle of Davis's embrace, clinging to him for support, pouring out her heart in broken sobs. He lovingly stroked her hair, caressed her cheeks, and gently brushed his lips against hers. The sweet sensations washing over her eased her troubled mind until her grandmother, still yelling, hurled a vase against the parlor wall. Madeline jumped and trembled anew, wanting nothing more than for Davis to ease her taunt nerves.

Disoriented, Madeline sat straight up in bed and gazed around her bedroom in confusion. Her temple and hair were moist with tears. Her body was damp with perspiration. Her insides felt as if they were twisting into tiny, tight knots.

A dream. She had been dreaming about that night before she moved to New York. Everything had been exactly the way it really happened. Everything . . . except Davis hadn't been in the cottage that night. He hadn't kissed her. He hadn't been there to wrap his arms around her. And even though the whole thing had been a dream, Madeline's lips still tingled with the feel of his kiss.

Scrubbing the back of her hand against her mouth, she slid from the deep feather bed and continued reliving the past. Until the night she overheard her grandmother slapping her mother, Madeline had not understood her mother's desperate desire to leave her childhood home and drag her daughter with her. Deep inside, Madeline had nursed a mounting resentment toward her mother, fueled by her grandmother's carefully placed, caustic remarks. But when Madeline stood at the banister and heard her grandmother's railing at her only child, all vestiges of resentment vanished to be replaced with blind loyalty for her mother.

Now wide awake, Madeline walked toward the dwindling fire. She swiftly laid several small logs on the glowing coals. Immediately the telltale crackling began. She sat back on her heels and peered into the rock fireplace as the infant flames suckled the logs. The sparks and crackling seemed a metaphor for Madeline's emotions. Old forgotten embers had lain dormant until they were stirred by her encounter with Davis.

Why had she dreamed of his kiss?

Wanting to sweep all thoughts of Davis from her mind, the troubled Madeline reached for her house robe and snugly cinched the ties around her slight waist. She donned her mink house slippers, retrieved a candle from the mantel, and lit it in the fire. As the downstairs mantel clock produced four deliberate chimes, she stepped into the short, cool hallway and crossed to her grandmother's room—the room she had claimed after she sold the mansion to the McCumbys. Madeline had yet to visit her grandmother's grave, but she felt drawn to her bedroom, as if a visit to the room could somehow reproduce the childhood feelings Madeline had held for her grandmother. Because of the mother-daughter conflict, Madeline held only a reserved fondness for her grandmother. But before the conflict, she remembered embracing a granddaughter's love—a genuine love.

Madeline entered the small, sleepy bedroom and set the brass candleholder on her grandmother's dresser. Gently she stroked the silver-plated hairbrush full of gray hair. An unexpected rush of tears stung Madeline's eyes as she remembered strong, wrinkled hands stroking her temple and singing lullabies. With a sigh, Madeline sat on the dressing stool. For the first time since the argument between her mother and her grandmother, she ached over what that conflict had cost her. If only her grandmother hadn't been so bent on having her own way and sacrificing the family relationship.

Trying to clear her troubled memories, Madeline abruptly opened one of the dresser drawers. Sooner or later she would have to sort through her grandmother's belongings. Why not begin now? The first two drawers produced only personal clothing, which Madeline set aside to give to Anna. In the third drawer she found a pile of old receipts and the accounting ledger that showed her grandmother's gradual, interest-free sale of the cotton plantation to the deserving McCumbys.

Setting aside the ledger, she glanced through the stack of receipts.

Not until she noticed the recurring New York address did she begin scrutinizing them. Upon thorough perusal, she discovered names with which she was familiar: "Miss New York," the shop where Madeline purchased all her tailor-made clothing, right down to the fur house slippers now warming her feet; "Mrs. Wright's Academy," the finishing school where Madeline had learned the rules of propriety; "New York University," the college from which Madeline had graduated; "Studebaker Brothers Manufacturing Company," the manufacturer from which Madeline ordered the finest of carriages. She went back to the first receipt to discover her name scrawled across the bottom.

Her heart pounded out hard, even beats at the implications of nearly a decade's worth of receipts. They were ample proof that her grandmother had supported Madeline almost from the time she moved to New York. Why hadn't her mother ever told her?

Davis's earlier words ricocheted through Madeline's mind: *It seems you're more interested in money than in fulfilling the dying request of a saint of God.* Once more Madeline remembered that horrid night her grandmother had slapped her own daughter—hard enough to leave a tiny bruise beneath Mother's right eye. Those were not the actions of a saint.

But these receipts were. Did Davis know something she didn't know?

Madeline looked into the mirror to see a young, sophisticated woman bathed in candlelight, cheeks pale from lack of sleep, long wavy hair cascading around her shoulders, dark eyes full of questions . . . questions . . . questions.

When she had arrived at the plantation, Madeline carried

with her a pocketful of dogmatic notions, fueled by her mother's resentment. She had never imagined finding a bundle of receipts with her name on them. Could the conflict between Grandmother and Mother be more complicated than Madeline ever dreamed?

Her first thought was for Davis. He could answer that question. Today. Today she would ask him. But Madeline once more recalled their argument, and her stomach twisted. How could she face Davis after their heated dispute and the horrid things he had said to her?

CHAPTER FIVE

Later that afternoon Davis walked toward the family cemetery that lay between the cottage and the mansion. He was certain of finding Madeline there. Anna had told him she had walked to the cemetery over an hour ago.

During Sunday dinner, Faye Allen and her family had been congenial as always. Yet Davis's thoughts had hovered with Madeline, who had rushed from church that morning without so much as a hello. Nonetheless, he asked Conrad Allen, Faye's father, not to run an advertisement for the sale of the cottage should Madeline request it. Conrad promised to refuse to run the ad and also to influence the other newspaper publishers in Atlanta to do likewise. Ironically, even while thwarting Madeline's efforts to sell the cottage, Davis had ached to see her.

Davis glanced back to where his parents sat in front of the mansion, soaking up the warm afternoon sunshine along with Davis's younger sister and her husband. Their three rowdy children played chase, their squeals adding a gleeful quality to the whole countryside. The unusually mild autumn morning had given birth to an afternoon unpredictably warm. Davis had long since shed his overcoat. With Christmas less than a month away, he knew they might not have another day like today until spring. Therefore, he jealously embraced the afternoon sunshine.

As Davis ascended the small hill to the cemetery, the cawing crows seemed to echo his silent prayers for God's wisdom. He didn't want another confrontation with Madeline like yesterday's. Some sensible voice inside him insisted the best way to avoid such confrontation was to avoid Madeline. She obviously wasn't going to change her mind about selling the cottage. And the stars would fall from the sky before Davis changed his mind.

Obviously, Madeline held a pathetically erroneous view of her grandmother. For to Davis, Mrs. Pritchard had been nothing but a source of joy from his earliest memories. Madeline was wrong about her. Terribly wrong. He began to suspect that perhaps Madeline didn't even know that her grandmother had supported her for the last ten years. Would that truth have any effect on Madeline's staunch opinions? Given her heated defense of her mother the day before, Davis wondered if *anything* would alter Madeline's prejudice. So due to their opposing views, Davis knew the safest measure would be not to even approach her today. Nonetheless, some force within Davis tugged him toward the girl of his childhood, despite what common sense warned.

Near the cemetery, he noticed her sitting on the same bench he had used to grieve the passing of the woman who had been his surrogate grandmother. The simple wooden bench sat against a massive oak's trunk on which Madeline's head drooped delicately. Her eyes were closed as in slumber, her hands clutching a white, lacy handkerchief. Nearby, an identical white handkerchief graced her grandmother's new tombstone. The sight of the freshly covered grave left Davis's eyes stinging.

At closer observation, Davis realized that tears streaked Madeline's pale cheeks. Her eyes, although closed, appeared swollen. Her thin lips were also swollen. Apparently Madeline had shed more than a few obligatory tears at the passing of her grandmother. She must have truly mourned her death.

He mumbled several invectives to himself. Davis had made some rather severe statements the day before. He not only called her a society snob, he also insinuated that she cared very little for her grandmother. It appeared he had been wrong on at least one count. His gut twisted with guilt once more. Perhaps if he gave Madeline a second chance he would learn he had been wrong on both counts. Maybe she was simply trying to keep her word to her mother, just as he was trying to keep his word to Mrs. Pritchard. If Davis were completely honest with himself, he would admit that he had been on the defensive from the moment Madeline walked into the cottage. Could the naive, intelligent, sweet girl from his childhood have changed as much as he accused her of changing?

As if these thoughts, so poignant, triggered his memory, Davis recalled that lonely, dreadful spring day he had watched Madeline and her mother ride away with Gerald Wilson III. He was standing in the mansion's ornate drawing room, stonily gazing out the front window, listening to Mrs. Pritchard's soft sobs echoing from the hallway. Davis wanted to cry. How he wanted to cry. But he wouldn't let himself. His emotions felt as if they were tightly encased within a heart throbbing in agony. Letting those emotions spill forth seemed to cheapen his burning sorrow. Madeline—his Madeline—was riding out of his life. And he might never see her again.

From the massive, chandeliered entryway, Mrs. Pritchard's sobs increased in fervency. At last Davis rushed to her side, wrapped his arms around her, and gently stroked her heaving back. "She was my only—only child," the grieving woman cried. "I lost my husband last month, and now I'm—I'm losing her—her and Madeline too. I c-can't bear it. I simply cannot bear it. Why has she hurt me so?" She weakly struck Davis's chest with her curled fists. One dry sob escaped Davis. As if his sob abated her agony, Mrs. Pritchard calmed. Once the storm of her emotions was spent, she pulled away from Davis and flung open the front door.

"I will never forgive you for this, Lily!" she called toward the now-empty yard. "Do you hear me? I will never speak to you again. I will—I will disinherit you! You are no longer my daughter!" With those turbulent words flung toward the surrounding trees, Mrs. Pritchard slammed the formidable door and ran past Davis to race up the curving, marble stairway.

Stunned at the memory, Davis blinked in confusion. He looked at the fresh grave, pondering the woman that lay beneath that dirt, the woman who had become a saint in his eyes. The behavior he just recalled was not that of a saint. He had never forgotten holding Mrs. Pritchard as she sobbed. But somehow, he had forgotten her hateful words—words that were more than empty threats. She had indeed disinherited her daughter.

However, Davis forced himself to remember that none of the mistakes from the past would stop Madeline from selling the cottage. And he was duty bound to stop her. If only the past didn't taint their present so.

That thought, fraught with emotion, prompted Davis to slowly bow and kiss the handkerchief in Madeline's hand. He planned to simply turn and leave her, never to mention that he saw her sleeping near the cemetery. But when Davis raised his head, Madeline was observing him.

Her dark eyes seemed the innocent, disoriented orbs of a fourteen-year-old. She spontaneously produced an endearing smile and even reached for Davis's hand. For a brief wrinkle in time, Davis felt as if the years peeled away and the two of them were once more indulging in their fond friendship. An innocent friendship untainted, unspoiled, untested.

But just before Madeline's hand touched his, those innocent eyes clouded. The remembering began. And bit by bit she resumed the sophisticated demeanor of the woman who arrived yesterday. Subsequently Davis's dear, sweet, young Madeline disappeared.

"Hello," she said warily.

"Hello," Davis replied as an unearthly chill seemed to engulf them. He stood only inches from her, and although propriety insisted he step away, Davis found no power to act. As their silent appraisal of each other continued, something inside Davis mourned the loss of the young Madeline. Desperately he yearned to see her again. Now that he knew she did still exist, something inside urged him to call to her, to beg her not to leave. That yearning came out in the form of a question from their past.

"Remember all the baking we helped Anna with the Christmas Eve before you moved?" He stepped away from her and sat on the mat of dried grass near the bench.

Madeline blinked, as if his question had caught her off guard. "Yes," she said at last. "I do." The memory seemed to empower the old Madeline to once more reveal herself, for her expression cleared and all vestiges of the sophisticate vanished. "I remember I helped with the baking and you helped with the eating."

Davis returned her smile, his heart warming with her humorous response. "You do remember. I think I almost made myself sick that day."

"But you made Anna happy with all the raving," she said, staring toward Davis's rowdy nephews as they continued in their game of chase.

"Yes. And she also received a good bit of raving from all those who attended your mother's Christmas Eve party,"

Davis continued. But no sooner had the words left his mouth than Davis wished he could obliterate them from the air.

As if the very mention of that party startled Madeline, she diverted her full attention back to Davis.

He daringly held her gaze as the scenes from that Christmas party seemed to dance between them like taunting spirits of the past. Davis's betraying heart began the reactionary pounding of a seventeen-year-old who has almost experienced his first kiss. He remembered the kitchen fire . . . the flickering shadows making Madeline's eyes full of intrigue . . . the feel of her soft cheek beneath his finger.

What if he kissed her now?

The thought sprang upon Davis from nowhere and produced an ache to embrace the girl who had stolen his heart, taken it to New York, and left him bereft.

But amazingly Davis found himself enchanted not only with the Madeline of his past but also with the Madeline of the present—the young woman sitting in front of him *now*. He wondered about her likes and dislikes, about what she did with her afternoons, about what her lips would feel like against his—not the lips of a girl, but the lips of a woman, with a woman's response.

A slow, red flush crept up Madeline's face as her swollen eyes churned with the mist of mystery. Nervously she began twisting that fated handkerchief until Davis was certain it would turn to shreds of thread. At last she jumped to her feet, turned her back on him, and took three hurried steps toward the cottage, which was barely visible through the trees.

❄

Although she desperately needed to escape Davis, Madeline halted. For just as desperately as she wanted to escape him, she likewise coveted his presence. Some shocking force inside her even suggested she repeat the scene from her dream, turn back around, and fling herself into his arms.

These conflicting desires—urging her to run, insisting that she stay—paralyzed Madeline. And her mind seemed to resist any logical thought. Her face continued to heat, and Madeline possessed no power to slow her pulse or catch her breath.

Davis. Davis McCumby. How could she have forgotten the bond they once shared? As children. As teenagers. The years had done nothing but intensify what they had left behind. And that confounded patch over his eye only added to his rakish good looks. Madeline had lied to herself yesterday when she thought she could never be attracted to the likes of Davis. For now she realized she had never stopped being attracted to him. Not after that moment he almost kissed her in the kitchen. And Davis wanted to kiss her again. Upon awakening, Madeline even experienced the drowsy impression that Davis had perhaps kissed her hand. Or did he kiss her handkerchief? Regardless, the gesture left her feeling like a puddle of melting butter. Suddenly those effeminate society men in New York seemed only shadows of this man from her past.

If only . . . if only . . .

But despite all the *if only*s in the universe, nothing had changed.

"Did you know Grandmother supported me all the years I was in New York?" she blurted from nowhere, desperate to change the course of their present voyage.

"Yes. How did you find out?"

"I found the receipts in her room this morning," she continued, her back still to him.

Silence.

"She loved you very much."

"If only she had loved my mother as much," Madeline said, a slight sting in her tone. But anything, even an argument, was easier than dealing with this earth-shattering attraction that defied reason.

"She did love her as much," Davis insisted. "The day you left, your grandmother sobbed as if both of you had died."

"She put on a good act for you. The night before, she slapped my mother twice. And when we left, she promptly disinherited my mother," she said, peering toward the cottage where that brutal argument had occurred. "That's a grand way of showing her love."

"I never said your grandmother was perfect," Davis said, a trace of hesitancy in his voice.

Forgetting her need to avoid facing him, Madeline whirled around, stunned by his admission. "So you *do* think Grandmother was partly to blame for what happened?"

"Do you honestly think your mother was completely blameless?"

"I never said that," she hedged, those receipts dogging her blind loyalty. Why hadn't her mother told her that Grandmother was supporting her?

"Oh, but you implied it," Davis said.

"Well, you implied that you thought Grandmother was blameless." Madeline daringly held his piercing gaze as long as she could stand it, then looked down at her twisted handkerchief. "I'm assuming Mother knew that Grandmother was the one supporting me."

"How could she not know?" Davis demanded. After a pause, lengthy and tense, he stood to the accompaniment of his nephews' nearing squeals. "You haven't met my sister's husband or visited with Mother and Father yet," he said grudgingly. "I think this would be an appropriate time to extend your greetings." Davis sounded as if he doubted Madeline would accept the invitation and that he was using the offer as a means to escape her presence.

"No," Madeline said quickly, glad to give him his means of escape. "I'm terribly tired, and—"

"And feeling guilty?" he challenged.

"What's that supposed to mean?"

"That you know my parents and sister know you're going to sell the cottage, and you don't want to face them."

"I never said that," she snapped, her own heart proving there was a trace of truth in what he said.

"No, you didn't." He narrowed his eyes and crossed his arms, reminding Madeline of the way he had acted during the previous day's argument. "But that doesn't matter because I know you much better than you think I do."

Refusing to take his bait, Madeline briskly turned toward the cottage.

This time she had no problem separating herself from Davis.

"Yesterday I said I would stop you, Maddy," he called, the old endearing name arresting her steps. "I've already talked to the owner of the *Atlanta Constitution*. There's no use in your trying to run an ad in that paper or any other. Conrad Allen promised to talk with the owners and editors of the other papers as well as the real-estate agents in Atlanta. By next week the whole town will know we McCumbys won't give a buyer right-of-way to the cottage."

Once more she whirled around to face him, ready to stomp her foot in raging frustration and yell a resounding "How dare you!" Instead, she stayed her spontaneous reaction and produced a calculating smile. "Conrad Allen. He must be related to Faye. But you *are* using all your contacts on this one, aren't you?"

"How do you know Faye?" he demanded, his face draining of all color.

Madeline paused to enjoy the moment of victory. Having finally scored a point in this verbal sparring, she savored the accomplishment. "I saw her sitting beside you in church today. Remember? All I had to do was ask Anna a couple of questions to learn the whole story."

Madeline briefly relived the church service in which she had been overwhelmed with an onslaught of unexpected jealousy. Yes, jealousy of the gorgeous, fragile blonde who sat in the invalid chair next to Davis's pew. She had felt as if Davis had once again abandoned her, just as he had when she was fourteen. But this time he abandoned her for another love. Although none of those messy emotions made any sense to Madeline, she still experienced them. And even now they left an unpleasant shadow in her mind.

Presently, she didn't know how much longer she could keep up this subterfuge of composure. Inside she wanted to scream in rage and frustration. If Davis was this serious about trying to stop the sale of the cottage, Madeline might never sell it. She breathed a trembling sigh when Davis abruptly turned and strode away. Apparently it was his turn to retreat.

"When is the wedding?" Madeline taunted as he stalked off, despising herself for needling him but simultaneously glad she wasn't the one being needled this time.

He stopped and looked over his shoulder. "Probably by Christmas," he said coldly.

By Christmas? That was less than a month away. Madeline's mouth went as dry as the frost-burned grass teasing the hem of her skirt. Without looking back, she walked toward the cottage, all the more determined to sell it. Perhaps if she beseeched the kind Lawrence McCumby with her plight, he would agree to give a buyer right-of-way. Madeline desperately needed to be out of Atlanta before Davis married Faye. The thought of him married to another woman left Madeline wanting to sob anew. But if she were in New York, she could drown her pain with the ceaseless social functions she loved so well. Or perhaps Madeline would finally get married. That would make her mother happy, especially if the groom were wealthy. Much to her mother's dismay, Madeline had turned down several well-endowed matrimonial offers that she knew were still standing. For some reason, Madeline had never been able to develop a serious relationship with any of the men who courted her, regardless of their financial holdings. As she entered the cottage and trudged up the stairs to her room, she wondered if her lack of romantic commitment stemmed from the man who had just kissed her handkerchief.

CHAPTER SIX

Ten days passed before Davis finally delivered the note. If left up to him, he would never have written it. But Davis didn't belong to himself. He belonged to a righteous God who required his children to make restitution. Davis had said some wretched things to Madeline upon her arrival. The time had come to apologize. Yet he didn't trust himself to apologize in person. If he approached Madeline, either one of two things would happen: They would once again argue or Davis would take her into his arms.

Neither option was suitable.

Hoping to find Anna this frosty December morning, he lightly tapped on the cottage's back door. How many times had he stood at this same spot as a child, waiting for Madeline to come out and play? Something reminiscent and poignant twisted in Davis's stomach as he recalled the hours of innocent fun he and Maddy had shared.

He tentatively repeated the knock. At just past dawn, the hour was entirely too early for Madeline's rising. From what Davis understood, most New York society girls slept the morning away. If Anna wasn't in the kitchen, he would silently enter the cottage and leave the note on the dining-room table. When Madeline took her breakfast, she would find the letter.

As he was about to enter, the aging doorknob rattled, and Madeline stood before him. She wore a formal housedress in shades of sea green satin that enhanced the red high-lights of her waist-length hair, which was cascading around her shoulders. Her face, pale from sleep, reminded him of the velvet-soft petal of a white rosebud, the blush of spring perceptible to only the most discerning eye.

She bedazzled him. This was Madeline—his Madeline—the girl with whom he had attended church, the girl with whom he had prayed, the girl with whom he had fallen in love. But she was also a self-assured young woman. Given another set of circumstances, Davis would have courted her with fervor.

"Was there . . . hmm . . . was there something you needed?" she asked slowly.

"Uh . . ." Davis realized he had been staring at her as if she were a long-lost treasure. "I . . ." Why was he standing here anyway? The note. He was going to give Anna the note. "I had a letter to give to Anna." He extended the envelope.

She took it, glancing at the front. "But this is my name," she said curiously, a faint tremor in her voice.

"It *is* for you. I was trying to say that I was hoping to find Anna and ask her to give you the note. I didn't think you would be up so early."

"I've been rising earlier the past few days." She inserted the note into the front cover of a book she held. At second glance, Davis realized the book was a familiar one. Mrs. Pritchard's Bible. In order to preserve it, she had quilted a cover for it. Many times before she died, that saint of God had asked Davis to read aloud from the Word.

Before Madeline moved to New York, she had shared the love of the Bible with her grandmother. Even as a child, Davis often found her reading it. But he wondered if she still carried that passion for the Word of God. He hoped, for her sake, that she did.

Oh, Father God, please, make it so.

If Madeline would just pray about selling the cottage, perhaps she would see that selling it was wrong. But she had given her word to her mother. She was as duty bound to sell the cottage as Davis was to stop her.

Suddenly Davis wondered why he was even trying to stop her. Wouldn't he be less tortured if she immediately sold the cottage and went back to New York? This . . . this knowing she was within walking distance and not being able to hold her was almost more than Davis could bear. The last ten days had felt like ten weeks.

Within that ten days, he had tried to propose to Faye a dozen times.

But with each opportunity, words failed him. For Faye's sake, he hoped Madeline's visit was cut short.

"Er . . . is that all?" Madeline asked, her cheeks flushing scarlet.

"Yes. Yes, that's all," Davis hoarsely whispered, realizing once more that he had been boldly staring at her. Did she suspect his thoughts? Did she feel what he felt?

"Well . . . thank you. I must get back to my reading now." And she immediately closed the door.

❄

Madeline leaned against the kitchen door, her legs trembling, her heart pounding, her stomach churning. With shaking hands she extracted the note from the Bible, stumbled back to the cushioned chair in front of the kitchen fireplace, and brushed aside the patchwork quilt.

A week earlier Madeline had found the Bible among her grandmother's belongings. She had been drawn not only to the Word of God but also to the notes and scribbles Grandmother had left in the margins. Each day for the past week Madeline had awakened with the dawn and read the old familiar passages that had once given her strength. She found those passages just as meaningful now as they had been in her younger years. Madeline had been wondering how she strayed so far from the Word of God when she heard the faint knock on the back door.

Never did she expect to see Davis. And he stared at her as if he never expected to see her. The day she arrived, Davis had told her he had been in love with her when she moved to New York. In the ten days she had been here, Madeline wondered every time she saw him working on the plantation whether he still loved her. When she noticed him mending fences . . . *Does he still love me?* When she spied him masterfully riding toward the back fields . . . *Does he still love me?* When she observed him talking to the stableboy . . . *Does he still love me?*

This morning's encounter answered that question. Nothing but silent adoration shone from Davis's face. With his patch firmly in place, he looked like a young rogue, thoroughly smitten. And Madeline felt like a maiden just as smitten.

But Davis was planning to marry Faye. He had told her himself the wedding would be at the end of December. He had probably already proposed to the beautiful invalid, as well he should. Presently something whispered that perhaps she could marry Davis, despite their differences. In New York, the young ladies showed no mercy in stealing beaus from their "dearest friends." Madeline, reflecting on her own behavior, felt a sudden rush of guilt. She had behaved less than mercifully on several occasions. But Madeline could never steal Davis from Faye. Given Faye's physical condition, Davis was probably the only hope she had for a husband.

These musings left Madeline cold, despite the crackling

blaze lighting the room's pine walls. At once, she wanted to flee to New York, whether the cottage sold or not.

She peered at the white envelope with her name scrawled on it. Davis's letter. One part of her wanted to rip it open and consume the contents. Another part wanted to burn it unopened. Madeline suspected that the contents would only complicate her life. The last thing she needed was more complications.

On impulse, she extended the envelope toward the fireplace, held it near the flames, and tried to make herself toss it onto the blazing logs. After what seemed hours of internal battle, Madeline at last pulled the envelope away from the flames and aggressively tore at it. A single white page fell out. Her hands shaking, Madeline unfolded the letter and hungrily devoured the words:

Dear Maddy,

Madeline caught her breath at his use of the old, familiar nickname. Only Davis had ever called her Maddy. It had started when she was seven and he was bent on aggravating her. But the nickname that began as an aggravation eventually became an endearment.

Mom has a saying: "In most conflicts, there are three sides: your side, their side, and the right side." I'm afraid that we find ourselves in a three-sided ordeal. In my prayer time, God has shown me that I have been unfair to you, less than kind, and, to put it bluntly, an ornery bore. I said some things to you upon your arrival that were hurtful and untrue. I'm asking you to forgive me.

Madeline bit her lips as her eyes stung. Only a real man would apologize. She wondered how many of the men who had courted her would have the courage to admit they

147

weren't completely right? By the same token, Madeline felt a bit guilty. If the truth were known, she probably owed Davis an apology as well. She resumed reading the letter, this time more slowly.

> Although you have changed and I see only brief glimpses of the girl I once knew, I have no right to judge you. For that I am deeply sorry. I, too, have changed. I am no longer the boy you left but a man with a man's obligations.

He must be referring to his duty to marry Faye, she mused inwardly. Nonetheless, a very deep yearning rose from Madeline's soul. A yearning to better know the man Davis had become. Her heart twisting, Madeline gazed at the letter.

> I only wish your stay could be more pleasant and our motives weren't so crossed. I've seen you leaving for town on several occasions and know you are trying to sell the cottage. I will honestly tell you that I'm still trying to stop you. I must keep my word to your grandmother, and you must keep your word to your mother. I only wish the two of them were as deserving of our loyalty as we originally believed.

Instantly Madeline's emotions reversed. How dare Davis suggest Lily Wilson was not a deserving recipient of her own daughter's loyalty! But the same thought that had harassed Madeline all week began to torment her once more. *Why didn't Mother tell me Grandmother was supporting me . . . the clothing . . . the readiness school . . . the college . . . everything?* Madeline had naturally assumed that her stepfather paid the bills. But given her mother and stepfather's incessant need for money to fund their luxurious lifestyle, Madeline should have known. The whole thing fit perfectly into place.

But despite what Davis said, Madeline had yet to try to get a real-estate agent to represent her. Several times she had driven the carriage into town and stopped in front of one of the numerous real-estate offices. Her plan had been to get a real-estate agent to agree to approach Lawrence McCumby with her in hopes he would relinquish the right-of-way. But each time, all she could see was that pile of receipts with her name on them. Somehow Madeline must learn to put aside the effect of those receipts and move toward the reason she came. She must sell the cottage, regardless of what her grandmother had done for her. Her mother had decreed that she must sell the cottage. Madeline had never gone against her mother's wishes. She had no choice but to sell. With only a few lines of the note left, Madeline grudgingly finished it.

> Mother has asked me to invite you to dinner, which is usually served by six. There is no need to keep your distance from my parents. They love you and harbor no harsh feelings because of your plans to sell the cottage.
>
> Your friend,
> Davis McCumby

Madeline stared into the flames in the rock fireplace until her vision blurred. The whole conflict between her grandmother and her mother began to unfold once more, this time in a different light. Perhaps Grandmother Pritchard had been deeply injured at the untimely parting of her daughter and, out of blind pain, disinherited her. The motive in no way justified the cruelty, but Madeline never once remembered her mother's trying to repair the relationship. That was part of what Madeline had grieved at the cemetery—not only the loss of her grandmother but also the loss of their relationship. For Madeline had taken on her mother's grudge, and that affected the closeness she and her grandmother once shared. But despite Madeline's aloofness with her grandmother, Regina Pritchard still supported Madeline and left her the cottage and money. Her only stipulation had been that Madeline keep the cottage. Was that such a terrible request?

According to Madeline's mother, yes.

A clanging in the kitchen diverted Madeline's attention. The wiry Anna had just added wood to the cookstove and was preparing to begin breakfast. Madeline suspected that only two things kept Anna serving at the cottage—love and loyalty. Now that Anna's brother owned the whole plantation, she could easily retire to the mansion and be waited on herself. But she had spent her whole adult life working for the Pritchards, and so here she was, wearing her ever-present white apron, ready to cook the morning meal.

"Why don't you let me cook breakfast for you this morning?" As Madeline stood to stretch drowsily, she wondered about the source of that offer. She had never cooked breakfast in her life.

"Oh, no, I would never do that," Anna said, her keen blue eyes alight with a morning smile.

"It's probably for the best." Madeline returned the smile. "I don't know how to cook."

"I know!" Anna produced a wooden mixing bowl, and the two laughed companionably.

"Would you like to have the evening off?" Madeline asked.

"Whatever for?" Anna's wind-worn face seemed to collapse in dismay. "I'm enjoying being with you. I'll have plenty of nights off after you go back to New York."

"Oh, Anna." Madeline gave her childhood confidante a sideways hug. "You're so sweet. Actually, I just received a dinner invitation from Mr. and Mrs. McCumby. I was thinking maybe the two of us—"

"Now that's different. I think that's a fine idea. And it's high time you paid a visit to them. I think they're feeling a little left out of things."

"I never intended to make them feel that way. Everything just seems so awkward at this point . . ." Madeline left the implied meaning unsaid, and Anna nodded her head as they shared a moment of silent communication.

"Would you like me to tell them to expect us tonight?"

"Would you?"

"I'll be delighted to."

As a cozy silence settled amongst the kitchen's pine walls, Madeline wondered what, if anything, Anna knew about her family's conflict. "Anna . . . ," she began, retrieving a paper-thin china cup and helping herself to a generous dose of the freshly brewed coffee. "I've . . . um . . . through the years I've never heard Grandmother's side of the argument between her and mother. Naturally, I took Mother's side—especially after the way Grandmother slapped her the night before we left. But lately I've been wondering . . ."

"It was a nasty battle that night, wasn't it? Might as well have been the War Between the States all over again," Anna said quickly, as if she had been awaiting Madeline's question.

"You heard them too?"

"Yes. I was in the kitchen. Your grandmother told me she was coming down from the mansion to beg your mother not to go."

"But Mother wanted her own life," Madeline said, a defensive thread still in her voice despite her recent musings.

"I'm not saying I blame her for wanting to marry again and all that. Any woman would feel that way." Anna began kneading the dough for their day's supply of bread. "I just . . ." She shrugged and warily eyed Madeline. "I don't want to make you angry, but I just thought it all happened too soon after your grandfather's death. He had been gone only a month. I think if your mother had waited six months or so—"

"But none of that justifies those horrid things Grandmother said or the fact that she slapped my mother. She even bruised her!"

"I agree, but—" Anna shrugged—"your grandmother's wrong doesn't cancel out your mother's lack of concern for her feelings."

"Do you know if Grandmother ever tried to make amends with Mother?" Madeline rushed, suddenly not enjoying this updated view of her mother. If Anna confirmed that Grandmother Pritchard never wrote, Madeline could maintain the blind loyalty to her mother.

"I think Mrs. Pritchard's Bible will answer that question." With a flour-covered finger, Anna pointed toward the book lying in the chair near the fireplace.

Confused, Madeline peered toward the chair. "How?"

"Between the back flap of that Bible and the quilt cover, you should find a letter. That letter will answer all the questions you ever wanted to know. I watched your grandmother read it tearfully more times than I can remember."

A fist full of dread sank into Madeline's stomach. Another letter. As she had wanted to turn away from Davis's letter, she once more dealt with the temptation to simply burn this letter sight unseen. A part of her wanted to delude herself into believing that if she didn't face the contents, then somehow she could maintain her present view of reality. But another part of her insisted that she face the absolute truth. As if drawn by some terrible force, Madeline neared the Bible. Silently she picked it up and walked toward the doorway.

"If I'm not down when breakfast is ready, just eat without me, Anna," she called over her shoulder.

CHAPTER SEVEN

Clutching the Bible to her chest, Madeline settled in the chair by her bedroom window. Hands trembling, she removed the quilt cover and discovered the letter, worn and yellowed. Seeing her mother's own handwriting in no way startled Madeline. The letter was addressed to Regina Pritchard. As if she were in a nightmare, Madeline slowly extracted one page from the envelope. Gently she unfolded it to see a tearstained date of March 7, 1882—two years after their departure for New York.

Regina,

The coldness of her mother's using her grandmother's first name dug at Madeline's soul.

I received your apology. But you need to remember that two years ago, you made your choice. You have hurt me so deeply that I do not believe I can ever forgive you. As you requested, I will allow Madeline periodic visits, but I will return to you what you have dealt me and vow to never speak to you again. Please do not further contact me for personal reasons. I will send a telegram the summers it is convenient for Madeline to visit. In return, I will accept your offer to support her and send the receipts as you requested. Don't think I don't understand your motive there. You want to make doubly sure I spend none of the money on me. You can be certain that after the way you have treated me, I would never take your assistance for my personal upkeep.

Lily

Madeline's tears fell unchecked. How could her mother have been so calloused? But Grandmother Pritchard had displayed similar callousness when she vowed never to speak to her own daughter. As if to support her musings, Madeline glimpsed a small note at the bottom of the letter—this time in her grandmother's spidery scrawl: "Exodus 34:6-7. I have sinned. Dear God, forgive me."

Now openly weeping, Madeline hastily fumbled through the Old Testament until she found the passage that twisted at her heart: "The Lord God . . . visit[s] the iniquity of the fathers upon the children, and upon the children's children, unto the third and to the fourth generation."

The implications were painfully clear. Madeline's mother sinned when she coldheartedly walked away from her own grieving mother. Madeline's grandmother sinned when she responded by disinheriting her daughter. Lily Wilson then returned sin for sin and refused to mend the relationship. Even though it would appear that Madeline's mother initiated the sin cycle, Madeline pondered what Grandmother Pritchard had done to make her mother so desperately want to leave for New York, even in the face of Grandfather Pritchard's death.

One word blazed through Madeline's mind. *Control.* She remembered all the years growing up when her grandparents had virtually dictated their widowed daughter's every move. That was the original sin in the situation—the need to manipulate, even beyond God's authority. And that sin had bred Mother's sin, which had bred Grandmother's sin, which had bred more sin.

A new reality sprang upon Madeline like an unexpected hurricane: She was part of the cycle of sin from one generation to the next. As the Scripture stated, she was the third generation, and she had adopted her own mother's unforgiving attitude. Taking on that sin resulted in God's displeasure and the rift in the relationship with Davis. He had been right. Neither her grandmother nor her mother deserved the blind loyalty she and Davis had pledged to their respective "sides." With a groan, she slid from the chair and onto the braided rug. Covering her face, Madeline beseeched God to forgive her sin—not only the sin of unforgiveness but also the sin of neglecting her relationship with him. Humbly she begged her Creator to restore the passion that had once burned for him.

Oblivious of the time, she prayed fervently until a wave of peace swept over her, until a renewed awareness of Christ's love for her filled her, until the flame of what she had long ago cherished blazed within her heart. Dashing aside the tears, Madeline realized that by coming back to this cottage, she had somehow forged a bridge between the past and the present to reconnect with the girl she once had been, the girl she stuffed away in the deepest cave of her soul. As Madeline stood to peer out her bedroom window, she felt as if that girl likewise stepped out of her internal cave and stretched into full existence.

Dabbing at the remaining tears, Madeline watched as unusually early snowflakes carelessly drifted from their icy haven to the welcoming earth. Already, the rolling hills and awaiting trees were powdered in clean whiteness. Inside, Madeline felt as pure as the falling snow. If only she could stand in this spot and bask in the simplicity of her youth.

But life in the here and now wasn't that simple. Madeline was still faced with a miserable choice. Did she sell the cottage as her mother had dictated, or did she acquiesce to the dying wish of her grandmother and keep the cottage? In distress, she tightly folded her arms and frowned as she contemplated the outcome of keeping the cottage.

The truth left her breathless. Lily and Gerald Wilson believed they desperately needed the money to secure their continued stance in upper society. Furthermore, her mother was too much like Grandmother Pritchard. If Madeline went against her wishes, she would undoubtedly disown her own daughter. Lily Wilson was all the family Madeline possessed. Thoughts of Davis teased her mind, but Madeline knew beyond a doubt he would marry Faye. He should marry Faye. If Madeline didn't sell the cottage, her mother would probably tell her not to come home. She would be stuck in Atlanta with no family. Stuck in Atlanta with Davis and Faye, happily married, and in clear view. Stuck in Atlanta with a broken heart.

Regardless of the fact that she now realized her mother wasn't the complete innocent in the conflict with Grandmother Pritchard, Madeline had no choice but to follow her original plan. She would sell the cottage. She must sell the cottage. And sell it before Davis married Faye. Before Christmas. That left her only two weeks.

Desperately she twisted her handkerchief as she once more noticed Davis at the door of the woodshed. During her visit, Madeline had periodically seen him entering and leaving that shed, usually in the morning. After the first time he caught her watching him, Madeline had been careful to prevent that from happening again. But as she had wondered in recent days, so she wondered again why he persisted in going into that darkened shed. The answer evaded her. Suddenly the answer didn't even matter, because Davis abruptly turned to look up at her. For the second time he had caught her peering at him. With the snow falling around him, Davis appeared forlorn, bereft, chilled.

Madeline resisted the urge to bolt from her window, race outside, and fall into his arms. At last she realized that he was the reason she hadn't accepted any proposals. In the deepest recesses of her heart, hidden far away from even her own introspection, Madeline harbored an aching love for the boy he had once been and the man he had become. Without preamble, she stepped toward the window and rested her forehead against it. Gently, she placed her opened palm against the cold, cold windowpane.

Davis, still bathing her in his admiring gaze, rushed forward as though he would burst into the cottage and sweep her off her feet. Immediately he stopped as if he had slammed against that invisible barrier between them. His obligations to Faye. Madeline's obligations to her mother.

Abruptly she turned from the window and ferociously stoked the dwindling fire, a fire that seemed a metaphor for her love for Davis. That love had begun to germinate the night of the Christmas Eve party all those years ago. Looking back, Madeline was certain of one thing: If she had never moved to New York, she and Davis would have long since been married.

How could she have forgotten their sweet love? How could she have let it grow cold? How would she ever be the same again?

CHAPTER EIGHT

Davis descended the mansion's winding marble staircase, pondering the approaching dinner with both dread and anxious anticipation. Shortly after breakfast, Anna had arrived at the mansion to inform Davis's mother that she and Madeline would join them for dinner. The news greatly pleased Marjorie McCumby. "We'll have a Christmas party! We'll sing Christmas songs and plan how we should decorate the tree this year!" she exclaimed. Yet Davis lacked her enthusiasm because one of the guests would be none other than Faye Allen. Davis had invited her last week. This morning he never imagined Madeline would so expediently accept the dinner invitation. Creating a tense or embarrassing situation did not appeal to Davis. Yet try as he might, he could fathom no escape from what promised to be a horribly awkward evening.

As he walked across the tiled entryway toward the ornate drawing room where Faye awaited him, Davis breathed yet another silent prayer. Was this some sort of cruel heavenly joke? How would he ever survive an evening with dear sweet Faye on one side and the enchanting Madeline on the other?

Davis recalled that very morning when he was entering

159

the woodshed for his morning prayer. Once again, he felt as if Madeline were watching him. A swift upward glance confirmed his suspicions. Her appraisal both warmed and disturbed him. Despite his vacillating emotions, he had used every vestige of willpower within his grasp to keep from dashing into the cottage, up the stairway, and into her waiting arms. Why, oh why, was life so difficult?

Determinedly he stepped into the drawing room, a mixture of crystal and fine tapestry and scarlet Persian rugs. Faye, sitting in her high-backed invalid chair, turned from her contemplation of the open marble fireplace to smile serenely. Davis's heart twisted in admiration for her pale beauty. Her father had brought her to the mansion only an hour ago. She would spend the night with the McCumby family, and Davis planned to return her to Atlanta the following morning.

What would stop Davis from proposing to her tonight? Hadn't he kept the poor girl waiting long enough?

There was no way he could ever marry Madeline. Even if the selling of the cottage wasn't an issue between them, Madeline was from a different world than Davis. True, the McCumbys were highly respected in the community, were prosperous business owners. But they had worked hard their whole lives. Therefore, Davis possessed a completely different mind-set. He scoffed at the idea of living an elite lifestyle. He was just Davis McCumby, not above any amount of hard work, not above being seen with the poorest of the poor. That was one of the many areas in which he and Madeline now differed.

He knelt beside Faye's invalid chair and took her slender, chilled hand. Her rose perfume seemed all the sweeter mixed with the smell of burning wood. He thought of the hours the two of them had spent in prayer for the Lord's touch on Faye's body and the spiritual depth they both had developed due to her condition. True, Davis wasn't in love with Faye as he was with Madeline. But once Madeline went back to New York and he married Faye, that love would develop. Already, they shared a deep friendship, an infinite respect.

All this pondering at last convinced Davis he should propose. Now. Before Madeline arrived. In short, he fully realized he could never live with himself if he didn't supply for Faye what the accident had stopped her from pursuing—a husband, a home, security. Most likely, Faye could never give Davis any children. But there were other things in life to compensate, for instance, the comfort of knowing he made honorable decisions.

"Faye," he began, gently stroking her hand.

She smiled, her kind blue eyes alight with the mutual respect they shared.

"I think with Christmas approaching this would be the perfect night for us to announce our engagement."

Blinking in surprise, Faye remained silent. As the ancient grandfather clock ticked off the seconds, Davis wondered if his suggestion had swept away every word from the poor girl's vocabulary. Hadn't she been waiting for this very moment?

She removed her hand from his and nervously rubbed her palm against her red velvet skirt. At last she spoke. "Does your proposal come because of your love for me or because of your duty to me?" She turned her penetrating gaze to his as if she were a prospector searching for one tiny nugget of gold.

Davis never dreamed she might question his intent. And he had no answer. At last, he parried her question with one of his own. "If you were to accept, on what grounds would your acceptance stand? Love or duty?" The irritation in his tone surprised even Davis.

Faye simply turned her attention back to the fire. "I care a great deal for you."

"And I you."

"But I cannot imagine that you would truly want to marry an invalid." Gently she dabbed at a lone tear as it trickled down the side of her nose.

"If I didn't want to marry you, I wouldn't have proposed," he said softly. Trying to soothe Faye's taut emotions, he touched her hand in brotherly concern.

Averting her face, she tugged her hand from his grasp once more.

Nonplussed, Davis removed himself to the front window. At a complete loss for words, he stared mutely out the window to observe the early snow, which had continued on and off all day and now covered the countryside in a thin white dusting. This snow reminded him of another night ten years before, the night he had vowed to marry Madeline. As if the memory produced her presence, Davis heard her hesitant hello? from the drawing room's entryway. Surprised, he whirled to face her and his Aunt Anna observing him.

"We came in through the kitchen door," Anna said with a familiar smile. "I wanted to chat with Camilla about what she's preparing for dinner."

"You mean you wanted to advise her on the meal," Davis teased, stepping forward to take his beloved aunt's hands. "I don't know how you'll ever retire to the mansion without driving the kitchen staff to distraction."

"You know me too well," Anna said through a chuckle.

He lovingly tucked his aunt's hand into the crook of his arm and nodded toward Madeline in what he had planned as only a brief acknowledgment of her presence. Yet when he made eye contact with Madeline, the world seemed to halt. Her searching, questioning, guileless eyes left Davis with impressions of the godly girl he had once ardently admired. And as much as he wanted to deny it, he admired the woman she had become all the more.

Purposefully, he forced himself to move to Faye's side. Beseechingly he glanced toward her to find her curious appraisal more than disturbing. Did she suspect the feelings he held for Madeline?

❄

Madeline nodded politely toward Faye, and they exchanged appropriate pleasantries. Her face felt as if it were as stiff as the frozen countryside. If she had known Faye was going to be present for this dinner, Madeline would never have accepted the invitation. Did Davis plan this whole wretched affair? Although he chatted amiably with Faye and his aunt, Madeline observed the hint of desperation nibbling the corners of his mouth. The answer lay blatantly before her. Davis never intended this encounter to occur. Mutely, Madeline stared toward the oak grandfather clock near the drawing room's doorway and tried to still her pounding heart. She and Anna were fifteen minutes early. She desperately wished for a way to discreetly depart before Mr. and Mrs. McCumby appeared for dinner.

A movement at the entryway dashed aside any potential for escape, for Marjorie and Lawrence McCumby entered the room, offering a radiant welcome.

"Madeline," Mrs. McCumby exclaimed, rushing to take her hands. "It's so good to see you!"

The two hugged, and Madeline felt as if she were truly coming home. How many times had Mrs. McCumby opened her arms to Madeline? Too many to count! Madeline breathed a silent prayer of thanks that this saint of God held no harsh feelings concerning Madeline's need to sell the cottage. Even though she had seen Marjorie and Lawrence at Sunday worship, Madeline had maintained her distance due to uncertainty about her reception. She had endured enough censure from Davis. The last thing she needed was a double dose of disapproval from his parents.

She and Mrs. McCumby pulled away from the embrace, and Madeline looked into dancing blue eyes, so like her son's, the only physical likeness Davis derived from his plump, fair mother. The rest of Davis's looks came from his father—the height, the slenderness, the rakish curl of his dark hair.

"We have so much to catch up on," Mrs. McCumby said, steering Madeline toward the library.

"Oh, no, you don't," Mr. McCumby tugged on Madeline's other arm. "I won't let you steal her away to yourself. We all want to visit with Madeline."

"Oh, all right," Mrs. McCumby said with a smile.

A firm knock at the front door arrested everyone's attention, and Davis curiously glanced toward his parents. He obviously wasn't expecting more company.

"That should be our final guest," Mr. McCumby said as the doorman answered the knock. Soon a tall distinguished, gray-haired gentleman stood on the drawing room's threshold.

"Allow me to introduce our new friend," Mr. McCumby said, cordially shaking the man's hand. "Arthur Shipley, the new president at Atlanta National Bank . . ." Mr. McCumby continued the introductions until he came to Madeline.

"And this is Madeline Devry, the young lady I was telling you about. She owns the cottage that is for sale near the brook."

Mr. McCumby ushered Madeline forward. As she politely curtsied, she wondered why Mr. McCumby had referred to the cottage.

In answer to her mental musings, Mr. McCumby continued, "Mr. Shipley is interested in buying your cottage, Madeline. He's particularly taken by the fact that your great-grandfather structured it as a model of the original Pritchard cottage in England." With a fervent glance toward his son, he firmly stated the next words. "Furthermore, I told him we would gladly permit him the right-of-way to access the cottage should he buy it."

❄

Davis, stunned by his father's words, gaped at Madeline and the refined gentleman. Madeline herself appeared momentarily nonplussed by Mr. McCumby's admission but soon regained her societal composure.

"Weren't you trying to stop her from selling the cottage?" Faye whispered.

"Yes," Davis hissed, his lips stiff with anger. Betrayed. His own parents had betrayed him. Even worse, they had betrayed Mrs. Pritchard, the very woman who enabled them to own the whole plantation. What was wrong with them? Had they lost their minds? The two acted as if linking Madeline with a potential buyer was the grandest accomplishment since the invention of the wheel.

Davis reflected on all those endearing years during which Mrs. Pritchard had taken him under wing, as she called it. She had treated Davis as her own flesh and blood and had been beyond generous, especially at Christmastime. The Christmas season seemed barren this year without her kind presence.

Soon Madeline and Mr. Shipley were engrossed in pertinent facts about the cottage, and Davis was powerless to stop them. The longer he stood near the fire and remembered Mrs. Pritchard's endless kindnesses, the warmer he became physically and the hotter he grew emotionally. As a rule, Davis had always been a respectful son, and his parents had likewise respected him. But this . . . this . . . this betrayal went beyond belief.

As the minutes dragged by, Davis's anger grew to fury, and the fury mounted until he became livid. By the time dinner was announced, he could control himself no longer.

"Mother . . . Father . . . ," he uttered through gritted teeth,

"I would like a word with you."

The two exchanged a knowing glance that left Davis even more angry. Once the room emptied of all the guests, he discreetly closed the drawing room door and turned to his parents. A voice deep within him whispered that he should dampen the explosion of emotions that threatened to erupt. Miraculously, Davis managed one simple question.

"How could you?"

Lawrence McCumby took his wife's hand and squared his lean shoulders. Davis was reminded of the times when he, as a child, had been particularly mischievous and his parents stood firm on a punishment. But this wasn't childhood, and it involved something far more serious than mischief.

"Your mother and I have discussed this at length."

"Yes, and we've prayed about it as well," his mother added.

"And we've come to the conclusion that what Regina Pritchard requested of you was unfair to both Madeline and you."

"Unfair?" Davis countered, still restraining his fury. "She was the fairest woman I ever knew! But her generosity to *us* many times went far beyond what was *fair!*"

"Not this time," his mother said, her plump cheeks a bit pale. "Regina was a very good and generous woman in many ways, but she had a tendency to want to control everybody and every situation, Davis. Because of your love for her, we feel that you were blind to this side of her. We believe she was trying to extend her control even beyond the grave by asking you to stop the sale of the cottage. *That* isn't fair to you. Don't get me wrong, Son; we loved Regina as much as you did—"

"You couldn't have or you wouldn't have gone against her wishes!" he accused, recalling Mrs. Pritchard's beloved wrinkled hand gripping his only moments before her death. "She was like my own grandmother!" he said with a suppressed sob.

"Yes, we know that," his father said soothingly. "But you must realize that what she requested of you was unreasonable. How can one person dictate to another what she does or doesn't do with inherited property?"

"You're on Madeline's side," Davis said incredulously. "She has somehow gotten to you and convinced you—"

"She has convinced us of nothing!" the two said in unison.

"Davis, calm down." His mother reached for his arm, but Davis stepped away from her, feeling as grief-stricken as he had felt the day of Mrs. Pritchard's funeral. He was simply too confused, too aghast, to endure the further complications of receiving comfort from the one who betrayed him, had betrayed Mrs. Pritchard.

With a resigned sigh, she let her hand fall. "Do you honestly think Madeline will sell the cottage?"

"What?" Davis scrutinized his parents, unable to comprehend this new avenue of thought.

"We don't think that, given the freedom to choose, Madeline will actually sell the cottage," his father explained. "But it needs to be her choice, not something that her grandmother dictated. That cottage has belonged to the Pritchards for a century now. Madeline understands all that. She's a good girl. She'll do what's right."

Davis suppressed the urge to tear out his own hair by the roots. "You don't know her! You think she's the same person who left ten years ago! But she's not! The Madeline who moved to New York would have never even considered selling that cottage. But she's no longer the woman I loved! Don't you see? She's a—"

"Son!" Mr. McCumby interrupted.

Ignoring his father, Davis continued, determined to make his point. ". . . a deceptive socialite who would rather be holding a bag of money than cherishing a family heirloom."

"Davis, please!" Mrs. McCumby begged.

"No, Mother, you need to realize the truth of what you have done!"

"It seems Mrs. McCumby isn't the only one to realize a truth," Madeline rasped from behind him.

Horrified by his own words, Davis whirled around to face Madeline standing in the doorway, her face ashen, her dark eyes pools of sorrow. "And in the light of your seemingly sincere apology this morning, it would appear that I'm not the only one who is deceptive." A lone tear trickled down her cheek. Davis recalled the same sorrowful expression the day of her grandfather's funeral. The day Madeline claimed Davis had crushed her.

He wanted to rip out his own tongue. He *had been* sincere in his apology that morning. Why had he spewed forth those words to his parents? Because his parents had shocked and angered him, and Davis had reverted back to the shock and anger he felt upon Madeline's arrival—the dismay of knowing that Mrs. Pritchard's wishes were being flaunted only weeks after her departure.

"Was there something you needed, dear?" Mrs. McCumby soothed.

"No. Nothing." Another tear, followed by a sniffle. "I just felt that I had been the reason for a rift between you tonight, and I came back to tell you . . . tell you . . ."

Confused by his own behavior, Davis stalked to the marble fireplace, doubled his fist against the mantel, and rested his forehead on his fist. He suppressed a groan—several groans—and wondered how he had managed to undo what little spiritual growth the Lord had accomplished in him this past year. What had he been thinking? He hadn't been thinking; that was the problem. He had allowed his fury to think for him.

The telltale noises from behind left his stomach in knots. Several more sniffles. The rustling of skirts. Mrs. McCumby's whispered, "He didn't mean it, dear." More movement, more skirts swishing. Then silence.

When Davis turned from the fireplace, he thought he was alone. Facing Faye as she rolled her chair into the room intensified the implications of the whole evening. Her grim expression spoke of a new disillusionment.

"You're in love with Madeline, aren't you?" she asked simply.

The denial posed on his lips, Davis stopped himself. Lying had never been his strong suit, basically because displeasing God left him less than comfortable. Despite his behavior this evening, he still desperately wanted to please his Lord. "Why would you ask that?" he said, sidestepping the answer.

"I suspected there had been something between you during your first encounter at church. I managed to brush the suspicion aside until she arrived tonight. I saw the way the two of you looked at each other." Her voice quivered. "Then a few moments ago you confirmed my every suspicion when you mentioned that you loved her upon her departure for New York."

"You heard me?"

"Everyone heard you," she said simply. "You were yelling."

This time Davis was unable to suppress the groan. He wearily rubbed his face and admitted the truth. "Yes, I'm in love with her," he said in a tired, hollow voice. "I have been since I was seventeen."

"Yet you proposed to me?"

"My proposal still stands."

"So does my refusal." She concentrated on her hands, firmly clasped together in her lap. "I hope that doesn't hurt you. It isn't my intent." Faye appraised Davis as if she were truly concerned for his feelings.

"I can't say that I'm hurt, Faye. I guess more than anything else, I'm surprised," he admitted. "You need to understand that even though I do have feelings for Madeline, she and I will never marry. She will go back to New York, and we will never hear from her again, I'm sure. Then as time marches on—"

"No. There's more that you don't know about," she said with unusual firmness as the quiver vanished from her voice.

"Oh?"

"Yes. This week, my father has learned that there's a doctor in Boston who—" her face began to take on new light, new hope—"who might be able to help me. He seems to think that with the appropriate exercise and care I might be able to walk again. Oh, Davis . . ." Gripping the chair's arms, she eagerly leaned forward. "Do you know what this means to me?"

"I can only imagine," he said, kneeling at her side.

"That was the reason I challenged you on your proposal. I wanted to know how much my being an invalid and your being involved in the accident figured into your proposal and whether or not you would have proposed had we not been linked together by tragedy."

"I . . ."

"I know the answer to my question," she said serenely. "And it's quite all right. I care a great deal for you. You will always hold a special place in my heart, but I'm not certain we're in love enough—either of us—to get married. Furthermore, I don't think you should marry any woman as long as your heart belongs to Madeline."

Davis took her hand in his and gently bestowed a brotherly kiss along the tops of her fingers. "You're a wonderful woman, Faye."

"And you're a wonderful man." She gently stroked his cheek. "Thanks for being my friend these last months. I will always remember . . ." Her voice cracked as a tear splashed to her cheek. "But now it's time for both of us to move into another part of our lives."

"You're heading for Boston," Davis said, trying to sound cheerful despite his own throat's thickening.

"And you'll marry Madeline," she said firmly.

Davis didn't argue with Faye. He had argued with enough people for the evening, had hurt enough feelings. But Faye was sadly mistaken. Davis would most likely never marry. He couldn't give his heart to another because of Madeline. And any minuscule chance he might have had with her, Davis had obliterated only minutes before.

CHAPTER NINE

Madeline entered the chilled, shadowed cottage with Anna close behind. Contemplating the evening, she didn't know how she had survived it. Despite Marjorie's valiant attempts to keep the evening festive, there were too many emotional undercurrents that ranged from tension to hostility. And Madeline experienced the hostility, the tension, and every emotion in between. How could Davis have said those hateful things about her?

His behavior was the exact catalyst Madeline needed to once and for all put the vision of those guilt-producing receipts behind her. If everything went as planned with Arthur Shipley, she would be free of the cottage, Atlanta, and Davis McCumby by Christmas Eve. And the way Madeline felt presently, Christmas Eve couldn't arrive soon enough.

"Why don't you go snuggle down in your bed, and I'll bring you up some hot tea and pecan crisps before you go to sleep," Anna offered gently.

The dear woman never mentioned what had happened at the mansion, but Madeline suspected she knew Davis had somehow hurt her. "I can't let you do that," Madeline replied firmly but kindly. "I'll be quite all right. But I do believe I'll turn in now if that's all right with you."

They halted at the base of the stairs, and Anna laid a consoling hand on Madeline's shoulder. "I might as well tell you that we all heard Davis's yelling. I don't know why he lets his temper take over. He's such a delightful young man when he's not riled. And he cares so much for you—"

"No, Anna," Madeline said stubbornly, peering into the clear blue eyes of her childhood confidante. "He says he does, but his actions speak otherwise." She bit her lips to stay the stinging tears. "Unknown to me, Mr. Shipley has already viewed the cottage from the outside at Mr. McCumby's invitation. Tomorrow he is coming to inspect the inside. If all is as he wishes, we have agreed to complete the sale at his bank on Christmas Eve. That will give me the time I need to finish going through the rest of Grandmother's belongings and give him the time he needs to prepare for the move."

"Are you sure you want to sell the cottage? I was certain this morning after you read the letter from your mother that you—"

"The letter . . ." Madeline searched for the right words. "The letter showed me that both Mother and Grandmother were to blame for the rift between them. And I think Grandmother finally realized that. I just wish Mother would." She sighed, feeling as if she had aged fifty years since her arrival in Atlanta. "But I still need to sell the cottage. Mother wants me to sell it. If I don't do as she wishes, she will be furious with me, and Mother is . . ." Torn by the conflicting emotions raging within her, Madeline once more fought the threatening tears. "Mother is the only family I have. If I anger her and she decides to—to do to me what Grandmother did to her, where does that leave me? I don't have a husband or . . . or other family or . . ."

"I understand," Anna said sadly, and Madeline saw that her friend understood all too well. "The sins of the father . . . ," she added.

"And the mother," Madeline said in defeat.

"The two of them were just too much alike."

"Yes."

"But you don't have to continue in—"

"I know," Madeline whispered. "And I won't. Things will be different for my children. I'll break this—this family cycle of control and fighting. I promise."

"I believe you will," Anna said kindly, squeezing Madeline's hand. "I believe you will."

Madeline trudged up the narrow stairway and into her room. Immediately, she spied Davis's letter nestled into the folds of the multicolored quilt on her bed. Beside that letter lay her grandmother's beloved, worn Bible. On impulse, Madeline grabbed the Bible, clutched it to her chest, and simultaneously crumpled Davis's letter. Ironically, she had re-read his apology just before leaving for the mansion. Madeline had naively hoped the two of them could completely end their feud that very evening. She had even planned to also apologize during the dinner.

She hurriedly stepped toward the fireplace and did what she wished she had done before ever opening Davis's letter. She tossed the crumpled note onto the dying coals and watched it gradually turn black around the edges then ignite with an instantaneous *poof.*

Still gripping the Bible, Madeline turned to kneel beside her bed, closed her eyes, and recalled the moment that morning when she had begun her journey back to the God of her childhood. She would continue in that journey, despite what Davis or anyone else said or did. New tears dampening her cheeks, Madeline envisioned herself as a child crawling onto the lap of a loving, healing, heavenly Father. The peace that had invaded her soul that very morning once more settled into every crevice of her inner being.

Madeline recalled the day a decade before when she left this very room on her journey to New York. She had been gently weeping, kneeling beside her bed, praying that God would ease the ache in her heart, still raw from her grandfather's death. Madeline was also torn about leaving her home, Davis, her grandmother . . . the familiar. She was scared. And God had comforted her with his own gentle, fatherly touch, through his own supernatural peace. Now ten years later, Madeline again drew strength from the same supernatural comfort.

If the truth were known, on some level she was back where she had been at the age of fourteen. Tonight, on her knees, huddled beside her bed, she had journeyed full circle to where she was, to whom she was. That young woman once more didn't want to leave her cherished cottage behind. The creaky floors, the aged kitchen, even the watermark on her room's ceiling, all seemed incredibly dear to her. Furthermore, the appeal that New York held for her upon her arrival here had now grown garish in the face of her reawakened love for her Lord. Nonetheless, Madeline would return to New York. She saw no other choice.

❄

Christmas Eve morning dawned with a heavy frost. The whole countryside appeared to have been decorated in sparkling crystals just for the celebration of Christ's birth. The last few days had been a whirlwind of activity for Madeline. Through numerous bouts of tears, she at last sorted through all of her grandmother's personal possessions. Several pieces of furniture she arranged to have shipped to New York. Other pieces she sold or gave away. A few items Mr. Shipley himself purchased. The only thing left to do on this cold December morning was load her trunk in the carriage, go to the bank and sign the appropriate paperwork, then on to Union Station to board the next train to New York.

As she silently observed Anna cleaning up the kitchen after their final breakfast together, Madeline wanted to ask her about Davis. She hadn't seen or spoken to him since that dinner two weeks before. Madeline had avoided church because she couldn't bear the sight of Faye and Davis together. Even though both Marjorie and Lawrence had come to the cottage more than once to assist Madeline in her tedious chore, Davis remained out of sight. Madeline hadn't even noticed him making his usual trip to the woodshed. Last week Marjorie had vaguely mentioned the woodshed's being Davis's prayer closet. Madeline had stopped herself from retorting that he needed to pray. At that time, Madeline still vowed that the man was insufferable!

Nonetheless she now stood in the kitchen, aching to see that insufferable man. Regardless of what he had done or said, Madeline hated the thought of returning to New York without telling Davis good-bye. He had been an important part of her childhood, and she might never see him again. She wanted to bid him a peaceful adieu, if not for what they presently shared then in honor of what they had once meant to each other. But that possibility was quickly fading, for Madeline planned to leave within the half hour.

Anna, holding a dishpan full of sudsy, gray water, walked toward the kitchen door. Madeline deposited her reticule and leather gloves on the worn kitchen counter and immediately opened the door for her. With one powerful swish, the water slapped against the frost-covered ground to create a gray splash imprint against the white frost.

"I think I see Davis walking this way!" Anna's wrinkled face, grim all morning, brightened with relief.

Madeline herself was washed in a sense of relief. Even if she and Davis no longer saw eye to eye and even if he did hold the most detestable opinion of her, Madeline had prayed that God would give her the opportunity to depart in peace. Davis wasn't the only one who needed to apologize. Madeline had sported a few bad attitudes herself. And despite Davis's wrongdoing, she had no right to repay wrong for wrong. That was what had characterized the whole nasty sin cycle between her mother and grandmother.

Within minutes, Davis entered the kitchen, wearing his worn overcoat, his usual white shirt, snug riding pants . . . and an uncertain smile.

"Hi," he said warily as he removed his black leather hat and hung it on the rack beside the back door.

Anna discreetly excused herself.

"Hello." With trembling fingers, Madeline nervously toyed with the hem of the short jacket that completed her somber gray traveling frock. Searching for any words, she walked toward the kitchen's rock fireplace and stopped.

Davis followed close behind, and Madeline felt him stop only inches behind her.

Madeline recalled a similar situation on a Christmas Eve . . . the night Davis had almost kissed her. If only they had both been older that night, perhaps that kiss would have sealed their engagement, which would have stopped Madeline's move to New York and ultimately this wretched decision to sell the cottage.

Not able to bear the tension, Madeline whirled to face Davis.

"I'm sorry," she blurted, only to hear him blurting the same.

The two chuckled nervously, and Davis gently took her hand in his. "If there's any way you can forgive me for what I said the other night . . . I know it's hard for you to believe, but I didn't mean it. I . . . I was just angry at my parents . . . and still grieving the loss of Mrs. Pritchard . . . and I reacted from what I felt when you first arrived. I never intended to hurt you that night."

"I know," she whispered, recalling what Anna had said after the dinner, that Davis sometimes allowed his temper too much control of his tongue. Madeline also recalled one cold winter's morning when they were children and they came upon a pack of boys beating up a smaller boy. Davis, twice the size of all of them, had scattered the pack and given them all a good tongue-lashing. Madeline remembered all this about him—all this and more. Peering into his honest face, she resisted the urge to stroke his temple, marred by the patch's black band.

Abruptly she removed her hand from his and stepped away to stare into the crackling fire. This fire might as well have been the very one into which she had spilled Anna's pecan crisps all those years ago. But it wasn't the same fire. And she and Davis weren't the same people.

"I never intended to hurt you when I came," she said. "But I must admit that I haven't behaved in a Christlike manner the whole time I've been here. So I don't feel that I can condemn you. I think . . . I think . . ." She gulped for air. "I think you have matured into a fine man and that Faye is a fortunate woman."

"No, she isn't."

Confused, Madeline looked at him.

He produced a tight smile. "We are no longer courting. I assumed you had heard, but I guess you haven't."

"No, I haven't." Madeline couldn't deny the glee dancing through her soul.

"She . . . er . . . rejected my proposal."

"Oh, really?" Madeline stifled a chortle. Why did this news so thrill her? She was going back home to New York, and Davis's matrimonial prospects should in no way affect her.

"Yes, and it seems she is soon to be traveling to Boston. There's a doctor there who might be able to help her."

"I know you're glad—I mean about the doctor, not the . . . not the . . . um . . . rejection." Madeline faded to a stop. Biting her lip in chagrin, she stared at the toes of her black ankle boots peaking from beneath her skirt.

After a pregnant pause, Davis spoke again. "About your selling the cottage . . ." He hesitated, and Madeline's back stiffened. "I've discussed it at length with Mother and Father, and I think they are right. It wasn't fair of your grandmother to ask me to stop your selling it. I'm not going to pretend that I want you to sell it. But by the same token, I hold no harsh feelings toward you. You are simply keeping your word to your mother."

"About Mother . . ." Madeline gazed out the frosted window near the fireplace, determined not to look back at Davis. Looking into his face left her stomach fluttering and muddled her mind. "I fully realize that she was as much to blame for the conflict as Grandmother. And quite frankly, I don't think it's quite fair for her to ask me to sell the cottage, but I gave her my word, and she's the only family I have. If I anger her . . ." She left the rest understood. "Actually, I've been praying about the whole thing—"

"Really?" he asked expectantly.

"Yes." The tone of his voice made Madeline forget her pledge to avoid eye contact. "Does that in some way shock you?" Despite her attempt at being congenial, a sharp note rang in her words.

"No. That was in no way what I meant to imply. I'm just thankful . . . uh . . . never mind!" With a frustrated growl, Davis turned and paced toward the potbellied stove. He abruptly stopped and turned to face her. "Oh, Maddy, I didn't come to start a new argument. I came to tell you good-bye and to say I'm sorry. Can't we just leave it at that?"

"Yes," Madeline said tightly, aggravated at him all over again and not even certain why. She was so touchy.

"All right. Then we'll leave it there. Now do you need someone to load your trunk into the carriage?"

"That would be nice, thank you. It's in my room." She walked toward the worn kitchen counter and began putting on her soft leather gloves in short, jerking movements. As

Davis swiftly and silently exited the kitchen, Madeline wanted to lambaste the infuriating man. But she simultaneously wanted to fling herself into his arms and beg him to beg her to stay.

But he would never do that, no matter how much she pleaded.

❄

Davis stood on the mansion's front lawn and watched as the stableboy assisted Madeline and Anna into the elegant Victoria carriage and they began their short journey toward Atlanta. He desperately prayed that they would turn around, that Madeline would change her mind. But once the hooded carriage rounded the final corner in the narrow, winding lane, Davis knew she wasn't coming back. As a cold Christmas breeze rattled the barren trees, a fist full of loneliness settled in his stomach. Once more Davis began to pray, this time a prayer of relinquishment.

He would accept defeat. He had no choice.

As his parents had encouraged him to do, Davis freed Madeline to make her own choice regarding the sale of the cottage. For the last two weeks, he had avoided the possible sight of her. He had given her the right to make her own decision. Despite what his parents theorized, Madeline still planned to sell the cottage. And for the first time Davis grasped a small grain of understanding about her reasons for persisting in selling it. Earlier she mentioned angering her mother if she chose not to sell the cottage. Most likely, Madeline's mother possessed Mrs. Pritchard's controlling tendencies and might disown Madeline as Mrs. Pritchard had disowned her.

Yet when Madeline mentioned praying about the whole situation, Davis had recognized a glimmer of spiritual fire in her dark eyes. Since the last time he saw her, she seemed more the Christ-centered girl who had left him ten years ago and less the socialite who had returned. In short, their differences were becoming less and less pronounced. At this point, Davis would gladly open his arms and give Maddy a home if her mother was to disown her.

But she had chosen to sell the cottage and return to New York. Davis would abide by her choice.

CHAPTER TEN

The granite-blocked streets of Atlanta teemed with holiday activity. People called Christmas greetings to one another from the sidewalks. On one corner, a young father, carrying a wrapped present, ran with his children toward their mule-drawn wagon. Down the street, a group of carolers sang outside a restaurant, serenading potential diners. Christmas bows decorated electric light poles. Christmas trees filled store windows. Even the sound of the electric streetcars and the whistles of the trains at Union Station seemed to proclaim holiday cheer.

Amidst it all, an infinite sadness dampened Madeline's holiday cheer. The stableboy guided the black mare toward the bank. The closer they drew the more Madeline wanted to burst into tears. She couldn't believe that her visit "home" had finally ended and that Davis had actually allowed her to drive away.

From the moment he told her he had once loved her, Madeline had secretly hoped his love still burned. When he delivered the apology note two weeks ago, her hope had soared. This morning, through the grove of elms between the mansion and the cottage, Madeline had spied Davis watching her departure. Up until the moment she pulled away, she prayed Davis would run after her, confess his undying love, and beg her not to leave. But Madeline's question was once and for all answered. Davis no longer loved her. What he once felt must have vanished.

So she would continue in her effort to sell the cottage. Mr. Arthur Shipley seemed a very deserving recipient of the family heirloom. He would care well for what the Pritchards had preserved. That would have to bring Madeline comfort.

At last they turned onto Alabama Street, stopped in front of the two-story brick bank, which reflected the Greek-style tradition of the whole city. Madeline stepped from the carriage. "I shouldn't be long, Anna. Would you like to wait inside where it's warm?"

Anna turned tear-filled eyes to Madeline. The desperation lining her leathery face almost snatched away every ounce of Madeline's resolve to sell the cottage. Clearly, Davis and Grandmother weren't the only ones who loved that old home. Madeline nervously chewed her bottom lip and once again tried to think of her options. As before, she determined she had no options. She must sell the cottage, regardless of what her heart told her.

Squaring her shoulders, she grabbed Anna's withering hand and tugged her from the carriage seat. Anna silently acquiesced, and together they walked into the bank's warm interior. The narrow, tiled main lobby hummed with holiday activity, and the air was filled with the smell of pine branches generously placed over office doorways and the tellers' barred booths.

"Miss Devry!" Arthur Shipley, dressed in a dark business suit, approached from amidst a group of laughing men near the front window. "I've been anxiously awaiting you."

Madeline produced a strained smile.

"Won't you step into my office?" The distinguished, graying gentleman respectfully placed his hand against Madeline's elbow and guided her down a narrow corridor and into a massive office. "I know you have a train to catch. So I have arranged this to be as expedient as possible. We can even transfer the funds for you to your bank in New York if you like."

"Yes. That would be nice." Madeline seated herself in the black leather chair and felt as if the books lining the walls were spinning. What would happen if she bolted and ran? But she couldn't. She didn't have a choice. Over and over again, she reminded herself of that fact. She listened absently as Mr. Shipley explained the various documents. Finally he dipped an ostentatious, gold-trimmed pen in ink and handed it to her. Her fingers trembling uncontrollably, she gripped the pen and reached for the first document.

❉

Davis stood on the mansion's front lawn for a full five minutes after Madeline's departure. The more he prayed and the more he pondered their recent conversation in the cottage's kitchen, the more he became convinced he had made a mistake. A terrible mistake! What he hadn't realized at the time, he now saw with clarity. Madeline had been thrilled that he was not going to marry Faye. That could mean only one thing.

She must be in love with him! How could he have allowed Madeline to ride out of his life without telling her he still loved her? Without at least giving her a chance to accept or reject a proposal? She was his enchanting woman who had courted his dreams for a decade, who had stopped him from falling in love with another. And Davis had let her get away! Had he been crazy?

He had convinced himself he should accept defeat in the whole situation. But when had Davis McCumby ever accepted defeat?

A single thought that began as a whisper in his soul escalated to thunder in his mind: *Go after her!* Castigating himself anew, he lost no time in racing to the stables and helping the stableboy prepare their fastest stallion. Within minutes, the winter wind numbed his cheeks as his horse galloped along the spruce-lined lane.

❋

The tears surprised Madeline. What had started as a stinging mist soon pooled to distort her view. She was actually selling the cottage. What she had traveled to Atlanta with the express purpose of orchestrating, Madeline now bemoaned. So much had happened to her in the last few weeks—mentally, emotionally, spiritually—that she felt as if she had been in Atlanta for years. The thought of returning to New York twisted her stomach in nausea. With a jolt, she realized that she had been so busy trying to be somebody in order to please her mother that she had forgotten how to be herself.

Madeline didn't belong in New York. Not really. Oh, she could feign the composure and the gay laughter and the propriety, but deep inside there was a girl who just wanted to sit and watch the redbirds on the front lawn as they pecked up bread crumbs . . . or the cotton as it sprouted and began its journey to full maturity . . . or the dogwoods as they bloomed in spring. New York City couldn't offer those treasures.

But she didn't have a choice. She must sell the cottage and return to New York.

Once more, she scrutinized the official document in her hand. Once more, she prepared the pen. Once more, she hesitated.

Mr. Shipley discreetly cleared his throat, and Madeline nervously glanced at him. He appeared somewhat perplexed, and her attempt to smile failed.

What would happen if she didn't sell the cottage? Her mother would very likely throw a temper tantrum and tell Madeline not to come back to New York until it was sold. But what was worse? Being a grown woman controlled by her mother? Or being free of that control caused by her mother's temper?

Free!

The word reverberated through Madeline's mind. And she realized that her mother's control only brought captivity. She recalled the last few years—years of maternally selected courtship, years of developing friendships with only the wealthiest because that was what her mother approved of. If she went back to New York, she would once more enter that world. She would be figuratively locking the door on her own cage.

The sins of the mother . . .

That Bible verse began to resound through her mind like a recurring chant, and Madeline once more contemplated her grandmother's sins, passed to her mother, passed to her. Finally, Madeline encountered the brutal truth: If she sold the cottage, she would be participating in her mother's sin. For her mother's grudge against Grandmother Pritchard manifested itself in her attitude toward the cottage. Selling the cottage was Lily Wilson's final blow against her own mother. By ridding herself of everything Grandmother Pritchard loved, she would once and for all gain the ultimate control. But the cottage legally belonged to Madeline, not her mother. Therefore, Madeline had the legal right to make the decision.

With determination, she firmly relinquished her pen and stood. She was no longer willing to participate in the sins of the mothers. If her mother disowned her, so be it. Madeline would not respond in like manner. She would forgive her, show love, and be ready to resume their relationship once her mother got over the anger. Madeline had enough money from her grandmother's estate to modestly support herself for some time. She would build a life for herself here in Atlanta. She would contribute to the community, perhaps teach school. She desperately loved Davis and hoped he could be part of that life, but if he wasn't, she would survive. She had her Lord, and he would be her strength.

With an apologetic smile she looked at Mr. Shipley. "I know this will come as a grave shock to you," she said in her most polite, most refined manner. "But I've been reassessing all my possibilities, and it would seem . . . I'm—I'm sorry to inform you, but I've had a change in plans. I cannot sell the cottage," she said gently. "I've—I've decided to stay here in Atlanta."

And she walked out of the office, leaving a gaping bank president in her wake.

❄

When Davis turned on to Alabama Street and the Atlanta National Bank came into view, Madeline was exiting with Anna close to her side. Davis was certain she had finalized the cottage sale. Although his heart momentarily sank with regret, he soon swept aside the disappointment. Whether Madeline sold the cottage or not in no way affected his love for her . . . the love he had nourished for a decade.

He slowed his cantering stallion to a walk, then stopped beside the Victoria and the waiting stableboy. As if she had been expecting him, Madeline gradually turned and held his gaze. The love shining from her eyes was enough to make a strong man weak. Without breaking eye contact, Davis slid from his stallion and slowly approached her to take her trembling hands in his.

With streams of people bustling by, he simply said, "I love you. I never stopped loving you."

And those incredible dark eyes that had long ago snared his heart filled with tears. Madeline placed her hand over her mouth to stifle a muffled sob. "I . . . I . . . I love you t-too."

Dashing aside all propriety, Davis wrapped his arms around Madeline and gently kissed her temple, reveling in the softness of her hair against his cheek. Pulling only inches away, he hungrily devoured the sight of her. He had been waiting for ten years to hear her say she loved him. He had also been waiting for something else—the kiss long denied him. But they were on a busy city street. The kiss would have to wait.

"I know you've sold the cottage—"

Madeline produced a teary smile. "But I didn't sell the cottage! I decided to stay in Atlanta, and—"

"You didn't sell the cottage?" he asked incredulously.

Her giddy grin increasing, she shook her head.

A joyous shout erupted from Davis's very soul. He picked up his enchanting woman and twirled in circles until they both were dizzy, not only from the spinning but also from the poignancy of their love, sweetened by a lifetime.

❄

That night Davis paced in front of the parlor's fireplace, awaiting Madeline's descent from her room. He had yet to formally propose and desperately wanted to ensure she was his, once and for all. The creak at the top of the stairs sent him rushing to the entryway. As he suspected, Madeline descended the stairs, dressed in a festive green velvet gown that reminded him of the very one she had worn Christmas Eve ten years before.

With the anticipation of a man who has waited a decade, he eagerly took her extended hand as she stepped onto the floor.

"Let's go to the kitchen," Madeline whispered, grinning mischievously. "I think Anna's been baking pecan crisps today. She might let us test them."

Feeling as if he were dreaming, Davis tucked Madeline's

hand into the crook of his arm, and they walked into the kitchen.

Anna turned from the cookie jar. "I've got a plate full of cookies for you and some hot coffee."

"Thanks, Aunt Anna," Davis said.

"I'll be in the parlor with some needlework." A conspiring smile lighting her weathered face, Anna whisked out of the kitchen.

After stepping aside for Madeline to precede him, Davis walked toward the straight-backed chairs sitting near the fireplace.

Madeline turned to face him, her face aglow with joy. "I . . . there's something I think we need to discuss."

"Oh?" Davis could think of several things he wanted to discuss, not the least of which was his proposal and the kiss long denied him.

"Yes. The day I arrived you asked me about my relationship with the Lord."

"I did . . ." Davis began apologetically. "But—"

She held up her hand. "No. The truth is, Davis, your doubts were well founded. I wasn't as concerned with spiritual matters as I should have been. All the distractions of New York and—and life . . ." She turned to stare into the fire. ". . . had moved my focus from the Lord. But I want you to know that since I've been here—"

"Yes, I know. I can see it in your eyes."

She turned those loving eyes back to him, and Davis's renewed love poured from his heart.

"I also understand the implications of your going against your mother and not selling the cottage. And I'll be here for you, Madeline, regardless of what she does."

"Even if she disowns me as Grandmother disowned her?" Her lips quivered, and Davis understood there was a strong possibility of that happening.

"Yes. I'll be here . . ." Hesitating, he took her hands in his.

"As your husband, if you'll agree."

"Oh, Davis." Madeline stepped into the arms that encircled her. "You know I'll agree."

The smell of Madeline's lilac perfume seemed to urge Davis to kiss her. As their lips met, his heart was filled with her and her alone. Madeline's sweet nature. Her ebony eyes. Her strength of character. Her dark, wavy hair piled atop her head. Her lips trembling against his. The deepening kiss sealed their engagement and testified to the passion bottled for a decade. Davis McCumby at last had captured the woman of his youth, the woman of his dreams, the woman who would always enchant him.

RECIPE

❄

There are two methods to make pecan crisps: the old-fashioned way, which Anna McCumby used, or the quicker modern method, which I use.

PECAN CRISPS (modern method)

1 yellow cake mix
1 cup oil
1 egg
1 cup chopped pecans

Mix ingredients in a large bowl. Spread and press onto a large cookie sheet. This will create a thin layer and is a bit awkward to spread evenly, but it's doable. Bake at 350° for approximately 15 minutes. Allow to cool about 15 minutes, then cut into squares. (If you cut the cookies when they are just out of the oven or after they are completely cooled, they tend to crumble some. A 15-minute cooldown is usually about right.)

Note: The recipe may be altered by using a different flavor of cake mix or by adding chocolate chips or almonds (in addition to or instead of pecans).

Old-fashioned method: Simply mix up the dry ingredients of a cake recipe instead of using a store-bought cake mix. Everything else remains the same.

A Note from the Author

Dear Reader,

Christmas holidays are often a difficult time, especially if a family conflict is involved. I wrote "Christmas Past" with the purpose of showing how complicated many conflicts really are. As Marjorie McCumby told Davis, "In most conflicts there are three sides—your side, their side, and the right side." Many times potentially good, Christian people, such as Madeline's mother and grandmother, find themselves at each other's throats, returning sin for sin to create a family cycle, which thrives from one generation to the next and deteriorates the family's spiritual fervor. It's very easy in such situations for onlookers to blindly take sides, as did Davis and Madeline. But the truth is that until each party involved responds in a Christlike manner, neither side is completely right. In other words, someone else's un-Christlike behavior never justifies my own un-Christlike behavior.

Is there a conflict in your own family this Christmas season? If so, I pray that you will bathe the situation in prayer. And if you are involved, be the first to make restitution. Even if the opposing party still accusingly points a finger at you after your apology, remain Christlike—as Madeline plans to do with her mother—and repay evil with good. Yes, "Love your enemies, bless those who curse you, do good to those who hate you, and pray for those who spitefully use you and persecute you" even when they're in your own family (Matthew 5:44, NKJV).

Merry Christmas!
Debra White Smith

ABOUT THE AUTHOR

Debra White Smith lives in east Texas with her husband and two small children. She is an editor, writer, and speaker who pens both books and magazine articles. She has twenty books to her credit, both fiction and nonfiction. Her works have appeared on the CBA best-seller list. A portion of her earnings goes to Christian Blind Mission International. Both Debra and her novels have been voted favorites by Heartsong Presents readers. She has  written novellas for Tyndale House anthologies *A Victorian Christmas Quilt, A Bouquet of Love,* and *A Victorian Christmas Cottage.*

You can write to Debra at P.O. Box 1482, Jacksonville, TX 75766, or visit her Web site at www.getset.com/debrawhite smith. She loves to hear from her readers!

A Christmas Hope

Jeri Odell

To Kathy, Becky, and the HeartQuest Team.
Thanks for taking a chance on me and making my
dreams come true. Also to Kathy, Monica, and Valerie—my
prayer partners who faithfully lift me before
the throne of grace. I love you guys.
And always to Dean . . .

CHAPTER ONE

What is faith? It is the confident assurance that what we
hope for is going to happen. It is the evidence of
things we cannot yet see.
HEBREWS 11:1

SAN FRANCISCO, 1875

G abrielle, you are late!"
"I'm sorry, Father." Gabrielle Fairchild screeched
to a halt halfway to her empty seat at the dinner table. Her baby blue eyes danced with merriment. "Please forgive me, but San Francisco is much too beautiful in August
to close oneself indoors." She seemed to float the rest of the
way to her chair.

"Hello." Her smile shined across the table and warmed
Nathaniel Morgan. "I don't believe we've met. I'm Gabrielle
Fairchild."

"Nathaniel Morgan. Pleased to make your acquaintance."
He rose, waiting for her to be seated. Glad she sat in his line
of vision, for a lovelier creature he'd not seen in a long while.
Her pale blonde hair was pulled off her face into a chignon.
He'd never seen hair quite that shade before, and it re-
minded him of the soft rays of sun in the early morning.
Quite different from her two younger sisters and their vary-
ing shades of red.

"Gabrielle, where have you been?" Her mother sounded
as annoyed as her father had.

"I've been enjoying our fair city with Jonathan."

"Without a chaperone?"

"He came by in his shay. You know they only seat two. Surely you didn't expect me to turn down a buggy ride because Magdalene wouldn't fit." She cocked her head to the side and batted her eyes with a practiced innocence. "Jonathan is harmless. You know that."

"And you know the rules of this house." Her father's disapproval showed in his brown eyes. "We shall have a word in the library later this evening."

Nathaniel watched Gabrielle's lips settle into a pout. She apparently wanted to argue her father's mandate, but wisely chose not to. Nathaniel knew that Edward Fairchild was not a man to reckon with. As their friendship had grown over the past year, Nathaniel had found him to be fair and honest but never a pushover.

Gabrielle Fairchild might be beautiful, but she also seemed spoiled and headstrong. Nathaniel was not impressed with her. The old adage "Beauty is only skin deep" rang true once again. He was not surprised. Experience had taught him that ladies with looks tended to lack character, and he'd never be fooled by one again.

After the servants cleared the table and served generous slices of cherry pie, Edward cleared his throat. "Ladies, I have an announcement to make." His gaze rested on each his three daughters in turn. "At 2:40 this afternoon the Bank of California closed its doors." He paused, looking again at his daughters.

Gabrielle finally broke the silence. "What are you saying, Father?"

"I am saying that my job as president of the board of trustees is no more."

Gabrielle gasped. "No, that can't be true!"

"Ah, but it is, my child. Mr. Ralston, the founder and main stockholder, is over nine million dollars in debt. Closing was our only recourse. We had no choice."

"Surely you can hire on at another bank."

"Possibly."

"What do you mean? Father, what are you saying?"

Nathaniel heard panic in Gabrielle's words.

"Your mother and I have chosen another direction. We are selling this mansion and returning to Rincon Hill."

"Rincon Hill! You can't mean that. What will my friends think?"

"Child, if they're your true friends, it won't matter to them where you live."

"Where *will* we live?"

"I've purchased a Victorian cottage overlooking the bay. Mr. Morgan, here, will be our closest neighbor."

"A cottage? I can't live in a cottage! What are you thinking? You're the one who said we were an innovative family, leaving Rincon Hill while it was still the place to live. You said we were ahead of our time, choosing to build the grandest three-story home on Nob Hill. Now you want to go back, when everyone who's anyone is leaving?"

Edward hung his head and answered Gabrielle softly, "I was wrong." Looking at her, he continued, "Since then, God has shown me the important things in life, and they aren't living on the right hill or having the right job."

"Then what are they?" A frown creased Gabrielle's otherwise perfect face.

"It's taken me a long time to discover that they are God and family. I want to reorder my life and find peace. I no longer want to work in banking and be responsible for other people's losses. With the closing of the bank today, our money is gone. All we have left is this monstrosity of a house. By selling it, I can help the bank return part of the depositors' money."

Again Nathaniel was reminded of what kind of a man Edward Fairchild was. More concerned with others' losses than his own, he possessed enormous integrity. Edward was a godly man—one whom Nathaniel felt honored to call his friend.

"How can you care more about strangers than your own flesh and blood?" Sparks now flew from those beautiful eyes of Gabrielle's.

"Someday you'll realize this move is best for you and best for the people who trusted my bank to care for their money. I have to do whatever I can to see that that trust is honored."

"Mother, do something! Surely you don't agree with this plan?"

Mrs. Fairchild sent a gentle smile in Gabrielle's direction. "I'd much rather be married to a man of honor than a man of means." The shade of her eyes matched Gabrielle's exactly.

"I won't go!" Gabrielle rose from her seat. "I'll marry the first man who asks me. I will not live in some hovel by the sea!" She stormed from the room.

"Please forgive my daughter's ill-mannered display, Nathaniel. I invited you here, hoping to soften her reaction. I thought you could share your passion for the sea, and she would capture your vision in the same way I did. Gabby is opinionated, but she will come around." Edward sounded sure of his daughter. Nathaniel had his doubts.

❄

After dinner, Nathaniel was invited to stay for a while. "Shall we make our way to the billiard room?" Edward asked the younger man. "I enjoy a good game while talking business."

"Certainly, sir." Nathaniel followed Edward. The plush surroundings took him back to his childhood. He much preferred his little cabin overlooking the bay.

Once in the billiard room with the door closed behind them, Edward racked up the balls on the table. He offered a cue stick to Nathaniel. "You take the first shot, my boy."

"I'm not very good, sir." His shot verified his statement.

"That's quite all right. Have you considered my offer to work for me for the next month?" Edward asked as he took his shot.

Nathaniel paused for a moment. He had prayed about it since Edward had made the offer a couple of weeks ago, and he felt certain that helping Edward was something God was directing him to do. After all, Edward Fairchild was a good man and needed help. But Nathaniel enjoyed his reclusive life, just him and the sea. Was he willing to let anyone, even a friend, intrude into his solitude? His heart stirred, and he knew he had to if he wanted to please the Lord.

"Yes, I'll help you with the move."

Edward lined up his next shot. "I'll also need help purchasing my equipment and learning the trade."

Nathaniel nodded. "Are you sure you want to be a fisherman?" Some men romanticized the sea, but fishing was hard work, and there was nothing romantic about it. Edward dropped another ball into the side pocket. "I am. I've always loved the sea. The more time I spent down at the docks getting to know you and the others, the more certain I became. As I told you before, I have seen this day coming for a couple of years, so I had much time to plan my future. Jacqueline and I invested two years of prayer into those plans. I tried to warn Mr. Ralston, but he wouldn't heed my advice. I stayed on until the end for the sake of our depositors."

"I admire you for that, sir."

"Remember, you agreed to call me Edward. We'll be spending a lot of time together. Let's not be so formal."

"It's hard to go against my upbringing. If my father were still alive, he would have my hide for being so familiar, but Edward it is. Thank you."

"No, thank *you*. I couldn't do this without your help. I don't even know what sort of boat to buy. Did you say you'd been fishing for ten years?"

Nathaniel nodded. "I started at fifteen, right after my father died." Most of Edward's balls were gone now, but Nathaniel's still covered the table.

"And you're still at it. Word on the dock is that you're one of the best."

"I work hard and love the ocean. There's nothing like the peace that envelopes me as I glide across a calm sea on a clear day. I feel closer to God there than any other place on earth."

"I've done some yachting and find that to be true myself." Edward's eyes took on a dreamy, faraway look. Maybe he did have what it took to be a fisherman. Then his last ball fell with a clunk into the end pocket. He straightened from his shot. "Can you start helping with the move tomorrow?"

Nathaniel nodded and shook Edward's hand, sealing their agreement.

❄

On his ride home Nathaniel pondered the Fairchild family. Edward had his utmost respect. He'd enjoyed their conversations at the dock and looked forward to spending more time with him. Nathaniel had longed for a father figure, even when his own father was still alive, and Edward Fairchild seemed the ideal father.

Mrs. Fairchild supported her husband fiercely. Nathaniel had noticed the way Edward took his wife's hand in his own when he made his announcement to his daughters. Nathaniel had once longed for a marriage like that, but not anymore.

The delicate face of Gabrielle floated into his mind; she was far more beautiful than any woman had a right to be. If he were a shallow man, winning her heart would be his desire. He'd loved a beautiful woman once, and once was more than enough. His experience had taught him that beauty and character did not reside in the same package. Only the sea would hold his heart now and forevermore. The sea never used a man, or lied to him, or laid a trap for him.

❄

Shortly after her abrupt departure, Gabrielle heard her sisters racing up the stairs. They charged into her bedroom uninvited.

"Gabrielle, I cannot believe you walked out on Father." Magdalene, sixteen, scrunched up her freckled pug nose in disapproval.

"He was appalled by your behavior and apologized for your rudeness to our guest," ten-year-old Isabel informed her smugly.

"What do you two ninnies know? Are you willing to move to Rincon Hill without so much as a word? Think about it. No self-respecting beau will come to the slums to court you."

"Would you like Nathaniel to court you?" Isabel asked with a dreamy look in her eyes.

"Certainly not!"

"I liked him. He was nice." Isabel spoke with the naïveté of a child.

"Izzy, I hope your tastes change before you're old enough to have boys come calling. Otherwise you'll end up with some *fisherman!*"

"Mother says it doesn't matter what people do. It matters what they are inside," Magdalene enlightened her.

"She has to say that; after all, Father is becoming a fisherman." Gabrielle almost choked on the very word. It was that distasteful to her.

"Honestly, Gabrielle, sometimes you are such a snob." Magdalene continued. "He's not so bad. His eyes are the color of molasses, and they dance when he smiles."

"Then *you* court him. Now, if you'll excuse me, I'm going to the library as Father requested earlier."

Gabrielle made her way down the grand staircase. She had planned to descend these stairs one day as a bride. Not anytime soon, but one day. Now it would never happen. The thought of leaving this house brought a lump to her throat. She loved all the beauty and wealth it exuded. Living here made her feel like a princess. Living here made her feel like *somebody*. How could she give it all up? She ran her hand over the rich, shiny wood of the banister. She loved her friends, her silk dresses, and the velvet furniture. She adored attending parties and going to the theater. *I will not give all this up!* she vowed. *I just won't!*

She spotted her father sitting in his favorite chair near the fire. He was reading his Bible with a look of rapture upon his face. How could he appear so calm and content at a time like this? Wasn't their world tipping upside down? He must have heard the rustle of her skirt, for his gaze rose to meet hers.

"Gabrielle, thank you for not making me send for you." He set his Bible down and looked at her steadily. "Your behavior at dinner disappointed and embarrassed me. You acted rudely in front of our guest. What do you have to say for yourself?"

Gabrielle hung her head, staring at the polished wood floor. "I'm sorry, Father." She longed to say more but knew she'd already said too much.

"You will have kitchen duty for the first month in our new home."

Kitchen duty! What exactly might that consist of? She only nodded, knowing that opening her mouth could be a fatal mistake. Disrespectful words wanted to pour forth like rain falling from the San Francisco sky. Her father still insisted on treating her like a child instead of the mature young woman she was. *Did you act mature tonight?* a little voice questioned. She ignored it.

"Another thing. Do not go out unchaperoned again. Your

mother must know where you are and whom you are with at all times. Your sister Magdalene must accompany you on all outings. Is that understood?"

"Yes, Father." He acted so old-fashioned sometimes.

"Sit down, child. We must talk."

Gabrielle settled on the velvet fire bench not far from her father's chair.

"I have failed you in so many ways. I've led you to believe that one's station in life is of greater importance than one's character. I've taught you to value things more than people. Now I regret how much my lack of spiritual maturity has influenced your thinking and your heart." His voice cracked with emotion, "Gabrielle, please forgive me for misleading you."

"Certainly, Father." She didn't think he'd misled her at all, but she wanted somehow to make him feel better. "May I be excused? I shall stroll under the moonlight through the rose garden. There is much I must think over."

"I know that adjusting to this move will be difficult for you, but please trust me, Gabby. I'm doing this for you and your sisters."

"I shall try. I must admit I don't understand. I love this life. Why would you want to trade it for a silly cottage and a boat?" Tears filled her eyes. She knew by the set of his jaw that there would be no changing her father's mind.

"Trust me. Someday you, too, will see the wisdom in my decision. Someday you'll thank me for rescuing you from our current position."

"With all due respect, Father, I highly doubt it." She raised her chin a fraction. "I will be back on Nob Hill by the end of the year, or at least on my way back with a shiny engagement ring on my finger."

"Child, please don't marry in haste. Marriage to the right person can be wonderful . . ." A slight smile touched his lips, and she knew he was thinking of her mother. "But to the wrong person and without love—"

"Father, I don't believe in love. I know what kind of life I want and will marry whomever can provide that for me. I will bear his children, and in return, he will shower me with clothes, jewels, and trips to faraway places. I will love the lifestyle and its provider. That will be more than enough to keep me happy."

"Ah, child." Her father's voice sounded sad. "I pray that you will learn the truth before it's too late. Go ahead and take that walk. Enjoy the night."

"Thank you, Father. Sleep well." Gabrielle leaned over, placing a kiss on her father's cheek.

As she entered the rose garden, the night air felt cool against her skin. Whether or not there were roses on the vine proved immaterial. This was still her favorite place to go when she needed to think. She walked through the rows of bushes, wondering if she should pray. It seemed to her that God had gotten her into this mess. After all, if her father hadn't decided he wanted to be a godly man a couple of years ago, life as she knew it wouldn't be grinding to a halt. No, she wouldn't pray. She might say things to God she shouldn't.

Let's see, whom could she persuade to marry her? Gabrielle looked up at the night sky. Most of her gentleman friends were of the same mind-set as she, avoiding the responsibility of marriage as long as possible. They'd all rather enjoy life's amenities than saddle themselves with a wife and children. But surely one of them would want her. She'd not give up her dreams of seeing the world. Gabrielle promised herself she'd visit Boston, New York City, and maybe even Europe. No, her father's newfound spirituality wouldn't detract from that goal.

Tonight she'd make a list of the qualities she'd require in a husband. Then she'd make a list of suitable men. Tomorrow she'd set her plan in motion.

CHAPTER TWO

Gabrielle stayed awake late into the night. By the time she turned off the gas lamp, she felt certain she'd found at least five men suitable for marriage. They all traveled in her circle, and all had called on her before. She must convince one of them he couldn't live without her.

Now morning light beckoned her to rise and face the new day. Instead she rolled over, snuggled down into her feather bed, and pulled her covers higher. Must the sunshine intrude into her day without being invited?

Suddenly she remembered her plan from the night before. She jumped out of bed and rushed into her sisters' room. "Magdalene, quick, wake up!"

"What?" her sister asked in a groggy voice.

"We have to get dressed and start my husband hunt. Father said you must chaperone me whenever I leave the house."

Magdalene groaned. "Who's being punished, you or me?"

After a quick breakfast, they headed down the hill. "Where are we going?"

"I thought we'd just walk for a while and see whom we run into." Gabrielle kept her gaze alert for a possible prospect. Her heart beat a little faster as she anticipated the hunt.

This could end up being a lot of fun. No wonder men enjoyed stalking their prey with guns, traps, or nets.

"Look! There's Jonathan down the block. Hurry, walk faster." Gabrielle saw him look at her for a moment and turn down another street without so much as a nod. She stopped dead in her tracks. What in the world?

"Maybe he didn't see you."

"Of course he didn't." But she knew he had.

They walked in silence as Gabrielle tried to understand what had just occurred. "Let's call on Amanda." They strolled up the walkway to a house almost as elegant as their own. Gabrielle tugged on the bellpull. A maid answered.

"Hello. We're here to call on Amanda," said Gabrielle.

"Amanda is not available." Before Gabrielle knew what had happened, the door closed in their faces.

"Why, I never! Can you believe a servant's treating us with such disrespect? Let's go home, Magdalene." A dread settled in Gabrielle's stomach as they climbed to the top of Nob Hill. Why were her friends treating her like a leper? Had the news of their current financial state already spread throughout the city?

Gabrielle grabbed Magdalene's arm as they entered their marble-tiled entry hall. "Please don't tell Father what just transpired," she said in a low voice. "I don't want him upset. You know how he hates prejudice." Magdalene nodded, and Gabrielle continued, "I knew this would happen. I felt horrified by Father's announcement. Our neighbors must be also. I mean a *fisherman!* I can think of nothing worse. Can you?"

"Don't you want Father to be happy?" Magdalene furrowed her brow.

"Of course I do, but he is ruining my life. I love this house. I love the parties we attend. Do you think a fisherman can afford the theater? Do you think we'll ever travel again, except perhaps a Sunday jaunt in his stinky boat?"

"I think you're being selfish. Mother says all those things

aren't as important as we make them."

"Yes, well, you certainly enjoyed the game of tennis last weekend with Jonathan and his brother. I didn't hear you complain when Father took the family for an outing to the Cliff House last month. Did you see any fishermen or their families enjoying such privileges?"

Magdalene gasped. "You are just as prejudiced as your snooty friends and their families."

"I am not prejudiced. I'm realistic. Nothing will ever be the same! Don't you understand, Magdalene? My friends won't be comfortable rubbing elbows with a pauper. Why, just last week five different men called on me. How many will want to escort a girl from Rincon Hill?" Gabrielle's voice had risen from a quiet tone to near yelling. "My life was perfect and now it's ruined!"

"You'll make new friends."

"Like that dreadful Mr. Morgan? I don't want new friends. I don't want a new life! Until yesterday, I didn't think my life could get any better. Now I'm certain it can't get any worse!" A sob escaped at the end of Gabrielle's passionate outburst. She ran up the stairs, not stopping until she lay facedown on her bed.

She cried for over an hour. At ten and sixteen, her younger sisters could adjust to this new way of living. At twenty, she felt certain she was much too old to adapt. *God, please, please help me find a way to stay here on Nob Hill. If you'll help me, I promise I'll never be mad at you again.*

❄

Nathaniel rocked on the cottage porch, waiting for the Fairchilds to arrive. He and Edward had worked hard the last few days to make this humble abode a home for his wife and daughters. Nathaniel dreaded Gabrielle's reaction. He didn't want her words to hurt her father. Edward so badly wanted his family to love this little place.

Their wine-colored carriage pulled to a stop. The gold scrolling that drew the rich to this fancy model made it look terribly out of place in this neighborhood. Nathaniel rose and went to meet them. He helped the girls step down from the coach. Gabrielle exited last and appeared quite subdued. *Good. Maybe she'll not upset anyone.*

"Ladies—" Edward bowed toward them—"your new home." He led the way with a flourish.

Suddenly all of them were talking at once, all except Gabrielle. She'd not opened her mouth. At the sound of their excited chatter, Nathaniel released a sigh of relief. *Thank you, God. I know how important this is to Edward.* Nathaniel waited on the porch while the family toured their new home.

Nathaniel's thoughts returned to a few days before when he'd been packing books for Edward in the library. He hadn't meant to eavesdrop on Gabrielle and Magdalene, but the library sat just off the entry hall where they were talking, and he'd heard every word. So, Princess Gabrielle thought there was nothing worse in life than being a fisherman. Instead of feeling insulted, he felt sorry for her. She'd been born with the proverbial silver spoon dangling from her lips. Her parents had obviously pampered and coddled her, and now Miss Gabrielle had not an inkling about what things in life held real value and what did not.

Magdalene had been right on three counts. Gabrielle appeared spoiled, selfish, and prejudiced against the lower classes. Normally this would evoke anger in him, but probably because of Edward, Nathaniel only pitied her. How a man of Edward's caliber had ended up with a child as shallow as Gabrielle was beyond Nathaniel's comprehension.

The porch creaked as Gabrielle stepped out into the sunlit morning. The pale blue of her dress matched her eyes. He wanted to say something to her, but other than their brief introduction at dinner last week, they'd never spoken. He nodded in her direction.

"You must think me a dreadful snob."

Nathaniel was startled at her words. He had never expected her to speak to him, let alone wonder about his opinion of her. "Ah . . ." His tongue felt tied in knots. He could think of no decent reply. Finally, he opted for the truth. "A bit of a snob, maybe. Dreadful? Never." Ironically, that was the exact word *she'd* chosen to describe *him*.

She swallowed hard and walked to the edge of the porch, facing the bay. Her back was to him when she spoke again. "I don't know how to do this." Her voice sounded flat and emotionless.

He strode up beside her. "Do what?"

Her hand gripped the porch column as if it were her lifeline. "Be poor." A tear trickled down her cheek. She faced him. "I don't know how to live like this. I don't know how to have no friends. Everything in my entire life has changed. Everything."

Gabrielle no longer seemed snobby. Instead he realized how frightened and vulnerable she felt. "If you ever need a friend to talk to—"

"I do. I have not one friend left."

"Well, now you have me." He recalled her saying she'd never be that *dreadful* Mr. Morgan's friend. He smiled down at her. In her frail state she looked even more beautiful to him than she had the night at dinner. *But remember*, he warned himself, *beauty and character are two very different things.*

❄

What am I thinking? What am I saying? Gabrielle looked into Mr. Morgan's molasses-colored eyes. The tenderness she'd seen there invited her to be real. In front of her family she acted tough and headstrong. In front of her friends she was the fun-loving, happy-go-lucky Gabrielle. Why, with this complete stranger, did she feel comfortable enough to reveal her true self?

When he'd smiled at her, she had felt accepted just the way she was, without pretense. Nathaniel Morgan was so different from the dandies of her world. He counted God as a friend, something many would scoff at. He cared about people. It showed in his actions and in his eyes. Her father already valued him as a dear friend.

Behind his outdated, close-cut, coffee-colored beard and sun-browned face was a man who genuinely cared about her family. She felt ashamed by her earlier assumptions that he wasn't worthy of her time or her friendship. He might end up being the only true friend she'd ever really had. After all, where were all those rich friends now that she was poor?

Gabrielle needed to escape from her own thoughts. They brought too much pain. "Would you walk with me down to the beach?"

"Not without a chaperone. I heard your father's mandate." He sent another warm smile in her direction.

Add *honorable* to his list of positive qualities. "I'll invite Magdalene to join us." She hoped he didn't think this was anything but two friends taking a walk. A poor friend she could cope with. A poor beau—never!

Moments later, Gabrielle and Magdalene rejoined Mr. Morgan on the porch. Magdalene chattered as they walked down the path toward the bay, keeping her gaze on Mr. Morgan the way a child eyed a piece of candy.

"Where do you live?" Magdalene questioned.

"See the little cabin up and to the right of yours?"

Gabrielle spotted the small place.

"I have the best view on the hill," he continued. "The one from your porch almost matches mine. There are grander homes on the other side of the hill, but I wanted to face the sea."

"Why do you love the sea?" Gabrielle asked.

"It's wild and free. It's powerful and incredible. It reminds me of God. When I'm on the sea, I feel alive. When I walk beside it, I'm awestruck."

His passion called to Gabrielle's heart, and suddenly she was enthralled by the majesty of the sea. *Wait!* she warned herself. *Don't start liking this place, or you'll never get out. It's going to be hard enough already.*

She turned away from the bay and faced Rincon Hill. "Did you know that in the sixties many rich and important people lived on this hill?" She noticed that now even the bigger places looked run-down. "This hill had a short-lived decade of glory. Now many consider it the slums."

"It's all in your outlook, Miss Fairchild. I'd rather live here, where a man has room to spread out and a porch facing the bay, than on the right hill with the wrong neighbors."

"So you're a snob, too," she teased. "You think you're too good to live near the rich and important."

"Not too good, but hopefully too smart."

"If you ever had the chance, you'd never come back here."

"I did have the chance, and that is why I *am* here."

"You lived on Nob Hill?" She doubted that very seriously.

"No, but I lived in Sacramento's most exclusive area. A nice neighborhood can't warm a cold heart, fill the lonely life of a little boy, or save a lost soul."

Gabrielle realized there was more to Nathaniel Morgan than just a simple man with a simple job and a simple home. She watched his eyes roam over his beloved mistress, the sea, and she knew somewhere inside was that lonely little boy.

"Where was your family?" Gabrielle asked softly.

"I was an only child. My mother died in childbirth, and my father never forgave me for that. I don't think he could ever stand to be around me because of the unpleasant reminder, so I lived in a house filled with servants but devoid of love. My father was a mine owner, so he had the perfect excuse to stay away."

"Oh, Mr. Morgan," Magdalene spoke with tears in her

eyes, breaking the tender exchange between Mr. Morgan and Gabrielle.

Mr. Morgan patted the hand Magdalene had laid on his arm. "It was a long time ago." He sounded as if he hoped to assure himself as well as them that it no longer mattered. But Gabrielle knew it did. No wonder he'd chosen a reclusive lifestyle. In one morning she had learned more about him and had shared more with him than with any of her shallow friends on Nob Hill.

She hated to admit—even to herself—how superficial they really were, and how much their rejection hurt. Not one friend, not even Amanda, had come to say good-bye. How could they betray her like that? Surely if one of them had had to move, she wouldn't have abandoned them. Or would she have? She glanced back at Mr. Morgan and knew instinctively that he would never forsake a friend or even an acquaintance.

"Shall we get you back? Your father said you needed to return in time to fix lunch."

Gabrielle groaned at the same time Magdalene laughed. "You won't think it's so funny when your time rolls around."

"As often as you get into trouble, my time may never come around," Magdalene informed her with a grin.

"So Gabrielle is the feisty one of the family? I would have never guessed." Nathaniel winked at Magdalene, and she giggled back.

"Absolutely. I, on the other hand, rarely displease my father." Magdalene informed him with a smile.

She is flirting with him! Something inside Gabrielle minded. *This is silly. Why would I care if Nathaniel courted Magdalene?* She knew not why she cared—only that she did.

CHAPTER THREE

Nathaniel walked toward his boat into the stillness of the morning. He'd spent much of his time the last three weeks helping Edward. He'd helped with the move, helped Edward purchase the right equipment for fishing, and helped prepare a spot for their garden. Edward knew nothing about manual labor, but he worked hard and willingly did what needed doing.

Though Nathaniel enjoyed his days with Edward, a part of him felt more than ready to return to his beloved sea. He missed the solitude, but most of all, he missed his all-day talks with God. Today he and Edward planned to go out in Edward's new boat, and Nathaniel could hardly wait.

Edward and Nathaniel cast off and anchored the boat off-shore. Midmorning arrived before either man said much. The gentle rocking of the waves filled Nathaniel's heart and mind with praise for his Savior. Edward was only watching the routine of a fisherman, so talking was unnecessary.

"Do you ever plan to marry?" Edward's abrupt question startled Nathaniel out of his quiet contemplation.

"I beg your pardon?"

"Do you ever plan to marry?" Edward repeated. "Nothing makes me happier than knowing the Lord and sharing life with Mrs. Fairchild. I just wondered if you were looking for that kind of happiness yourself?"

Edward never indulged in idle conversation, so Nathaniel knew where this might lead. He took his time, trying to choose his words with care. He had noticed Magdalene flirting coyly with him, but she was much too young in his opinion. At sweet sixteen, she seemed a giddy, giggly child most of the time. Two qualities he found annoying.

"I fell in love once—briefly. I found once to be more than enough. Now God and the sea hold my heart captive. There's no room for a wife or children in my affections."

"Are you content, fulfilled?"

"I am, Edward."

"In view of your firm stance on bachelorhood, would you consider calling on Gabrielle? Only to fill her life with a little friendship."

Shocked by his request, Nathaniel said nothing for several minutes. Magdalene was one thing, but Gabrielle? Something about her made him want to bring a smile to those often pouty lips. He wanted to take her and teach her the joy in simple things. He wanted to show her the God he knew, his best friend. Gabrielle represented danger because his heart responded to beautiful women, even though his mind knew better.

"I'm not sure that would be a good idea."

"Why not? Neither of you is interested in marriage, so there would be no harm. You could just help her get through this move. I'm concerned about her." Edward's eyes held a faraway look. "Gabrielle was always so alive, so vibrant. Her laugh danced through the halls of our home. Her eyes sparked with life and joy. Now all I see is sadness. It's tearing my heart out. I don't know how to help her."

How could he tell Edward no, but how could he say yes?

He'd be placing himself in peril. He had vowed to never allow himself to let another beauty gain access to his heart and life. The mistake came when he looked into Edward's face. The pain and fear for his daughter ripped at Nathaniel's heart. Could he say no and rob this tender father of his hope? "Why do you think I can help her? I don't live on Nob Hill. That's what she wants, Edward, not me."

"That's what she *thinks* she wants. She is mourning the loss of that lifestyle and the loss of her so-called friends. I know there is more to her than that. I know that deep inside Gabby is a person who values more than a lifestyle. Help me find her. Please, Nathaniel. She's feeling rejected and unworthy. Just having a man call on her will restore her faith in herself, and I'm hoping your love for the Lord will draw her to him as well."

Nathaniel, too, had noticed the black cloud following Gabrielle wherever she went. These past weeks, since their walk by the sea, she'd become more withdrawn and subdued. Could God use him to draw her out and lead her to the Savior? Again he looked at Edward and knew he could not tell this father—who fought for his child—no. "Yes, Edward, I'll call on Gabrielle—if she'll permit it."

Why did he feel as though he had just signed his own death sentence?

❄

"You're getting pretty good at cooking. Does the accomplishment give you satisfaction?"

At the sound of her father's voice, Gabrielle looked up from the bread dough she was kneading. She wanted to throw the mass at him, scream, and run from the room. But something in his eyes caused her to react in a more civilized manner. His eyes looked at her with a combination of fear, hope, and sadness. "Thank you, Father, for noticing I've improved since that charred roast I served on my first attempt."

His smile of relief made her glad she'd chosen a gentle response.

"Nathaniel and I spoke yesterday about his calling on you," he said.

She dropped the dough on the counter with a plop. "Father, you know—"

"Wait, let me finish."

She leaned back against the counter, the breadmaking forgotten. "Yes, Father."

"I know you are sad and lonely. Perhaps if your dandies from Nob Hill see you around town with Nathaniel, they'll realize you're still worth pursuing."

Her heart leapt in hope. "So he wouldn't actually be courting me?"

"No. He doesn't want to marry, nor do you, or at least not to him. It would be two lonely young people enjoying each other's company."

"Mr. Morgan doesn't seem lonely to me."

"I believe he is. I just don't think he's realized it yet."

She thought of Nathaniel and doubted that he could evoke jealousy in anyone, especially the socially elite of her crowd. His hands were work-worn and rough, not soft and pampered like those of the men she knew. His clothes were plain and practical; none spoke of the latest styles. The only thing he'd elicit from her old friends would be pity. Yet for some reason she felt intrigued about having him call on her. "I don't know, Father."

"Nathaniel is the son I never had. He is a humble man who loves the Lord. There is nothing he wouldn't do for me or this family. Would it hurt to enjoy his company?"

"I suppose not." Still, reservations filled her.

"Perhaps you could teach him to relax occasionally and have fun. I think he is often far too serious and needs a touch of joy in his life."

"What about Magdalene?"

"What about her?"

"She is quite taken with Mr. Morgan. Maybe he should call on her instead." Even as she said the words, she hoped her father wouldn't like the idea.

"No. I don't think Magdalene is what Nathaniel needs in his life. After all, who knows joy better than you?"

"Not anymore, Father. I don't know how to have fun. I just feel so very sad all the time. I can't help myself."

"Then you and Nathaniel need each other."

"I suppose. As long as he understands we have no future together."

"He does. And he wants you to realize that as well. May I invite him for supper?"

Gabrielle wasn't sure she wanted anyone but the family to experience her cooking skills yet. But maybe it was a good idea. Having Mr. Morgan taste her fare might help him remember the casualness of their relationship. After all, a man wanted a woman who could cook for him, unless he could pay someone else to do it. Mr. Morgan wasn't in that category. "Certainly, Father."

"He is bringing our catch for the day and will teach you to prepare salmon."

"Why did you bother asking me then?"

"If you'd said no, I'd have asked him to wait until another time."

Gabrielle returned to her bread dough. Was her father hoping more would come from this? She hoped not because Mr. Morgan wasn't her type.

The man himself knocked on their door a short while later. "Good day, Miss Fairchild." He bowed from the waist as if in the presence of royalty. "I've brought tonight's dinner. Do you think the two of us can make it edible?"

"I doubt I'll be much help, but I'm sure you'll do fine."

"Ah, but this is a joint effort. Pass or fail, we're in this together." He took her hand and led her to the kitchen. Something about him seemed charming today. He'd even dressed up for the occasion, not that his being dressed up compared to what she was used to. "Sit with me for a moment." He motioned to the table and chairs, very plain in comparison to the ones they'd dined at in the mansion.

"Miss Fairchild . . ." Suddenly he seemed serious. "Your father gave me permission to call on you from time to time. How do you feel about it?"

"Why would you want to? Father says you have no plans to marry."

He looked directly into her eyes, and her heart reacted to the tenderness residing there. "I want to know you better. I thought we could have some fun. Enjoy life together. You seem so sad—"

"I don't want your pity." Anger sparked within her at the thought of his calling on her because she acted forlorn.

"Nor do I want yours. I chose this life and I love it. Don't think everyone must live on Nob Hill and drive a fancy carriage to enjoy life."

"I never said that!"

"But you believe it."

"I just think that you don't know what you're missing."

Gabrielle felt incensed by his insight. How dare he think he'd figured her out?

"And I'm convinced you have no idea what is important in life and what is not."

"So you're planning to teach me? How very thoughtful! But don't bother. I don't need your pity, and I don't need your benevolent charity toward the poor little rich girl!" She stood, knocking her chair over in the process.

"Gabrielle!" Her father's voice came from behind her.

Why? Why must he always catch me at my worst? "I'm sorry, Father." She lifted her chin. "Mr. Morgan, please forgive my rude behavior. Excuse me."

She quietly strolled from the room, wishing that a lady

could yell, stomp, and throw fits. She did occasionally give in to such behavior, but she focused on refinement today. How dare that man think he could rescue her from herself and her materialistic ideas? If anyone needed rescuing, it was he—the poor, pathetic man.

Gabrielle strolled along the beach, trying to bring her anger and frustration under control. What bothered her most about Nathaniel Morgan—that he was good, or that he was kind? Both, she decided. He made men like Jonathan look selfish, lazy, thoughtless.

Mr. Morgan spent his days serving her father. He was constantly underfoot helping someone in the family do something. At this very moment, he planned to teach her to prepare salmon for dinner. Why must he be so bothersome?

His eyes always looked tender, compassionate, and thoughtful. When he spoke of God or the sea, they danced and sparkled with a passion that made her want to feel that strongly about something.

Why did she find him intriguing and infuriating at the same time? The only reason he wanted to call on her was to rescue her from herself. Well, she didn't need changing. She felt perfectly fine just the way she was.

"You liar," she scolded herself out loud, heading up the path toward her humble new home. *You're not fine at all. You're miserably unhappy. You hate this life, and you hate fishermen and boats, and the stinking sea! God, I beg you, get me out of here!*

❄

Nathaniel watched Gabrielle climb the path from his spot at the kitchen window. What a pair they were. He did want to change her obsession with the rich, and she wanted to rescue him from his dislike of the very same. But more than anything, he longed for God to free her from her life of self-absorption.

"I'm sorry, Miss Fairchild," he said as he met her on the

porch. "You're right. I hoped to change your way of thinking. I wanted you to see how possible it is to be happy in any surroundings if you let God fill your heart with joy."

"Even in these miserable surroundings?"

"Anywhere."

"And *I* want *you* to see how much happier you could be in a world of luxury and ease."

Nathaniel laughed. "We're at a standoff. I guess spending time together is a bad idea."

"The worst."

"Well, your family still needs dinner. Do you want help?"

"Please."

Nathaniel held the door for her and followed her to the kitchen. Even amidst the hundred and one things he disliked about her, something appealed to him. Something more than sunshine hair and summer-sky eyes. Inside, Gabrielle was a fighter. Someone who took life by storm and made things happen. She was a survivor, and she'd survive being a fisherman's daughter.

They worked side by side, preparing the meal. "For someone who's determined to leave this wretched poverty behind, you also work hard at learning the ways of this new life."

"I believe in doing everything well."

"Why bother?"

"All my life Father and Mother have taught me to do my best. It's so instilled, I don't know how to live any other way."

"I like that about you."

"Thank you. You know what I like about you?"

"Nothing?"

She laughed, but he knew she liked him at least a little. He'd caught a few glimpses of admiration in her eyes.

"I like to hear you talk about God and the sea."

"You do?" That comment opened a door for him to share

his faith with her more often.

"Your enthusiasm makes me wish I cared that deeply about something."

"You do. You're pretty determined about getting out of your current lifestyle."

"That's different. I'm passionate about a goal. You're passionate about your life."

Nathaniel knew Gabrielle had it in her to be fervent about life, too. She just needed to find something that moved her the way God and the sea moved him. He saw in her a zest few people possessed. *Lord, may she find her reason in you.*

"How are your sisters adjusting to this new life?"

"It's been hard on all of us, except Father. The worst part of poverty is having no servants. I know that sounds like snobbery, but I don't mean it that way. We're all good at looking pretty, behaving properly, and using the correct fork. Now every one of us—including Mother—must learn to cook, clean, wash clothing, iron, garden, and put up preserves. Mother doesn't complain, but sometimes I hear her crying and know she feels as overwhelmed as the rest of us. We must seem dreadfully shallow to you."

For the first time, Nathaniel caught a glimpse of how big this change really was. How hard the adjustments were. He turned her away from the stove to face him. "No, Miss Fairchild, you seem amazingly brave." Shock registered in her eyes. "I know this hasn't been easy, and I'm sorry for thinking it should be. When I look at you I see courage. I see a headstrong woman who will survive however and wherever she must. And I see a young girl who longs for life as it was, filled with friends and pleasure and laughter."

What he saw before him was an incredible fighter whose character just might match her beauty.

CHAPTER FOUR

Gabrielle swallowed hard. The passion in Mr. Morgan's eyes matched the passion in his words. He understood. He truly understood and felt compassion for her plight. He laid his hand against her cheek, and the tender gesture brought comfort to her anguished soul.

"Thank you," she whispered past the lump in her throat. She turned back toward the stove to attend to her dinner preparations.

"I'll set the table while you finish up here."

She nodded, glad to have a moment alone. She wiped her eyes with her apron. This new life was so hard. Was she really courageous or a dreadful coward? She may have fooled Nathaniel Morgan, but she hadn't fooled herself. She would willingly marry any man with money to buy her way out of this hovel. She wanted servants and cooks. If she never stood before a hot stove again, it would be too soon.

Gabrielle remained silent through the entire meal. Magdalene flirted outrageously with their guest, and her behavior grated on Gabrielle. Mr. Morgan and Father entertained the family with tales of fish and boats. The young man's gaze rested on her often, as did her father's. Both looked concerned. She couldn't even force her lips into a reassuring smile. *God, please send someone to rescue me from this place.* Why bother? Not even God cared if she was happy.

"Would you mind if Gabrielle and I walked on the beach?" Mr. Morgan directed his question to Father. "There's a full moon tonight. We'll take Magdalene, too, of course."

"Magdalene is responsible for kitchen cleanup tonight. I'm certain Gabby will be fine with you alone this one time."

"I appreciate that, sir. I won't abuse the trust you've placed in me."

Anger rose in Gabrielle. How dare her father make allowances for Nathaniel that he refused to make for her other friends? It was his fault she'd lost everything near and dear to her heart. For the first time in her life, she realized what a selfish man her father was. Because he no longer wanted to work in a bank, her mother, she, and her sisters had become his personal slaves while he spent all day off in some stupid boat.

She'd walk with Mr. Morgan, all right, and give him a piece of her mind as well. Not that it was his fault that her father made self-seeking choices, but she needed an excuse to let off steam. And he acted so patronizing. What was it he had said? *"I won't abuse the trust you've placed in me"*!

They walked the path together in silence. Mr. Morgan held tightly to her elbow. He probably considered it his duty to keep her from stumbling. Somehow that just made her fume even more. She pushed his hand away. "I can make it fine by myself—thank you very much."

"Why are you suddenly so angry?"

She spun around to face him. His face showed shadowy concern in the moonlight. "I'll tell you why I'm angry. I'm angry that I had to move here! I'm angry that I have no friends! I'm angry that I've spent the last month in the kitchen! I'm angry that my father ruined my life! I'm angry that you want to call on me, and most of all I'm angry that my father lets you escort me without a chaperone!"

Nathaniel nodded but didn't say a word. How could she pick a fight with him if he refused to disagree?

"My parents don't approve of my desire to marry a wealthy man. You probably don't either."

"It's not my place to approve or disapprove. I hope some-day—before it's too late—you discover that money and happiness aren't necessarily partners."

She ignored his statement. "They think I'm worldly. What do you think?"

"I think you'd be happier if you set your heart on things above."

"What is that supposed to mean?"

"If you put your energy into trying to know God instead of trying to move back to Nob Hill, you would find what you're looking for."

"And what is it I'm looking for, since you seem to know everything about me?"

"I think you're looking for something to fill the empty spot in your heart. But it's a place only Christ can truly fill."

"You're just as old-fashioned as my parents. You think God is the answer to everything."

"He is. Your father learned that the hard way, just as I did. Now his heartfelt prayer is for his daughters to put Christ in the center of their lives. He wants your relationship with the Lord to be more important to you than money, power, or living on the right hill."

"That's absurd."

"You see, Miss Fairchild, whatever is at the center of your heart and thoughts is your god."

"And you think money is my god?"

"I don't know. Only you know the most important thing in your life."

Nob Hill, the right house, the right friends . . . God isn't even in the top five, Gabrielle realized. She stopped and looked out over the water. The moon glowed above it, shining its reflection over the waves. *Could Nathaniel be right? Am I the one who's wrong?*

❄

Nathaniel stood back, watching Gabrielle struggle with her own inner demons. He'd stand there all night if it would help her understand the truth. *Lord, please open her heart to you,* he silently prayed. *May she find that you fit perfectly in the lonely, empty space.* His heart ached for her. He felt torn between shaking sense into her and taking her into his arms to offer comfort. He did neither. He just waited for her to speak.

A sob reverberated through the stillness of the night. Nathaniel went to her, to hold and console her. She caught him by surprise when she pounded on his chest with her fists. "I hate you! I hate my father! I hate the sea! I hate Rincon Hill!"

He pulled her into his arms. She laid her head against him, and he wrapped his arms around her. He could barely remember why he'd chosen a life of solitude. Truth be known, he could barely remember how to breathe. Crazy feelings erupted in his heart, feelings of rightness and joy. Feelings of fear and loneliness. And overriding them all, a yearning to hold Gabrielle in his arms forever.

After what seemed like hours, Gabrielle's sobs calmed. Tenderly, he touched her hair. It felt like silk against the roughness of his fingers. Reverently, his lips placed a silent kiss at the tip of her forehead. "I need to get you home." His voice came out deep and raspy.

She only nodded. He took her hand in his, finding comfort in its velvet softness. He expected her to pull away, but she didn't. She seemed to need his reassurance as much as he needed to give it. They wound their way up the path, stopping at the edge of her porch.

His hand dropped hers and moved to her face. Her dazed eyes rose to meet his, and he longed to kiss her. Instead, he let his hand fall to his side and stepped back, putting some distance between them.

"Good night, Gabrielle."

She only nodded. Was that disappointment on her face? Had she wanted the kiss as much as he had? She turned and slipped inside.

What am I doing? I'm every kind of fool. I don't even know if she knows you personally, Lord. I must be crazy. I'm falling for her. Her hurting is ripping me apart. Edward's longing for her to marry a godly man for love has affected my ability to reason. Dear Lord, what do I do now? How can I call on her and fight these feelings? How can I not call on her when I want so badly to help her father out?

Nathaniel spent his walk home and the hour after he arrived in prayer. His heart played tug-of-war with his brain. The thing that scared him most was the possibility of his heart's winning. He knew in the end it would be handed back to him, broken into a million pieces.

❄

Gabrielle faced the arrival of Saturday morning with mixed feelings. A part of her longed to see Mr. Morgan—or Nathaniel, as she was beginning to think of him—but another part of her dreaded it. She had wanted him to kiss her. She closed her eyes and relived his tender kiss on her forehead for the thousandth time. She'd been kissed before, even on the lips. Why did this one seem so different and much more romantic?

"He's here! He's here!" Isabel danced into the sleeping quarters the three girls shared. "Are you ready, Gabrielle? We're all waiting for you."

Gabrielle took a deep breath and nodded. Thinking of

spending the day at Woodland Gardens with her sisters and Nathaniel brought a knot into the pit of her stomach. Why did that man affect her in ways no other had? "Because he's so bothersome!"

"What?" Isabel looked confused.

"Nothing! I'm thinking aloud."

Nathaniel's eyes lit up when she and Isabel joined the others on the porch. A disarming smile lit his face. Gabrielle's heart quickened its pace. Her eyes lingered on his lips, as she once again remembered. Heat born from embarrassment touched her cheeks.

"Are you feeling ill, darling?" Mother questioned. "You're quite flushed this morning." She laid her fingers against Gabrielle's forehead.

"I'm fine, Mother." Gabrielle pushed her mother's hand away. She stole a look at Nathaniel. His amused smile assured her that he knew the cause of her rosy cheeks.

Oh, that man! "What are we waiting for?" Gabrielle snapped.

"*You*, silly," Isabel informed her.

Father had lent Nathaniel the carriage for the outing. On the ride to the gardens her sisters chatted, but both Gabrielle and Nathaniel remained silent.

"I thought we should take advantage of the late October weather. Next month our rainy season starts, and we may not get another chance to enjoy a dry day in the outdoors until next spring," Nathaniel commented as they disembarked from the carriage.

Gabrielle nodded. She tried to remain cool and distant. Inside, strange and unrecognizable feelings churned in her heart and stomach. What was happening to her? She must be going crazy. Why would she want this man, who didn't impress her in the least, to look at her again the way he did the other night? She longed to feel his hand against her cheek, rest her head against his chest, and feel safe, loved, and valued.

"Can we go to the sea lions first?" Isabel pleaded.

Nathaniel smiled down at her and took her hand. "Certainly, milady." None of Gabrielle's old beaus had treated Izzy with such tenderness. They'd all considered her a nuisance. Nathaniel and Isabel led the way to the sea lion tank. As her sisters crowded close, Gabrielle stood back.

"Miss Fairchild?" Nathaniel stood close but didn't touch her. "Don't you want to enjoy the exhibit up close?"

"No. I don't care to be jostled about in the crowd."

"What's your favorite part of the gardens?"

"The gazebo on the Italian terrace. What's yours?"

"I have to say the sea lions and the deer park."

They stood in silence for several minutes, watching Isabel and Magdalene enjoy the sea lions. "Why are you opposed to marriage?" Gabrielle wondered aloud.

"I'm not opposed. I just never plan to enter into it myself."

"Why? You must have a reason." She turned her gaze from the tank to Nathaniel's face.

He sighed. "It's a long story."

"We have all day," she pointed out with a shrug.

"Well, as a young child, I discovered people only hurt and disappoint you. The people you love the most cause the most pain. As a young man, I made the mistake of falling in love. Lilly's beauty drew me to her."

"Tell me about her. What was she like?"

"Lilly was the most beautiful woman I'd ever seen," *until now*, "coal black hair, violet eyes, and skin the color of ivory. From the moment I saw her, I was smitten. I wanted her for my wife. I courted her. I thought she loved me." His voice sounded far away.

"The truth was she loved my inheritance. She was a con artist who claimed to be a missionary's daughter on sabbatical. I donated lots of money to help her parents leave Africa. After she'd drained me dry, she laughed in my face, informing me I'd been a fool."

Gabrielle's heart ached for Nathaniel. It was the first time in her life she'd ever hurt for another person. How could anyone treat him that way? He was so sweet and honorable. "I'm sorry."

"I'm not. You see, that's when I really gave my all to God. I was broke, alone, and hurting. Over the last five years, I've spent all my time and energy on him. Paul's words in Philippians became my determined purpose: 'That I may know him, and the power of his resurrection, and the fellowship of his sufferings.' It's in suffering we really begin to search for God. It's in suffering we find he is all we need."

His words moved her. She was suffering. Could God be all she needed?

"Gabrielle?" A familiar voice called from her right.

"Amanda! Jonathan!" She ran to them. No, God wasn't what she needed; she needed these friends and a way back to Nob Hill.

❄

Nathaniel watched her rush toward her high-society friends. They hugged and laughed. Before his eyes, Gabrielle changed. Suddenly there was an air about her. She acted coy and openly flirted with the young man. She laid her hand on his arm, cocked her head to the side, and looked at him adoringly.

Nathaniel's heart ached. Holding her the other night had only solidified the growing feelings in his heart. He'd stayed away since then, trying to convince himself that spending time with her was the most foolish thing he could do. Seeing her here now with her so-called friends reminded him again that he and Gabrielle weren't compatible socially or spiritually.

Jonathan—as Gabrielle called the young man—made Nathaniel feel every bit the fool. Jonathan wore a sailing suit and canvas shoes. Both were new on the fashion scene, worn by the rich for leisure. He wore a cap to match and sported a mustache. His blond hair curled below his cap. *Why did I think I could compete for her?* Nathaniel wondered. *Father God, why did I hope that she would find you, be freed from her love of money, and fall in love with me?*

"Mr. Morgan, these are my dear friends Amanda and Jonathan. This is Nathaniel Morgan, a friend of my father's. He escorted us here today, at Isabel's insistence—I believe."

Nathaniel greeted her friends. He sensed their disapproval of him and his attire. Worse, he sensed Gabrielle's embarrassment. *A friend of my father's.* Wasn't he also a friend of hers? What would her friends think if they knew he'd almost kissed those beautiful full lips? An ornery part of him longed to wrap his arms around her waist and say, *Darling, don't be so modest. You know I'm much more than your father's friend. I'm sure if they'd seen us on your porch the other night, they'd realize you and I have a special relationship all our own.*

"You'd adore our quaint little cottage." Gabrielle's voice brought him back to the present. "It's simply charming."

"I didn't realize anything left on Rincon Hill fit that description."

"Oh, come now, Amanda," Jonathan said, "let's give Gabrielle the benefit of our doubt. After all, it's been years since either of us ventured down there. Perhaps one or two decent places remain."

"Of course, you are right. Please forgive my presumptions, Gabrielle. Do tell us about your life now. Are beaus still fighting over you?"

Nathaniel hated this game of one-upmanship they played, but even more he hated how small they sought to make Gabrielle feel. He watched her as she struggled to answer their questions and save face. "Don't be modest, Miss Fairchild. Tell your friends how many moonlight walks you've taken with a gentleman at your side." He smiled at the surprised look on her face. "If they'd seen you the other night on the porch with a certain caller, why, they'd not worry about how you're faring."

Gabrielle's face lit up like a Christmas tree covered in candles.

"Why, Gabrielle, do tell."

"A lady never tells. You know that, Amanda." Gabrielle sent a most grateful look in Nathaniel's direction. Though he didn't actually lie, his implications left him feeling unclean, even if he had done it as a good deed for Gabrielle.

CHAPTER FIVE

Wh
hat a dear you are," Gabrielle said, the minute her friends departed. "For a moment I feared you might mention it was you and I on the porch. That certainly wouldn't impress anyone." The moment the words left her lips, she realized the thoughtlessness of her error.

"No, it certainly wouldn't." His voice sounded flat. Looking into his eyes, Gabrielle realized she'd hurt his feelings.

"I'm sorry. I didn't mean that quite the way it sounded."

"How else could you mean it? I saw your embarrassment when you introduced me as your father's friend. I thought we were friends too."

She bit her lip, feeling ashamed both of her behavior and of anyone important knowing she truly liked Nathaniel. "We are. You know that."

"But only if no one's looking?"

"Isabel, it's time to move on." Gabrielle avoided his question. "Let's go find the stuffed monkeys and birds you like so well." They began to move away from the sea lion tank.

"I already know the answer," Nathaniel informed her. He wasn't fooled by her abrupt change of subject. They walked in silence. When Isabel and Magdalene became absorbed in the stuffed birds, Nathaniel pulled Gabrielle away from the crowd. "Explain to me who that was back there."

"I introduced you. It was Jon—"

"Not them. Who was the woman who looked and sounded like you?"

"What do you mean?"

"Come now, Miss Fairchild. That wasn't the you I know. Don't you tire of all the silly games? *Here, let me impress you. Well, I can outdo that.* Nothing you said to each other was real."

"I don't expect you to understand."

"That's the problem. I understand too well. Why do you want to be treated like that? Do you enjoy being made to feel small and insignificant?"

"No, but they didn't mean it like that."

"How did they mean it? Were they encouraging to you? Did they build you up?"

"No, but why do you care? Why are you so angry?"

"I'm angry at you because you play their silly games, and I'm disappointed that my friendship means so little to you that you'd lie about who I am."

"I did not lie. You are my father's friend."

"No wonder your father wanted to get you away from their influence."

"My father could not afford to live in the mansion any longer. Our move was financial."

"And spiritual. Your father and mother are troubled by the direction of your life. They made a personal sacrifice to get you and your sisters away from all the materialism and emptiness of high society."

"You act like he had a choice."

"Maybe he did. Had he wanted another banking job,

don't you think he could have obtained one?"

"Yes, but he said he wanted to fish."

"Partly to get you three girls out of the lifestyle that broke your parents' hearts. I beg you, Miss Fairchild, think about it. Don't settle for these friends when God can give you real ones."

A part of her knew he was right. Just as she'd felt embarrassed to call Nathaniel her friend, so Jonathan and Amanda were ashamed to be *her* friends. She felt more confused than ever. Had they even been glad to see her?

"I'm hungry." Isabel tugged on her sleeve.

"I'll get the picnic basket." Nathaniel walked away without sending his usual smile in Gabrielle's direction. He'd been hurt badly by that Lilly woman. Now she'd hurt him by denying their friendship. The strange thing was she really cared about him, just not enough to put her own reputation on the line. Why did she even care? Her own reputation lay in ruins because of the move to Rincon Hill.

❄

Nathaniel felt grateful for the time to walk to the carriage and fetch their lunch. Emotions simmered within him. Guilt for playing the game with Gabrielle's friends. Anger with Gabrielle for not seeing how shallow those people really were. Hurt that he meant so little to her that she couldn't even claim him as a friend. Frustration that Gabrielle didn't understand how much God loved her.

"Here we are. One picnic lunch for one special little lady." Nathaniel spread a blanket on the ground and all found a spot to sit.

"Gabby, can we play a game of My Favorite Things while we eat?" Isabel asked.

"I suppose. Mr. Morgan, you must finish the sentence. My favorite color is . . ."

"The blue green color of the sea."

"Now you ask one of us a question," Isabel informed him. "Pick me," she whispered.

"Isabel, why are there freckles on your nose?"

She giggled. "No, you have to start with 'My favorite something is . . .'"

"Isabel: My favorite freckle is . . . ?"

"You're not playing right! Gabby, make him play right!"

"I'll try one more time." All the girls laughed at his antics except Isabel. He looked at her adorable freckled nose. "My favorite animal is . . . ?"

"A kitten! Gabby: My favorite flower is . . . ?"

"A rose. Magdalene: My favorite book is . . . ?"

Nathaniel listened as the sisters giggled their way through lunch. He answered when it was his turn. He wondered how he'd survived the past five years with so little human contact. Could he ever return to his reclusive lifestyle? Even now, he dreaded the thought.

"Mr. Morgan—" Isabel's voice brought him back to the present—"my favorite girl is . . . ?" She giggled and covered her mouth with her hand.

"You, Isabel. Only you're too young for me." He tickled her. "Let's clean up our mess and walk up to the gazebo. It's your sister's favorite spot in the gardens." He winked at Isabel.

❄

"You're so good with children," Gabrielle told him a few minutes later as they walked together. "It's a shame you'll never have any of your own. Don't you ever get lonesome for people?"

It was as if she had read his thoughts. "Not yet."

"I love crowds and people. I love parties and dances. I love the theater. I could never be happy alone."

"That's just it. I don't feel alone. God is there with me. I may not always live such an isolated existence, but I needed that time with him so he could heal me."

"Heal you from what?"

"The hurts of life."

"Did you have a painful childhood?"

"I had a lonely childhood."

"Tell me about it."

He was surprised by her request. As they climbed the steps to the gazebo, he changed the subject. "What do you like about this spot?"

She looked out over the gardens. "I like seeing the whole park from up here. It's as if I can see forever."

"What are your hopes and dreams, Gabrielle?"

She glanced at him and smiled. "I really didn't have many plans for the future—too busy enjoying the day, I guess."

"That's not a bad thing, forgetting what lies behind and not worrying about what is ahead."

"Many girls dream of husbands and babies. I dreamed of seeing faraway places. I didn't want to marry for years to come. If it wasn't for the fact that I'd be classified as an old spinster, I might never marry."

He chuckled at her response. "Your parents seem happily married. Why are you so opposed?"

"A wife becomes a slave to her husband. Even look at my mother. She's suddenly living a life of poverty because my father has a whim to fish."

"I'd hardly think you qualify as a poverty-stricken family. Surely you realize it's a long way from middle class to cold and hungry? As for your mother, I believe she is exactly where she wants to be."

"And I believe you've been brainwashed by my father. What woman would choose to relinquish a life of ease for a life of hardship?"

"Can we go watch the deer now?" Isabel seemed to prefer the animal exhibits.

Gabrielle nodded and took one last look out over the horizon before they descended the stairs.

"If you feel so negative, why are you wanting a husband?"

"Even being married has to be better than being middle class. I'm not just searching for a husband, but the *right* husband."

"Meaning the richest one you can find?"

"Exactly."

His heart felt heavy at her response. "Money can't buy happiness."

"But it can buy everything I want."

"Which is?"

"Luxurious gowns, jewels, a mansion on Nob Hill, the right friends—"

"If you have to buy your friends, are they worth having?"

"They are to me. I know you can't possibly understand. Even though you're close to my age, you come from my father's generation. Your ideals are much like his. You don't understand the new way of thinking. You believe God is the answer to all. I believe money is."

"I feel sorry for you."

"And I for you. I adore the life of the socially elite, and I will do whatever it takes to return there." She raised her chin in a determined gesture.

"When you take a man's name, don't you want to be in love with him?"

"No. I want to be in love with his bank account. I know you're appalled by my honesty, but for me marriage is a means to an end. I plan to travel, attend parties, and be pampered by servants."

"What if you have children? Won't they mess up your plans?"

"I'll hire a nanny," Gabrielle stated matter-of-factly.

No response seemed appropriate. He shook his head. Why had he thought she was softening, changing? Because he wanted it so badly, he fooled himself into believing she had. Did she truly believe money could give her contentment?

❈

Gabrielle knew she sounded sure of herself, but in reality doubts assailed her. Her pat answers rolled forth with ease because she and Amanda had discussed those same things many times, but was that the life she really wanted? Nathaniel's claim, *"Money can't buy happiness,"* echoed again and again through her thoughts. She'd been happy, hadn't she? Weren't people like Jonathan and Amanda overflowing with happiness?

She watched a baby deer nibble at the grass. Did she really want a nanny to raise her children?

She remembered Mother's tucking her in at night, even on Nob Hill. How could a child sleep well without a mother's kiss and prayer? A nanny's good night would be cold and impersonal.

"When you take a man's name, don't you want to be in love with him?" She remembered telling her father she didn't believe in love, but somewhere deep inside she knew she did. Was love something she wanted and needed?

She glanced in Nathaniel's direction. He was down on one knee next to Isabel, talking quietly with her about the deer. Gabrielle loved his gentle, humble demeanor—*even though I don't like him,* she reminded herself. Always so tender with her and her sisters, he would be a wonderful husband and father someday . . . if that was what a girl wanted.

CHAPTER SIX

Dawn on Thanksgiving morning revealed a sky laden with storm clouds. Rain drizzled down from the heavens, but Gabrielle's heart soared on wings of anticipation. Today Nathaniel planned to join the Fairchilds and share their feast. She could already hear her mother in the kitchen beginning the preparations.

Gabrielle slipped out of bed and dressed quickly. She chose her favorite outfit, a navy gown with overskirts. The color accented her eyes. She pinched her cheeks and thought of the entire month that had elapsed since she'd last seen Nathaniel. She missed him terribly, much more than she missed Amanda or Jonathan. How strange.

Today she decided to leave her long, blonde ringlets free. She swept the front up but left the rest cascading down her back. Nathaniel had never seen her hair down. Would he like it? She hoped so.

As she worked with her hair, she thought about their last day together at Woodland Gardens. She'd behaved horribly, as usual. Was that why he'd stayed away from the cottage since then? She'd regretted not being more honest with him. Why had she let him believe that nothing mattered to her but money?

She'd spent this past month paying attention to the sermons in church and reading the Bible for herself. She sensed changes taking place within her, mostly changes in her attitude. She had also spent a great deal of time thinking about her neighbor. Her admiration of him grew by leaps and bounds as she'd compared him to her other friends.

She was filled with a longing to see Nathaniel, the man she tried to despise. She missed their walks together by the sea, his laughter, and the light that danced in his brown eyes. His absence had intensified her yearning to spend time with him, and today she'd see him at last.

Her heart soared at the thought. She'd been so blue lately; it felt wonderful to be excited again. Life often played funny tricks. Who would have guessed that seeing Nathaniel would have such an effect on her? Who would have guessed how important his friendship would become? She chuckled at the irony and headed for the kitchen to help her mother.

"Good morning, darling. You look exceptional today. You're even smiling! Some days I wondered if I'd ever see that again."

"Thank you, Mother. I feel exceptional today. I feel as if a long storm has moved on, and the sun has returned to shine down upon me."

Her mother gave her a knowing look. "Does this have anything to do with a certain young man who is coming for dinner?"

Gabrielle felt heat in her cheeks. "Of course not! At least not in the way you're implying. But I have missed Mr. Morgan. He's such a dear friend."

❄

Nathaniel's breath caught somewhere in his chest. Both at the sight of Gabrielle and the words she'd just spoken. She'd never looked more lovely to him than at that moment. *She missed me! Gabrielle Fairchild missed me!* He'd missed her too, more than he cared to think about.

"Good morning, Miss Fairchild." When her eyes met his, fireworks exploded in his heart.

"Mr. Morgan! How good to see you." They stared across the kitchen at one another for countless moments.

He cleared his throat. "Edward let me in. I thought I'd come early and help. Is that all right with you, Mrs. Fairchild?"

"I never turn down an extra pair of hands. Why don't you and Gabby make the dressing for the turkey?"

He and Gabrielle gathered knives, celery, and onions, and took seats at the table. "I've missed you," he said in a low tone, once they'd begun their dicing.

She looked up at him, a soft smile touching her full lips. "And I, you."

He hadn't even realized how much until this moment. He'd spent many an afternoon debating with himself about the right thing to do. A part of him had fallen in love with her. Avoiding her seemed smartest and safest.

"How have you been?" he asked.

"I've had an awful bout with the blues, but I'm finally feeling better."

"Any of those Nob Hill dandies figured out how much they miss you?" He really hoped not.

"Not yet." Her eyes reminded him of the sky on a warm summer afternoon. "I'm doubting they ever will." She didn't seem all that upset by the prospect.

"Their loss."

Gabrielle finished her stalk of celery and began to tear corn bread into tiny pieces. "The strangest part is, it no longer seems so important. Do you think I'm crazy?"

"No." He couldn't stop the grin that spread across his face. God was answering prayer! Dare he hope?

"Sometimes I feel crazy. First I'm angry; then I'm sad. I cry and cry, unable to stop. I'm even starting to like the sea."

From his porch he'd often seen her walking along the beach. "There's nothing wrong with liking the sea."

"But the things I hated, I'm starting to like, and the things I loved no longer seem so important. I feel confused by all the changes taking place inside me." She looked soft and vulnerable. "I've even been reading the Bible. I'm actually enjoying it."

"I'm glad." He'd desperately wanted Gabrielle to change her thinking. He'd even tried to help her see the truth. Now he understood; only Christ can change hearts and perspectives. More than anything, Nathaniel wanted her to realize that Christ could fill her heart and that Nathaniel could give her so much more than any dandy ever could. *Lord, my prayer is that she'll find you, and then she'll find me.*

He had convinced himself that loving Gabrielle was hopeless. Now hope soared within him like a kite on a windy beach. Maybe he could truly win this beautiful woman's heart, and maybe some beautiful women did have character. A dream for the future settled inside him as he watched her mix the dressing in a large bowl.

The dinner tasted wonderful. Sitting at the Fairchild table next to Gabrielle, dirt probably would have tasted wonderful! He'd missed this dear family. He belonged to them and they to him. Though it sounded strange, his heart knew the truth of those feelings.

❄

Since Gabrielle had helped to prepare the meal, her sisters were responsible for cleaning up afterward. "Would you walk with me to the beach?" she asked Nathaniel when they finished eating. He nodded his agreement. His gaze warmed her each time it rested upon her.

When she spent time in his company, her father didn't feel

they needed a chaperone. She knew her father hoped that love would blossom between them. Of course, Nathaniel was only a dear friend, but her father could dream.

"I truly have missed you," she said again as they carefully trudged down the muddy path toward the shore. "What has kept you so busy that you've had no time for us?"

"I'm a loner." He held tightly to her arm as they slipped and slid down the path. "Once I'd finished working for your father, I returned to my normal existence."

"Don't you miss being around people?"

"I never have before, but I did miss you and your family."

The news warmed her. "Maybe you're changing, too."

"Maybe."

"It's not bad to need people, is it?"

"No."

"You don't have to be a recluse anymore. We can be your family."

"Thanks. I'll keep that in mind."

"That is, if you want a family."

"Suddenly, it sounds very nice."

They'd reached the bottom of the hill, and he loosened his hold. Her arm felt cold where his hand had been. "Does God care if I'm happy?" she wondered aloud.

"I guess I'd be inclined to say no."

"But I thought he loved me." Gabrielle shivered, and Nathaniel drew her close, wrapping an arm around her shoulders.

"He does, more than you can imagine. He wants you to have joy in all circumstances, but that comes from him. He wants you to be content—anywhere, anytime. He wants you to be holy, but I think happiness is man's idea."

"I don't understand."

"What makes you happy?"

"I'm not sure anymore. What makes you happy?"

"The sun, the sea—because they are made by God. But I

could find happiness without those things because my happiness comes from God, not things."

"So he does want me to be happy with the things he gives me?"

"Exactly! Not from the things we find in the world. He wants you to be just as happy living in a cottage as in a castle. I guess it might be considered contentment rather than happiness."

"I used to think God was at church on Sunday morning, and we went there to visit him. When we left, he stayed behind. But you and my father keep talking about a personal relationship. What does that mean?"

"A hard question." He was glad she was thinking about such things. "In the Gospel of John, Jesus talks about being a vine and we're the branches. A branch remains attached to the vine. We do that by spending time in the Bible and in prayer each day. That's the way we get to know him and stay attached to him. How did I become your friend?"

She felt her cheeks grow warm. They'd stopped walking and stood overlooking the bay. He still held her close. She liked being close to him. "I got to know you?" She wasn't certain of the answer he was looking for.

"Exactly. Correct me if I'm wrong, but you had no intention of befriending that 'dreadful fisherman.' Once you got to know me, I guess I wasn't quite as bad as you originally thought. You discovered you even liked me a little."

"Actually, a lot," she confessed.

He grinned down at her, and a warmth flooded her heart. "Now that you know me, I told you that I was a lonely little rich boy. Strangers aren't aware of that. I only reveal my intimate self to friends. It's the same with God. As you spend time with him, you get to know and understand him. The better you know him, the more you love him."

Gabrielle wanted to understand, but it was all so confusing. She'd asked Jesus into her heart as a little girl because she wanted to go to heaven. Now it seemed like so much more than that simple decision. Was she even a Christian?

✻

Rain started drizzling from the sky. Nathaniel grabbed Gabrielle's hand, and they ran toward the path. They'd wandered at least a mile or more down the beach, so he knew they'd be drenched before arriving home. He let her set the pace, realizing she wasn't used to such exertion.

Long before they reached the path, she stopped, gasping for air. She bent over, resting her hands on her knees. Her beautiful ringlets lay soaked and flat against her back. "I'm sorry. Can we stop for a moment?"

He knew she was spent. He let her rest against him, trying to shield her from the pouring rain. She laid her head against his shoulder, and he found himself praying for her.

He knew she'd spent the last month pondering many things. He saw differences in her that encouraged him. She'd softened toward both him and God. Again his hopes soared as he admitted to himself how much he loved her. He could no longer imagine a life of solitude. He needed her to complete him. He needed her family, too.

Once she had caught her breath, they moved on, only this time more slowly. By the time they reached the path, both were soaked to the bone.

"Can you make the climb?"

She nodded. The path was even slicker than before, so she ended up using her hands to keep her balance. She slipped to her knees a couple of times but fought her way to the cottage. Nathaniel stayed right behind her, helping her when she stumbled.

Finally they reached the porch. She fell against him, laughing. A mud streak covered one of her cheeks.

"You're a sight. I hope your dress isn't ruined."

"I hope not, too. It's my favorite."

That information stirred something in his heart. So she'd worn her favorite dress, knowing he'd be there. His heart insisted that must mean something.

Her father came out with a quilt for each of them. "Come in and sit by the fire," he instructed.

"In just a moment. I'd like a word with Mr. Morgan first, if that's all right?"

Nathaniel's heart turned over at her declaration. Edward nodded and returned inside. Gabrielle walked to the edge of the porch, watching the rain fall. Finally, she turned to face him. "I owe you an apology. I behaved badly the last time we were together. I'm sorry I felt embarrassed by you. I know I hurt you. Can you forgive me?"

Her words touched him deeply. Her eyes pleaded with him to understand. He took her hands in his; they were damp and cold. "Forgiven and forgotten."

"Thank you. You've become very dear to me. I missed you terribly and hated how rudely I behaved. I hated knowing I was probably the reason you stayed away."

He longed to pull her into his arms and whisper the words of his heart, but he didn't. This time he would go at God's pace. Gabrielle must get things right with God before she and Nathaniel had a chance.

"Please, promise you won't stay away that long again."

"I promise."

She turned back toward the bay. They silently watched the rain. Then her hand reached for his. "Mr. Morgan?"

"Yes?" His heart felt like it might explode with love for her. He suddenly was certain she'd be his one day.

"Will you be my escort for this Christmas season?"

His heart plummeted toward the ground. "What do you mean?" Was she asking him to take her places so she could leave him standing alone at the punch bowl?

"I'd hoped you'd take me to the theater and a party or two."

What a fool I am! She just played me like an old fiddle.

She kept her eyes focused on the rain, not even looking at him, probably afraid he'd see she only used him. "Please, Mr. Morgan?" Now she cocked her head to one side the way he'd seen her do with her father.

Against his better judgment, he agreed. Why, he wasn't certain, except that it offered the chance to spend time with her again.

She lit up, giving him a quick kiss on his cheek. "Thank you! Now let's go in and warm up." She waited at the door for him to join her.

"I think I'll head on home and get out of these wet things." Did he imagine the disappointed look that crossed her face?

She nodded. "I'm glad you came today."

I just bet you are. He left without another word. Disappointment bubbled up within him. Nothing about Gabrielle had changed. She played the role so her wish would be his command. Her plan worked. He'd fallen prey to her charm like some lovesick puppy. The only thing she'd missed about him was having a fool around to get her out of the house.

He dreaded the next month, but he'd given his word. Too late to back out now. He'd pray she'd see how empty that world really was. He'd pray. God could still change her, but truthfully, he had no hope of that happening.

CHAPTER SEVEN

As Gabrielle dressed for the theater, she wondered why Nathaniel had seemed cool this week and avoided being alone with her. She didn't understand what had happened. They'd shared a wonderful Thanksgiving. Then suddenly he acted icy. Although he'd agreed to be her escort to the play tonight, she sensed he faced it with about as much excitement as a man facing a firing squad.

It had been too long since she'd visited the opera house. Tonight a traveling company would present *A Christmas Carol* by Charles Dickens. She didn't know which appealed to her more, seeing the show or spending more time with Nathaniel. Their month apart had changed her opinion of him. She'd missed him. He was her dear friend—actually, her only friend.

She so looked forward to the coming weeks. Not only was December her favorite month, she adored Christmas. She loved the decorations, the parties, the festive atmosphere, even the smells associated with the holiday. She pulled out a green velvet dress and rubbed a sleeve against her cheek. She'd be the only girl there without a new dress. Oh well, there were worse things in life, she supposed. At least she was going.

A part of her felt concerned about what Nathaniel might wear. She'd made up her mind that no matter how bad he might look, she would be proud to be at his side. She'd treated him poorly at the park and refused to do that again. "After all, it's what's inside that counts," she reminded her reflection in the mirror. She hoped she really believed that.

When Nathaniel arrived to pick her up, his appearance surprised and pleased her. He looked quite fashionable in a long sack coat, ascot tie, vest, and trousers. A handkerchief even peeked out of his front pocket. His eyes showed his approval of her gown.

He led her out to a beautiful, shiny black shay. "Wherever did you get this?"

"It belongs to a man who owed me a favor."

"Thank you for agreeing to take me tonight. I don't think I could bear one more night in that tiny cottage."

Nathaniel nodded stiffly at her remark but said nothing. He'd been acting so different this past week.

"Mr. Morgan, is something troubling you? You seem distant."

"I'm just wondering about your purpose in this outing." His voice sounded harsh and accusing.

"I love the theater, especially at Christmastime."

"Whose eye are you hoping to catch?"

She felt hurt by his implication. "Just yours, I assure you."

"Until someone richer walks by?"

"Truly, I only wanted to see the play. I've heard about it but never seen it."

"And I guess I'm better than no escort at all. I'm certain your invitation stemmed from a need to escape the confines of the cottage, not a desire to spend time with me."

She felt perplexed by his behavior. "That is not true! I told you I missed you. I discovered I enjoy spending time with you."

"That was mighty sudden." He sighed. "You don't have to play games. I know you're using me to find a way back to your wealthy friends."

"You don't know anything, Nathaniel Morgan!" She fumed inside. How dare he imply she lied. Who did he think he was anyway, a mind reader? Now she just wanted this dreadful night to be over. "Take me home."

"What?"

"You heard me. Take me home." Now it was her turn to sound icy.

He stopped the shay and pulled over to the side of the street. "We're almost there."

"I don't care. I no longer want to go, if that's what you think." Her voice cracked. "I've treated you unkindly in the past, but you said you forgave me. I thought we'd become friends. Perhaps I was wrong."

❉

Why do I quit thinking clearly around this woman? Nathaniel asked himself, not for the first time. She seemed so sincere, he felt hard-pressed not to believe her. "I'm sorry. You're right. We did agree to put the past behind us, so let's enjoy our evening."

Gabrielle looked at him for a moment, then agreed. "All right. Thank you."

Upon arriving at the theater, Nathaniel helped Gabrielle down from the shay. His hands wrapped around her tiny waist. She accepted the arm he offered, once her feet touched the ground. They walked together through the entrance.

Many heads turned their way. Certain he was escorting the most beautiful woman in the city, he walked proud and tall. He noticed that Gabrielle also held her head high. She smiled and nodded at a few people, but kept her arm entwined through his. He'd dreaded a replay of the scene in the park, where she had barely acknowledged his existence.

They made their way to their seats, high at the back of the fourth level. Gabrielle most likely used to sit up close, but she didn't comment or complain. Nathaniel noted with amazement how many seats this building held.

Just as they sat down, a couple of dandies approached them. "Miss Fairchild, is that you?"

Surprise filled him when she slipped her hand into his. "Yes, it is. How are you? Tom Owens, Jim Jacobson, this is my dear friend, Nathaniel Morgan."

Dear friend? Nathaniel rose and shook each man's hand, noticing the way these two men eyed Gabrielle, much the way a thirsty man eyed a cup of water. It made him want to punch them.

"I've been meaning to call on you, but I wasn't sure how to find you," Jacobson, the taller of the two, informed her.

She smiled up at him but didn't offer directions to the cottage. "I understand. It's quite all right. I hope you'll enjoy the performance tonight." With a bright smile, she pointedly turned away from them and toward Nathaniel.

What game was she playing? Both men appeared surprised by her abrupt dismissal. They bid them good evening and left.

She removed her hand from his and placed it into her lap. "Forgive my forward behavior. I wanted no doubt about whom I'm with tonight—even in your mind."

At that moment a hush fell over the crowd as the lights dimmed and the curtain opened for the first scene. Nathaniel struggled to pay attention. He kept thinking of how different Gabrielle's behavior was. He knew she must be up to something but couldn't figure out what.

❄

Gabrielle watched with intensity as the scenes unfolded before her. She loved the theater and losing herself in someone else's story. When the play ended, she'd seen parallels with her own life that frightened her.

"You're awfully quiet," Nathaniel commented as they made their way down the long flights of stairs to the bottom.

She only nodded her agreement. Her hand again lay in the crook of his arm. As she looked around at the many men in the crowd and then looked back at the man beside her, she saw for the first time beyond Nathaniel's normally dowdy attire to the man underneath. He wasn't overly tall, but he had the strength of a bull. She could feel the muscle under his coat sleeve.

She remembered being held in those arms when he tried to protect her from the rain. The memory brought a blush to her cheeks and strange feelings shooting through her heart. He looked down at her and smiled. She loved his warm, encouraging smile. She smiled back, her heart feeling tender toward him.

"You're the most beautiful woman here tonight, Gabrielle." His low, soothing voice reminded her of the sea on a calm day.

"And you are the most handsome gentleman." As she said the words, she realized they were true. She saw the doubt in his eyes. "Really," she whispered her assurance. His nose stood chiseled and proud under two small and incredibly expressive eyes, but his smile was what she loved the most. When he smiled, it wasn't something he did with just his mouth. His whole face lit up, and his eyes danced with either mischief or tenderness.

She looked at his mouth and wondered how it would feel against hers. She longed to find out. What was she thinking? She'd never had silly schoolgirl thoughts like these before, even when she was a silly schoolgirl! *You're falling for him*, a little voice inside her head accused.

"No, I am not!" she insisted.

"What?" he asked with a confused frown.

Heat filled her cheeks. "I'm afraid I was thinking aloud." His grin caused her stomach to somersault. *You are, too!*

"Gabrielle!" She turned her head and caught sight of a group of her Nob Hill acquaintances. She hadn't wanted to see any of them. The hurt from their rejection still hadn't healed. She needed time before facing any of them.

She tightened her hold on Nathaniel's arm, hoping to draw strength from him. He smiled down at her. Again her heart did a little dance all its own. *I am falling for him.* New feelings bubbled within her. She, Gabrielle Fairchild was falling for a fisherman. Oh, the irony of life!

❄

Nathaniel expected her to drop his arm like a hot potato, but instead she clutched it tighter. "Hello, everyone." The sweet sound in her voice seemed forced.

Amanda stepped forward and hugged Gabrielle. "I'm so glad you didn't miss the opening night. That would have been tragic."

"Mr. Morgan was kind enough to bring me, even though it's not his favorite form of entertainment." She looked up at him with light blue eyes that expressed her thanks. She looked softer, and again he felt confused by all the changes he saw in her. Were they real or all part of some elaborate scheme to catch a Nob Hill husband?

"Oh, yes." Amanda sent an insincere smile his direction. "I remember Mr. Morgan—your *father's* friend."

"Actually, he's also a dear friend of mine." Her look dared Amanda to dispute the facts. She took Nathaniel's hand in hers, pulling him toward her old friends. She raised her chin a fraction. "Everyone, I'd like you to meet *my* dear friend, Nathaniel Morgan."

She introduced them one by one, but he didn't catch a single name. All he heard, again and again, was Gabrielle declaring him a dear friend. All he could think of was the possessive way her hand held his. He tottered somewhere between hope and dread. Hope that this was not an act, and dread that she was only using him to evoke jealousy in one of these young men's hearts.

Each man shook his hand as they were introduced. Each young lady smiled at him and nodded. He almost chuckled aloud at the questions he saw etched on their faces. Whatever Gabrielle's ploy, it seemed to be working because she suddenly had their attention.

Jonathan approached Nathaniel and spoke in low tones close to his ear. "So you're courting the elusive Miss Fairchild? How ever did you manage to get her undivided attention?"

Nathaniel felt certain this man was hunting for information. He hated to admit the truth. "We're not courting—"

"But you are the only one I spend my time with." Again Gabrielle was at his side. She seized his arm and smiled up at him. "The only one I *want* to spend my time with," she added as if she'd read his thoughts about being the only one available. He swallowed hard. *Don't toy with my heart, Gabrielle. You have no idea how fragile and uncertain it is.*

"Well then, why don't the two of you come to our annual Christmas party next week?" Gabrielle's face lit up at Jonathan's invitation. So this was what she'd been after.

"I do love a good party, but Mr. Morgan prefers quiet walks on the beach. I think we'll pass." She rested her head against his arm. His head spun, seeing this new side of her.

"Surely you can sacrifice one quiet evening alone with her and share her with old friends." Jonathan's comment held some sort of challenge, as if he were daring Nathaniel to put Gabrielle's desires ahead of his own.

If he only knew . . . "If Miss Fairchild would like to attend, I shall escort her. After all, Miss Fairchild usually gets what she wants." He sent his own warning look, *including you, if that's what she's after.*

"Good. I'll see you both there, then. Don't forget to save a waltz for me, Gabrielle. After all, you always said I was your favorite dance partner."

"Not anymore," she said before looking up at Nathaniel with a shy smile.

Jonathan lifted a disapproving brow before striding off without another word. If provoking Jonathan to jealousy was her goal, Nathaniel felt certain she'd succeeded. Gabrielle might yet receive her Nob Hill proposal before the year ended, just as she'd assured her father she would. A heaviness and hopelessness settled in Nathaniel's heart.

CHAPTER EIGHT

Will you take me home now?" Gabrielle's party face disappeared as she slumped against Nathaniel like someone battle weary.

He wrapped his arm around her shoulders and led her out into the night. Gabrielle remained quiet. He spent the ride home pondering the evening. She certainly mystified him.

"Good night, Nathaniel," she said softly when they reached her porch. "Thank you so much for a lovely evening." She stood on tiptoe, placing a kiss on his left cheek. He longed to turn his head ever so slightly and meet her lips with his own, but he didn't. Instead, he stood very still, breathing in the sweet smell that was Gabrielle. It took him a moment to notice that she had used his first name.

"Would you join us for church tomorrow? Then afterward you could help us decorate the tree. Father could use an ally." Her soft eyes tugged at his heart. Could he build these memories with her, only to watch her marry another?

Against reason, he let his heart decide. "Yes. I'll be here in the morning." *At least I'll have someone to share my pew,* he justified. "See you then . . ." He left her standing in the moonlight—a picture he felt certain would be etched in his mind forever.

❄

Gabrielle watched Nathaniel go, knowing he carried a piece of her heart with him. The more she grew to care for him, the less he seemed to feel toward her.

Now that she'd realized Jonathan didn't possess the qualities she longed for in a husband, he appeared to be interested in her. She believed she'd seen jealousy in his eyes tonight. He could be hers for the taking; she felt certain of that. She just didn't want him anymore.

As her friends spurned her and left her hopeless and alone, she'd finally turned to God. Gently, tenderly, he had opened her eyes to see the emptiness of the things she'd held near and dear. Slowly, the truth dawned. In Nathaniel she had seen a deep, abiding contentment that testified to the reality of the words she'd read in Scripture. His peace came from inside and had nothing to do with status, money, or clothes.

She'd spent too much time grieving over the loss of all the privileges and possessions that came with wealth and the people she'd called friends. At the Gardens with Nathaniel, her eyes had opened to the depth of his feelings—not just for her, but for her entire family. Jonathan, on the other hand, had known Izzy for most of the youngster's life and had never spoken more than three words to her. He was shallow and self-serving. She saw that clearly now.

Nathaniel had worked his way into her heart, not with flattery but with humility. His gentle ways melted her icy attitudes toward him, and now she, Gabrielle Fairchild, had discovered deep feelings for him. She closed her eyes and leaned against the porch column. Would he ever have similar feelings for her?

As she climbed into her bed that night, Gabrielle thanked the Lord that Nathaniel had agreed to join them in church tomorrow. She so wanted him to be present when she rededicated her heart and life to Christ. After all, even if he was never to be anything more than a friend, he had had a profound impact on her ability to see and understand Christianity lived out on a daily basis.

❄

Nathaniel was taken aback at the sight of Gabrielle in a red Christmas dress. Of all the colors he'd seen her wear, red was his favorite. It brought out a glow in her face. She was beautiful.

They spoke little. Gabrielle seemed preoccupied, almost nervous. She fidgeted during the ride to church and throughout the sermon. He did enjoy hearing her soprano voice sing out during the songs, though. At the end of the service, when the Reverend Smith invited those needing prayer or making decisions to come forward, Gabrielle glanced Nathaniel's way before heading off down the aisle.

A deep sense of gratitude filled him. He closed his eyes, thanking the Lord for the work he'd done in Gabrielle's life. Whether or not she ever belonged to Nathaniel paled in comparison to this decision. At least now she belonged to the Lord.

Reverend Smith stood next to her at the front of the church. "This is our sister in Christ, Gabrielle Fairchild. She's coming today to publicly rededicate herself to our Lord. She invited him into her heart as a small child, but now she is inviting him to be the Lord of her life. She wants to live the rest of her days seeking his will instead of her own way. Will the congregation please come by and welcome her back into God's loving arms. We know from Scripture that God saw her coming from a long way off, and he has run to meet her. May we do the same."

Reverend Smith closed in prayer. Then many members of the congregation made their way to the altar to encourage Gabrielle. Nathaniel followed behind her family. A lump sat planted firmly in his throat. He wondered if he'd be able to tell her all the things his heart longed to say.

He watched Edward take Gabrielle into his arms. Tears streamed down both their faces as her father hugged her tightly. He whispered something meant for her alone. Then he kissed his daughter's cheek and moved aside so her mother could hug her. Nathaniel stood back, not wanting to intrude on this tender family moment.

As her mother and sisters gathered round Gabrielle, Edward shook Nathaniel's hand. "Thank you for the impact you've had on her decision." Then Edward hugged him with tears still glistening in his eyes.

"I didn't do anything except pray. This is the work of the Lord." Nathaniel noticed Gabrielle's mother and sisters had stepped away, and it was his turn. Her sky blue eyes met his, and he swallowed hard.

"Go on, my boy." Edward gave him a slight push toward Gabrielle. "Tell her your heart."

Unable to mutter a single word, he took her into his embrace. He held her tight for countless seconds. When he loosened his hold, he touched her satin cheek with his fingertips. Tears shimmered in her eyes.

"Thank you, Nathaniel, for your prayers on my behalf," she said. "Thank you also for being an example to follow. When I look at you, I see Jesus in your life, your words, your actions."

He could only nod. She kissed his cheek before she joined her family waiting at the back of the church. *Thank you, Lord, for drawing her to yourself. Thank you for allowing me to have a small part in that. Thank you if she saw you in me. I find that hard to believe, since I so often fail you.*

❊

"I'm glad you came today," Gabrielle whispered to Nathaniel once they were back at the cottage. The two of them lingered on the porch after the others went inside.

"I'm glad you invited me." She noted that his eyes glowed with tenderness under thick, heavy brows.

She wanted to stand there forever, looking into his compassionate face. "I suppose I should go help Mother with dinner." Still their gazes remained fastened together like two magnets with no will of their own.

"Yes, and while you ladies prepare the meal, your father and I have a date with a Christmas tree." Finally he broke the spell by walking to the door and holding it open for her.

The smell of pine filled the small cottage. How fitting that she recommit her life to Christ in December, the month set aside to celebrate his birth. She went through the motions of setting the table, but her mind contemplated the baby lying in the manger who was God. How incredible. *For God so loved me that he sent his only Son.*

The meal flew by in a time of chatter and laughter. After dinner they all went into the front room to join in decorating the Christmas tree. Nathaniel and Edward were in charge of the top of the tree since they were the only ones tall enough to reach it. A couple of hours later, an evergreen stood dressed in the splendor of Christmas, dominating their small sitting room.

"Could we sing carols, Father, please?" Magdalene asked.

"Yes, like we used to," Isabel pleaded.

"Why not?" Edward asked. "Nathaniel, would you care to join us around the piano?"

Nathaniel glanced at Gabrielle. She wondered if he could see how much she wanted him to. She smiled slightly, waiting for his answer.

"Sure. Sounds like fun."

And it was fun. They gathered around the piano while Mother played. Gabrielle enjoyed the rich timbre of Nathaniel's baritone. They sang every Christmas song they could think of, ending with "Silent Night."

"Father, tonight after supper, could we go caroling?"

Isabel had learned to cock her head to the side the same way Gabrielle did. Gabrielle used to think it was cute the way her sisters imitated her. Now she hoped to be a better example.

Magdalene joined the pleading, and soon Father gave in. "If Nathaniel will agree to come along, so I don't have to sing the low notes alone."

"I've never gone caroling before. I think I'd like that."

"It's so much fun," Isabel assured him. "You'll love it."

After a light supper, Edward brought the carriage around. They all huddled inside under blankets. Isabel managed to worm her way between Gabrielle and Nathaniel. He smiled at Gabrielle over Izzy's head, and she thought his eyes said he'd rather be next to her. She knew she'd rather be next to him.

They sang until their throats ached. Gabrielle listened to the words with a new ear, feeling amazed by God's love. Nathaniel carried Isabel when her legs gave out. Her father offered to take her, but Isabel insisted she preferred Nathaniel. Gabrielle wasn't the only Fairchild who'd fallen in love with Nathaniel. Both of her sisters adored him.

By the time they returned home, Isabel was sleeping in Nathaniel's arms. Gabrielle found herself a tiny bit jealous. She'd like to find a way into those safe, strong arms. She waited in the parlor while her mother showed him where to lay Izzy.

"It's been a nice day," Nathaniel said when he joined her on the sofa. "You have a nice family."

"I know."

"Thank you for allowing me to share them."

"My father loves you. He'll always want you around."

❄

What about you, Gabrielle? he wanted to ask. *Do you love me? Will you always want me around, or are you telling me that once you've married another man, I'm still welcome to share your fam-*

ily? "Shall we take a walk?" he asked instead.

"I'd love to." After they had bundled up again in their coats and scarves, she slipped her arm through his, and they headed down the path toward the beach. "It's very dark tonight. Do you think we can maneuver the path without any moonlight?"

"I could find my way down this hill blindfolded," he assured her.

They walked in silence, listening to the waves hitting the beach. He thought back over the day's events. He now knew where Gabrielle stood with God. His big question was where she stood with him. He'd find out soon enough when they went to Jonathan's party on Friday evening.

"Do you still want to attend the party next weekend?" He hoped she would say no.

"Well, you said we would. They're expecting us. Have you changed your mind?"

"I thought perhaps you had. After today and all . . ."

She stopped. He wished he could see her expression. "Would it be wrong to go? I don't want to displease God."

"No, it's not wrong to attend a Christmas party together, unless you dishonor him with bad behavior while you're there." They started walking again, back toward home.

"I wouldn't do that. If you're uncomfortable attending, I'll send word to no longer expect us."

He wanted to cancel, but a part of him needed to go. He needed to figure out why Gabrielle longed to attend. He needed to know her intentions toward Jonathan. Was she hoping to push Jonathan into a proposal, or had she let go of those dreams at the altar where she'd surrendered to God? He could ask her, but sometimes a picture was worth more than words. He needed to *see* the answers to his questions.

She tugged on his sleeve. "Mr. Morgan? Did you hear me?"

"I'm sorry. I got lost in thought. I know it's important to

you, so we'll go. Do you mind if I wear the same clothes I wore to the theater? It's my lone dress outfit."

"No." He heard the smile in her voice. "I thought you looked quite handsome in it. Do you mind if I wear the same dress? We didn't get any new Christmas clothes this year."

Who could have guessed that the snooty little thing he met last summer would be so calm and agreeable about wearing last year's fashions? "I truly wouldn't mind if you wore a flour sack. I'm certain you'd still be the prettiest girl at the party."

She giggled. "Too bad all men aren't as easy to please as you are. I'm sure every girl in the world would be happy if they were."

Did he have his answer? Was she still trying to please the dandies of this world? If only he could figure her out. She kept him guessing, and just when he thought he'd discovered the answer, she changed like the wind.

More important, though, he needed to seek God's will in this. He'd never asked God if marrying Gabrielle was his will. He'd been afraid to look that far ahead in case she never committed to the Lord. Now he had some serious praying to do.

CHAPTER NINE

The evening of the Christmas party arrived. Gabrielle floated into the sitting room, not sure if her feet even touched the floor.

"Miss Fairchild," Nathaniel's voice sounded awestruck. He rose from the sofa when she entered. Admiration shown in his eyes. She noticed his Adam's apple bobbed when he swallowed.

"Gabby," her father's voice took her attention from Nathaniel. "I've never seen you look lovelier."

"Thank you, Father." She and Nathaniel moved toward the front door.

"Have a wonderful evening," her father said. Then he directed his next words to Nathaniel. "Jonathan's family has a tradition of throwing the most festive party in the entire city. It will be an experience. Have fun, you two." He placed a kiss on her cheek, and the door closed behind them.

"I see you have the shay again," Gabrielle commented as he helped her board.

"Yes. Your dress is beautiful. I believe red is your color. What happened to wearing the green one you wore to the theater?"

"Magdalene offered to lend me hers from last season. I'm glad you like it." She laid her hand on the velvet skirt, enjoying the softness against her skin.

"I like your hair down, too. I meant to tell you that on Thanksgiving. You should wear it that way more often." She felt warmed by his compliment.

"Thank you. I'll remember that."

They rode in silence to the party. Gabrielle had mixed feelings about tonight. She'd always loved dancing, and it was a good excuse to find her way into a certain fisherman's arms. But she wasn't the same person her friends remembered. She hoped her behavior would please God and Nathaniel. Not for anything did she ever want to hurt Nathaniel again.

Jonathan's house stood in splendor near the crest of Nob Hill. Together they climbed the steps to the porch. Nathaniel tugged the bellpull, and a maid answered the door. She took their coats in her chubby hands and directed them to the festivities. Gabrielle took Nathaniel's arm, proud to be at his side. He'd grown from plain and outdated in her eyes to a handsome specimen of a rugged man, and on the inside of this fisherman she'd discovered a boatload of character.

"Gabrielle, so glad you could make it!" Jonathan greeted her with a wide smile. "Morgan, welcome." His words to Nathaniel lacked the enthusiasm she'd heard in his voice when he addressed her. "Come, darling, let's dance." He took her hand from Nathaniel's arm and attempted to lead her off.

"Jonathan, I'm dancing with Mr. Morgan tonight. Perhaps later I'll squeeze you in." She removed her hand from his, returning it to Nathaniel's arm. How dare Jonathan treat Nathaniel with such rudeness? She smiled up at Nathaniel's surprised expression. "Shall we?"

"We shall." Then he directed his attention to Jonathan. "I'm certain we'll talk again, Jonathan, old chap, if Gabrielle allows me to take a break. You know how she loves to dance."

❄

Nathaniel wondered if Gabrielle knew what a gift she'd just given him. He feared she'd leave him standing alone in the doorway when Jonathan tried to whisk her away, but she hadn't. He smiled as he pulled her into his arms for their first waltz together. "I'm not much of a dancer. I hope I don't disappoint you."

"I'm certain you won't." Her words sounded like a deeply felt promise.

As they glided across the floor, he loved how she fit in his arms. He loved the silkiness of her hair against the back of his hand. He loved the way she smelled, sweet and soft like the roses she adored. Most of all he loved the way she'd made him feel special when Jonathan wanted him to feel insignificant.

"Thank you for not dumping me at the doorway."

She smiled up at him, her eyes bright. "I didn't want anyone else to steal my dance partner."

They stayed on the floor for several songs. He concentrated on his dancing, so they didn't talk much, though talking seemed unnecessary anyway. Just as the musicians finished another tune, Jonathan and Amanda approached them.

"Let's switch partners for the next number," Amanda suggested. "I've never danced with a bearded man." Though she acted flirtatious, Nathaniel wondered if her words were a subtle insult. He realized fashion dictated that only mustaches were acceptable right now. Beards were for old men and him.

"I'm not ready to share him just yet," Gabrielle informed Amanda in her sweetest voice. "And I love his beard." Taking Nathaniel's arm, she said, "I'm parched. Shall we go find something to drink?" She led him away from the stunned twosome.

After a stop at the punch bowl, they went out onto a patio. He sensed anger boiling within her. He waited for her to say something, but she didn't. Finally he commented, "The view from Nob Hill is beautiful at night. No wonder you love it up here." He looked out over the lights.

"Why can't they just leave us alone? How dare Amanda insult your beard. I happen to like your beard!" He smiled when she stomped her foot to emphasize her words.

"Why don't you go ahead and dance with Jonathan? I think Amanda's willing to keep me company, so I'll be fine."

"If you want to dance with Amanda, just say so!"

"I don't want to dance with Amanda. I'm just trying to keep peace. Jonathan is our host. You can't very well turn him down all night." Though a part of him wished she could.

"Fine. I'll dance with him the next time he asks. I'm cold. Let's go back inside." He shook his head and followed her in. Why was she suddenly so angry?

"Ah, there you two are." Jonathan and Amanda were back at their sides. "Come on, Gabrielle—" Jonathan took her hand in his—"Amanda will take good care of your friend while we're gone."

Nathaniel saw Gabrielle look back at him as Jonathan pulled her toward the dance floor. Nathaniel winked at her, wondering if she was angry to be stuck with him. Maybe she was unable to enjoy her old friends with him tagging along but felt responsible for him.

"Looks like it's just you and me." Amanda laid her hand on his arm. Her dark hair glistened under the gas lamps. "Shall we dance or just get to know each other better?" She wet her top lip with the tip of her tongue, and he thought of the adulteress woman in Proverbs. He had no desire to become better acquainted with her.

"I'll just wait here for Miss Fairchild." He hoped he

sounded polite but firm.

"I'm sure she'll spend the rest of the evening in Jonathan's arms. It's always been her favorite place to be." Amanda's words inflicted pain and fear into his heart. What if she was right?

He watched Jonathan twirl Gabrielle around the dance floor. She laughed up at him when he drew her close again. Nathaniel's heart ached with the reality of Amanda's words. Gabrielle had probably arranged for Amanda to divert his attention. He turned to Amanda. "Let's dance."

❄

The thought of being in Jonathan's arms again scared Gabrielle. What if all the old feelings returned? What if she forgot Nathaniel while in Jonathan's arms? What if dancing with Jonathan made her forget the shallowness she'd seen in him these last months? Could he twirl her back into that old Gabrielle that she no longer wanted to be?

She'd never admitted it to anyone, but the reason she'd allowed so many beaus to call on her was because her feelings for Jonathan frightened her. He was the one she'd planned to marry one day, but he hadn't been ready to settle down. She refused to let him see her pining away, so she had flirted outrageously with all his friends. She'd loved knowing it bothered him.

As Jonathan twirled her, she considered the differences between him and Nathaniel. Jonathan was tall and thin. Nathaniel was stocky and strong. Jonathan's blond curly hair and blue eyes were opposites of Nathaniel's molasses-colored eyes and straight dark hair. Their personalities contrasted too. Nathaniel was everything wonderful, and Jonathan was selfish, self-centered, and self-indulgent.

She smiled up at Jonathan, realizing she truly was a new person in Christ. In his arms she felt nothing except a longing for Nathaniel. The old feelings for Jonathan were dead and gone. The desire for this empty lifestyle was gone as well. Her smile grew bigger as she threw back her head and laughed out loud, free from all this nonsense and worry.

Gabrielle knew that dancing with Jonathan left Nathaniel at Amanda's mercy. Amanda had stolen more than one beau from her. The thought of Amanda in Nathaniel's arms troubled Gabrielle greatly. Amanda wasn't shy about kissing a man. What if she tried to kiss Nathaniel? Gabrielle's eyes sought him out.

She stopped dead still on the dance floor. Another couple collided into her. Jealousy squeezed into her heart as she watched Amanda wrap her arms around Nathaniel's neck as they waltzed around the floor. She pulled him closer, and her fingers slid into his hair. She pulled his head down toward hers, and Gabrielle's heart stopped beating. Amanda planned to kiss Nathaniel. Gabrielle wanted to scream.

❄

Nathaniel felt Amanda's fingers curl into his hair and was disgusted. She pulled his face toward hers. *She's going to kiss me!* Stunned by her forward behavior, he grasped her arms, pulling them from around his neck. "I think I've had enough dancing. Excuse me." He knew his actions appeared rude, but the Bible said to flee from temptation. That's just what he planned to do. He stepped out onto the patio for a breath of fresh air. He tugged at his collar and sighed.

"Nathaniel?" Gabrielle stood in the doorway. He turned to face her. His heart throbbed with pain as he remembered her laughing up at Jonathan. "Are you all right?"

He nodded. "Yes." He turned back toward the city lights.

"I noticed that Amanda wanted to capture your attention." She joined him at the edge of the patio.

"She's a little too forward for my liking. I feel like I just escaped a harrowing experience." He chuckled at his inexperience yet felt thankful for it all the same. "You seemed to have old Jon Dandy's attention. You looked right at home in his arms." He looked over at her, hoping to read her expression and hoping she didn't hear the jealousy he felt.

"They don't feel quite the same anymore." She smiled up at him, and he wondered if that was a small sign of hope. No, he'd seen the look on her face when she laughed up at Jonathan.

"What now?"

"We can either dance a while longer or leave. Which do you prefer?"

That wasn't what he meant. He wondered "what now" between her and Jonathan. "We'll stay and dance, if I don't have to share you." This would probably be his last night to claim her attentions, and dancing gave him just the excuse he needed.

"I'm not giving Amanda another chance in your arms, so that's a deal." She laughed, taking his hand.

They danced for over an hour. No one approached them to switch partners, and he felt grateful. He held her at a respectable distance and gazed into her pale blue eyes. He longed to whisper tender words to her that he had no right to say.

Jonathan waltzed with Amanda and scowled at Nathaniel each time they passed on the dance floor. Nathaniel knew that he'd scowl, too, if someone else held his intended. Nathaniel felt certain that Jonathan planned to visit Rincon Hill soon to ask Edward for Gabrielle's hand, and he knew from the joy he'd seen on her face when they'd danced that her answer would be yes. That knowledge didn't make him love her any less.

He'd known better than to allow his heart to care for her. He remembered countless talks with himself on this very subject. "She'll break your heart," he'd said to his image in the mirror. And now it was so.

Tonight when he took her home, he'd walk with her one

last time to the beach. He'd cherish the time with her, and then he'd turn and walk toward home, leaving his heart at the cottage with her. Hopefully, one day he'd forget Gabrielle Fairchild with her summer sky eyes and silky golden hair.

❄

Joy, incredible joy, filled Gabrielle's heart as she floated through dance after dance with Nathaniel. *Thank you, God, that he didn't let Amanda kiss him!* She'd felt such relief when he pulled out of Amanda's hold. She'd embarrassed Jonathan by stopping and staring in the middle of a dance, but she didn't even care. She could still hear his words accusing her of making a fool of herself over some lowly fisherman. She had spoken similar words only months before. *Thank you, God, for changing me.*

She felt like Cinderella at the ball, and she'd found her prince. She loved this man, this wonderful, incredible man. There was nowhere on earth she'd rather be than in his arms. It amazed her that he didn't despise her after the way she'd often behaved.

Her feet ached when they finally quit dancing and headed to the cottage, but when Nathaniel invited her to walk on the beach, she couldn't bring herself to say no. She loved being with him, tired feet or not.

As they walked in comfortable silence, her heart overflowed with peace and contentment. She smiled, remembering her father saying that one day she'd thank him for getting her off Nob Hill. Tomorrow she must remember to do just that.

She'd grown to love the sea and their little cottage. Moving here had led to the two most important events in her life—making a wholehearted commitment to Christ and growing to love her tender neighbor. Yes, moving to the cottage on Rincon Hill had proved to be the best thing for her after all.

"You're awfully quiet tonight," she commented as they climbed back up the hill.

"Just pondering life."

"Thank you for tonight. I promise never to ask you to take me to another party. I did enjoy dancing with you, though."

They'd returned to her porch. He turned her to face him. His hand rested lightly on her waist. His eyes looked sad. "I enjoyed being with you tonight, too, but honestly, that's all I enjoyed."

"I'm sorry about Amanda. She considers every man her personal challenge."

"And what about you?"

"I consider only one man my personal challenge." She hoped he knew she was speaking of him.

"And are you winning, losing, or is it a draw?" He brushed her hair back off her cheek.

"I hope I'm winning."

Slowly his mouth moved toward hers. Yes! She was definitely winning. She met him halfway. His lips on hers brought an explosion of joy into her heart. The tender kiss lasted but a moment, yet she knew it would live in her memory forever.

"Good-bye, Gabrielle." It sounded so final.

Tentatively she laid her hand against his bearded cheek. "Not good-bye, only good night," she whispered. He turned his head and kissed her palm. Then he was gone.

She sighed with contentment, realizing she wouldn't trade Nathaniel for one hundred wealthy beaus. She loved him! *Thank you, God, for bringing him into my life! I love him. I really love him!*

CHAPTER TEN

Nathaniel hiked down the path between his cottage and the Fairchilds.' Gabrielle's words had echoed around in his head since the party two days ago. *"I consider only one man my personal challenge."* She meant Jonathan, of course. No matter how badly Nathaniel wanted to believe otherwise, Gabrielle would marry Jonathan.

Nathaniel had spent the past two days pleading with God to change her mind, but he knew that God gave each person—including Gabrielle—a free will. She was free to choose, and she'd never be content as a fisherman's wife. Even if she had feelings for him, Jonathan offered her so much more, and material riches were her weakness.

He'd considered telling her he wasn't as destitute as he appeared. He wasn't as rich as Jonathan was, but he could provide her with a nice life. He'd checked around and learned that he could even afford one of the smaller mansions on Nob Hill, if that's what she wanted. But he didn't want to buy her love. He didn't want to wonder if her feelings ran as deep as his. He hoped he'd not live to regret that decision.

Since the party he had stayed away from the Fairchild home, not wanting to hear the news. Now he couldn't stand wondering any longer. Besides, the thought of spending Christmas Day cooped up alone in his tiny cabin was more than he could bear. He knew that with or without Gabrielle, he could never return to his previous lifestyle of solitude. He now needed and wanted human contact. He'd also learned that beauty and character could reside in the same woman. Gabrielle was living proof of that. Not only was she the prettiest girl his eyes had ever rested on, she had also turned out to have depth and courage and character.

He stopped dead in his tracks. A shay stood near the Fairchild cottage, and his worst fears were confirmed. He spotted Jonathan and Edward talking on the porch, and even out of earshot, he knew exactly what they were discussing. Edward shook Jonathan's hand and left him alone while he went inside.

Nathaniel knew he should leave, but his feet felt like lead in his boots. His chest ached with the weight of his sorrow. It hurt to breathe. His vision blurred as the scene unfolded before him.

Beautiful, sweet Gabrielle moved gracefully out onto the porch. She wore a dress he'd not seen before. The blue green color reminded him of the sea. Jonathan went to her, taking her hands in his. He kissed both her cheeks. Then he knelt before her. Nathaniel could stand no more. He turned toward home. He'd lost the most important person in his life.

❄

"Jonathan, what a surprise!" Gabrielle dreaded what lay ahead. Her father had informed her of the reason for Jonathan's call. *Lord, help me to handle this in a way that would please you. Help me not to give him a piece of my mind for the way he hurt and rejected me.*

Jonathan crossed the porch, reaching for her hands. It took

all her effort not to yank them from his grasp. As he placed a kiss on each cheek, she wanted to duck. A few short months ago, she'd yearned for this with an aching heart, and now she was so thankful to God it hadn't happened. She'd have spent a lifetime with the wrong man.

Jonathan went down on one knee. Gabrielle bit her lip to keep a straight face. Earnest blue eyes gazed up at her. He possessed a cocky assurance, and she knew he thought he was offering her the chance of a lifetime. She felt certain her answer would provoke his wrath.

"Gabrielle, I've asked your father for your hand. With his blessing, I now ask you to marry me."

She moved away from Jonathan to the edge of the porch and looked out over the sea. How she wished it were Nathaniel asking. A lump formed in her throat as she wondered where he'd been these last two days. Maybe his good-bye the other night really had been good-bye.

"Gabrielle?" Jonathan now stood next to her at the railing. The cockiness had disappeared and he looked vulnerable.

"I can't marry you, Jonathan. I don't love you."

He put his hands on her waist, turning her to face him. "What happened to my beautiful friend who scoffed at love? I hope you've not changed your mind."

"My heart changed my mind for me. Love is real and incredible. To settle for less would be a crime. Someday you'll be glad I said no."

"I cannot believe you're turning me down!" Anger turned his face to a reddish color. He grabbed her upper arm, and his fingers bit into her tender flesh. "You're settling for a man who stinks like fish when you could have *me?* You'll live to regret that decision, Gabrielle."

He let go of her and strode away in anger. She watched him leave in a cloud of dust, rubbing her arm and feeling regret. She'd hoped to have a chance to tell him about the Lord, and now she never would.

She looked up the hill toward Nathaniel's cabin and wondered if he'd ever want her to be his wife. It seemed doubtful. She had nothing to offer him. She barely knew how to cook and was just learning to sew. Besides, her father had once said that Nathaniel had no intention of getting married. The possibility of Nathaniel's interest waning loomed before her in stark reality. Maybe she'd only imagined that he cared.

But even if Nathaniel never wanted her, she knew she'd not feel sorry about turning Jonathan down.

Gabrielle went into the house, grabbing three gaily wrapped presents lying under the tree. "I'll be back in a few minutes," she told her mother in the kitchen as she quickly wrapped a plate of freshly baked Christmas cookies and added them to her armful of gifts.

If Nathaniel wanted to spend Christmas alone, he'd have to say so to her face. She'd not let him disappear without a word. He at least owed her some sort of explanation, didn't he? She suddenly felt angry with him for leaving her confused and hurt.

She'd never been to Nathaniel's cabin. As she mounted the porch, she turned to look at the bay. He was right—his view left her in awe. She stopped and laid her hand on the old rocker resting there. She imagined herself in it, waiting for Nathaniel to return from his day at sea, a babe in her arms.

The poignancy of that dream stole her breath and her confidence. He didn't want her. He'd called on her only to please her father. He'd spent December escorting her only because she'd insisted and he was too polite to turn a lady down. She laid the gifts and cookies in the rocker and turned to leave.

As her foot touched the bottom step of the porch, she heard the cabin door creak open.

"Gabrielle?"

She turned back to face him. His eyes looked tired and sad. No smile greeted her, only a questioning look. He must be wondering why she was there.

"I'm sorry to interrupt your day." Her voice wavered with uncertainty. How she wished she could tell him she loved him. "I dropped off some things for you that were under our tree." She pointed toward the rocker.

His eyes followed her finger, and he nodded. Then they returned to her. Why didn't he say something—anything?

"Well, Merry Christmas."

Just as she started to leave again, he spoke. "Merry Christmas, Gabrielle." Despite the intimacy of using her first name, his voice sounded strained. It brought a deeper ache to her heart.

She turned back to him. "You know we'd love to have you join us for Christmas dinner—if you would like to."

"I appreciate the invitation, but I think I'll pass this time."

She nodded. "Certainly, I understand." But she didn't really, not at all. "Good-bye, Nathaniel." And she knew it really was good-bye. The tears began to fall the moment her foot hit the dirt path. She didn't look back. She wanted to run but held her head up and walked slowly toward home. He'd never know that a waterfall of tears ran down her cheeks. He'd never know she'd fallen in love with him. He'd never know . . .

❄

Nathaniel swallowed a lump and watched Gabrielle walk out of his life forever. He didn't take his eyes off her until she disappeared into her own cottage. Then he gathered the three gifts from the rocker and carried them inside. His eyes blurred as he read the tags. The smallest one was from Izzy—the heaviest, from Edward and Mrs. Fairchild—and a soft, flexible one came from Gabrielle.

He'd seen the disappointment on her face when he turned

down her invitation. Perhaps one day he could sit at the same table with her and Jonathan, but not today. He laid the packages aside, unable to open them right now. One day he'd probably be grateful for her gift as a reminder of her, but not today.

He sat at the table and rested his weary head in his hands. Had he made a mistake not telling her about his money? In his heart he knew he hadn't, but part of him wanted to fight for her with every weapon he had.

A knock at the door freed him momentarily from his painful thoughts. He wondered if it was Gabrielle. Feelings of hope and dread filled him at the possibility of seeing her again so soon. Instead, Edward greeted him when he opened the door.

"Merry Christmas! Gabrielle said you had other dinner plans. I don't smell anything cooking."

"No." He opened the door wider and stepped back to allow Edward to enter. "Have a seat." He pointed to the sofa.

"It's dark and cold in here. Are you sick?"

Nathaniel weighed the opportunity and decided he had to talk to someone. Edward was probably sent by God. He swallowed hard and forced the words out. "I'm heartsick." Instead of joining Edward on the sofa, Nathaniel paced back and forth.

"Gabrielle?"

He faced her father. "I love her."

"Have you told her?"

"How can I, when she's spoken for?"

"Did she tell you that?" A frown creased Edward's brow.

"I saw Jonathan at your house earlier today. It's what she wanted. She must be beside herself with joy."

"Last I saw her, she was moping around as if she'd lost her best friend, much the way you look now. She's down on the beach—alone. I think you two need to talk things over."

A tiny glimmer of hope ignited in the core of Nathaniel's

heart. "Why would she be moping on the day of her engagement?"

"I think you should ask her that yourself."

Nathaniel pondered Edward's suggestion. Maybe there was no engagement; otherwise why would she be moping? The flicker of hope grew into a small flame. "On the beach, you say?"

Edward nodded and rose. "Go talk with her."

Nathaniel picked up the presents and headed out the door. Edward wouldn't mislead him. Now that small flame filled his entire heart with hope, and he ran down the path toward Gabrielle.

He slowed at his first glimpse of her. She sat on the sand resting her chin on her knees, her dress tucked around her legs. She looked solemn and sad, not like a joyous bride-to-be. He longed for assurance that he wasn't fooling himself as hope and fear dueled within him.

Lord, give me the courage to share my heart with her. He took a deep breath as a mantle of peace settled on his shoulders. He approached her slowly, praying all the way. By the time he sat down next to her in the sand, he knew he had to tell her everything, even if she had said yes to Jonathan. He loved her too much to leave it unsaid.

"I didn't want to open these alone," he said, indicating the gifts in his hands. "Will you share the moment with me?"

"Nathaniel! I thought you were Father." She looked at him in surprise. She smiled slightly, but a deep sorrow resided in her eyes. They were red-rimmed, and he knew she'd been crying. He touched her face, reverently, tenderly, and more tears began to fall.

"Did he do this to you?"

"Who?"

"Jonathan. I saw him at your cottage earlier today. Did he say something—"

"No. This has nothing to do with Jonathan."

"Because if he hurt you . . ." He faltered, then asked, "Then why are you crying?"

"Just wishing things had turned out differently."

"Didn't he ask you to marry him?"

She nodded. "He did. I turned him down."

"You what?" Nathaniel felt more confused by the minute.

She smiled slightly again. "I said no."

"And now you wish you'd said yes?"

"No."

"But I thought you'd marry anyone to get back to Nob Hill."

"Not anymore."

"So . . . what do you wish had turned out differently?" he asked, barely daring to breathe.

"It doesn't matter."

"It matters to me," he assured her.

"Why?"

"Don't you know?" She shook her head, and he continued. "I love you, Gabrielle."

The tears started again, but joy replaced the sorrow in her eyes. "You do?" She sounded astonished by his declaration.

"I do." He again laid his hand against her cheek, wishing she'd say something.

❉

Gabrielle could hardly believe his words. She'd hoped for so long, but today she'd finally given up. She looked into his molasses eyes and glimpsed the depth of his feelings for her. "And I love you, Nathaniel."

"Really?" She sensed how much he needed her assurance.

"With all my heart. I feared you'd lost interest in me. I thought I'd waited too long, and your heart had changed its course."

"And I thought you'd accepted Jonathan's proposal, and I loved you too much to spend Christmas with you and your new fiancé." Nathaniel stood, pulling Gabrielle to her feet. He placed his hands on her shoulders.

"I'd rather be alone than marry someone who doesn't love me and God."

Nathaniel grinned at her. "For a girl who didn't believe in love, you've obviously rethought your position. Would you consider marrying me—a man who loves both you *and* God?"

Her heart leaped with joy. "I thought you'd never ask. Yes, Nathaniel. A thousand times, yes!"

He gathered her into his embrace. Then his lips claimed hers for a tender moment. "I have enough money to buy you one of the smaller houses on Nob Hill, if that's where you want to live," he whispered against her hair.

She stepped back so she could look into his eyes. She remembered her daydream on the porch with the rocker and the baby. "I don't want to go back."

A surprised but pleased look settled on his face.

"I want to move forward with you and God at my side. Nob Hill wasn't all I thought it was, and you, Nathaniel Morgan, are far more than I hoped for."

"As are you, Gabrielle, as are you . . ."

RECIPE

❄

These cookies are a favorite of my husband, Dean. Hope your family enjoys them, too!

CHRISTMAS COOKIES

1 cup butter
1 cup shortening
1 cup powdered sugar
1 cup sugar
2 eggs
2 tsp. almond extract
4 cups flour
1 tsp. baking soda
1 tsp. cream of tartar

Cream together butter, shortening, powdered sugar, and sugar. Add eggs and almond extract; mix well. Then add flour, baking soda, and cream of tartar. Form into small balls and press flat with a drinking glass dipped in sugar. (We use red and green sugar to make them more festive.) Bake at 350° for about 10 minutes or until lightly browned around the edges.

A Note from the Author

Dear Friend,

Christmas is my favorite time of year. I love the lights, the tree, the presents. I love the feeling in the air and walking through the crowded mall with Christmas carols playing in the background. More than that, I cherish the sense of unity, family, and togetherness.

But the greatest thing about Christmas is the knowledge of a Savior who came to earth two thousand years ago. He came because he loved me more than I can even imagine. He came to die in my place. And he came for you. Do you know him? Have you invited him into your heart and life? Please don't spend another Christmas without Jesus. Discover, as Gabrielle did, that Jesus offers so much more than the things of this world can offer. He will fill your heart with love and joy and peace, if you will only ask. He's waiting—with arms outstretched—for you to run to him.

My prayer for each of us this Christmas is that we may know Christ in a more real and more personal way. Jesus truly is the only reason for the season!

In his amazing love,
Jeri Odell

ABOUT THE AUTHOR

Jeri Odell enjoys writing, teaching, and speaking on marriage, parenting, and family issues. She is a firm believer in true love, knowing that God holds marriage and the family dear to his heart. She has been active in her church and community for the past twenty years.

Jeri is happily married to her high school sweetheart; they recently celebrated their twenty-sixth anniversary. She loves reading Christian romance, leading Bible studies, and spending time with family and friends—especially her husband, Dean, and their three kids. All three of their almost-adult children migrated to California to attend Christian colleges, so she has an empty nest, except in the summer when the two youngest come home.

Jeri's novellas appear in the anthologies *Reunited, A Bouquet of Love, A Victorian Christmas Cottage,* and *Dream Vacation.* Her articles have appeared in *Focus on the Family, New Man* magazine, and *ParentLife* as well as other publications. She thanks God for the privilege of writing for him.

Jeri welcomes letters written to her in care of Tyndale House Author Relations, P.O. Box 80, Wheaton, IL 60189-0080, or by E-mail at JeriOdell@juno.com.

The Beauty of the Season
PEGGY STOKS

For my mom, Judy.
Your courage in the face of adversity has been
one of my life's greatest lessons.

CHAPTER ONE

N ow, Eli, if I'd known there were so many lovely women in Maple Grove, I never would have wasted all those years at veterinary college down in Ames."

A face of wrinkled brown leather split into a delighted smile while matching, corrugated hands pulled the team and wagon to a halt. "Maybe you got some good sense after all, Clark. You mighta just spared yourself some special Iowa sayin's I been savin' up," the thin, elderly man called down to the younger.

"You haven't heard the last of our Minnesota sayings, either." A deep-throated laugh escaped the other man whose hair and beard were the color of a rusty nail. He stood on the well-worn dirt in front of Eli Woodman's barn, in his hands a large, shiny black bag and a wide-brimmed hat that had seen better days. His eyes lit with interest on the young woman seated next to Eli.

"I been tellin' him all about you, Rebecca," Eli Woodman whispered to his grandniece before making what he considered to be a proper introduction. "Miss Rebecca Belanger of

Minneapolis, I'd like you to meet this new fellow here, Hugh Clark. He ain't a farrier, but a full-schooled veterinarian just moved up to the area from Iowa." He cleared his throat and nodded after drawing out the last syllable of the state, pronouncing it *weigh*. "We been usin' him through the summer for differ'nt things an' he been doin' a fair job, I s'pose. Today he thinks he's gonna fix up our new horse." He shook his head in disgust. "Ain't had her three months and she's dead lame already."

"I'll give her my best, Eli." The veterinarian laughed again, a warm and pleasant sound. "With such praise and confidence in my skills, it's a wonder I've gotten any other work in these parts." His gaze shifted briefly from Rebecca to her uncle, then back again. A welcoming smile curved his lips in a most handsome way. "Good afternoon."

"Pleased to meet you," Rebecca managed to state, feeling heat rise up from beneath the high collar of her blouse. Instinctively, she lowered her gaze and turned her face toward the left. At the same time she tucked her left hand into the folds of her skirt, even though she wore a concealing pair of gloves.

Lovely, he had said? His eyes must not work the same as everyone else's. Yet, all the same, his words brought a quick rush of pleasure amidst Rebecca's discomfiture.

"It's a pleasure to meet you as well, Miss Belanger." To her dismay, the veterinarian's voice was much nearer her ear than before. Before thinking, she swung her head to see that he was practically standing at her elbow, extending his hand to her. "May I help you down?"

"That would be right kind of you," Eli replied, unmindful of Rebecca's embarrassment. "Saves this old back a little wear and tear." He swung down from his perch and landed in the dirt, spry as ever for a man just past his sixty-fifth year. Heading toward the house, he called over his shoulder. "I'll tell Jo we're home, Bell; then we'll put your things in the cottage."

Left with no reasonable choice but to give Hugh Clark her hands, Rebecca took a deep breath and murmured her thanks. It was too late; he'd already seen her face and the enormous purple birthmark encompassing its left hemisphere. Accustomed to twenty years of people's reactions to her port-wine stain, she waited for the shock to reflect in his eyes. Or pity. Or disgust.

"Did he just call you 'Bell?'" Nothing more than puzzlement showed in his brown-flecked gaze. "I thought he introduced you as Rebecca."

As she was assisted to the ground, Rebecca turned her attention to a stand of maples just beginning their autumn turn from green to what she knew would become magnificent shades of orange, red, and yellow. Puzzlement echoed through her mind, as well. Why didn't this man react like others? Whenever she met new people, she steeled herself to their various reactions, saving her feelings of hurt and rejection until later when she was alone. Consequently, she kept the world in which she circulated quite small.

Her next-door neighbor and best friend Jane Eberley had always tried to change that, but now Jane was married and expecting a baby, her time and thoughts occupied by the many concerns of being a new wife and mother-to-be. In June she had moved to her new home with her husband, leaving Rebecca happy for her and bereft all at once. With all the changes that had taken place, the two miles that separated them often felt like two thousand.

Rebecca was her parents' only child, and she lived with them yet in their comfortable Minneapolis home. In an unspoken manner, they also seemed to encourage her isolation from society. She would get a better education at home than at public school, they had decided for her when she was quite young. That didn't mean they weren't loving—for they were, and they had not spared any expense in engaging the finest tutors for her education. In the back of her mind, though, lurked the thought that once they had seen the disfigured infant they had created, they had not dared bring any more children into the world.

And that they were ashamed of her.

It was only at Uncle Eli and Auntie Jo's farm that her feelings of unworthiness melted away. Perhaps it was the exposure to the beauty and grandeur of God's creation, to the harmony and rhythms of making a living from the land. Or maybe it came from Eli and Jo themselves, the childless pair who had lavished their love and attention on her all through her childhood and growing-up years.

With her father's parents back east and her mother's parents long-ago deceased, Eli and Jo were the closest thing to grandparents Rebecca had ever known. Sometimes it seemed impossible that only twenty miles separated the modern city life of Minneapolis from this idyllic piece of nature . . . as well as from a life of self-consciousness to one in which she sometimes went days without thinking about her markings.

"Uncle Eli always called me 'Beckybell' when I was young," she found herself replying, recalling countless sunlit mornings and afternoons she'd trailed behind her uncle as he tended to his work, "and somehow over the years it just dropped down to 'Bell.'" Chancing a glance at him, she saw once again the handsome smile.

"Ah, yes. Bell. I'm learning that your uncle can be quite clever with words when he wants to be."

"You think shortening 'Beckybell' to 'Bell' is so very clever, then?" She failed to see his point, the challenging contradiction escaping her lips before she thought the better of speaking. Perhaps Uncle Eli had been a bit premature in boasting of Dr. Clark's college education. Openly, she studied his face, noticing that the arrangement of his features caused a curious feeling in the base of her stomach. Or was it a slight hunger for air?

A gust of wind ruffled her hat and threatened to knock his from its perch atop his bag, so he walked over to retrieve the battered piece of leather. Placing it atop his head, his grin became mischievous. "Quite so if you speak French, *belle.*"

Her breath caught in her throat at the combination of wind, sun, handsome man, and outrageous flirtation. *Belle,* indeed. She had studied the Romance languages. This wooing was just the sort of thing that happened to the heroines in the novels Jane used to smuggle into her bedroom. Yet for a moment, she gave herself over to the feeling, a giddy, glowing, floating sort of feeling, that had been oh-so-inadequately described in the stories she'd read.

No man had ever called her beautiful before.

But scarcely before it had begun, reality grounded her soaring flight of fancy. No man would be likely to comment favorably on her appearance, ever again. Beautiful was one thing she wasn't—her birthmark had seen to that.

"Je ne crois pas qu'Oncle Eli parle Français du tout," she replied in a clipped tone, turning the marked side of her face away from him. Tears that she was normally able to keep at bay threatened to spill from her eyes.

Was Hugh Clark nothing but a scoundrel, toying with her emotions? Her first impression was that he was a kind and friendly man. Her second was . . . what? To dare hope that such a nice-looking man might be interested in her? *Not likely, Rebecca,* she told herself. *You know that courtship and marriage are out of the question for you. Who in his right mind would dare take the chance of producing burgundy-splotched children? Remember, you learned long ago that the worst cruelty often comes from the most unexpected people.*

"Your grasp of the language is much better than mine, but I think you just told me that your uncle doesn't know French."

"I'm sure of it. Now, if you'll excuse me—" She turned on her heel, blinking back the itchy hotness behind her eyelids.

"Wait," he called, taking a half-dozen rapid steps to close the ground between them. "Please wait." In place of the grin was a contrite expression. "I can see I've offended you." He was so near that she could smell the soap from his clothing . . . or was it the man himself? It was both foreign and pleasant, and she marveled that a man who likely spent much of his time in barns did not smell like one.

"With the rigors of schooling and setting up a practice, I must plead ignorance in the matters of male conduct in the presence of the fair sex. I beg your forgiveness, Miss Belanger. I hope you might give me another chance . . . your uncle speaks so highly of you."

"Just what has my uncle said about me?" With each word of Dr. Clark's heartfelt speech, Rebecca's confusion mounted.

"Oh, he mostly says things about the brightness you bring to their lives. That you're thoughtful and kind and compassionate and loving as the day is long. He also says you can be full of mischief and give back every bit of rascality he dishes out."

The curious feeling returned to her stomach while Hugh spoke. If his friendliness was sincere and did not spring from impure motivation, then why had he asked for another chance? What kind of man was he? she wondered. She'd never met anyone quite like him.

"Maybe you want to know a little about me," he offered, as if he followed the direction of her thoughts. "I grew up on a farm outside of Ames and always loved tending to animals. Getting through veterinary college was always my aim, if you'll pardon the pun, and now that I've done that, here I am in Maple Grove starting my practice. A few other things happened here and there along the way, but I figure we ought to leave some things for the sake of future conversation." His grin was infectious.

Hinges squeaked and Uncle Eli reappeared from the

house. For just a moment as he came down the porch stairs he looked old and tired. But then, squaring his shoulders, he walked across the yard to join them, the spring back in his step.

"How is she?" Rebecca asked, sudden shame washing over her. The reason she'd come to the farm, after all, was to help out during Auntie Jo's recuperation from a broken hip. But with the veterinarian's flattering words flowing as deep as the Mississippi River, she'd been entirely distracted from her original purpose.

"Snoozin' away," her uncle replied. "Be a good time to get you settled in the cottage. Since her tumble down the steps, neighbors and church folks have been takin' turns seein' to Jo durin' the day." His voice softened with tenderness. "I see her through the nights."

"Are you sure you wouldn't rather have me stay in the house, Uncle Eli? I can help at night as well as during the day."

"I'll see my darlin' through the nights, Bell. You'll have plenty to do with the harvest comin' in. 'Sides, we know how much you like the cottage."

Reflexively, all three heads turned toward the small, wooden structure tucked just inside the nearest stand of maples. Situated a good forty yards away from their present house, the cottage was Eli and Jo's original Maple Grove dwelling. Rebecca's dauntless great-aunt forbade Eli to tear it down while she had breath in her body, declaring that their first Minnesota home held too many memories to be turned into kindling.

So that was how Eli had come to add the duties of maintaining the cottage to his already busy life of farming. Once shingled with bark, the small dwelling now boasted a proper roof. Thirty years of changing seasons had weathered the split-log siding to gray, adding only to the cottage's charm, in Rebecca's opinion. The once-sagging front porch had been replaced with a new one, and the flower box beneath the small front window was never without foliage or pine boughs, depending on the time of year.

Auntie Jo kept the indoors of the cottage as tidy as she did their newer, larger frame home. Already Rebecca could picture herself waking in the cozy, homemade bed beneath a pile of her aunt's sunshine-dried quilts. The rustle of leaves and calls of birds scarcely known in the city were as splendid a symphony as she could ever imagine. The cottage had always been a wondrous place to her, a private sanctuary that she could pretend was her very own.

But it stood second only to the warmth of Eli and Jo's home. Auntie Jo always had an enormous eight o'clock breakfast waiting for her and Eli—sausages, bacon, flapjacks, eggs. The town had been aptly named for its many groves of maple trees, and delicious syrup was made by many of the local residents.

Dr. Clark was the first to break the silence, speaking in a professional tone. "Well, I came to tend a hoof, and I'd best get to it. Thank you, Eli, for the introduction to your most remarkable niece. She is indeed everything you said and speaks French like a Parisian, to boot." A hint of the previous grin played about his mouth.

"Speaks French? Now why in tarnation would you two be talkin' in French?" He shook his head. "I can't understand a word of it. *Oui, oui, oui . . .* sounds like hog-callin', if you ask me."

Rebecca couldn't resist meeting Hugh's amused gaze, her brows lifting a scant quarter inch at her uncle's admission. *Told you so,* she communicated.

". . . entirely too much book learnin' between the two of you," Eli went on, though pride was evident in his voice. "Bell here gots herself a pile of learnin', but better'n that is her heart. Solid gold—just like Jo's."

"You've got a good woman," the veterinarian seconded in

all seriousness. "Please give your wife my best when she wakes and tell her she's in my daily prayers for a swift recovery."

"She'll be sorry she missed you, Clark. She always enjoys your visits."

Though his reply seemed to be to her uncle, Rebecca's impudence vanished when, a moment later, the brown-flecked gaze sought her own. "You might mention to her that I'll be by tomorrow." With long strides he retrieved his bag, then was swallowed up by the shadows of the barn.

"Speakin' French? If that don't beat all." Eli chuckled, a twinkle evident in his blue eyes. "Oh my, yes, Bell, it's good to have you back with us again. Come on, honey. Let's get you settled before Jo wakes up."

Settled? With Hugh Clark coming by again tomorrow? Rebecca knew she would fit back into her relatives' lives like a hand in a glove, but after this afternoon's extraordinary meeting, "settled" was one thing she doubted she would be for a long time to come.

CHAPTER TWO

"Those weren't the best eggs I ever ate, but they weren't the worst, neither."

"I know, I know," Rebecca replied to her uncle with mock weariness, "I'll just have to keep practicing until I get them right." Sunshine streamed in the east windows of the kitchen, illuminating the breakfast table and Eli's grizzled head. Taking a bite of her flapjack, she watched her uncle wipe the remaining egg yolk, syrup, and melted butter from his plate with the last slice of bacon.

"Not bad," he commented, chewing thoughtfully, "but tomorrow you could fry the bacon a tad more crisp."

Auntie Jo interrupted her husband's ritual teasing from her bed in the next room. "Eli Woodman! Just be thankful Bell put a hot breakfast before you this morning, you old rascal."

Rebecca giggled. "He thinks I don't know he's trying to trick me into making more food for him. It's the same old carrot he dangles whenever I make molasses cookies. 'They're not half bad, Bell, but you'd better try again tomorrow,'" she mimicked in a gruff tone. Leveling her fork toward her uncle, she lifted her brows. "I'll never make the best cookies you ever ate, will I, Uncle Eli?"

"That," he replied, reaching for the peg that held his hat, "is something you will never know unless you keep trying." A self-satisfied grin played about his lips as he rose from his chair and headed toward the bedroom.

"Pay him no mind, Bell," Auntie Jo directed. "He's always been a scoundrel in the kitchen."

"Among other places," he remarked, silencing Auntie Jo's whoop of surprise with a loud kiss.

Rebecca smiled at the older couple's exchange. Unlike her parents, who rarely touched, Eli's and Jo's love was plain for all to see. *What would it be like to have such an affectionate and devoted husband?* she wondered, thinking of Auntie Jo's radiance whenever Eli was near. Face tilted upward expectantly, lips curved into an indulgent smile, the older woman's fine-wrinkled cheeks bloomed like wild roses as often as not. Rebecca often thought her aunt's bright blue eyes and expression held the sparkle of a young girl's.

With a sigh, she stacked her plate on Eli's. The wine-colored birthmark that stained her face had also, to a lesser degree, mottled, blotched, and whorled its way down her left arm to her fingers. With her sleeves rolled up a few turns, the discoloration was stark against the white of Auntie Jo's china plates.

"Leave those dishes, Bell," her aunt called, "and come sit. Martha Denning said she'd come by later this morning and do whatever needed doing."

"Hope she don't get a notion to bring more chowchow," Eli muttered, walking through the kitchen. "I was eatin' on that for days after last time she was here, an' it wasn't even good." He made a face as he put his arms into his coat. "Too sweet."

"You mind your complaints and count your blessings, Eli Woodman! If not for the generosity of our neighbors, you'd be staring at an empty table."

"Ain't your hearin' ever gonna go, woman?" In a quick movement, he put on his hat and turned, with a rueful expression, toward Rebecca. "Hears like an elephant, smells like a bloodhound, an' has eyes sharper'n a hawk. A fellow ain't got half a chance when his wife's senses are more animal than human."

As Jo's quiet laughter filtered toward them, Rebecca was overwhelmed with the love she felt for this unique couple. Married over forty years and they still chortled and joked like youngsters. Yet she knew things hadn't always been easy for them.

Not long after they'd come from Vermont as newlyweds, Uncle Eli had enlisted to fight in the War Between the States, leaving Auntie Jo on her own to battle the Midwest frontier on their fledgling farm. More difficult than that, though, was the fact that the older woman had never been able to carry a babe in her womb past seven months; one small stone back East and three markers in Rush Creek Cemetery gave testimony to their crushed dream to bring forth new life.

For some people, such great loss would be reason enough to welter in bitterness, but somehow Jo and Eli had persevered through each demise, emerging with quiet, strong faith that Rebecca imagined could indeed move a mountain.

"Would you like another cup of tea, Auntie Jo?" Rebecca asked, entering the generous-sized bedroom. Against the opposite wall sat a handsome bed of maple, next to which stood a bedside table. Completing the room's furnishings were a dresser, mirror, wardrobe, two chairs, and a sewing machine. Lacy curtains had been drawn back to admit the morning light.

"You made a good breakfast, Bell, but I'll wait on more tea till later." Propped on two pillows, the stockinged sole of her great-aunt's foot hailed her, toes waggling in greeting. "The more I drink, the more I'll have to trouble you for the pan."

"You know it's no trouble."

"Maybe not for you, but hoisting this old body up and down plumb wears me out!"

"Josephine Woodman worn out? I've never heard such talk." This was the closest thing to complaining she'd ever heard from her aunt, yet Rebecca saw traces of suffering around the blue eyes she loved so well. These past two weeks had to have been difficult for Jo and Eli both.

"I wish you would have called for me right away," she said with gentle reproach, slipping into the chair at the bedside. "I would have been on my way in the time it took to pack a bag."

"I know that, honey, but for a week we didn't have any idea I'd broken anything. I took to bed after the fall, thinking I'd be fine in a day or two, but when the soreness only got worse, I figured I must have done myself some serious damage."

"How's the pain?" She took the hand her aunt offered, warm and strong and small. How many tasks had these hardworking fingers accomplished in sixty-two years? she wondered. This confinement had to be something near to torture for Jo, a farmwife who rarely ever stopped moving.

"It doesn't hurt so bad today. At first I used some of the opium Dr. Janery left me, but it locked me up something fierce, if you know what I mean." The face she made was at odds with the elegant silver hair framing her features. "That's about the last thing I need on top of everything else."

"Uncle Eli said it may be some time till you're up and around."

"The doctor figures I fractured the neck of my thighbone when I fell and says I'll need to keep to bed for a few months. After that, I'll walk with crutches . . . maybe always."

Rebecca's other hand came up to clasp her aunt's hand. Her eyes grew moist. "I'll stay as long as you need me . . . even always."

"Oh, Bell." Jo's eyes closed for a long moment, and when

they opened, their azure depths glistened with tears. "What would we do without you?"

"I don't know what I would do without you," she whispered, quite honestly, in reply. "I love you and Eli so much, Auntie Jo."

"As we do you, sweet Bell."

A gust of autumn wind rattled the windows while beyond, a noisy flock of grackles gathered in the trees. Motes of dust performed a slow waltz on the morning sunbeams. The moment stretched on, sweet and painful, until Rebecca noticed fatigue growing on her beloved aunt's face.

"Oh dear, you're tired and I'm keeping you from a nap." With a final squeeze, she withdrew her hands and stood.

"I don't know why I've been sleeping so much," Jo replied, almost irritably.

"Your body's working on knitting those bones back together so you can toss a few more forkfuls of hay before you depart this earth."

The choleric cast of the older woman's lips gave way to a grin. "You're remembering back aways. I haven't forked hay in quite a few years now." Changing the subject, she asked, "What did you think of our new veterinarian, Bell?"

"He was—" Rebecca felt her face warm, remembering the things Hugh Clark had said to her . . . the way he had said *belle*. "He seemed like a good man."

"Yes. He's only been here since July, but Eli and I think highly of him. As far as we know, he's a bachelor." Her snowy brows lifted, her voice turning speculative. "And I heard you two got on quite well."

"I . . . I only made his acquaintance."

"In French?" The blue eyes twinkled.

"I . . . he . . . oh!" Rebecca's tongue seemed wont to trip over itself before she regained control of the unruly organ. "He made a comment about my name."

"Really?"

311

"He . . . wondered why I was called Bell, so I told him."

"And what was his comment?" Jo persisted, looking remarkably alert now.

The flustered feelings she'd felt the afternoon before returned full force. She also remembered Hugh Clark's smile. "He said Eli was clever for naming me Bell."

"Because . . . ?" Jo supplied.

"Because in French, *belle* means . . . 'beautiful,' " she finished miserably.

"Well, he's absolutely correct—you are beautiful." Jo nodded, a smile playing about her lips. "I knew he had intelligence. Pull that cover up over my leg, Bell, will you? I believe I'll take my nap now." Closing her eyes, the older woman settled back into her pillow. She let out a deep breath. "And mind you don't let me sleep through Dr. Clark's visit today."

❄

At precisely noon, Hugh Clark turned down Territorial Road, the long dirt lane that would bring him to the Woodman farm. The stray dog he'd taken in and named Lucky rode beside him, the mongrel's paws disheveling the small bouquet of asters he'd placed on the seat. The abscessed hoof he'd tended did not require a following-day visit—two would be more like it, but he had the matter of Miss Rebecca Belanger to attend to.

Allowing for the sixth-grade crush he'd had on Emily Tessier, he'd never given himself over to the pursuit of courtship. Science and animals had been his passions for as long as he could remember; whatever spare time he'd had after chores was spent learning about one or the other. This interest was strongly encouraged by his father, a gentle-hearted man who shared his love for animals.

Hugh's acceptance to the Ames Veterinary College was a cause of great celebration in his family, second only to the jubilation caused by his graduation. Owing to the number of veterinarians in the Ames area, however, he knew the feasibility of setting up practice in his nearby hometown was poor. His sister, Deborah, who had moved to Minneapolis with her husband in '86, suggested he move north and try Hennepin County. The city itself held no appeal, but upon visiting some of its outlying areas, Hugh's heart had been captured by Maple Grove, a land of gentle, rolling hills dotted with small lakes and majestic stands of hardwood.

After renting a modest house, he'd set to advertising his specialty in the local paper. Eli Woodman had been the first to use his services, making no bones about the fact that he would personally run him out of the area if he wasn't what he said he was. His care of Woodman's colicky cow was efficient, however, and the older man had done him a great service by word-of-mouth endorsement.

Hugh had immediately taken to the dry, wisecracking farmer and his sprightly wife. It hadn't taken long for him to witness their deep faith in the Lord as well as their uncommon love for one another. Eli Woodman was a born talker, his favorite topic being persons near and dear to his heart. Next came farming, local residents and events, and if he was allowed to wax on unchecked, eventually would come precise recountings of the months he'd spent on Tennessee soil during his time in the volunteer infantry.

It was during these long, lazy dissertations he'd learned of Rebecca. So skillfully did Eli paint descriptions of both appearance and character with his speech that Hugh felt as though he knew the persons of whom the older man spoke. All summer and into fall, the old farmer had shared accounts of his grandniece from Minneapolis, stirring a place within Hugh that had not been seriously affected since the days of Emily Tessier.

He'd been wanting to meet Rebecca Belanger for some time, but what he couldn't understand was why he'd been so brash and forward upon their introduction. True, he might feel as though he knew her, but she didn't know the first thing about him. No wonder he'd drawn the reaction he had.

Eli hadn't exaggerated, either, about her sensitivity regarding her birthmark. She had visibly shrunken from him upon their introduction, turning the affected side of her face away. Perhaps he had tried too hard to let her know he didn't care one whit about the stain on her skin. "Careful there!" he admonished Lucky, glancing at the rapidly deteriorating bunch of flowers. "Or my second impression will be worse than my first."

Tail thumping, the multicolored canine received the advisement with gratitude, assuming that any words his new master spoke were words of praise. Unable to resist the tilted head and expressive brown eyes, Hugh reached over and gave his pet a good scratching behind the ears. A blissful yawn escaped Lucky's jaws, and he lay down upon the upholstered bench.

The scenery rolling by the carriage was peaceful, tranquil, utterly pastoral. His family and roots were in Iowa, but he was beginning to think Minnesota had quite a charm of its own. He chuckled, remembering Eli's response to his expression of such thoughts. "You might want to reserve judgment there, son, till you been through one of our winters. More than a few fainthearted folks have packed up an' tore back south at first thaw."

Hugh's smile faded when he passed by the Scruggs place, a small, forlorn home standing amidst a collection of ramshackle outbuildings. Eli's lips thinned when he spoke of Barter Scruggs, a man whom Hugh had not yet met. It was commonly believed that Scruggs made and sold liquor illegally, and he was reputed by many to be a mean drunk.

Standing in sharp contrast to the surrounding beauty of so many neatly tended farms, the Scruggs property looked seedy. Weeds sprang forth from the driveway and yard; no smoke rose from the chimney. A family dwelled in this sad place, he thought, shaking his head and realizing how fortunate he was to have been raised by the parents he had.

Catching sight of the edge of the Woodman property, his mind turned again toward Rebecca. Was it foolishness on his part to think so much of a woman he, in all actuality, barely knew? Just what was it about Woodman's grandniece that had so captivated his attention? he rather sternly asked himself.

It was her heart, he decided only a second later, remembering the common threads of Eli's recountings. Rebecca sounded so much like Jo, fun and selfless and giving. That the young woman held a special place in Eli's affections was plain to see. Hugh sighed and readjusted his hat. Maybe this attraction to Rebecca had something to do with watching Eli and Jo together and longing for a woman with whom to share such a relationship.

Could mere foolishness explain the quickening in his chest as he directed the team of bays down the Woodman drive? Lucky seemed to sense his anticipation, awkwardly pushing himself to a sitting position and mangling several more blooms in the process.

"Thank you kindly. I'm sure Miss Belanger will be delighted to receive these flowers you have so thoughtfully crushed."

Sometimes Hugh was certain animals smiled. Grinned, even. Tongue lolling, Lucky turned his head toward his master and seemed to lift an eyebrow.

He couldn't resist a chuckle. "You'd do well to be on your best behavior today, dog. I'm already on unstable ground."

Something between a grunt and a second yawn escaped Lucky. Regarding his master a moment longer, the canine turned his attention forward. The crystal song of a cardinal sounded from a nearby tree, carrying clearly on the sun-warmed autumn air. "Tell me, Lucky, how do I go about convincing this young woman I couldn't care less about a big old birthmark?" he mused. "People's insides count for a whole lot more than their outsides—it's a fact your kind knows much better than mine."

The thumping of the white, black, and brown tail was the end of the asters. Hugh shook his head and fingered what had been a simple but attractive bunch. "No flowers. Now I'll have to rely on my charming personality . . . and that didn't get me very far yesterday." Though his words were light, he contemplated what he would say to Rebecca . . . Bell . . . *belle.*

She was a lovely woman. He remembered how her glossy dark hair had peeked out from beneath her stylish traveling hat, framing a face filled with graceful planes and angles. Her eyes were dark, snapping with fire when she'd spat that snappy line of French at him. There were no thoughts in her mind of her birthmark at that moment, he'd wager.

A slow smile curved his lips. Yes, Rebecca Belanger was a very interesting woman. If he wasn't mistaken, Eli was not-so-subtly maneuvering the two of them together, the old rascal. How Rebecca felt about that—or even if she was aware of it—he didn't know, but he imagined that once Eli Woodman set his mind to something it was as good as done.

"All right, Lord," he spoke aloud with a brief glance overhead, "between you and Eli I've fallen half in love with her. But knowing someone by proxy and knowing her in person are two different things. I'm ready and willing to go the other half of the way, but you've got to give me some help. I think you know what I mean. Amen."

Satisfied, he brought the bays to a halt in the Woodman yard. "Lucky, you stay put," he ordered, eyeing first the dog, then the flowers. "I've had enough help from you already today."

CHAPTER THREE

Rebecca's hands were submerged in dishwater when, out of the corner of her eye, she saw Hugh Clark's carriage turn into the drive. Quickly, she dried her hands and smoothed the apron she wore over her blouse and skirt, her heart thumping at the sight of the veterinarian sitting tall in his seat. Though she would never admit it to another soul, her eye had been drawn to the window all morning.

"Looks like you got company," Martha Denning remarked as she mashed a heap of boiled potatoes. The energetic, middle-aged woman had arrived a little before nine and in that time had not only swept and dusted the entire house, but had put together such a fried chicken dinner as to make the angels weep. Adding another splash of milk to the potatoes, she stirred with even more vigor, her voice a little breathless. "It's that new fellow, if I'm not mistaken. People are talking about him . . . saying mighty good things. Rebecca, dear, why don't you set another place, and we'll invite him to stay for dinner."

"Is that Hugh Clark you're talking about?" Auntie Jo's

voice called. "You'd best not let him get away without feeding him, Mart. You never know what those bachelors are eating on their own."

"Isn't that the truth! You know my neighbor, Mr. Harbaugh? He makes himself nothing but fried eggs every morning, noon, and night. I don't believe he's ever washed the pan, either." All morning Martha had been conversing with Jo from whatever room she happened to be in, just as naturally as if they'd been facing one another across a table.

"I've seen worse." There was no satisfaction in Jo's voice.

"You're meaning the Scruggs place, I reckon. What were you ever doing inside those walls?"

"Oh, I've brought a few baskets down. Bread, jam, things from the garden. It'd like to break your heart to see how those people live."

Rebecca listened carefully as she added another place setting to the table. She was acquainted with some of her aunt and uncle's neighbors, but of the mysterious Scruggs family living in the dilapidated house down the road she'd heard little.

"I'm not sure Mrs. Scruggs is right in the head," Jo continued. "She can be looking square at you, and it's as if she doesn't even see you."

"It can't be good for a person to be shut away like that. And what of the little ones? I couldn't even tell you how many there are."

"Just two . . . that I know of, anyway, but they're always kept out of sight. I'd like to do more for Lavina, their mother, but their father hangs so close that I can barely say half a dozen words without him telling me it's time to go home. If not for the food, I'm sure he wouldn't let me on his place."

"Barter Scruggs is a dangerous man. . . ."

Rebecca's heart went out to Mrs. Scruggs and her children as the older women talked, the stir she'd felt at Hugh Clark's arrival taking a backseat to her compassion. It did not surprise her in the least to learn of Jo's charity toward the least fortunate of her neighbors. But the thumping of boots on the wooden steps outdoors a moment later brought the conversation to a close and Rebecca's concerns about the veterinarian back to the forefront.

"How do, Miz Denning? Forgot to tell you ladies there'd be two more for lunch," Eli called, entering. "Arthur and Jake are hired on through the harvest."

Rebecca had met both men in the past, hardworking locals. They greeted her and Martha politely as they came in, their hands and faces damp from washing. Bringing up the rear was russet-haired Hugh Clark.

Eli sought Rebecca's gaze and winked. "Best make it three. S'pose we'll have to let the new fellow sample your cookin' as long as he showed up right at mealtime." Cocking his head toward the veterinarian, he added conspiratorially, "In my courtin' days I was treated to several fine meals by Jo an' her mama by takin' such a tack."

Hugh threw back his head and laughed. "I wasn't expecting a meal, but I won't turn it down . . . especially since I smell fried chicken."

White teeth gleamed in the reddish-brown beard, and Rebecca was both dismayed and overjoyed to see that Hugh Clark was every bit as nice-looking as she remembered. His gaze sought hers, his broad smile reaching all the way to his eyes.

"Good day, Miss Belanger," he spoke warmly as she busied herself with setting two more places. "I hope having me will be no trouble."

"No trouble at all," Eli answered, clapping the veterinarian's shoulder while Rebecca's inner voice shouted that the man's presence would indeed trouble her nerves a great deal. "Sit down, everyone, and load up your plates while I see to my bride."

Rebecca helped Martha dish up while Eli made a brief

visit to Jo and the men settled around the table. Self-consciousness made her movements seem unnatural. How was she going to manage sharing a table with him? Worse yet, what might he say in front of all the others?

"Is that for your aunt? Let me." Shivers shot down her legs at the sound of his voice near her ear. Taking the plate she was fixing for Jo at the stove, he added a biscuit to the chicken, potatoes, and baked squash. "I owe her a visit, so I'll have my meal with her." With that, he set the plate on the tray, took his own, and disappeared around the corner.

Though Rebecca had been hungry after a morning of vigorous housework, her appetite had fled with the appearance of the hazel-eyed man. She picked at the meal, her stomach tied in knots. Much laughter came from Jo's bedchamber; she and her noontime guest seemed to be having a wonderful time.

Several times last night Rebecca had awakened, thinking of Dr. Clark's parting remark . . . *you might mention to her that I'll be by tomorrow.* After what had transpired between them yesterday, had she been mistaken to read double meaning into his message? She had thought his words spoke to her as well, but it seemed as though she was mistaken.

Why was she so disappointed?

The buttered squash tasted terrible in her mouth, and she set down her fork. Martha ate as heartily as the men. Jo's laughter pealed yet again, followed by Hugh's, causing Eli's eyes to crinkle with pleasure.

Thick wedges of warm apple pie, accompanied by steaming cups of strong coffee, capped off the dinner and were fairly gobbled down by the men before Eli announced it was time to return to the fields. Rebecca sighed while they departed, studying her uneaten food . . . listening to the happy sounds of Auntie Jo's and Hugh's conversation.

"You can consider it done," came Hugh's voice, preceding his appearance in the kitchen by just a moment. He handed his and Jo's dishes to Martha. "If your niece agrees, that is."

Looking up, she saw the hazel gaze seeking hers. Feeling suddenly silly to be sitting alone at the table before a plate of barely touched food, she pushed back her chair and began piling plates. "If I agree to what?" she asked, focusing her attention on the task at hand.

"Pick grapes!"

"Pick grapes? What are you talking about?"

"Your aunt tells me she's sick about missing the wild grapes, and she wonders if we would be so kind as to take some buckets and see what the birds have left." His eyebrows rose entreatingly. "Grape jelly *is* my favorite."

"I . . . we? I . . . I'm not certain if I remember where to look," she hedged, knowing exactly where wild grapevines grew in profusion. She and Auntie Jo had been there many times over the years, their visits ultimately culminating in clouds of grape-scented steam pouring from the bubbling jelly pot.

"I'm willing to make it an adventure then. Why don't you get directions while I see to that hoof? It just so happens that I have the next few hours free."

"But I—"

"No buts," Martha interrupted firmly, whisking the stack of dishes from beneath Rebecca's hands. "You go on and find Jo some grapes, and while you're at it, enjoy this lovely weather for the rest of us. You've already scrubbed up the worst of the pots, so I'll just wash the rest."

"Your escape on a purple platter, Miss Belanger." Hugh's grin was infectious; Rebecca felt the beginning of an answering smile tugging at the corners of her mouth. "How about you produce two buckets and meet me outside in ten minutes?"

"Ten minutes," she found herself agreeing, feeling very much like a small leaf that had just been swept aloft by a surprising gust of wind.

❄

The grapes were a disappointment after all, puckered and leathery on the vine. Down the hill and deeper into the woods, Rush Creek flowed at a lazy pace within its winding banks. The sun shone warm upon their shoulders, but the breeze carried with it the promise of cooler temperatures. Lucky trotted beside the pair, his gait both peculiar and efficient, as they walked on the gravel road back to the Woodman farm.

"It's amazing how he keeps up so well." Rebecca had been astounded when the three-legged dog had jumped from the veterinarian's carriage, tail wagging. As if Lucky understood she was speaking about him, he turned his head and regarded her in a friendly manner. "I keep wondering what happened to the poor thing."

"We'll never know. He was near dead when I found him." Hugh swung the empty bucket he carried, shaking his head. "I don't understand how some people can treat animals so cruelly . . . or people," he added softly, after a pause.

Rebecca's heart thundered at the gentle words spoken by the man beside her. Beneath the close-cropped beard she could see the strong set of his jaw. His form was as fine as any she could imagine, his height exceeding her own by five or six inches. What she liked best about him, though, was the kindness that shone from his brown-flecked eyes. Laughter, tenderness, and empathy seemed to be stored in his gaze, free for the dispensation.

He should have been claimed by some beautiful young woman long ago.

She couldn't understand why he had chosen to spend this afternoon with her, engaging in pleasant conversation and seeking to tickle her rib with his funny stories, making her feel as though he truly enjoyed being with her. *And what would he know of the cruelty of others?* she wondered. He was . . . normal.

"People would say terrible things about my father. Snicker . . . stare . . . whisper," he continued in a ruminant tone.

Answering grief rose inside Rebecca, for he had just described her entire existence. Tears blurred the colorful countryside before her.

"He never let on that it bothered him, but I wonder, deep down, if it did. It bothered me, though, an awful lot."

"What . . . why would people treat your father so?" she asked, finally trusting her voice enough to speak.

"Because of his scars. He was burned in a barn fire when he tried to rescue the stock."

"Oh."

"I was too young to remember anything, but my mother told me he nearly died." Strong teeth flashed amidst the copper glints in his beard. "I'm sure glad he didn't, though, because if not for him I doubt I'd be where I am today."

"Where? In Maple Grove, Minnesota, not picking grapes?"

He threw back his head and laughed. "Your tongue is quick in any language, *belle*. It's good to become acquainted with the lady Eli told me about."

"Just how much talking has my uncle done?" She strove to make her words casual, but inside, a thrill threatened this disguise of her emotions.

"Enough to spark a healthy interest in spending time with you."

The glow of excitement left her in a rush, and she dropped her head. "You can't mean that."

"I can't? Pray tell me why not."

"Because I . . . because of . . ." Tears threatened yet again. Oh, why had she thrown aside her caution and agreed to walk with this man? A courtship like Jane Eberly's was just not possible for her. "Because," she averred, studying the dirt at her feet.

"Because of a little dab of color on your cheek?" His voice was a smooth caress on the autumn air.

"We both know there's more than a 'little dab of color' on my cheek. Why don't you just say it—I'm ugly." Rebecca stopped walking, hot wetness spilling over the area in question. "Ugly," she whispered angrily, her fist coming up in a quick, jerky motion to wipe her tears.

Hugh stopped in the road also, allowing a respectful distance between them. Lucky sat on the side of the road, head cocked, glancing first at his master then at the anguished woman.

"Please just leave me alone." Anguish and defeat welled up inside her, and she dropped the bucket in the weeds at the side of the lane. How many afternoons had she spent curled up on her bed at home, in tears over her disfigurement?

"Oh, but then I couldn't be a gentleman." Reaching in his coat, he pulled out an ironed square of linen. "My mother told me to carry a clean wiper for just this situation. 'You never know when you'll meet a damsel in distress,' she told me when I left for college. Besides reminding me to say my prayers and brush my teeth, I believe that was the only advice she gave me." He held the handkerchief aloft for a moment before closing the distance between them. "You're my first damsel in distress," he said gently, pressing the soft fabric into her hands.

Accepting the cloth, she wiped her eyes.

"Do you really believe that little dab of color prevents me from seeing your lovely dark eyes?" he asked, guiding her chin upward with a light touch of his knuckles.

Rebecca's heart seemed to skid to a stop at the contact of his fingers. With a shaking breath, she met the steady hazel gaze. The warm fingers traced upward, grazing her cheek, the soft hairline just above her ear.

"*Belle*," he asserted, "I see before me a woman with a

beautiful oval face, whose hair and skin are silkier than anything I've ever before imagined. She smells a little like fried chicken, but underneath that is something mysterious and flowery that makes me want to keep smelling and smelling. Her mouth is—" She was powerless to move as his head bent toward hers. Stopping just short of a kiss, he touched two fingers to his mouth before brushing her lips with them in a featherlight caress.

He'd nearly kissed her. She swallowed in shock.

Taking a step back, he smiled wryly. "Rebecca, do you believe your aunt and uncle would love you more if you had no marks on your skin?"

"I believe my parents would." Finding her tongue, she was surprised at the contentious words that had escaped.

"Ah, but I asked you about Eli and Jo. Give me the truth. Do you believe they would care more for you without this birthmark?"

"No," she replied after a long pause, lowering her gaze.

"Is it possible, then, that others might feel the same?"

"I . . . I . . . you don't understand—"

"I think I have some understanding, *belle*. Will you answer just one more question for me?" The soothing timbre of his voice was such that she could imagine sick and injured animals lying down in surrender before him.

"What is it?" With a deep sigh, she looked back up into the earnest features of the man before her.

"Do you believe God is good?"

CHAPTER FOUR

More so than his demonstration of his feelings, Hugh Clark's question burned within Rebecca the remainder of the day and all through the evening. Did she believe God is good? Why had he asked such a thing? *Did* she believe God is good?

Jo, as if she sensed a matter weighing on her niece's mind, had handed her a stack of letters after the supper hour. "I've been looking through these today. Why don't you take them with you out to the cottage?"

To her questioning look, her aunt had replied, "They're the letters Eli wrote me from his enlistment."

"From the war? Why do you want me to read them?"

"There's a pressure on my heart to give them to you tonight, Bell." The blue eyes had shone as bright as a midsummer sky, gentle and warm. "You've not been courted before, and I expect your feelings must be running somewhat out of order."

"My feelings? . . . Who says I'm being courted?"

"I say so, dear, for two reasons." A winsome smile had curved Jo's lips, melting years from her features. "The first is observation. The second is because a certain young man asked if I thought you would be amenable to being called upon."

"Oh . . ."

"Already knowing Eli's mind on the matter, I was pleased to tell Dr. Clark that he may indeed call upon you."

Holding the bundle of letters in her lap, Rebecca had sat quiet a long time. "I don't know what to think. I've always loved staying with you because it's . . . safe here. But this time everything seems all wrong. You're hurt, and I worry so about you, and I don't know what to think about this man who looks at me like—"

"He looks at you that way, Rebecca Belanger, because you are a beautiful young woman," had come Auntie Jo's forceful words, "inside *and* out. I know I should hold my tongue, but I've got to say I've never had a minute's time for the way your mother and father have kept you squirreled away from the world. You need to get out and live!"

"If this is what 'living' feels like, I'm not sure I like it."

"Yes, it can be mighty strange and even frightening at times—painful, too—but there's no doubt it's all worthwhile."

"Auntie Jo . . . do you believe God is good?"

"Yes, child, I do."

"Even when bad things happen?"

"That all depends on who's deciding what's bad, I reckon. God's ways are often a mystery to his children."

"Well, what about falling and breaking your hip? Or . . . not being able to have children?"

"Or being born with a birthmark?" The gentle blue gaze held fast upon her. "Bell, you need only open the Scriptures to be affirmed of the Father's love for you. What you have to decide for yourself is if God—who loves you so much that he sent his only Son to die for your sins—is for you or against you."

Outside the cottage the wind gusted, breaking Rebecca's

reverie as it rattled the window on the small structure's south side. Braiding her hair into a thick plait, she readied herself for bed, thinking that now she had not one question to ponder but two.

The small fire she'd built had taken the chill out of the air, and she settled into the well-worn rocker with a quilt and the letters Auntie Jo had pressed upon her. The reason Jo had given them to her still wasn't clear in Rebecca's mind, but perhaps reading them would distract her from her cumbersome thoughts.

Thumbing through the stack, she noted various postmarks and Eli's distinctive script. Beginning with what seemed to be the first missive, dated September 24, 1864, she read of her great-uncle's sadness to be separated from his wife and home. Rebecca couldn't help but think that the more formal style of his written word stood in contrast with his colloquial speech.

> . . . just before we got to St. Paul a little girl came out and stood by the gate and waved her handkerchief and cried. I don't know if she had any friends in the troop or not, but I felt like crying along with her. An old woman also came out and waved her bonnet and said, "God bless you boys. May you live to come back."
>
> After the boat started, I could not help but think of you and wonder when—if ever—I shall see you again. . . .

Immediately engrossed in a story of which she'd only heard bits and pieces over the years, Rebecca realized she was most likely sitting in the same place, before the same stove, that Jo had sat reading these letters some twenty-six years before. How difficult it must have been for Jo to be alone, managing the farm on her own. And for Eli, journeying through adverse conditions to a fate unknown. A letter dated October described his travels.

> Rain, rain, rain. I never seen so much of the blame stuff in my life. We been marching. . . . I was never so happy to lay on the soft side of a brick floor as I was when we finally got through Indianapolis. Many of our rations are stale. . . .

Through both tears and smiles she read through the next several letters. Even in the face of such hardship, Eli's and Jo's love for one another radiated from these pages written over a quarter-century ago. Her uncle often gave voice to his conscience, as well, as advice for Jo's management of their farm.

> My dearest wife,
> Perhaps I write too often, but I am impatient to hear from you. I keep your picture with me and gaze often at your face, missing you. . . . I feel badly that so much has fallen to you while I am away, but I do not doubt our home is in capable hands. . . . We have landed in Tennessee. . . . Several of us have had the jaundice and I am feeling sore. All day today and yesterday we heard cannons. I am saddened to think of the fellows who have been sent to their Maker, leaving widows and orphans beyond any reckoning I care to do. . . . Don't let Harlan Loucks take down those trees on the east side of that clearing till a line is run. If they're on my side, I want them. If not, I don't care what he does.

The fire burned low, no longer keeping pace with the cold radiating from the walls. Shivering, Rebecca glanced up at the clock and was shocked to see the hour. A busy day of cleaning the cellar awaited her on the morrow, and here it was past eleven o'clock. With longing, she eyed the remainder of the letters, knowing it would be best to save them for later.

Yawning, she felt weariness both physical and mental. Looking around the shadowed interior of the cottage, she thought of the good life Eli and Jo had made here in Maple Grove. Eli had come home from the war uninjured, their farm had prospered, and their love for each other had grown stronger each year.

What, in her twenty years' experience, could remotely compare to the richness of their lives? She could barely conceive of encountering such challenging circumstances, let alone knowing such love. A nervous flutter danced across her ribs when she thought of Hugh Clark and the idea that he wished to court her.

If things were to . . . progress, would they realize such love as Eli and Jo? she wondered. What adventures lay in their future, or did a peaceful destiny await them? Would there be children?

No! She couldn't let herself think of such things. No man would dare sire children with a woman such as she. Some years ago, her parents had taken her to Dr. Neibling, a St. Paul physician specializing in skin diseases. She had overheard the serious-eyed doctor telling her parents it wasn't likely she would pass on the extensive *naevus vascularis* to any children she might bear, but that one could never be certain.

Though she'd never spoken of it to another soul, a dream had died inside her that day. From that point on she had never allowed herself to think of becoming a wife or mother. And now Hugh Clark with his kind hazel eyes had burst upon her life, daring to challenge her way of thinking . . . daring to call her *belle*. Beautiful.

Daring to ask her if she believed God is good.

Troubled, she added another log to the fire, blew out the lamp, and climbed into bed. "Just think about it," he'd urged after she'd first fumbled for an answer, then grown incensed at her failure to find a smooth reply.

For the most part, things had been on an even keel by the time they'd walked back to the farm with their empty buckets. Turning down Eli's invitation to stay for supper, the veterinarian had parted with a warm smile and the promise of joining them the following evening.

Tomorrow. He was coming again tomorrow . . . courting her . . . asking her questions she couldn't answer. The wind gusted again, sounding frigid and mournful. Between the cold sheets Rebecca tried to pray but soon gave up, feeling ashamed. She had always loved Jesus, but what if she did indeed doubt the Father's character?

Then what?

All of a sudden her life had taken a turn she had never anticipated, and she was finding it all too much to take in at once. Even the familiar milieu of the cabin failed to soothe her frayed feelings. Her mind continued to whirl while she sought one position after another, to no avail.

Sleep was a long time in coming.

❄

With a fresh bouquet of asters tucked safely out of harm's way, Hugh drove to the Woodman farm at twilight. Had he pushed Rebecca too hard by asking her about God yesterday? he wondered. It had just popped out of his mouth before he knew it. What about nearly kissing her? Would she even be glad to see him this evening?

By her demeanor, it was plain to see when she was thinking about her birthmark and when she wasn't. Perhaps he was too impatient about wanting her to believe he didn't care about the color of her skin, but he found the Rebecca who wasn't thinking about her markings an absolutely captivating young woman. Saucy, bright-eyed, witty, quick to smile. In his ardor he had pressed his fingers to those lovely lips, unprepared for the tender, protective feelings that had surged through him.

Rebecca. *Belle.* She was so beautiful, and it pained him to know she regarded herself as ugly. His father had been a grown man when his tragedy occurred, so the unkindnesses of others did not penetrate as deeply into his interior as they apparently had into Rebecca's.

Eli hailed him as he pulled in the drive. "Take your team on into the barn," he directed, "and come wash up. Bell's got supper just about ready."

After he'd seen to his horses, Hugh reached for the asters. "At least I can give her these tonight," he said aloud.

"Hoo-eeh! Flowers an' all!" Eli came up alongside the carriage. "You talkin' to yourself in here? Practicin' what you're gonna say?"

"No, but maybe I should," he said reflectively. "Things have been coming out my mouth lately that I have no intention of saying."

"It's been my experience that women manage to have a way of jumblin' a man's tongue," the older man agreed, chuckling. "That Bell, she's somethin', ain't she?"

"She is, indeed."

"Pretty, too, only she don't think much of her looks." Eli grew serious. "Over the years, Jo an' I have come to think of Rebecca as the granddaughter we never had. Stiff as a board, she was, when she first started coming to visit as a little tyke, but she soon loosened up an' became herself. It's funny, she's almost like two differ'nt people at times."

"You mean when she's thinking about her face and when she isn't?"

Eli gave him an assessing look in the lantern light. "You've got a quick understandin', young fellow. Don't let her shake you off."

"I'm not one to be easily shaken off," he replied with the beginnings of a grin. "But she's given it her best effort a time or two."

The older man sighed in agreement. "If you knew the things people have said to her face . . . about her face, well, you could see where a bit of defensiveness comes out when she meets strangers. After a while, once she figures they ain't gonna go on about her face, she settles back down an' is herself. I been prayin' she'll take a shine to you."

"Me too," Hugh replied, holding aloft the asters. "My father always knew how to bring a smile to my mother's face. I figured it couldn't hurt."

"Yep. Flowers. That'll get 'em every time." Eli nodded knowingly. "Come on inside now an' let's have some of that Eye-talian macaroni she's been talkin' about this afternoon. I don't recall eatin' such a dish before, but if it ain't no good, I know she's made a pile of molasses cookies for dessert. An' they're better'n good. Have I ever mentioned what a fine cook Bell is? Jo's taught her just about all she knows, an' . . ."

Hugh let the farmer talk as they walked to the house, wondering if he—and his bouquet of flowers—would be a welcome sight to the dark-eyed girl whose inner wounds he longed to heal.

CHAPTER FIVE

I don't believe I've ever eaten such tasty macaroni before. What do you think, Eli?"

"Not half bad," the older man replied to the younger, "but a bit heavy on the cheese."

"That's just what I like about it," replied the auburn-haired veterinarian, taking a large forkful of tender beef, noodles, and cheese coated with well-seasoned tomato sauce. "Your niece is skilled in the kitchen."

"Jo's turned her into a fair cook," Eli commented with a wink, "but don't swell up her head with too much sweet talk an' flattery."

"Yes, that's probably wise," Rebecca dished back, "considering what happened with those poor molasses cookies this afternoon. Pity . . ."

Her day of cellar cleaning and reorganization had been blessedly shortened by the arrival of Addie Unsell, a woman of impressive strength and work ethic whom Rebecca had known for years. Together they had scrubbed and disinfected the storage area beneath the house, removing every questionable food item and restocking the shelves with fruits and vegetables to last the winter.

Of course, Jo kept that room as tidy as every other and had already gotten a good start on putting away produce from her garden. Crocks and barrels lined the walls on a system of well-constructed shelves and supports, while bunches of herbs hung from hooks in the ceiling.

Rebecca couldn't explain how her short night of sleep had given her sufficient energy for her tasks, but when she had awakened she'd felt well rested and alert. The sharpness of the disquieting emotions she had experienced the evening before had dulled, leaving her state of mind contemplative rather than frantic.

Through the day, she had thought a great deal about Hugh's question—and Jo's, as well. And if she had forgotten, last evening, to turn her attention to the startling display of interest the handsome veterinarian had pressed on her lips, she had more than made up for it today. Thrice, the kindly Mrs. Unsell had teased her about woolgathering.

After their work in the cellar was finished, Rebecca had returned to the cottage to shed her dirty clothes. Washing from head to toe, she paused to inspect her face in the glass. The birthmark hadn't changed, of course, but she studied her lips, her eyes, her hair, pretending to see them as a stranger might. Her brows rose like elegant wings above nut-brown eyes, matching the lustrous locks framing her face. If she turned her head three-quarters to the left, she imagined someone might find her features . . . fair.

"What about 'em?" Eli's words brought her back from her thoughts as he strained to look over Hugh's shoulder, first toward the counter, then the pie safe. "Where's those cookies?"

She shrugged, feigning wide-eyed innocence. "Oh, Uncle Eli, they spread more than usual on the pan, so I thought it best not to serve them to company. You understand, I'm sure, since you always seem to find them lacking in some way. Thank goodness the batch didn't go to waste. Mrs. Unsell said her boys wouldn't mind if their cookies were flat or not."

"Dad blame! You went an' gave the whole batch to Mrs. Unsell?"

From the bedroom came delighted chuckling. "You've been had, you old rascal! Bell hid them in here, and if you don't stop making mischief about her cooking, I just might not tell you where they are."

"I got ways of makin' you talk, Missus Woodman." Eli's grin was roguish as he pushed his chair back from the table. "An' I'm comin' to find me some cookies!"

"I can see why you like it here," Hugh said through his laughter, his hazel gaze falling warm upon her. "I've never met a pair quite like these two."

Rebecca's heart came to another curious standstill as she studied Hugh's face over the supper table, remembering how his fingers had touched her cheek, her ear, her hair. And then how his lips had hovered over hers for just a second. The touch of his fingers on her lips had been warm and startling, and she wondered how his beard would have felt against her cheek. . . ."

"A penny for your thoughts, *belle*."

Dropping her gaze as quickly as she would a hot potato, she felt such a furious blush arise that she was sure her birthmark was indistinguishable from her unblemished skin. Quickly she stood and began gathering dishes, the pounding of her heart more than making up for its seeming cessation a few moments earlier.

His hand stayed hers. "I'd like to talk with you again. If I help you with dishes, will you take a ride with me?"

"I don't know if . . . I . . . where?"

"Just down the road aways. The moon is nearly full and orange as a pumpkin. I'll ask your uncle's permission . . . that is, if you'd like to go."

Nodding, Rebecca couldn't suppress the joyful smile that curved her lips. Of course she would like to go! For heaven's sake, she was being courted! Actually, truly, really courted. Happiness made her voice clear and strong as she lifted her gaze.

"Do you prefer to wash or dry, Dr. Clark?"

❄

A sheer veil of clouds had come up to mute the moon's vivid coloring. The wind blew from the northwest, tugging dried leaves from branches overhead and scattering them at will to the countryside below. The temperature was low enough to chill the end of Rebecca's nose and transform her breath into puffs of steam, but she found it refreshing.

Or was it simply being in Hugh Clark's company she found refreshing?

A mile passed while they alternately shared the details of their day and slipped into companionable silences. Hugh's grip on the reins was loose as the horses clopped along the gravel road at a slow, steady pace.

"Thank you for coming out with me tonight," he said, glancing over at her. "I wasn't sure if you wanted to spend time with me after the way I seem to blurt out what's on my mind. I must seem insufferably forward."

"You *are* a bit forward."

He sighed, shaking his head. "I fear I've acted like Lucky where you're concerned, bounding too far ahead for my own good. I'll try and slow down some."

"Actually, I've never been courted before, so I don't know the difference," she quipped, trying to lighten the heaviness she heard in his voice.

"We're even, then, because I've never called on anyone, either."

"You can't be telling the truth!" Rebecca was astonished at this revelation.

"I can't? Why not?"

"Because you're so . . ."

"Because I'm so?" The familiar grin reappeared, and he cocked his head toward her. "Because I'm so what?"

"Intelligent. Funny. Nice-looking." She all but whispered her disclosure. "I never thought any man would look at me twice."

"Well, you're selling yourself short, *belle.* I've looked at you more than twice and I plan to keep looking."

The gleam in his eye backed up his words, and Rebecca once more experienced the breathless, heart-stopping feeling with which she had recently become acquainted.

"I've never had the time nor inclination for courting," he said in a more serious tone. "I knew it was a financial strain for my parents to send me to veterinary college, and along with that came courses in medicine, surgery, chemistry, zoology, histology, ophthalmology, pathology, and any other 'ology' you can think of. Heifers were the closest things to girls I saw for the better part of three years."

"But . . . did you leave a girl back home?"

"Yes, I must confess I left Emily Tessier—"

At his reply, Rebecca's bubble of happiness burst. She should have known Hugh Clark's calling on her was too good to be true. Undoubtedly Miss Emily Whoever had the milkiest white complexion in all of Iowa—

"—back when I was eleven or twelve years old. She never did like me much, and I heard she married Tom Stratton a few years ago. So I come to you unencumbered by romantic entanglements. Excluding the heifers, of course."

He was teasing her. Without thinking, she raised her muffler and whapped the fluffy accessory soundly against his arm.

His deep-throated laughter filled the air. "Had you worried, did I?"

"Not a bit," she replied primly, finding it difficult not to succumb to his merriment.

"I've been thinking about something," he said, pulling the horses to a halt. "I know you're here to help your aunt, but next month I'm invited to spend a few days with my sister Deborah in Minneapolis—she's throwing a big party for her husband's thirtieth birthday. If Eli thinks he can spare you, well, I'd be honored to have you accompany me."

"I can't." Every trace of joy, gaiety and anticipation was swept away by an icy current of dread. She knew about the people of Minneapolis . . . how they whispered . . . and pointed . . . and stared.

"As my parents are so far away, I was hoping you might like to meet my sister." She heard the question in his voice but was powerless against the tide of self-disparaging thoughts rushing through her mind.

She felt his touch through the sleeve of her coat. "Rebecca, you look as though you're about to cry. Please tell me what you're thinking."

"I . . . I can't."

"Yet another 'I can't'? Does this have anything to do with what we talked about yesterday?"

She shrugged, fighting back the tears.

"Well, just for the sake of continuing this conversation, I'll assume that little dab of color on your face is the reason you won't consider going to Minneapolis with me."

"Oooh! You and your 'little dab of color'! Did you ever consider that I might know something about Minneapolis—after all, I *live* there!"

"Oh, of course. I'll have to speak to my sister, then, about how she treated you."

"You know I've never met your sister!" she cried in frustration, trying to make him understand why she had to protect herself. A sob choked her voice. "Every so often my friend Jane would talk me into going out in public, to the library, to a concert. My parents frowned on it, but she kept after me. 'Come on, Becky, it'll be fun. This time it's going to be different.' Well, it was *never* different."

Short of breath, she gulped in a lungful of cold air before continuing. "The only place I ever went was to church, and that wasn't much better. Only there I was known as 'John and Henrietta's poor daughter.' Maybe those don't sound like very good reasons for not going out in public, Dr. Hugh Clark, but they're good enough for me."

Two strong arms engulfed her shaking frame, pulling her toward a solid, manly torso. The dampness of her cheeks was absorbed by the coarse fibers of his wool coat, while gentle fingers untied her hat ribbons and stroked her upswept hair.

"Rebecca," his deep voice rumbled in her ear, "if I could take this pain from you, I would. You know all people aren't unkind or insensitive. Think of Eli, Jo, their fine neighbors . . . think of me. How about we do some reasoning together, *belle?*"

Reasoning! What could he possibly say that would stop the flood of unworthiness flowing through her?

"Remember what I asked you the other day?"

"Yes," came her grudging whisper.

"Well, I have another question for you: In whose image were you created, Rebecca Belanger?" His arms steadied her as she struggled to sit up. Reaching inside his coat, he produced a neat square of white linen and handed it to her.

"I suppose you're going to tell me God has a great big birthmark on his face." She accepted his handkerchief but not his words, dabbing her eyes and blowing her nose in a most unladylike manner.

"No . . . but I've heard his Son has a few scars."

"You shouldn't joke about God like that! It's just not . . . respectful."

"I'm not joking." Urgency showed in both his tone and expression, and he took her hands into his. "Think about it, *belle.* How much respect does it give the Almighty to declare that his creation is ugly?"

"What . . . what do you mean?" Rebecca's emotions were a jumble; his concepts struck her ears as both confusing and complex.

"I mean that the Good Book tells us we were created out of God's love—*in his image*—and because of that fact, we are good. *Very* good, the book of Genesis tells us. Rebecca, our dignity as persons rests in the fact that we are unique, beloved creations of the Creator. When I was younger, I used to take it to heart when people would say cruel things about my father. His burns were extensive—and so are his scars—and more than once I was sent home from school for using my fists to try and shut the mouths of the boys who taunted me for how my father looked. Yesterday you called yourself ugly." His voice dropped. "What was hardest to hear was the certainty in your voice."

"But—"

With a squeeze of his hand, he stopped her protest. "Let me ask you one more question: Do you think your life would be perfect if you didn't have a birthmark?"

"No," she whispered to her lap after a long silence, his syllogism crystallizing into perfect clarity.

"I realize I have known you only a few days, but I would like to know you many more, Rebecca . . . if you'll give me the chance. I'd like to make you a promise, too, if you'll make me one in return."

Taking a shuddering breath, she lifted her gaze to his.

"I promise I won't railroad you into doing anything you don't feel you can do, if . . ."

"If what?" she replied, feeling both weariness and hope course through her. Even in the near-darkness, she could see kindness, acceptance, and conviction shining from his countenance.

"If you promise to never again say you're ugly. You are a

lovely young woman, and I want you to repeat that ten times each day." His lips twitched with the beginnings of a grin.

"Only if you promise to limit yourself to asking me one question per day. I don't think I can cope with any more than that."

His laughter rang to the treetops. "I did just tell you I was going to stop blurting out what was on my mind, didn't I?" With a final squeeze of her hands, he shook the reins and set the horses back to walking, regaling her with a tale from his days of veterinary college.

Though traces of dampness lingered on her cheeks, a curious lightness of heart stole over her while she listened to his deep voice. What manner of man was Hugh Clark? She had never met—nor ever imagined—anyone like him. She knew she had much thinking to do about the things he had said, and she might even consider telling herself ten times a day that she was a lovely young woman.

But one thing was for certain: She wasn't going to his sister's party in Minneapolis.

CHAPTER SIX

Autumn dug in its heels, spitting northerly winds from leaden skies. Skeletal branches emerged from trees previously decked in carmine glory, and nightly coats of frost covered the land, freezing the topsoil and turning the creek edges into sharp, delicate lace. For the most part, the *clackety-clack* of threshing machines had fallen quiet. The harvest was in, and winter would soon spread its white cloak over the land.

Hugh Clark knew both joy and sadness as he thought of Rebecca. She had come a long way out of her shell in the weeks they had been seeing one another, yet there was a part of her that he couldn't seem to reach, no matter how hard he tried. When she was at ease, she was a charming and often witty conversationalist, as well as the most empathetic of listeners. As Eli had once said, her heart was pure gold.

She had been deeply moved by the missives her uncle had written home from the war and had shared excerpts and sometimes whole letters with him. After adorning the outside of Jo and Eli's house in anticipation of the upcoming holiday season and the first real snow, she had also placed

345

fresh pine boughs in the window boxes of the cottage. Her delight in having a domicile of her own was evident, the few glimpses he'd had of the interior revealing feminine warmth and hominess.

That womanly touch was something from which he could benefit, he acknowledged with longing as he glanced around his plain bachelor surroundings. Licking his finger, he tested the iron. Not quite hot enough. He sighed, wondering what the Lord had in store for him as far as Rebecca Belanger was concerned. If he was halfway in love before he'd even met her, he was at least three-fourths of the way there now.

As he had come to know her better, he discovered her earnest spirit of wanting to do the right thing. That she had faith in God he did not doubt, but years and years of believing something so wrong about herself—and the Lord—had built roadblocks to her having a vital and growing relationship with him. But what could be done to help her? Worse, her life experiences had only reinforced the falsehood. Jo and Eli had provided a loving sanctuary for her over the years, but only to a limited degree. It was impossible to completely shield Rebecca from the unkindness of others.

His love he offered freely, but even that wasn't enough. What had to change was something inside her, and that was up to God and Rebecca. For now, he must practice patience.

This time the iron sizzled when he touched his wet finger against its surface. Laying a starched white handkerchief across the ironing board, he smoothed its wrinkles and began the series of movements that were becoming second nature the longer he kept house. Fold, press, fold, press. A grin tugged at his lips as he guessed that his *belle* was responsible for approximately half of his soiled hankies.

She hadn't changed her mind about accompanying him to Minneapolis to attend Deborah's party, nor was the topic open for discussion. Whenever he broached the subject, she archly reminded him of his promise not to railroad her into anything she wasn't ready to do. Of course, in return he made her recite a full decade of "I am a lovely young woman."

Much laughter usually ensued such an episode, for she would roll her eyes and pull horrid faces while repeating the phrase. Deep down, though, sadness lingered inside him as he waited for her to truly believe the words she spoke.

Later today he would depart for Minneapolis—alone. But first he would drive out to the Woodman farm, for Rebecca had offered to care for Lucky while he spent the few days away. Who knew? Maybe she had changed her mind about going with him since he'd seen her yesterday. Fold, press, fold, press. Lucky dozed on his rug in the corner, opening one eye from time to time to observe his master's strange movements.

If you don't have hope, you don't have anything.

An oft-quoted saying of his mother's popped into mind as he set aside a handkerchief and reached for another. Perhaps Rebecca was packing right this minute, planning to surprise him. He had written both his parents and his sister about her, asking for their prayers.

He guessed he was just an optimist at heart. With God, anything could happen—anything at all.

And in just a short time from now, he would know if anything had happened.

❄

Watching the light and expectation leave the hazel eyes she had come to find so dear felt a little like dying, Rebecca discovered. She felt sick at heart for refusing to accompany him to meet his family, for no one had ever brought such joy into her life as Hugh Clark.

Over tea with Auntie Jo just a few days past, she allowed that she was falling in love with him. Whether or not he loved her in return she couldn't say for certain, but Jo was convinced he did. Eli, too. Uneasiness filled Rebecca as she wondered if she wasn't being horribly selfish about this whole situation.

"You're sure, then?"

"Yes."

"Well, then . . . I guess I'll be off."

"I'll take good care of Lucky for you," she called, reaching down to pet the tail-wagging mongrel sitting at her feet. She wished she could say more . . . she wanted to, but couldn't.

"I'm sure you will. So long, Rebecca. I'll be back for him when I return." His shoulders were stiff as he climbed into the carriage, his voice strained. With a nod, he shook the reins and was off.

He said he'd be back for the dog, but would he be back for her?

Lucky started after his master, but she held fast to his collar while the carriage departed. Smart dog—she should have the same inclination. If she valued her relationship with Hugh at all, why didn't she just shout his name? It would be so simple to tell him she'd reconsidered . . . tell him she'd go.

But she didn't.

Smaller and smaller the coach appeared, until it was swallowed by a distant bend in the road. With a deep, sad sigh, she walked up the path to the steps, Lucky trailing behind her. "I don't know how Auntie Jo will feel about having you in the house, but we'll give it a try," she spoke to the canine.

As it turned out, Jo welcomed Lucky's presence in her sickroom. "As long as he behaves himself," she admonished. Obediently, he lay down on the scatter rug next to her bed and closed his eyes.

"Goodness, Bell, you look as though you lost your last friend." The sharp blue eyes swept over her appearance, not missing a thing.

"I think I just did."

"Did you quarrel with Hugh?"

"No, but maybe it would have been better if we had. I know I hurt him by not going . . . only he was too polite to tell me so."

"I see."

She heard no condemnation in her great-aunt's voice, yet Rebecca felt ashamed before her. She shook her head. "I should have gone."

"You could still go, Bell. Eli would take you to the train . . . or heavens, take you all the way to Minneapolis, if you wanted. We'll make out fine here without you for a few days. I can eat on that roast you've got in the oven from now till next week."

Meeting Hugh's sister wasn't what brought up the old, familiar feelings of dread. It was the thought of facing a roomful of staring strangers, enduring the discomfort that would certainly follow.

Is that too great a price to pay for being Hugh Clark's friend? Think of what kind of friend he's been to you . . .

"Auntie Jo, would you excuse me? I need to get out . . . take a walk."

"Mercy, Bell! It's heading on towards dark, and the mercury's dropping like a stone. You don't want to be out there. Why don't you just go out to the cottage for a spell?"

"I need to walk," she persisted, the urge to move—to get away—running high. Her emotions were agitated and comfortless, and she was sure the elements couldn't make her feel any worse than she already felt. "I'll take Lucky with me, and I'll be back to make gravy before you know it." Forcing a smile as she arose from the chair, she called the dog and left the bedroom before the gathering tears spilled from her eyes.

❄

Forgetting her gloves was a blunder she sorely regretted. Not immediately, for at first her distressing thoughts overrode all tactile sensations. It was when she turned to walk back to the farm, a good mile down the road, that she felt the cutting edge of the north wind. She also became aware that darkness had almost completely fallen, its descent accelerated by the gray, forbidding skies. A fine mist stung her cheeks.

Shivering, she pulled her hands more deeply into the sleeves of her coat. "Sorry you have to share my misery, Lucky," she said, noticing that the dog headed into the wind with his nose pointed to the ground. He stopped midstride to look up at her, cocking his head with what appeared to be sympathy. His tail beat back and forth like a brush.

"You're such a good dog," she said with a sigh, wondering why animals could display more virtuous traits, oftentimes, than humans. "Hugh sure found himself a champion when he—Lucky!" Her compliment ended in an outcry as the multicolored dog suddenly growled and streaked from the road to the dried underbrush, his missing limb not seeming to hamper his progress whatsoever.

"Lucky! Come back here! Lucky!" she cried again and again, quickly losing sight of him. He barked once, twice, then fell silent. The crashing of branches and leaves grew more faint until the only thing sounding in her ears was the bluster of the wind.

"Now what?" she spoke aloud, pacing back and forth. The mist had changed to tiny, sharp grains of sleet. "Lucky!" she tried again several more times to no avail. They were still a mile from the farm, and his flight had taken him even farther away.

What was she going to do? Worse yet, how could she tell Hugh she'd lost his dog? He had entrusted Lucky to her care, and she had disappointed him in even that simple thing. The sleet grew more forceful, hissing as it hit the trees and ground. "Lucky!" she called again, her cries swallowed by the inclement weather.

She eyed the underbrush and woods with indecision, not knowing the wisest course of action. Not a soul was in sight, nor did she see any houses or lights. Returning to the farm to enlist Eli's help would be futile . . . full darkness would be upon her before she traveled even half the distance. Too, upon returning, how could she be sure of the exact place where Lucky had disappeared?

Her decision was made when she thought again of Hugh, of the hurt and sadness she'd seen in his eyes when he'd departed. She'd wounded him with her refusal to go to his sister's party; she couldn't hurt him again. Into the underbrush she hastened, her skirt catching on spiky stems and branches.

"Lucky!" she tried again, the crisp tangle of low-growing vegetation finally yielding to a stand of hardwood. Here the ground was easier to traverse, but large, dark trunks and branches blotted out what little light there was. Her eyes strained in the gloom. "Oh, Lord," she half prayed, half sobbed, "please help me find this dog. I know what Lucky means to Hugh, and I just can't let him down again."

Bewilderment set in as she looked first to the right, then to the left, trying to discern in which direction to begin searching. "Lucky!" she called, stepping forward, only to trip over a good-sized branch buried by leaves.

"Ooh!" she cried, the heels of her hands stinging from the sudden impact. Dampness soaked her skirt and chilled her knees, intensifying her icy state. Her shoes and socks were sodden.

"Come on, boy," she entreated, picking herself up and moving ahead. "Please, Lucky!" Her progress was slow on the slick forest floor, its relative flatness soon giving way to a significant downward slope. She realized the creek would be ahead of her. Fresh worry filled her. What if Lucky, on his three legs, had tripped or fallen down the hill . . .

Had she just heard a voice? She stopped, grabbing hold of

a sapling for support on the slippery incline, while she strained to listen. Again she heard something and very nearly shouted her position, but there was a quality to the sound that raised a chill having nothing to do with the weather.

Instinctively she knew it was evil.

Physical discomforts forgotten, Rebecca shrunk against the trunk of the sapling, wishing it were big enough to hide behind. The voice was louder now, more distinct, its owner clearly in a rage. Filthy words and dreadful threats spewed from his mouth, directed toward the person he was searching for.

Scarcely breathing, she held fast to the tree, guessing that the dangerous-sounding man was sweeping the creek bottom. The dual cover of storm and darkness suddenly became her friend, and amidst her prayer for deliverance, she thanked God for the disguise he'd provided.

After what seemed like endless hours, the man's voice grew faint. Waiting until she no longer heard anything but the hiss of the storm, she collapsed at the base of the tree. Muffled, hacking sobs escaped from her throat as she realized the direness of her situation. Not only was Lucky lost, but she was lost as well.

Tears spent, she resolved to try and find her way out of the forest. If she walked directly up the hill in the direction from which she'd come, perhaps she would eventually make her way back to the road. The danger came in losing her direction once she reached level ground. Too, fear of the snarling man kept her from crying out for help. What if she was trespassing on his land? He'd made no secret of the fact that he was more than willing to do bodily harm. . . .

A branch cracked behind her. With a gasp she spun her head while trying to maintain her hold on the sapling. Fresh fear made her arms and legs rubbery, inefficient, putting her in danger of falling down the bank. Heart flopping within her chest, she tried to speak, to let the terrifying man know she was simply lost, that she meant no harm.

But the point of something thrust suddenly into the small of her back cut off the appeal lodged in her throat.

CHAPTER SEVEN

The familiar muzzle was insistent, pressing again and again into her back, her side. Relief washed over her, making her limbs weak and her quivering heart thump in hasty tempo. "Lucky!" she breathed, turning to enfold the dog in her arms. But he would have nothing to do with her embrace.

"You scared the wits out of me," she scolded in a low voice, mindful that the violent-sounding man might still be near. "What are you—ow! . . . Lucky!" she exclaimed as he dug his nose harder into her ribs.

"All right, I'm getting up. Let's get out of here and go home. You *can* get us out of here, can't you?" Her skirt sodden and heavy, she struggled to rise. "Come on, boy," she whispered, climbing a few steps up the hill. Reaching behind her, she felt for his wet coat, her hand swishing nothing but air.

"Lucky, where are you?" Squinting, she could just make out his silhouette, still beside the sapling. "Come *on*, Lucky. Let's go home."

He didn't move.

Exasperated, she step-slid back to the tree, determined to take him by the collar. "I mean it, dog. We're leaving. You dragged me out here in the middle of these woods on this wild chase and made me listen to that scary man shout those awful things that would scald my ears if I weren't so cold. It's storming, in case you haven't noticed!"

As her icy fingers fumbled for his collar, she realized she was babbling. "Come," she commanded in the sternest voice she could muster. But Lucky didn't budge, countering his weight against her tug. Instead, he whined, an urgent, plaintive sound.

"You're hurt!" Realization dawned upon her, redoubling her anxieties. Even if she could make her way out of the woods, she doubted she could carry the good-sized dog the entire way home. She groaned, sinking down beside him. "Oh no, boy, what are we going to do?"

With another whine, he vaulted from her, heading neither up nor down the hill, but sideways. "Ooh!" she cried, lurching to her feet. "You'd better not be hurt, because when I get ahold of you, you're going to think about changing your name!"

Onward they went, perhaps thirty yards, with Lucky whining and staying just out of her reach. Several times she fell, once striking her side hard against a leaf-buried stone. "Lucky," she pleaded through the lancing pain in her ribs. "I don't understand what you're . . . I can't do this anymore. I have to . . . stop." Sinking down upon her haunches, she bowed her head in surrender, utterly lost.

Lucky whined again before returning to her side, nudging the outside of her arm with his snout. "I can't play this game with you," she wept, noticing that the darkness was all but complete. "We're lost, you fool dog, and no one knows where we are."

With another mournful whimper, Lucky bounded from her.

"I'm not following you—," she started to say, her blood running colder than the night when she heard a child's voice.

"Doggy? Is that you again?"

Rebecca shook her head incredulously, wondering if she were imagining things.

"Oh, Doggy, I'm so glad you came back," the child spoke again, the voice coming from just ahead. "I think Pa's gone now. I don't hear him no more."

"Hello?" Rebecca ventured, the pain in her side forgotten. "Is there someone out here?"

Silence.

God in heaven, there was a small child out in this storm. A shudder of horror coursed through her as she realized this little one was most likely the object of the man's pursuit. "That nice doggy is with me," Rebecca called, her voice quavering with both cold and emotion. "His name is Lucky."

More silence.

Having little experience with children, she didn't know what to say to draw the youngster out. "He brought me out here to find you because he knew you were cold," she attempted. "I mean you no harm."

Several long seconds passed before a reply was forthcoming. "Do y'have any food?"

"I don't have any with me, but I know where we can get a nice, warm dinner. Where are you, sweetheart?"

"B'hind a tree."

"Can I come to you?"

Again there was a long pause. "I'll come out, but you have t'tell me where you're at. I cain't see nothin'."

"Lucky will help you find me," she suggested, scrabbling along the hillside toward the sound of the child's voice. "What's your name?"

"Hannah."

"Hannah? What a . . . lovely name." Exertion and distress

caused her breath to come in puffs. "Do you know . . . Hannah from the Bible?"

"No." The child's voice was near now, just ahead. Sleet continued to hurtle from black skies, grainy and frigid.

"I'm in . . . front of you now, Hannah. If you keep walking, you'll come right to me."

"What's your name?"

"Rebecca."

"I get whopped for talkin' to strangers."

"Well, we're not strangers any longer. I know your name and you know mine." Her fingers closed around a tiny, thin wrist. Like hers, the hand was bare. Rebecca's heart clenched when she pulled the child close and discovered she wore no coat. Without a thought, she began unbuttoning hers. "We're going to sit by this tree for a spell, Hannah," she said, "and help each other warm up."

"I *was* gettin' cold."

"Why, in this weather, I'm certain you were!" she exclaimed, her nose protesting at the unwashed odors arising from the girl. Bracing her back against a tree, she enfolded the bony child in her arms and lapped the front edges of the overgarment about her. "See? We both fit."

"Oohh!" Hannah breathed as they made a clumsy pitch to the ground. Lucky pressed himself close beside them. "It feels good to be out of the wind."

"Are you lost, Hannah?" she began, not knowing how to ask the youngster about her troubles. The ravings of the girl's father had left Rebecca still feeling weak in the knees. No one, least of all a child, deserved such treatment.

"Not if it wasn't night. I come out here a lot when my pa gets nettled. I go back in the mornin', when he's sleepin'."

She stayed outdoors all night? Rebecca swallowed, judging that the child couldn't be more than seven years old. "Do you have a mother?"

"Yes."

"Well . . ." Her thoughts raced as she searched for words. "What does she do when your father becomes . . . angry?"

"Nothin'. She don't talk much." The child sighed, snuggling more closely. "You smell good. Where does the other Hannah live?"

"I don't *know* the other Hannah because she lived a long time ago."

"Was she nice like you?"

"She was very nice, and she loved God with all her heart. Have you . . . do you know about God?"

The thin shoulders shrugged against her breast. "Pa says mean things 'bout him."

"Sometimes people get the wrong idea about God and believe things about him that aren't true. But God is good, Hannah, very, very good." Holding this neglected child in her arms, Rebecca felt the truth of those words penetrate deep into her heart. What would have happened to this little lamb tonight if Lucky had not brought them together? Was it possible that the Lord had woven together this mysterious set of circumstances to rescue Hannah's life? Her voice broke as she added, "Not only is he good, but he loves you with his whole heart."

"No one loves me." The words were so quiet that she might easily have missed them.

"Oh, Hannah, that's not true," she countered. "It's because of God's love for you that he made you . . . and he knows you better than anyone—inside and out. Why else do you think he sent Lucky and me along tonight? He knew you needed some help and that you were hungry and cold."

"I been hungry other times. Why din't you come then?"

A deep sigh escaped Rebecca, and she wrapped her arms more tightly around the child. "I don't know. I wish I could have come the very first time you were hungry or cold, but for some reason the Lord wanted me to come tonight."

A small hand came up and touched her benumbed cheek.

"You're nice. My aunt Sharlit, she's nice, too, but Pa don't let her come over no more."

"How about you come over to my house tonight, Hannah? The first thing we'll do is get warm, and then we'll eat a lovely dinner of roast beef and potatoes and gravy. I have a nice, soft bed with lots of covers, and I'm going to tuck you right in the middle of it."

"Is that where Doggy sleeps?"

She couldn't suppress the chuckle that burst from inside her. "I think Doggy can sleep just about anywhere he pleases tonight."

"I like your laugh." The little voice became wistful. "You're lucky. You're big. You got everything an' you know everything, even 'bout God. You're always happy, ain't you?"

"Oh, Hannah, I don't—"

"An' I bet you're a beautiful, beautiful lady. Like a princess."

If you only knew.

Her discomfiture at the youngster's words made the toll of the past hour too much to bear. As soon as they got home—if they got home—Hannah was going to see her face. What would she think of her beautiful princess then?

"I'd say it's time to go have our dinner," Rebecca announced with false brightness. "We'll have to travel a little ways, but I'm going to wrap you as snug as can be in my coat, so you'll stay warm."

"What about you?"

"I'll be just fine, sweetheart. Remember? I'm big."

Her words were a lie . . . all her words were lies. Could she honestly profess the kind of faith she'd presented to this girl? Hugh Clark had made short work of slicing through the tangled ball of falsehoods surrounding her heart, but she still didn't have the kind of faith it took to walk through life with her mottled face, blessing God at every turn.

The frenzy of the sleet and wind striking her was worse than she'd anticipated without her coat, nearly unbearable. As the three made their awkward ascent up the bank, Rebecca prayed aloud the words of Psalm 23, hoping that God in his mercy was indeed with them.

And that if they made it safely from this place, he would lead her in the path of righteousness, for his name's sake.

❄

Eli picked them up a half mile from the farm.

As Lucky had guided Rebecca to Hannah, he led them both from the woods to the road. Without the relative shelter of the trees, the wind was a dreadful thing. Staggering down the road with the weak, exhausted child in her arms more often than not, Rebecca felt as if she must be in the midst of a dream.

But then she saw a light in the distance and heard her uncle's voice calling her name over and over. Never had she seen him look as old as he did when he finally reached them. Without a word, he loaded child, woman, and dog into the box of his wagon, covered them with horse blankets, and turned his team into the wind.

After what seemed like an eternity, they were safely in the barn and the doors had been swung shut. The sound of the storm was subdued but echoing in the tall structure.

"What's your name, sweet pea?" he asked the ragged youngster. Burrowing her head in Rebecca's chest, the girl didn't answer.

"You can talk to Eli, honey," Rebecca assured the child. "He's my uncle, and he's taken us to his home. You'll be safe here, and well cared for." Though they'd been out of the wind a short time, her face was still numb, her words sounding as though they were too carefully formed.

"Can we eat?"

"That's the first thing we'll do once we get into some

warm, dry clothes." Over the girl's head she spoke to Eli. "Her name is Hannah. Lucky led me to her in the woods . . . her father was . . . after her."

"Am I right in guessin' you'd be a Scruggs, darlin'?" Eli's weathered face was set in a grim cast.

Against her chest, Hannah nodded.

"She says yes."

"S'what I thought. Think you can manage things, Bell? I've got a call to pay before the weather gets worse."

He intended to go back out into the night? In her opinion, the weather could hardly get worse. "But Uncle Eli—," she protested, fearing for his safety. She fell silent at the fire blazing from the blue eyes beneath the brim of his hat.

"Go on in the house, Bell, and take care of the child. I'll be back when I'm finished."

Chapter Eight

Once warmed, fed, and bathed, little Hannah Scruggs gave an account of her home life that brought tears of sadness and outrage to Rebecca's eyes. If she lived to be a hundred, she knew the things she learned from this child would never leave her memory.

Hannah and her brother Howie had been forced to hide during Jo's visits to their farm, but the girl recognized Rebecca's kindly aunt and took to her immediately. When Eli opened the back door some two hours after he had rescued them from the elements, Hannah was curled up next to Jo on the bed, sound asleep.

The lamp in the bedroom burned low, and Jo and Rebecca had long since finished their tea. The storm had lessened, bursts of sleet hitting the side of the house only infrequently. Neither of them had voiced their worry about Eli's safety, but Rebecca saw that Jo's relief at his return was as great, if not greater, than her own.

"Aw," he said, coming to the doorway and viewing the scene before him. Deep red suffused his cheeks exposed to the cold and wind, and he reached in his pocket for his handkerchief. "Poor little tyke. I bet she's never been warm an' dry an' all tucked in."

"Just where have you been, Eli?" Jo asked in a quiet voice, glancing at the sleeping child beside her.

"Don't worry, woman, I didn't go chargin' right into the Scruggs place, if that's what you're thinkin'."

Jo's expression said more than any word she could have spoken.

"First I went to see Chet Evans, an' then we got the constable." Eli stepped into the room and pulled up a chair beside Rebecca. She had heard of C. E. Evans, the justice of the peace living down the road.

"And then?" Jo persisted.

"An *then* we went chargin' into the Scruggs place. Only Barter was out cold from whatever poison he pours down his hatch. The missus jus' sat there starin' at the wall, but their boy—he's about nine—was only too happy to leave. Constable Owens took Scruggs away to lock him up, an' Evans took the woman an' her son to spend the night. Apparently there's an aunt who's wanted the children for some time." He shook his head. "It's my guess she'll get 'em now."

"Aunt Charlotte. Hannah told me about her," Rebecca said softly.

"As soon as the weather clears, Chet's holding an inquest." Eli looked gravely at his niece. "You'll be asked to testify before a jury."

Testify . . . before a jury? With all eyes trained on her? She hadn't had anything like this in mind when she'd scooped up Hannah and taken her home. But before she could protest, he went on.

"Chet suspects this'll be a criminal matter, so you'll most likely be testifyin' again before a Hennepin County jury when the trial comes up."

"I . . . I don't . . . I can't!" she burst out.

Hannah stirred but did not awaken, and Jo gazed at her

with tenderness before turning those expressive blue eyes toward her niece. "Take one thing at a time, Bell," she said. "The most important thing is that you saved this child and her brother from further maltreatment. We'll stand beside you with whatever comes next."

Eli buried his head in his hands. "I could just kick myself for not doin' anything before now. I knew things weren't right at the Scruggses', an' I did nothin'.'"

Jo sighed. "I stand just as guilty, but neither of us had any proof beyond what we suspected. Thank the Lord for moving his hand of justice tonight by puttin' Bell where he did. I have confidence that Barter Scruggs will get his due."

Eli shrugged. "Maybe."

"Let's all get to bed and have a good night's sleep," Jo suggested. "Perhaps things won't look quite so glum in the morning. Bell, why don't you stay in the house tonight?"

"As long as Hannah's asleep, I think I'll go out to the cottage," she replied, rising, feeling the exhaustion seeping from deep within her bones. Auntie Jo's broken hip . . . handsome Hugh Clark and all his challenges . . . a neglected child driven out into a storm . . . the specter of testifying before not one jury but two.

Why had all these things happened to her since her arrival in Maple Grove? she silently questioned, feeling all thoughts of peace spin wildly away from her. Eli and Jo's farm had always been a sanctuary, a haven from the many adversities of life. The cottage, especially, had always been a retreat where she found joy and renewal.

Why now, she asked the Lord, had her place of peace become home to a host of hardships?

❄

Humming, Hugh Clark drove out Territorial Road toward the Woodman farm. The sun shone from a sky of glazed sapphire, and a brisk wind threatened to yank his hat from his head. The evidence of the ice storm that had struck the area had melted, leaving the Saturday morning countryside looking much as it had before he left.

It had been wonderful to see Deborah and her family in Minneapolis, and the time away had given him fresh perspective about his relationship with Rebecca. He looked forward to sharing the details of the party and of his visit, hoping that she would one day soon be willing to meet his sister . . . and his parents.

Only a twinge of hurt remained when he thought of her refusal to accompany him. It had occurred to him that he had only had a few weeks to combat what had been, for her, a lifetime of hurts. If his instincts could be trusted, he suspected she was as interested in him as he was in her. Once the issue of her birthmark was laid to rest, they would be free to pursue whatever the Lord might have in mind for them.

He smiled, thinking ahead to that day.

Lucky was good medicine for whatever ailed a person. His bouncy, optimistic nature and soulful eyes could melt the heart of even the most cantankerous curmudgeon. Hopefully the canine had been able to provide Rebecca with his special brand of comfort.

Sunlight struck the shingles of the Woodman farm, making short work of the morning frost. He didn't have much time to spend with his *belle* today, but perhaps they could make plans for Thanksgiving . . . even Christmas.

To his disappointment, she did not answer his knock at the house. Strange, Lucky wasn't to be seen or heard either. He was ready to turn and seek Eli in the barn when he heard Jo's faint, "Hugh Clark, come in!"

"Hello?" he called, opening the door.

The older woman's voice was urgent. "I saw you coming up the drive. Bell's not here, but the inquest is being held over at the schoolhouse. If you hurry, you can still make it."

Had she said *inquest?* In heaven's name, what had happened in the few short days he'd been away? Alarm tripped his senses and sent him toward the bedroom with long strides. "Pardon my boots on your floor, Mrs. Woodman, but just what is going on? Why in heaven's name is Rebecca involved with an inquest?"

Five short minutes later he had a summary of the facts and was speeding toward the schoolhouse. If Rebecca had been fearful of going to a mere party, how was she going to handle giving such important testimony before the company of a justice of the peace, a jury . . .

And especially the accused?

❄

The school yard was filled with horses, wagons, and carriages. Hastening up the wide clapboard structure's front steps, Hugh heard an indistinguishable but commanding voice say something, followed by a woman's soft reply.

Trying to make as quiet an entrance as possible, he slipped through the door and took the nearest chair. His heart clenched at the sight of Rebecca seated at the front of the room, giving her answer to the white-bearded, distinguished gentleman occupying the teacher's desk. In his hand was a pen; as Rebecca spoke he made notations in a good-sized ledger.

Approximately fifty student seats faced forward, a full half of them occupied by persons who had long since outgrown their dimensions. On the front and side walls of the room hung blackboards and an assortment of maps. Six large, curtained windows lit the room, beside one of which stood two men.

"I see, I see." The justice of the peace paused after Rebecca's response, stroking his beard. "While you were in the woods, you heard Mr. Scruggs say some things. Would you tell the jury what you heard?"

Rebecca visibly shrunk. "I . . . I couldn't repeat that kind of language."

"For the record, Miss Belanger, you must tell us what you heard."

She closed her eyes, nodded, and took a breath. Upon opening her eyes, she fixed her gaze toward the back of the room, starting slightly when she noticed Hugh. "He said . . ."

If Hugh had been shocked at Jo Woodman's brief account of things, he was sickened as Rebecca recounted the terrifying, vile threats Barter Scruggs had bellowed out to his young daughter. On top of that, the man had chased his own seven-year-old child out into the woods, during a storm . . . apparently not caring if she returned home or not.

"Can you think of anything else?" Justice of the Peace Evans queried after Rebecca had finished.

"She didn't even have a coat," Rebecca added, her voice choking. "A defenseless little—"

"More like a willful, disobedient little brat!" a raspy, sardonic voice interrupted. "And where did you come up with this . . . this *woman* here? Why, I've seen boils on my backside better lookin' than she is!"

Three times the gavel struck the desk. "Mr. Scruggs, I must warn you again not to—"

"Well, look at her!" Scruggs persisted, rising from his chair to face the jury. "All blotched up an' ugly! Are you going to believe a person stained with . . . such devil's marks? She's a witch, a spawn of Satan, doin' his—"

Fury boiled inside Hugh as he watched his beloved endure the unkempt man's verbal blows, and he found himself on his feet, heading toward the front of the room. He noticed Eli had risen from the front row as well, body tight and fists clenched.

"Order!" shouted Evans, banging his gavel furiously. He nodded to the two men near the window, who came forth to subdue the offensive man. The room erupted in a clamor while Evans continued to strike the wooden mallet against the desk.

Through this, Rebecca continued to sit woodenly in her chair, her head bowed in resignation. She wore a dress Hugh had not seen before, a finely tailored blue and gray garment that showed the beauty of her feminine form in a tasteful, elegant way. Her hair gleamed in its upswept arrangement. He imagined she had selected her finest clothing for this ordeal, carefully preparing for the worst yet praying to God it wouldn't happen.

Finally, some semblance of order was restored to the proceedings. "I have heard enough," Evans proclaimed, setting down his gavel in a manner that spoke of his displeasure, "to render judgment in this examination. Besides hearing Miss Belanger's sworn testimony, I have also heard much from both young Scruggs children regarding their home environment." He leveled his gaze at Scruggs. "And I have, with my own eyes, witnessed their home environment. By law and fact, sufficient evidence has been presented to warrant this case a criminal matter, and I hereby judge and determine that the accused, Barter Scruggs, will be tried at Hennepin Country District Court for the neglect and endangerment of his children. He will be detained—"

The remainder of Evans's judgment was lost in the ensuing hubbub, as the two constables forcibly removed Scruggs from the schoolroom. Eli was the first to reach his niece, throwing a protective arm about her. But she did not raise her head, keeping it bowed, as if in shame.

"Rebecca!" Hugh called, pushing past the jurors rising from their chairs. "Rebecca . . . *belle!*"

At that, her head lifted. "Don't call me that anymore," she said, regarding him with hollow eyes. "And if you have another one of your 'questions' for me today, Dr. Clark, I don't believe I've got an answer."

Eli shot Hugh a helpless, sympathetic look as she rose stiffly from the chair and walked toward the door without a backward glance.

Chapter Nine

Finding little for which to be grateful, Rebecca passed Thanksgiving week miserably. Over and over Barter Scruggs's vicious words ran through her mind. All she could think of was that sometime early in the coming year she would have to endure the judicial process—and his malevolence—all over again.

The only bright spot in this entire matter was that Hannah and her brother had been removed to their Aunt Charlotte's home in Dayton. Mrs. Smith had been contacted and had come for her niece and nephew just before the inquest. Her manner was both gentle and kind, and Rebecca trusted that the maltreated children would soon thrive under her loving care. Mrs. Scruggs, her sister, had been taken to the state hospital in St. Peter for treatment of her insanity.

Curiously, not once during the time Hannah had spent with Rebecca had the girl said anything about her face. While the youngster was saying good-bye to Lucky, Rebecca had impulsively offered for her to take the dog until she was settled in. Eyes glowing, the girl had wrapped her arms first around Lucky's neck and then had flown into Rebecca's arms. With laughter, Mrs. Smith declared that Lucky would be set a place at the head of the table for all he had done. Rebecca hoped Hugh would approve of her gesture, suspecting he would have done the same thing in her position.

She need not have feared. Uncle Eli conveyed to her that Dr. Clark was pleased with her decision. He also wished to meet with her at her earliest convenience, Eli had passed on, not able to keep himself from expressing his opinion that she should do so at once.

But November slid into December and she continued to avoid Hugh Clark, and to a large degree, God, as well. From the cottage each night she cried out sad and angry prayers, expecting no replies. It wasn't fair that she'd been born with the curse of such a birthmark, not fair at all. She scoured the Scriptures, reread each of Eli's letters to Jo, finding consolation nowhere. Throughout her days she tended her aunt and moved from one chore to the next, consumed with dread at the upcoming trial.

The wind soughed about the cottage, sounding to her as mournful as her frame of mind. She eyed the bed, knowing sleep was far off. With a sigh, she picked up the stack of her uncle's letters and selected one at random.

February 13, 1865

South Tunnell
. . . what you wrote about waking up crying made me feel the most helpless and homesick I have been since leaving Maple Grove. What a tragedy it is that our newest daughter also rests in her grave rather than in your arms. Dearest Jo, please do not lose heart in this battle of life. Remember what cannot be cured must be endured. With the help of our heavenly Father . . .

What cannot be cured must be endured? Her eyes flicked back over that particular phrase, and she wondered how she had missed it in earlier readings. Tears came to her eyes as she imagined Auntie Jo sitting in this same place during the dead of winter, grieving the loss of her children with no sympathy or encouragement save a packet of letters written by a far-off husband whose fate was also uncertain. How had she ever managed?

Just then came a brisk knock at the cottage door, causing Rebecca to start violently. "Who is it?" she called, feeling as though her heart had come to rest somewhere near her tonsils.

"Hugh Clark, Rebecca."

Hugh? What was he doing here at this time of night?

"I spoke to your uncle. We saw that your lamp was still lit. He gave me permission to call on you, but he's standing out on the porch counting off five minutes and not a second longer."

"Just a moment," she called, not doubting for an instant that her great-uncle had said such a thing. In some form or manner he managed to mention Hugh Clark in every third sentence he spoke.

A burst of cold air swept into the cottage when she opened the door, and she noticed a light snow had begun since she'd left the big house. A white dusting covered the russet hair and broad shoulders of the man standing on her threshold. He held his battered brown hat in his hands.

"May I come in?" His breath rose in so many clouds, disappearing into the night. "The mercury's dropped since I left home."

Nodding, she opened the door to allow him entrance. Anxiety knotted her stomach as her thoughts raced one way, then another, trying to devise an explanation—or excuse?—for avoiding him. With her distress also came twin waves of longing and remorse, much stronger than she'd ever expected.

What kind of fool had she been to cut off all contact with a man whose heart contained so much goodness? Her eyes drank in the sight of his familiar form while he stamped the snow from his boots and hung his hat and coat on the peg next to hers. She recalled the sunny fall day they'd met, remembering how he'd all but swept her off her feet with his bold, wooing words. Such romance she had never expected in an entire lifetime.

And then there was his courtship of her in the ensuing weeks. Seeing Hugh Clark tonight brought back every wonderful emotion of the autumn, all the hope and expectancy, every flutter of burgeoning love.

"I hear the Scruggs children are doing well. Best of all, their father is locked up until the trial," he commented, pulling a straight-backed chair up before the stove. Rubbing his hands together, he held them near the radiant heat. "Ahh, much better. Aren't you going to join me where it's not so cold?"

At the mention of Barter Scruggs, Rebecca recoiled inside. The words the evil man had spoken about her appearance slithered through her soul with the coldness of a serpent. *All blotched up an' ugly . . . stained with the devil's marks . . . spawn of Satan . . .*

"Eli was telling me about the letter Mr. Evans got from their aunt this week," he went on, "thanking all of you for what you did for Hannah and her brother. Just think, Rebecca, if not for you . . . who knows what might have happened?"

"It could have been anyone," she said stiffly, dragging her feet toward the warmth of the fire and the pair of hazel eyes regarding her. "Anyway, Lucky found her—he's the real hero."

"Hmm, and you just happened to be in the right place at

the right time to meet up with her, during a storm, deep in the woods? And let's not forget who carried the little one to safety. A dog would have been hard-pressed to do that, or for that matter give his legal testimony, *belle*."

Belle? How could he say that? She was the furthest thing possible from beautiful. Molten anger sparked when she thought of her birthmark and of all the things she had suffered on account of it. Hands on her hips, she found herself unable to take her seat. "I thought I asked you never to call me that again," she challenged. "And what really brings you here tonight? I'm sure it wasn't to talk about Hannah Scruggs."

"Well," he said, his grin cautious, "I did have it in mind to ask you to the Dennings' Christmas party on Saturday night. Martha stopped me one day and—"

She shook her head and held up a hand. "We need to clear the air about some things, Dr. Clark."

"I agree, *belle*," he asserted, also taking to his feet, "and I *will* call you that because I *do* believe you are beautiful." Frustration colored his expression. "Rebecca, I thought for a time that you might have feelings for me. Was I mistaken? Was it only my imagination that you trembled when I touched your face that day out on the road?" He dragged his hand through his hair. "Do you realize how close I came to kissing you that day? I think you do, and what's more, I think you wanted me to."

Rebecca swallowed, remembering through her anger the wild mix of emotions she'd experienced that sun-gilded afternoon.

"*Belle*, I've wanted to kiss you a thousand times since then—no, make that *ten* thousand times—but I've held back, not wanting you to have the wrong idea about me." He held his palms upward in supplication. "Is it too much to hope that you might feel the same about me? I think I've fallen—"

"Stop. Don't say it," she interrupted through the tears

spilling from her eyes. Her voice sounded brittle in her ears. "I've been thinking about you, too—"

The tension left Hugh's face and he lowered his arms. A joyous smile turned up the corners of his mouth.

"—and can't help but wonder if you're confusing l-love with sympathy."

There. She'd finally given voice to the terrible suspicion weighing on her mind.

"Are you telling me I've been courting you only because I feel sorry for you?" Gone was the smile, the hopeful expression. Passion burned in his gaze, threatening to incinerate her where she stood.

Years of collective pain and unworthiness caused her to lash out. "Well, look at your father . . . look at me . . . look at your *dog,* for heaven's sake! I'm just one more cripple you've taken under your wing!"

The silence following her angry declaration was broken only by the doleful sound of the wind.

When he finally spoke, his words were so quiet she had to strain to hear them. "I know your life's been hard, Rebecca, and I don't disbelieve anything you've told me. What happened during the inquest . . . well, that was the evil of a sinful man warring with the ugly truths you brought to light. You did a good thing that day; you did the right thing, and such sacrifice always comes with a price. If it makes you feel any better, I wanted to cry for what you endured . . . and for every other painful thing you've endured your whole life long. If I said, 'There's more to a person than how she looks,' I know you would be the first to agree. You know your Scriptures, and you know that God looks on a person's heart."

His next words were choked, delivered in a whisper. "The sweetness that comes from inside you is what I love most about you, Rebecca."

Tears blinded her vision, and she reached the post of the rocker to steady herself.

"But there comes a time, *belle*, when a person has to make a choice about how he's going to live his life. It's when times get hard that you most need to remember whose child you are and what's really important. I can give you more time, more understanding . . . but if I give you as much as you think you need, I know you'll slip away from me. You already are . . . I can feel it happening."

"Hugh—," she began, longing for the shelter of his strong arms and at the same time wishing she could hide for shame at the pain she'd caused him.

"Your birthmark stands between us only because you let it, *belle*. I couldn't care less if your face were orange or pink or blue. It's *you* I love—all of you."

He loved her? "Oh, Hugh," she whispered.

"Can we build from here?" he asked, a hopeful thread running through his voice. "Start again with the understanding that people are going to sometimes treat you badly on account of your birthmark? We both know it's inevitable. But the difference, from now on, will come from in here. From the truth." His fingers tapped against the left side of his chest.

"But . . . it's so . . . hard . . . to . . . be . . . me," she sobbed. "I'll never be . . . normal."

"Pshaw! What's normal? Normal looking? Normal acting? Common? Usual? Ordinary? You're unique, *belle*, and when you're not thinking about your face, you're the most delightful and refreshing person I know. What you need to tell yourself—and believe—is that you are the way you are because God chose to make you that way. You please him, Rebecca."

"But I'm not pleased with the way he made *me!*"

"Have you ever told him so?"

"Oh, right! And just how would I do that?"

"By laying out your heart before him and telling him everything." A slow, tender smile curved his lips. "Do you re-

377

ally think you're keeping such a monumental secret? After all, he is God. I don't think you'll be telling him anything he doesn't already know. Surrender all your anger and pain to him, *belle,* and I promise he will do a wonderful and beautiful work in your heart."

"But not my face . . . or my arm or my leg, or any of the other places in between!" Once the bitter words had left her mouth, she blushed with embarrassment, realizing she had spoken immodestly. Dropping her gaze, she studied the rug beneath her feet.

"I didn't need any of my anatomy courses to know that the only place that counts lies just beneath your ribs." He paused, clearing his throat. "I'll leave now, but before I go, I want to give you one more thing to think about."

"What?" she finally asked, looking up. If she had thought her heart heavy before, its weight now was insupportable.

Stepping across the distance separating them, he cupped her face in his hands. Gently, slowly, he brought his lips to hers. Instead of being fleeting, however, his kiss was warm and lingering, a promise of glorious things to come. His right hand moved from her face to clasp her hand, and as he lifted his lips, he gazed deeply into her eyes and raised her hand to the hard expanse of his chest. "Feel that, *belle?* I may be a doctor of veterinary medicine, but I don't think what my heart is doing right now has anything to do with sympathy."

Rebecca's breath caught at the strong thudding of his pulse beneath her fingers. His brown-flecked eyes continued to gaze into hers, piercing her, while his warm breath fanned her face. Lord above, how could a person experience such great measures of agony and gladness at the same time?

"Come to the dance with me," he urged. "What's the worst thing that can happen?"

"Someone will make fun of my face."

"So let them. You're going to have a new heart."

"I don't know . . ." she whispered, stepping backward from his embrace. All her old fears and feelings of unworthiness threatened to rise up and choke her. Taking a panicked breath, she blurted out, "I can't . . . I just don't think I can."

Hugh's expression was patient, his gaze steady. "I have faith in you, Rebecca, and I have faith in our God. Give yourself over to him and let him work." With a final nod of encouragement, he retrieved his hat and coat and disappeared into the night.

She didn't know how long she stood staring at the closed door after he left. She wanted the things he had spoken of—and she wanted Hugh Clark, as well. Ever since her childhood she had said her prayers and believed in God, but Hugh's unique perspectives of the Almighty gave her pause.

Give herself over to the Lord? How was she supposed to do that? As far as she understood, she was already his. And even if she knew exactly what Hugh meant, what would be the result of such abandon?

The russet-haired man had outdone himself this time. In only five minutes he had given her more to think about than could be contemplated in five lifetimes.

Chapter Ten

B ell, you look as though you have more troubles than Job had boils."

Auntie Jo, who had advanced from strict bed rest to sitting up twice daily, readjusted her roomy yellow wrapper while occupying the comfortable, cushioned chair Eli had carried from the living room to the bedroom. Her affected leg was extended before her, supported by a footstool and two plump, soft pillows. Afternoon sunlight bathed the room in bright hues.

"I know that inquest was a wretched experience for you," she went on, her blue eyes filled with concern. "But Mr. Evans told Eli that if not for what you did, those poor children would still be suffering. I'm sure you're dreading the trial; how could you not? I wish you'd talk to me, honey, and tell me what's going on inside your head." She paused a moment, as if weighing her next words. "Especially about Dr. Clark."

"There's nothing to say," Rebecca spoke in a low voice. "There are just too many problems."

"Are those his words?"

Rebecca was silent as she finished changing the sheets. Since Hugh's visit earlier in the week she had thought a great deal about the things he'd said, not believing that she could live a life untroubled by her port-wine stain.

He also told you he loved you, Rebecca, her inner voice spoke, *and what you felt in his kiss affirmed that a thousand times. You know you love him, too. What are you going to do about that?*

Since that night she'd been thinking about returning to Minneapolis to await the trial. Dr. Janery was pleased with Auntie Jo's progress and had hinted at his last visit that she might soon be up on crutches. With her aunt on the mend, Rebecca's presence in the home wouldn't be as crucial as it had been when the older woman had been strictly bedridden.

It would be for the best if you just pulled out of his life. What he really deserves is an uncomplicated, unmarked woman who won't subject him to a life filled with problems.

"I've been wondering if it isn't time for me to go home," she announced, tucking the blanket at the foot of the bed with a series of efficient movements.

"Yes, I suppose playing nursemaid to an old woman can't be much fun for a young person."

"Oh, it's not that, Auntie Jo," she said quickly, stopping her work to convince the older woman of the truth. "I love being here."

"Do you? Eli and I have noticed that you've seemed most unhappy over the past month or so."

"It's not you, really. It's just . . . well . . ."

"Hugh Clark," the white-haired woman supplied with a knowing expression. She nodded. "You know, Bell, when Eli's courtship turned serious, I wanted to bolt like a jackrabbit into tall grass."

"You did? How come you told me you loved him when you were a young girl—even before he started courting you?"

"Because I did love him back then. It was when he started making noises about settling down that I got scared." With a half smile, she let her head rest against the back of the chair. "Goodness, that was a long time ago."

"But you married him . . ."

"I did, indeed, after doing some wrestling with the Lord."

Rebecca took a seat at the end of the bed." *You* wrestled with the Lord? I don't know anyone with stronger faith than you."

The ticking of the clock was the only sound in the room for a long moment. "Faith isn't always an easy process, Bell," Jo finally answered. "Time and many painful experiences go toward its building, and I've come to realize that the greatest gains are made through times of greatest adversity. To be honest, I wrestled with the Lord about getting married, moving to Minnesota from Vermont, losing each baby, and sending Eli off to war. After many unhappy years I finally quit my wrestling because I realized God was going to have his way no matter what kind of fuss I put up, and that it was a whole lot easier on all concerned if I just went along with as thankful and cheerful a heart as I could."

Rebecca was quiet, trying to reconcile the woman she'd just heard described with the great-aunt she'd known from her childhood.

"Did you get a chance to read through Eli's letters, honey?" Jo asked.

She nodded, answering slowly. "The one Uncle Eli wrote you from South Tunnell, where he urged you not to lose heart after your baby . . . well . . . was that a time you were wrestling?"

"It was a time I wished more often to be dead than alive."

"Oh . . ." Rebecca was speechless at this disclosure.

"Burying our third baby while Eli was off to war was the blackest moment of my life. The day I gave you the letters, Bell, I challenged you to decide whether God was for you or against you. I'll confess to you now that during the winter of '65 I believed he'd set his face against me."

Rebecca tried imagining such despair. They had dared much, Eli and Jo. Moving halfway across the country, far from family and friends, staking a claim and settling the land. Conceiving child after child, only to lay each one in the ground. Shouldering the burdens of the oppressed and believing in that cause so deeply that Eli had enlisted in the Union Army.

And yet through all this they'd loved, and continued moving forward, and grown in their faith. When she thought of such bravery and conviction, Rebecca felt very small indeed. What was the pain of a birthmark compared to all that?

Auntie Jo picked up her Bible and went on. "While I waited and hoped for Eli's return, I chose to read Job, of all things . . . maybe because I thought I could identify a bit with him. Do you recall the last chapters of the book, where God speaks?"

"When he tells Job to gird up his loins like a man because he wants to ask him some questions?"

"It's more than that, dear. The Almighty Creator challenges Job, a mere man, to give him the *answers* to unanswerable questions . . . beginning with 'Where wast thou when I laid the foundations of the earth?' Day after day I read those chapters and wondered how I would reply if I were in Job's place. One day my hardness of heart broke and my cry to God was the same as Job's: 'I know that thou canst do every thing, and that no thought can be withholden from thee.' From the depths of my despair I repented, Bell, and the Lord heard me. He restored my faith, making it stronger than it had ever been before." The Bible lay on her lap, unopened, while a single tear traced down the wrinkled cheek.

Was that what Hugh had been talking about? In her mind, she heard her beloved's words from the cottage. *After all, he*

is God. I don't think you'll be telling him anything he doesn't al-
ready know. Surrender all your anger and pain . . . I promise he
will do a wonderful and beautiful work in your heart.

Moisture gathered in Rebecca's eyes as she longed for the
same release. She felt so weak, so tired, so unworthy. Her
shoulders slumped and she hung her head in misery.

"Honey, I know that birthmark has made your life painful." Auntie Jo's voice was tender. "But there is one who is
greater than all that, one who promises that his yoke is easy
and his burden light. I know of your love for Jesus, child, but
there is a kingdomful of treasures that are yours for the taking. To claim them you must walk in victory, not defeat."

"How?" she sobbed, dropping her head to her lap. "I want
that more than anything."

"Then we won't wait a moment longer. Come over here,
my love, and kneel beside me. The one who calls you knows
of your suffering, Bell. He suffered much himself. . . ."

Her limbs felt leaden as she moved. "But what do I *do*? I
just don't know what to do."

Her aunt's hand was warm upon her head as she knelt before her. "Just speak to him as plainly as you would me,
child. Tell him of your sorrows, your fears, your longings.
Confess the error of your ways. Tell him of your desire to
live as he wants you to—in joyful freedom."

"Father," she began in a whisper, her mind and spirit in
turmoil, "my faith in you is weak." Fresh tears fell. "I haven't
been very good about accepting the way you made me, and I
think I've blamed you for all my unhappiness. I'm . . . so very
sorry, and I beg your forgiveness. Instead of wishing I was
different all these years, I should have been asking for your
help to live as you wanted me to. Hugh and Auntie Jo have
helped me see how much you love me—and my part in rescuing Hannah shows me how dearly you care for each one of
us. And that you would send a man like Hugh into my life—"

The thought of such undeserved love caused her to weep

at length, all the while her aunt's gentle fingers stroked her hair. "Please help me see myself as you see me," she finally spoke, "and live as you want me to live. Amen. Oh—and if Hugh Clark is still willing to court me, I would be grateful for another chance in that area as well. Amen."

"Oh, honey, you're going to be just fine," the older woman whispered, wiping her eyes with her other hand.

"For the first time, I have to agree with you." In her heart dwelt a smoothness, a peace she had never before known.

"Now what is to be done with our handsome veterinarian?"

"I . . . I don't know. He invited me to the Dennings' party tonight. He also told me he loved me, Auntie Jo," she confided. "I . . . just don't know how—"

"Hold on! Is this the old Rebecca talking, or the new Rebecca?"

Rebecca felt a chagrined smile steal across her lips while her aunt went on. "Martha told me the Rand Trio will be providing the music at her party. Eli and I have tapped our toes to their tunes many a time. Now, mind you, this is just my opinion, but I think you look particularly fetching in that dark pink dress with the cream stripes."

"Are you saying I should go to the party?"

"Absolutely." The blue eyes twinkled with glee. "And just maybe we'll be having ourselves another type of celebration before too long."

Instead of pushing aside the wave of joy and hope that rose inside her at her aunt's words, Rebecca allowed the marvelous feelings of anticipation to wash over her. With that came the memory of the lingering kiss in the cottage . . . the feel of Hugh Clark's heart beating beneath her fingertips . . .

She glanced at the clock and froze.

"How am I going to get ready in time?" she burst out. "What am I going to do with my hair? Oh, no! How will I get word to him that I've changed my mind?"

Jo chuckled. "Don't fret. Eli will drive you over to the Dennings, and you can just tell Dr. Clark you've changed your mind—in person."

A scant hour later, Rebecca was ready for the party. Eli whistled when she appeared in the kitchen, his wrinkled face lighting with pleasure. "I declare, Bell, I never seen you lookin' so lovely! That young fellow won't be able to take his eyes off you."

"Do you really think so?" The last rays of the setting sun shone through the window, catching her in the face as she twirled around.

"I know so. Now let's get you over there! Can you hold down the place for a while, Mrs. Woodman?" he called.

"Take your time, Eli. Have a cup of eggnog for me while you're at it. And Bell, remember that you're walking in victory, dear. I'll want to hear about your evening the minute you get home. Promise you'll wake me up?"

"I promise."

The horses were eager to stretch their legs in the frosty twilight, and the trip to the Dennings took scarcely a quarter hour. Recalling the events of the stormy night last month, Rebecca felt a shiver as they passed by the darkened Scruggs place. What wickedness those children had suffered! Thinking of Barter Scruggs brought another chill and the memory of his words during the inquest.

Many of Jo and Eli's neighbors she knew, but there would no doubt be many there at the party she didn't. Once again she would have to endure the stares, the snickering, the whispers. In her excitement to surprise Hugh, how had she forgotten what her life used to be like? *Remember you're walking in victory . . . there is a kingdomful of treasures that are yours for the taking . . .*

Did God have Hugh Clark in mind as one of those treasures?

"Looks like there's quite a crowd," Eli commented as they

turned in the drive. Warm yellow light spilled from every window of the Dennings' two-story structure, and horses and conveyances of every type were parked about their yard. Eli caught the tune of the cheerful carol being carried on the crisp night air and began humming "O Come All Ye Faithful" while the all-too-familiar apprehension began building inside Rebecca. Could she really walk into a crowd with her head held high?

As if Eli read her mind, he broke off from the chorus and turned his head. "I expect you're gettin' cold feet right about now."

"How did you know?"

"I been around a few years, Bell, an' been through a few things myself. Times like this is when we gotta let the Holy Ghost lead us on."

Rebecca smiled at her uncle's earnest expression. "Don't worry; I'm not going to bolt. I figure the worst that can happen is that someone will make fun of me."

"That's right, honey—sticks an' stones."

However, her nervousness mounted as Martha Denning warmly swept them into the house. A full three dozen adults had assembled, and Eli made his greetings as he led her through the throng. Rebecca tried not to worry about what people might be thinking of her face, but it was difficult. A fine mist of perspiration broke out on her forehead and dampened her back. If Hugh wasn't here, she reasoned, she would have Eli take her back home at once.

The musical trio played before the window in the Dennings' large sitting room; the room was lit with several wall lamps and the lovely glow of candles. Catching sight of Hugh across the room, Rebecca felt the tension drain from her like water from a pipe. An enormous grin split his face when he saw her, and he raised his arm in greeting just as "Deck the Halls" came to its drawn-out conclusion.

"Look at that lady, Mama!" cried a little boy with a loud

voice. He stood before Rebecca, pointing toward her cheek. The relative quiet left in the wake of the carol became dead silence as people glanced at one another with stricken expressions. "Would you look at her face! She looks just like a purple Holstein!"

But instead of hurt, a mysterious and joyful laughter bubbled up from inside her. Kneeling down, she smiled at the youth. "Why, I've often thought the same thing myself. I guess it pleased the Lord to make me with a few dabs of color."

"What does it feel like? Can I touch it?" he asked, stepping forward. His mother, nearly apoplectic with embarrassment, failed to reach him before his fingers swept across Rebecca's cheek.

"Hey, it doesn't feel any different at all," he said, disappointment evident in his voice.

"Mind your manners, Monty. This is the lady who put Barter Scruggs away," an older youth said from behind the boy. His nod toward her was respectful, serious. "'Member what Pa said . . . she's got more guts than you can hang on a fence."

"I'll second that. I was in the jury along with your pa," a deep voice warranted. "Miss, you done the bravest thing I think I ever saw."

Before she knew what was happening, the room erupted with whoops, cheers, and an abundance of applause. One of the fiddlers elbowed the banjo player, and the trio launched into a lively rendition of "For He's a Jolly Good Fellow." Person after person moved forward to shake her hand, offering her congratulations and welcome.

And from across the room, a pair of hazel eyes beamed their love and approval.

EPILOGUE

I n the pale moonlight outside the cottage, Hugh enfolded Rebecca in his arms and chuckled. "I'd say you just gave 'the belle of the ball' a whole new meaning tonight, Miss Belanger. That was some party." His tone became mischievous. "Remember the day we met . . . how you took me to task over by the barn there? You spit out that French so fast and hard I could barely understand what you said."

Rebecca smiled and gazed up into the face of her beloved. "I must confess to wondering at your intelligence . . . and being more than a bit bowled over by your forwardness."

"Well, that was really Eli's fault. Thanks to him and all his talk, I was halfway in love with you before I helped you down from the wagon—only you didn't know it yet." He pressed a kiss against her forehead. "I doubt I'll ever be fluent, but I must tell you I've been brushing up on my French. I thought it only fitting."

"Fitting for what?"

"For this." He knelt on the packed snow outside the threshold. "I spoke to your uncle tonight, and I intend to speak to your father, as well . . . but I can't wait, *belle. Je t'aime*, Rebecca. *Acceptes-tu d'être ma femme?"*

"Marry you! Are you . . . do you really . . ." Words failed her as she realized this moment was really, truly happening. A gentle wind blew through the trees overhead, its sound as familiar and comforting as the Voice in her heart.

"Yes, Hugh Clark, I'll marry you," she said with confidence and joy, taking hold of the hand he extended. "I love you, too," she managed to add just before she was engulfed in his embrace.

Somehow, she could imagine no better life than the one she was living.

RECIPE

❄

BEST EVER MOLASSES COOKIES

1 cup sugar
1 egg
3/4 cup shortening
2 tbsp. molasses
2 cups flour
1 tsp. cloves
1/4 tsp. salt
1 tsp. cinnamon
1 1/2 tsp. soda
1 tsp. ginger

Cream shortening and sugar. Add egg and molasses; beat well. Mix in spices and dry ingredients. Shape into approximately one-inch balls, roll in sugar. (During the holiday season, I often use red or green decorating sugar.) Bake at 350° for 9–10 minutes.

A Note from the Author

Dear Reader,

Even though an author thinks she might know at a story's outset how the tale will end, many surprising things often occur while writing everything between page 1 and The End. In this case, a box of musty treasures led to many twists and turns in "The Beauty of the Season" that I never expected when I wrote the proposal.

I was casually acquainted with the materials my grandmother, Ivy Evans Tasler, had collected as a genealogist and amateur historian. Maple Grove, Minnesota, is a real town that was settled, in part, by her grandparents—Chester and Helen Eddy Evans. Many of Eli's letters from the Civil War were patterned after Evans's letters home to his wife. I must tell you that the initial paragraph of the first letter Rebecca read in chapter 4 was taken verbatim from Chester's first letter home to Helen. I felt it captured the sadness and emotion of the troops' departure in a way fiction could not improve.

C. E. "Chet" Evans indeed served as justice of the peace of Maple Grove from 1875 to 1891. The Justice logbook is a fascinating account of many civil and minor criminal offenses committed throughout its thirty-plus years of recording.

It was a pleasure to discover that my great-great-grandfather was a gifted writer. His letters and essays were well written, touching, and often insightful. He was also a man of faith, who clearly trusted in God's providence. As a tribute to him, I would like to share with you the poem he wrote Helen on their fiftieth wedding anniversary:

FIFTY YEARS

Full fifty years of wedded life
Dear wife we've spent together
We've seen adversities, dark clouds,
And love's bright sunny weather.

We've had sad days and joyous ones
And laughed at fate's hard measure:
We've filled the cup of life with love
And quaffed it off together.

We've lived the lonely frontier life
And heard war's bugle call,
We've thanked God for the victories
That proclaimed peace for all.

We have kind friends and children dear
To fill our earthly measure
And when we drain the cup of life,
May we pass on together.

C. E. Evans
December 25, 1910

May the peace and joy of this holiday season be yours, and may your
life be blessed with the richness of a deeper relationship with our risen
Savior, Christ Jesus the King.

In him,
Peggy Stoks

About the Author

Peggy Stoks lives in Minnesota with her husband and three daughters. She has worked as a registered nurse for nearly twenty years. She has published two novels as well as numerous magazine articles about child care and pediatrics. In addition to her novella for *A Victorian Christmas Cottage*, she has written novellas for *A Victorian Christmas Quilt, A Victorian Christmas Tea,* and *Reunited*.

Peggy welcomes letters written to her at P.O. Box 333, Circle Pines, MN 55014.

Current HeartQuest Releases

- *A Bouquet of Love*, Ginny Aiken, Ranee McCollum, Jeri Odell, and Debra White Smith
- *Faith*, Lori Copeland
- *Finders Keepers*, Catherine Palmer
- *Hope*, Lori Copeland
- *June*, Lori Copeland
- *Prairie Rose*, Catherine Palmer
- *Prairie Fire*, Catherine Palmer
- *Prairie Storm*, Catherine Palmer
- *Reunited*, Judy Baer, Jeri Odell, Jan Duffy, and Peggy Stoks
- *The Treasure of Timbuktu*, Catherine Palmer
- *The Treasure of Zanzibar*, Catherine Palmer
- *A Victorian Christmas Quilt*, Catherine Palmer, Debra White Smith, Ginny Aiken, and Peggy Stoks
- *A Victorian Christmas Tea*, Catherine Palmer, Dianna Crawford, Peggy Sokes, and Katherine Chute
- *With This Ring*, Lori Copeland, Dianna Crawford, Ginny Aiken, and Catherine Palmer
- *Dream Vacation*, Ginny Aiken, Jeri Odell, and Elizabeth White— coming soon (February 2000)
- *The Rainbow Road*, Dianna Crawford—coming soon (February 2000)

Other Great Tyndale House Fiction

- *As Sure as the Dawn*, Francine Rivers
- *The Atonement Child*, Francine Rivers
- *The Captive Voice*, B. J. Hoff
- *Cloth of Heaven*, B. J. Hoff
- *Dark River Legacy*, B. J. Hoff
- *An Echo in the Darkness*, Francine Rivers
- *The Embers of Hope*, Sally Laity and Dianna Crawford
- *Home Fires Burning*, Penelope J. Stokes
- *Jewels for a Crown*, Lawana Blackwell
- *Journey to the Crimson Sea*, Jim & Terri Kraus
- *The Last Sin Eater*, Francine Rivers
- *Leota's Garden*, Francine Rivers
- *Like a River Glorious*, Lawana Blackwell
- *Measures of Grace*, Lawana Blackwell
- *Passages of Gold*, Jim & Terri Kraus
- *Pirates of the Heart*, Jim & Terri Kraus
- *Remembering You*, Penelope J. Stokes

Heartwarming Anthologies from HeartQuest

A Bouquet of Love—An arrangement of four beautiful novellas about friendship and love. Stories by Ginny Aiken, Ranee McCollum, Jeri Odell, and Debra White Smith.

A Victorian Christmas Cottage—Four novellas centerig around hearth and home at Christmastime. Stories by Catherine Palmer, Jeri Odell, Debra White Smith, and Peggy Stoks.

A Victorian Christmas Tea—Four novellas about life and love at Christmastime. Stories by Catherine Palmer, Dianna Crawford, Peggy Stoks and Katherine Chute.

A Victorian Christmas Quilt—A patchwork of four novellas about love and joy at Christmastime. Stories by Catherine Palmer, Ginny Aiken, Peggy Stoks, and Debra White Smith.

Reunited—Four stories about reuniting friends, old memories, and new romance. Includes favorite recipes from the authors. Stories by Judy Baer, Jan Duffy, Jeri Odell, and Peggy Stoks.

With This Ring—A quartet of charming stories about four very special weddings. Stories by Lori Copeland, Dianna Crawford, Ginny Aiken, and Catherine Palmer.

HeartQuest Books by Catherine Palmer

Finders Keepers—Home, family, security . . . three things that lovely, inde-
pendent antiques dealer Elizabeth Hayes is determined to provide for her
adopted son, Nikolai. And Ambleside, Missouri, is just the place to do it. The
beautiful Victorian mansion next door is an ever-present reminder of the stable heritage and gracious, old-fashioned ways Ambleside represents. Zachary
Chalmers is shocked to receive an inheritance from an aunt he barely remem-
bers—even if it is just a decrepit old mansion. Once cleared, the site will be
perfect for the architectural firm he's designing. Out with the old, in with the
new. That's Zachary's motto. Even as they clash over the fate of Chalmers
House, Elizabeth and Zachary begin to discover dreams of a shared future—
an idea vigorously supported by the irrepressible Nick! But are they willing to
surrender to God's plan, which is greater than their own? Then a surprising
revelation makes them wonder whether even a wrecking ball can put to rest
the shadows of the past.

Prairie Storm—Can one tiny baby calm the brewing storm between Lily's past
and Elijah's future? Evangelist Elijah Book is a fearless warrior for God—or so
he believes. When a helpless infant is entrusted to his care, his zeal becomes
sidetracked as the fate of an innocent child rests with a woman Eli must trust
in spite of himself. Stores of hurt and bitterness threaten to overwhelm Lily
Nolan after the death of her husband and child. If there is a God, how could he
abandon her so completely? Can she risk opening her heart to the orphaned
Samuel? United in their concern for the baby, Eli and Lily are forced to set
aside their differences and learn to trust God's plan to see them through the
storms of life.

Prairie Rose—Kansas held their future, but only faith could mend their past.
Hope and love blossom on the untamed prairie as a young woman, searching
for a place to call home, happens upon a Kansas homestead during the 1860s.

Prairie Fire—Will a burning secret extinguish the spark of love between Jack
and Caitrin? The town of Hope discovers the importance of forgiveness, over-
coming prejudice, and the dangers of keeping unhealthy family secrets.

A Victorian Christmas Cottage—Continuing the popular Victorian Christmas
anthology series, this collection of four original Christmas stories leads off with
a heartwarming novella by Catherine Palmer. In "Under His Wings," a young

widow leaves her home in Wales to settle with her beloved mother-in-law in a small cottage in England's Lake District. Finding work in the kitchen of the dashing earl of Beaumontfort, Gwyneth soon attracts his attention. He is charmed by her wit, her love for her mother-in-law, and her devotion to Christ. But unexpected developments at the lavish annual Christmas gathering threaten their growing love.

A Victorian Christmas Tea—Four novellas about life and love at Christmastime. Stories by Catherine Palmer, Dianna Crawford, Peggy Stoks and Katherine Chute.

A Victorian Christmas Quilt—A patchwork of four novellas about love and joy at Christmastime. Stories by Catherine Palmer, Ginny Aiken, Peggy Stoks, and Debra White Smith.

The Treasure of Timbuktu—Abducted by a treasure hunter, Tillie Thorton becomes a pawn in a dangerous game. Desperate and on the run from a fierce nomadic tribe looking to kidnap her, Tillie finds herself in an uneasy partnership with a daring adventurer.

The Treasure of Zanzibar—An ancient house filled with secrets . . . a sunken treasure . . . an unknown enemy . . . a lost love. They all await her on Zanzibar. Jessica Thorton returns to Africa with her son to claim her inheritance on the island of Zanzibar. Upon her arrival, she is reunited with her estranged husband.